PRAISE FOR THE BOOKS OF NANCY HERRIMAN

"In this latest Mystery of Old San Francisco, justice is served in ways that will leave readers thoroughly satisfied and have them cheering at the end."
—Alyssa Maxwell, author of the Gilded Newport Mysteries

"Nancy Herriman has penned a clever, atmospheric mystery with interesting, diverse, and compelling characters that transported me right back to late-19th-century San Fransisco! I can't wait for the next book!"
—Colleen Cambridge, Agatha Award-nominated author of *Murder at Mallowan Hall*

"Clever and ever-capable nurse Celia Davies once again finds use for her considerable skills in this compelling series addition. *No Refuge from the Grave* is a tightly plotted, engrossing mystery that is rich in historical detail and vividly brings to life 1860s San Francisco."
—Ashley Weaver, Edgar Award-nominated author of the Amory Ames Mysteries

"Highly recommended!"
—Historical Novel Society, Editors' Choice on *Searcher of the Dead*

"You'll love the intrepid heroine, nurse Celia Davies."
—Victoria Thompson, bestselling author of the Gaslight Mysteries, on *No Pity for the Dead*

"A tremendously riveting read . . ."
—*Newport Plain Talk* on *Searcher of the Dead*

"Skillful storytelling . . . a standout historical mystery."
—*Publishers Weekly* starred review of *A Fall of Shadows*

NO JUSTICE
for the
DECEIVED

NANCY HERRIMAN

No Justice for the Deceived
Nancy Herriman
Copyright © 2023 by Nancy Herriman

Beyond the Page Books
are published by
Beyond the Page Publishing
www.beyondthepagepub.com

ISBN: 978-1-960511-11-9

This is a work of fiction. Names, characters, places, and incidents either are the product of the author's imagination or are used fictitiously, and any resemblance to actual persons, living or dead, business establishments, events or locales is entirely coincidental. The publisher does not have any control over and does not assume any responsibility for author or third-party websites or their content.

To Teresa, a dear friend and amazing woman

℘ Chapter 1 ℘

San Francisco
February 1868

"It's rare to see a clubfoot in a female, Mrs. Davies," Dr. Schneider said. The physician tilted his head and squinted through the spectacles balanced upon his nose, eyeing Celia's cousin with unpleasant curiosity. "Did one of her parents happen to be afflicted?"

Barbara returned his scrutiny with a glare. She was used to being stared at, her half-Chinese heritage impossible to disguise. Her parentage showed in the beautiful sheen of her black hair, the shape of her dark eyes. How often, Celia wondered, had a young woman like Barbara ever entered the hallowed confines of this man's surgery? Where the fire in the tiled hearth warmed the room to the perfect temperature, his walnut desk gleamed as if polished daily, the leaded glass in the medicine cabinets was unmarred by fingerprints, and his credentials were proudly displayed in gilt frames. Where tastefully pale February light filtered through the surgery window's lace curtains, as white as the day they'd been hung and far whiter than the ones gracing the windows of Celia's medical clinic.

It was safe to say that a young woman like Barbara had never stepped inside the papered walls of this hushed room, faintly smelling of pipe smoke and ammonia.

I should not have brought her here, no matter the recommendation I was given.

"My Uncle Walford, her father, was not afflicted, Dr. Schneider," Celia replied, sensing more than observing the tension pinching her cousin's shoulders. "Her mother died long before I moved to San Francisco from England, so I cannot—"

"My *Chinese* mother did *not* have a clubfoot, Cousin Celia, Dr. Schneider," Barbara stated, her voice as taut as her shoulders. That she hadn't already jumped down from the examining table and run from the fellow's surgery showed an admirable amount of restraint.

The doctor frowned at her outburst.

"Is there anything you can do for her, Doctor?" Celia interrupted before he crafted a retort that might cause Celia to want to storm from the surgery herself.

Dr. Schneider exhaled and resumed turning Barbara's foot over in his hand. Her toes curled at an odd angle, contorting the bones. "She had surgery as a child?"

The old scars were clearly visible. "Yes, but as you can see, the operation was not fully successful," Celia replied. "On damp, cold days her foot causes her a great deal of pain."

"I can speak for myself, Cousin," Barbara said, her cheeks reddening. "I'm not a child any longer."

"Your ward is outspoken, Mrs. Davies," the doctor said. Why he'd not included a *tut* she could not fathom.

"I confess I admire that trait, Dr. Schneider."

He tutted at that.

"I had surgery when I was around four," Barbara said. "That's what my father told me, because I don't remember much about it."

"I see." He released her leg, and Barbara adjusted her skirt over her crinoline, the checked green wool falling to drape over her bare ankle and foot and conceal them.

"So?" Celia asked.

"There's not much I can do for her at her present age, Mrs. Davies. If I had attended your cousin when she was young and her bones and tendons were more pliable, I'm certain we would have achieved a complete cure," he said. "However, at this point, extensive surgery would be needed in order to repair what was previously done as well as attempt a further fix. Even if successful—which is doubtful—the treatment would also require a lengthy and uncomfortable recovery." He slid an assessing look at Barbara, who had climbed down from the examining table and was occupied in pulling on her stocking. "I expect your cousin may not wish to endure that."

"Barbara is both strong and courageous, Dr. Schneider, so do not doubt her ability to 'endure.' However, I accept your assessment that the situation is likely too far gone to correct." As it was, the money for the procedure would have been difficult to come by. "Thank you, though, for your time. I will be certain to tell Miss Bremerton when I see her next that I appreciated her recommendation, but that you are unable to provide any help for my cousin."

He stood up from the stool he'd been seated on. "The recommendation was from Miss Bremerton? How are you two acquainted?"

"She knows Cousin Celia through her charity work and wants to fund a women's medical clinic like the one my cousin runs," Barbara explained, tightening the laces on the inner sides of her low-heeled boots. "She recently visited us to ask for her advice."

"Ah, so that is your connection, Mrs. Davies."

"We are not acquainted because Miss Bremerton requested my services in an investigation, Dr. Schneider, if that is what you were wondering."

Perhaps Celia's notoriety *was* the only reason he'd agreed to examine Barbara in the first place. A relative of the notorious "female detective." The first time a reporter had written about Celia had been bad enough. After she discovered a dead body in an acquaintance's front yard last November, she'd become the subject of even more articles. A profusion of requests had followed the lines of print, entreaties to locate missing persons or confirm inheritances or prove the parlor maid was stealing from the lady of the house. Barbara had sulked with each new solicitation for help. Celia had turned them all down, because she was *not* a female detective, despite the number of criminal cases she'd managed to become embroiled in.

"I was simply curious, that's all, Mrs. Davies." Dr. Schneider turned to pluck a clean towel off a stack of them, using it to wipe his hands. "I know Miss Bremerton and she has never mentioned your name."

"She has had no reason to mention me, I presume."

"Will you be attending the masquerade ball her fiancé's family is hosting tomorrow evening?"

"Her fiancé? I was unaware Miss Bremerton is engaged to be wed." Proving the true and limited extent of her acquaintance with the young woman.

"I believe she and Mr. Sebastian Carr mean to formalize their engagement at the mask tomorrow." He glanced at Celia's black dress. Her widow's weeds. "Forgive me, madam. Undoubtedly, you won't be attending. My sympathies on your loss."

Celia accepted his sentiments with a nod. She had scant need for sympathies over her husband's death, however. She could not miss or mourn a man who'd abandoned her and whom she'd rarely had contact with in the final years of his life.

"I do regret that I cannot attend the ball," she said. "I've never been to a masquerade. I presume from your question, however, that you will be there and you may see Miss Bremerton before I do."

"Mrs. Schneider and I have been invited, of course, but my wife wants to attend the grand masquerade ball hosted by the San Francisco Verein Society on Thursday next and has only one costume to wear." He removed his spectacles and took to wiping the lenses with the towel he'd been using to clean his hands, peering nearsightedly at Celia while he rubbed the glass over and over. "She doesn't want to spoil the surprise by wearing it to the Carrs' fete tomorrow."

The San Francisco Verein Society was the largest German-American organization in the city, and an invitation to the masked ball they annually hosted in the week prior to the beginning of Lent was highly coveted.

"How very fortunate for you to be able to attend the Verein Society's event," Celia replied, helping Barbara with her cloak.

"It promises to be a fantastic evening. I may drop in at the Carrs' and give my regards, though," he said. "I had hoped to meet Miss Bremerton's parents at the mask, but they had to cancel their plans to make the trip to San Francisco. Mr. Bremerton recently suffered a severe attack of ague and his wife, of course, did not wish to leave his side."

"Miss Bremerton is in San Francisco without them?"

"She arrived last fall to stay with a relative but was quickly embraced by the Carrs, Mrs. Davies. Her parents fully trust Mr. Carr to watch over her," the doctor sniffed.

"Certainly."

He stared at his spectacles, at last realizing he'd been repeatedly rubbing the lenses, and tucked them into a pocket of his striped waistcoat. "Sebastian Carr is a lucky man to have snagged Irene Bremerton as his fiancée."

A comment that made Miss Bremerton sound rather like a prize trout hooked by an angler.

"Mr. Carr will indeed be fortunate to be married to such a generous and talented woman as Miss Bremerton. I was most impressed by her plans for the medical clinic her friend will oversee." She'd been told that a bequest to Miss Bremerton from a recently deceased relative would be financing that clinic. "We spoke for several hours about what she and her friend hope to accomplish."

"Ah, Mrs. Davies, Sebastian will see to it that Miss Bremerton is far too busy to be involved in founding medical clinics for destitute females, I assure you."

Barbara grumbled a complaint under her breath.

"For my part, Dr. Schneider, I hope you are mistaken." Celia took Barbara's elbow and guided her to the door, which the doctor rushed to open. "Thank you again."

They marched out of the examination room. In the hall waited the middle-aged woman who'd answered the front bell. She was as quick as the doctor had been to throw wide the door and usher them outside.

They reached the pavement and Celia gazed up the road, ascending toward Telegraph Hill and home. Alert to the stares of people passing on the crowded street. People likely wondering why a respectably dressed white woman was in the company of a teenaged Chinese girl in Western garb.

Barbara glanced back at the surgery. "I'm glad Dr. Schneider didn't want to operate on my foot, Cousin Celia. I don't like him."

"I do not much either, Barbara," she said, taking her cousin's hand and tucking it in the crook of her elbow.

"He was awfully mean about Miss Bremerton," her cousin said, walking alongside Celia with her head high, because she'd learned that displaying confidence was her best safeguard. "Talking as if he hopes both she and her friend's clinic will fail."

As if he hoped Sebastian Carr would crush her spirit. "I expect Dr. Schneider is like so many people who do not appreciate successful, independent women."

Barbara looked over at her. "Or he's simply mean."

• • •

"Would you mind if I knock off early today, sir?"

Nick Greaves looked up from the paperwork strewn across his desk. His assistant, J. E. Taylor, stood in the doorway to the detectives' office, his hat in his hand. Behind him in the main room of the station house, one of the other officers was hauling a resistant lawbreaker toward the jail. The sound of the man's pitiful wailing competed with the thudding of his boots as he kicked at every piece of furniture the officer dragged him past. Only midafternoon and they already had their first thoroughly soaked drunk.

Taylor shut the door to block out the noise of the commotion. Nick could still hear the yowling.

"Sir?" his assistant asked when Nick didn't reply. "I mean, Mr. Greaves. Sorry about calling you 'sir' all the time. I know you don't like it, but I can't seem to stop."

Shoving aside the report on a robbery they'd recently resolved, Nick leaned back in his chair. It creaked, like usual. One day he'd figure out how to permanently fix it. Or how to keep from leaning back. "It's okay, Taylor."

"Would you mind, though? If I left early today?" he said. "I've finished interviewing folks about that counterfeiting case and there's not much else going on. But I know what you always say about quiet days."

"That they never last." A fact as constant as the creaking of his blasted chair.

Taylor reached up to rub at his neck where the collar of his gray policeman's coat met his skin. "You don't mind, do you?"

"Go on ahead."

His assistant exhaled. "Thank you. I'm planning dinner with Miss Ferguson tonight."

Celia Davies's housekeeper. She and Taylor had been courting for months, starting around the same time that Nick had fallen for a pale-eyed Englishwoman with the stiffest back and sharpest mind of any woman he'd ever met.

"She's able to get away early on a Thursday?" Nick asked.

"Mrs. Davies is fine with Add—Miss Ferguson leaving after she's cooked dinner. We're heading out to celebrate Valentine's Day tonight."

"Valentine's Day is tomorrow, Taylor."

"Couldn't wait." Taylor perked his eyebrows. "Have you sent a valentine to Mrs. Davies?"

A valentine? Not when he kept expecting that husband of hers to rise from the grave, even though Nick had seen the man's body in the morgue after Celia had identified him. Maybe he shouldn't have gone, but Nick had wanted to prove to himself that the fellow was truly dead and not about to interfere in her life again. Had wanted to look on the man she'd thought she'd once loved, just to understand how a woman like her could have married a common criminal like Patrick Davies. All he'd seen was the battered, discoloring remains of the victim of a terrible stagecoach accident. He'd thrown up afterward.

"I take it you've sent a valentine to Miss Ferguson," Nick said, evading Taylor's question.

His assistant grinned. "I sure have, Mr. Greaves. A really nice one, too."

"Expect so."

Taylor peered at Nick. "So you didn't send anything to Mrs. Davies?"

Knuckles rapped on the door, saving him from having to answer.

One of the police officers opened the door and poked his head through the gap. "There's a lady in the station come to see you, Detective."

Nick got to his feet, smiling until he noticed the perking of Taylor's brows. "Show her in, Officer."

He ushered in a slim young woman wearing a mismatched bodice and skirt, as if she'd thrown on the first pieces of clothing that had come to hand. Most men would be too distracted by her striking face to notice. Nick wasn't too distracted, though, and she wasn't the lady he'd been hoping for.

"Miss Ingram," he said. "Thank you for coming back into the station."

Taylor dragged over a chair so she could sit across from Nick.

Her eyes—also lovely—were wide with expectation. "Tell me you've found proof that Sebastian Carr is responsible for this, Detective."

Louise Ingram lifted her right hand, swathed in bandages that concealed the acid burns on her skin. She was lucky she'd leaped aside as quickly as she obviously had and the vitriol hadn't splashed her face or more of her body. Several weeks ago, a seamstress who lived on Jackson had also been attacked with vitriol and hadn't been as fortunate. She'd lost the sight in one of her eyes. The policeman who'd been summoned by her screams had been burned, too, from touching the woman's soaked clothing. He wondered if Louise Ingram's assailant had gotten the idea from the news articles about that particular attack. That was all the city police needed. Copycats.

"That is why you sent for me, isn't it?" she asked, her initial hopefulness starting to fade.

"It's not that, miss." Nick drew in a long breath. "The boy you claim that Mr. Carr hired to toss the vitriol—"

"Claim? I know he paid that kid to throw vitriol on me. I *know* he did, Detective."

"I sent for you because the boy has died, Miss Ingram," Nick said with as much composure as he could muster. "Last night. From phthisis, I was told. At San Quentin. I thought you'd like to know."

"What?" She cast a look at Taylor, leaning up against the wall to her left because somebody had made off with the chair he usually sat on. The women who came into the detectives' office always preferred speaking with him. Taylor could calm them when they were upset—a skill Nick had never acquired. Maybe she was hoping his assistant might tell her something she'd rather hear. "He's dead?"

"I wanted to tell you before you read the news in the papers."

"And now the boy has taken the truth to the grave with him," she said. "Taken the evidence I need to show just how guilty Sebastian Carr is."

"The kid never named him," Nick said.

David Alonso had never named anybody. A Mexican boy of around fifteen, he'd stated that some person had paid him five dollars—a hefty sum of cash—to toss a liquid he'd been told was a harmless dye onto Miss Ingram as a practical joke. When she screamed in pain, he'd realized it wasn't a harmless dye but acid. Unfortunately for David, he hadn't been able to provide a name or more than a vague description of the person who'd hired him. Maybe the person didn't really exist and David Alonso simply possessed a macabre desire to disfigure a beautiful woman. Nick had believed him, though, when he'd claimed his innocence in his halting English. The jury hadn't, however. He'd been hastily convicted of assault and sent to San Quentin.

"I know Sebastian is responsible. I can't help that David Alonso never supplied the proof to indict him." Louise Ingram lowered her gaze to her hands, folded in her lap. "Now what will I do?"

A smudge of red paint marred the gray brim of her bonnet. According to what she'd told Taylor right after the attack, she worked at various theaters alongside her brother, who was some sort of musician.

She was employed to paint scenery, which explained the red staining her bonnet. Working at a theater was a risky occupation for a female, especially one as petite and lovely as Louise Ingram. Maybe she'd imagined having her brother nearby would provide enough protection. Obviously, it hadn't. And the hand she depended on to make her living had been the one she'd raised to shield herself.

"We did try to find evidence that Mr. Carr was involved, miss," Taylor said, his notebook at the ready in case she added more information to the scant details she'd provided the first time she'd come into the police station. "Detective Greaves and I both talked to folks who were near the theater that day, and all anybody saw was the kid running from the side alley after he'd splashed the acid on you."

In Nick's experience, folks suddenly going blind and deaf was normal. Sebastian Carr belonged to an up-and-coming San Francisco family; wouldn't want to ruffle the wrong feathers by ratting on him to the police. Especially if your evidence was nothing more substantial than a rumor. Especially if the woman doing the accusing worked in the theater and was probably a tossed-aside paramour.

"Plus, Mr. Carr seemed genuinely upset when I questioned him about what had happened to you," Taylor added.

She looked up from her lap and smirked. "And here I thought his brother Preston was the amateur actor in that family."

"Without evidence beyond your accusations, Miss Ingram, there's nothing else we can do," Nick said. "Furthermore, Mr. Carr swore he'd never met you beyond occasionally seeing you at a theater."

She set her jaw. Maybe she wasn't so delicate, after all. Rather like another female he knew.

"I'm aware that that's what he told you, Detective. But we *had* met." She paused to draw in a breath. "Often and in private."

"You two had a love affair."

"Yes."

Definitely a tossed-aside paramour.

Nick leaned back, the chair creaking even more loudly than before.

Taylor opened his notebook and readied his pencil. "Why didn't you tell me before?"

"Do women usually admit to their liaisons, Detective?" she asked. "My brother warned me not to get involved with Sebastian. Said that I'd never be employable if theater managers learned about us. As it is, I'll never work again because of . . ." She lifted her injured hand, wincing with the motion. The pain from the still-healing burns must have been excruciating. "I doubt I'll ever be able to paint again."

"You never know, miss," Taylor said, soothing. "You might."

She smiled at Taylor, making him blush. He was prone to it.

"Why admit to your liaison now, Miss Ingram? Unless you're with child." He felt sorry for her. Felt sorry if she'd dreamed that shared nights of passion with Sebastian Carr might lead to wedding vows.

"I'm not, thank God," she replied. "Maybe I should've kept my secret to myself, because what does it all matter, now that the Alonso boy is dead? No one has ever wanted to believe that Sebastian Carr could be a vindictive cur. Poor Miss Bremerton."

"Who's she?"

"A woman who is far wealthier than I am," she replied, a bitter edge to her voice.

"Ah." A rival.

"Sebastian brought her to the theater to take in a performance one evening. We had that soprano from Chicago in town and she was singing. I had a clear view of Sebastian and Miss Bremerton from behind the proscenium. I'm occasionally allowed to stand offstage on the nights my brother is playing." Her gaze drifted as she thought back. "I didn't know who she was. One of the grips told me her name. They were smiling together, laughing. He reached over and touched her cheek . . ."

Her voice faded, the silence eventually broken by the door to the lockup clanging shut out in the main station.

"Seeing them together upset you."

Her eyes focused on Nick's face. "Of course it did. I thought I loved him. That he loved me. I broke off with him."

"And you think that's why he paid David Alonso to toss acid on you? Revenge, maybe?"

"How do I know what motivates Sebastian Carr, Detective? Maybe."

Nick shot a glance at Taylor, who'd lifted his eyebrows but kept taking notes. "Seems like he would've been happy to be able to focus on Miss Bremerton without an encumbrance, Miss Ingram. No insult to you intended."

"You don't know Sebastian, Detective. He likes to eat his cake and have it, too," she said. "And now that kid . . ."

Was dead.

"We are mighty sorry, Miss Ingram," Taylor said.

"Sorry?" she spat and scrambled to her feet, catching the leg of the chair in her skirts and tipping it over. The word rankled her, too. "Your pitiful efforts weren't enough to convict Sebastian Carr, were they? And now some poor kid he duped is dead and Sebastian gets to merrily skip into the loving arms of another foolish woman. You might think you're sorry but you can't possibly be as sorry as I am."

Miss Ingram flung wide the office door, slamming it against the wall, and stormed out into the main room.

"Damn," Nick muttered.

"Isn't there anything else we could do to help Miss Ingram, sir?"

"If you think of something, let me know."

Nick retook his chair, turning it to stare out the street-level window at his back. One of the women striding past on the sidewalk noticed him staring. She leaned down to blow him a kiss before strolling off, her laughter loud enough to hear through the glass. A woman from the Bella Union theater, maybe, in her bright orange striped dress, or one who'd been to visit a courtroom in the upper floors of the City Hall building.

"You know what still bothers me the most, Taylor?"

"No, Mr. Greaves. What?"

"Why *didn't* David Alonso give us a better description of who it was who'd paid him to toss acid on Miss Ingram?"

"Because it was too dark, was what he'd explained."

"Too dark to have at least *some* idea? He was so vague it could've been anybody. A man. A woman. Another kid, even. Any age. Any race," Nick said. "And it couldn't have been too dark to get a clue from the person's voice."

"He said he thought it was a man."

"'Thought.' Why wasn't he more positive?"

Taylor shrugged. "Guess we might never find out, sir."

"No. We might never find out." A scattering of clouds obscured the sun, casting the room in shadows. A darkness matching Nick's mood. "We'll never find out what it was he was hiding."

"Or who it was he was protecting, right?"

"Right, Taylor." The clouds passed and the sun returned. His foul mood didn't lift. "And as for our Miss Ingram, you know what else I think?"

"What, sir?"

"That if anything unfortunate happens to Mr. Sebastian Carr, we know who to bring in first for questioning."

CHAPTER 2

Barbara was quiet on the horsecar trip home, her gaze fixed straight ahead to avoid the other passengers' prying glances. Most, though, were preoccupied with their newspapers or the passing scenery, the streets crowded with wagons and workers.

"We shall be home soon, Barbara." Celia took her cousin's hand, entwining Barbara's slim fingers with her own. Barbara surprised her by not pulling away. "I see our stop up ahead."

The horsecar rolled to a halt at the intersection of Stockton and Vallejo. Outside, the low afternoon sun bathed the wood and brick houses that tumbled down the side of Telegraph Hill in a warm glow.

Celia got to her feet.

"You can let go of my hand now, Cousin," Barbara whispered tersely.

Celia relinquished her grasp. Her cousin surged ahead, climbing down the horsecar's steps to the street as quickly as her foot would allow then marching up the road. Celia hurried to catch her up, striding past St. Francis church, its bells pealing the hour. The corner grocer, tidying a display of cabbages and onions arranged next to the door, nodded at them. Across the street stood a wagon, its side emblazoned with the name *Appleton's Valentine Express*, tethered to a team of horses. Ten in total, a quantity intended to impress the women receiving missives from their beloveds, Celia presumed.

"Barbara, there is no need to dash up the road," Celia called.

Barbara slowed. The effort to speed along had cost her, and she was limping. "I wonder who the lucky recipient of an Appleton's valentine is," she said, looking over at the wagon. She sounded envious; the valentine would likely not be for her.

"I believe the answer is straight ahead."

Celia nodded in the direction of their house. A man had descended the steps and was jogging down the street toward them. A crisp apron was tied over his clothing, and the name of the establishment he worked for was emblazoned on the bottom hem. *Appleton's.*

"He was at our house?" Barbara asked.

"It appears so." The fellow must have parked the wagon on the corner because Vallejo was too steep and muddy after a recent bout of rain to maneuver. Even with ten horses.

Barbara peered at Celia around the edge of her bonnet brim. "A card and maybe a piece of jewelry for you, Cousin?"

"And who would send me a valentine?"

The employee from Appleton's reached them, tipping his hat as he passed.

"Detective Greaves. Who else?" her cousin asked.

"Don't be silly, Barbara. He would do no such thing."

"He might."

Would he? After her husband's death, they'd admitted their feelings but had seen so little of each other in the weeks since. They had spent Christmas and New Year's together, and there were the occasional dinners, but should she expect more? When he was so busy with his police work and her notoriety had filled her days with new, inquisitive patients and the ever-expanding parade of folks requesting her investigative help. Maybe they might never have enough time for each other. Maybe he had already changed his mind about what he felt for her.

Honestly, Celia. You sound like an inexperienced schoolgirl.

"I sincerely doubt that Nicholas Greaves is predisposed to sentimental gestures such as expensive valentines, Barbara. I presume that was a gift for Addie from Mr. Taylor." He, on the other hand, *was* inclined to sentimental gestures.

"Do you think he'll ask Addie to marry him, Cousin?" Barbara came to a halt in front of the house, the lovely two-story brick she'd inherited from her father. "She'll move away from us, if he does. She'll go and live with him."

"It is far too soon to worry about Addie leaving us, Barbara."

"You think she won't accept Mr. Taylor?" her cousin asked hopefully.

"That is not what I meant," Celia replied. "I meant we shall still see her. She can continue to work for us during the day."

"But she won't be with us in the evenings," Barbara said, her apprehension plain. "And she won't be able to work f gprobably when the bottleor us once she and Mr. Taylor start having children."

What would either of them do without Addie? She'd been with Celia since London, since the early days of her unhappy marriage to Patrick Davies, and had become far more than a servant; she was a friend.

"This is all in the future, Barbara. We shall cross that bridge, as they say, when we come to it."

"At least Mr. Taylor isn't like that horrible Dr. Schneider."

"Addie would not love him if he ever attempted to crush *her* spirit."

They climbed the steps leading up to the house and passed beneath the sign publicizing Celia's clinic, which creaked in a fresh gust of wind.

Addie stood in the entry hall. "Oh, Mrs. Davies. Miss Barbara." She hastily concealed behind her back a card she'd been reading. "You've returned."

"Is that a valentine from Mr. Taylor, Addie?" Barbara asked, untying her bonnet ribbons.

Addie stuffed the card into her skirt pocket. "How was the doctor, Miss Barbara?"

"It *is* a valentine from Mr. Taylor." Barbara's eyebrows lifted. "Has he proposed?"

Addie's cheeks reddened. "Och no, he's nae proposed."

"Well, that's good."

"Barbara, that is enough," Celia chided. "Sending a valentine was very sweet of him, Addie."

"A letter came for you while you were out, Miss Barbara," Addie said, directing the conversation away from Mr. Taylor's valentine. "Looks to be from Miss Grace."

"Oh?" She snatched the envelope off the hallway table. "I think I'll go to my room to read it. And to work on my arithmetic assignment, of course," she said and fairly galloped up the stairs, her aching foot forgotten.

"Poor bairn," Addie said, her gaze tracking Barbara's departure. "She is missing her friend terribly. Could we not send Miss Barbara to Miss Grace's ladies' college too, ma'am?"

Celia sat to undo her half boots, swapping them for her soft kid shoes. "You remember how she was treated the last time we sent her to a school, Addie." Horridly. "And even if Barbara wanted to attend, I do not believe the ladies' college accepts Chinese students."

"'Tis their loss." Addie took Celia's bonnet. "You've nae valentine from Mr. Greaves, by the way, ma'am."

"I did not expect one." *But I may have wished for one.* "And the doctor cannot help Barbara. Even if he could, she'd refuse to accept it. He goggled at her like she was an exhibit in a traveling circus, Addie. As if the crookedness of her foot was somehow due to the fact that her mother was Chinese."

"'Tis just as well, if that is how he thinks."

"I completely agree." Celia gestured at the closed parlor doors. "Do we have company?"

"Miss Bremerton has come to see you. I did tell her I wasna certain when you and Miss Barbara would return from your appointment, but she insisted on waiting." Addie leaned in to whisper. "She seems verra bothered, ma'am. Nervous."

"I hope it is nothing serious."

Addie arched an eyebrow. "Ma'am, when folks visiting you are acting nervous, 'tis always something serious."

"Yes. Indeed."

"Should I serve tea?"

"If you would." Celia hastily checked the presentability of her gown before striding over to the parlor doors and sliding them open. The doors rattled on their tracks, and the noise made Miss Bremerton leap up from the blue-striped settee. Definitely nervous.

"There you are, Mrs. Davies."

Irene Bremerton was dressed in a very spring-like rose from tip to toe. The shade complemented the deep brown of her hair and lent color to her presently very pale cheeks. Coloring that almost disguised the smattering of pockmarks that marred her skin. She was lovely, nonetheless, and pockmarks were all too common. Even on the skin of well-off young women.

Celia smiled at her and slid the doors closed once again.

"I was not expecting a visit from you, Miss Bremerton. I thought our appointment to further discuss the clinic was set for tomorrow morning," she said. "Although you are welcome at any time, of course. And while I am thinking of it, thank you for recommending Dr. Schneider. Unfortunately, he cannot help my cousin."

"Oh. Oh, yes. I'm sorry to hear that, though."

"It is quite all right."

"About our meeting." She squeezed together her hands—clad in dusty rose kid gloves—and attempted to return Celia's smile. The expression slid off her face before it could even take hold. "I . . . You see . . ."

"Miss Bremerton, please do sit. I intend to."

Celia chose the thick-cushioned chair directly opposite the settee, the mahogany center table filling the gap between them. Irene Bremerton retook her seat, her unhappy demeanor a contrast to that of Uncle Walford's beaming face in the painting hanging on the wall above her. If the artist had attempted to convince Uncle Walford to strike a more sober expression, he'd failed.

"I am afraid that I have to cancel our meeting with Miss Vanmeter, Mrs. Davies," she said. "I wanted to inform you in person."

Sebastian will see to it that Miss Bremerton is far too busy to be involved in founding medical clinics . . . "Cancel? Or merely postpone?"

"I hope only postpone, Mrs. Davies."

"Nonetheless, I do hate to hear this, Miss Bremerton. The city is desperate for another free clinic for women in need," she said. "I can only manage so many patients, what with my other responsibilities."

"I regret that it can't be helped. You understand."

No, I do not. "Have you informed Miss Vanmeter?"

"Not yet. She'll be so disappointed," she said. "Katherine was truly looking forward to operating the clinic with my financial help and your wise guidance, Mrs. Davies. However, she thinks—"

Just then, Addie opened the doors connecting the parlor to the dining room and kitchen beyond, a tray of tea things in her hand. "Pardon me for interrupting, ma'am."

"You can set the tea on the table, Addie. No need to serve us," Celia said. "I shall pour it out."

Placing the tray on the table at Celia's knee, Addie glanced at Miss Bremerton, whose attention had shifted to the lace cuffs of her sleeves. Apparently, they required adjusting. "Aye, ma'am."

She hastily retreated, closing the doors again.

Celia leaned over to pour out a cup of oolong for the woman across from her. "What is it that Miss Vanmeter thinks, Miss Bremerton?"

She looked up, blinking a few times. She had enviably long lashes that drew a person's attention to her eyes, which were the pale brown of coffee diluted with milk and strikingly lovely. Were they the feature that had caused Sebastian Carr to fall in love with her?

"I don't remember what I was going to say, Mrs. Davies." She gave a laugh to suggest she was silly to have had a lapse of memory, but Miss Bremerton was far from silly. "I'm sorry."

Celia placed the strainer on its drip bowl and handed her the cup of tea. The young woman's hands were trembling. "How does your fiancé feel about your decision to postpone working with Miss Vanmeter on the clinic?"

She set down her teacup, which clinked loudly against the saucer. "Sebastian?"

"I should offer my congratulations, by the way. You hadn't told me that you intended to wed soon."

"It's all come about so quickly, Mrs. Davies," she said. "The official engagement announcement is set for tomorrow evening. During the masquerade ball Sebastian's father is hosting. I wish my parents could be here but it can't be helped."

"I have heard about the mask and the announcement."

"Don't believe the gossip, Mrs. Davies." This time, her smile was not accompanied by the artificial laugh. Its absence did not make her smile appear any more sincere. "We are both delighted and looking forward to the engagement party and our wedding later this spring."

There had been gossip suggesting one of them was not "delighted"?

Celia peered over the brim of her teacup, assessing Miss Bremerton, and took a sip. "I trust that your fiancé is not the reason you are delaying work on the clinic, Miss Bremerton," she said. "Although, I suppose Mr. Carr might be happy you've elected to postpone. You now have so much else to attend to, as you'll soon have a house and a husband to occupy your energies."

"Yes." She abruptly stood. "I hate to rush off, Mrs. Davies, but I just remembered another engagement that I have. You see? I am getting so forgetful."

She extended her hand. Celia stood as well and took it. "If you ever need anything, Miss Bremerton, anything at all, please let me know."

The forced smile made a reappearance. "What might I need? I have all that I could want."

Celia squeezed the young woman's hand, which she'd yet to release. "Anything, Miss Bremerton. I can be trusted. I can be useful," she said. "I am worried about you."

"You don't need to worry about me, Mrs. Davies."

She tugged her fingers clear of Celia's grip and hurried from the house.

• • •

"There's dinner, if you're hungry now, Mr. Greaves," Mrs. Jewett, Nick's landlady, announced. She wiped her hands across the apron tied about her waist, leaving behind a trail of flour. "And that dog of yours has been whining all day. I let him out into the yard earlier, but he's been at it again up in your room."

Nick removed his hat and scrubbed his fingers through his hair. True to her word, Riley let out a series of yaps, the sound echoing down the staircase. "Maybe he can smell your delicious cooking, Mrs. Jewett."

She smiled, the dimple in her left cheek hollowing. "I don't know what to do with you if you're going to start complimenting my cooking, Mr. Greaves. I can share my recipes with your ladylove, though, if you'd like."

Between her and Taylor, he wasn't sure who enjoyed teasing him more about Celia Davies. "I doubt Mrs. Davies would appreciate being referred to as my 'ladylove.'"

"When are you going to ask her to marry you?" She tapped his arm with a flour-coated finger, leaving a streak of white on his sleeve. She swiped at the mark with a corner of her apron.

"I thought you didn't like her."

"Now, Mr. Greaves, that's ridiculous. Of course I like her."

"I seem to remember differently, Mrs. Jewett."

"Well, that was in the beginning." Satisfied she'd eliminated the flour residue, his housekeeper stopped fussing over his coat sleeve. "We can all make mistakes about people, Mr. Greaves."

More than once, his mistakes had involved falling in love with the wrong woman. How could he be positive this time?

Mrs. Jewett was eyeing him. "Don't tell me you've gone and become faint-hearted. If you're not quick to grab her up, she'll get away from you," she said. "A pretty thing like her? And smart, too."

"She's too opinionated for most men."

"Which is why she's perfect for you, Mr. Greaves. Did you even send her a valentine today? No. I can see from that look on your face that you didn't."

"Celia Davies is in mourning, Mrs. Jewett."

"Mourning for a fellow who ran off to Mexico, abandoning her? Some sort of criminal? Bah."

He regarded her. "Who's been talking to you about him? Have you been gossiping with Taylor?"

Her expression didn't reveal a hint of guilt. Heaven help them all if Mrs. Jewett ever turned to a life of crime, because the woman could be as canny as the most stone-faced crook.

"Besides, Mr. Greaves, it's been three months since her husband died."

"She is in mourning," Nick repeated.

"Well, nobody around here cares, except for you. You're just insisting on being stubborn."

He was just insisting on being scared. "I'll be down to eat once I see what's going on with Riley."

She held out a hand to stop him. "Wait. A package was dropped off for you today. I found it on the front steps with your name on it." She hurried into the parlor, steeped in shadows from the sun having set, and brought back a small parcel tightly wrapped in brown paper and tied with string. "Something from your sister, maybe."

Aside from his name, there weren't any other markings indicating where it had come from or who'd sent it. The parcel couldn't be holding much, because whatever was inside weighed about the same as a regular letter in an envelope. "Doesn't look like her handwriting, Mrs. Jewett. And I can't imagine what Ellie might send me. Or why she would."

Mrs. Jewett fisted her hips. "Mr. Greaves, is it so impossible to conceive that people like your sister and Mrs. Davies—and me, for that matter—might care enough for you to want to give you gifts?"

Yes. Since his closest friend, Jack Hutchinson, had died on a battlefield from a bullet meant for Nick, since his little sister Meg had taken her own life while he'd been wallowing in an Army hospital recovering from a bayonet wound that still pained him, he'd stopped wanting anybody to care.

Until he'd met Celia Davies.

"I'll be down to eat soon."

Package tucked under his arm, he bounded up the steps and entered his set of rooms. Riley scurried out of the way of the door before Nick hit him with it.

"Sorry, boy. You okay, there?" Nick squatted next to the dog, whose shaggy brown-and-white tail wagged fiercely. "Seems you've been unhappy today."

Riley responded by licking him in the face then sniffing at the package Nick held.

"Once I've had a look at this, I'll take you outside, if that's what you'd like."

He ruffled the dog's floppy ears and stood. Unholstering the Colt he carried, he took both the gun and the package over to the table in the room Mrs. Jewett liked to call his parlor. He struck a match and lit the coal-oil lamp, turning up the flame to examine the parcel by its glow. Nothing at all on the outside to indicate who the sender was.

Riley dropped onto the floor by Nick's feet, his eyes watchful.

"You're curious, too, aren't you? Guess the only way to find out what's inside is to open it."

He removed his bowie knife from the scabbard strapped around his waist, cut the string, and peeled back the paper. A folded piece of heavy card stock, like that used for a photograph, was all that was inside. He opened it out, forcing it flat to smooth the creases cross-hatching the surface. A chill spread over his body and his old wound took to aching. It *was* a photograph. One he had a copy of. *Damn. Damn.*

Riley whimpered as Nick went to the dresser against the wall where the matching daguerreotype stood in its tarnishing silver frame. An image of three people in a photographer's studio, his youngest sister barely able to suppress her grin as she struggled to calmly sit on the chair she'd been given. How stiff they looked. How much younger, too. Ellie, her face smooth and eyes soft before a widowhood that was years in the future would sap her vivacity, her hand pressed on Meg's shoulder to quiet her. Nick, his hand tucked into his vest like a pompous idiot, itching to be finished with the whole process and get out of the studio, stifling hot on a Sacramento summer day.

He flipped over the copy he'd been sent. On the back, in fading ink, Meg had written out the date they'd sat for that daguerreotype. In the past few months, he'd had days where his memories of Meg, of her bright laughter and teasing smiles, hadn't haunted him. Where he hadn't been shaken by daydreams of her nimble fingers weaving daisy chains to wrap around his neck and Ellie's, too. And now this. Her copy. This photograph without any note or explanation. Who the hell had sent it to torture him?

Nick folded the photograph and jammed it into the top drawer of the dresser. He had a feeling whoever had sent the picture wouldn't keep him in suspense for long. He'd get an explanation. Whether he wanted it or not.

· · ·

Celia knocked on Barbara's door and eased it open. "Do you mind if I come in?"

Barbara was seated at the writing desk placed in front of the window, where evening darkness was beginning to stretch across the street beyond. She looked back over her shoulder. "Does it matter if I do?" Her voice was shaky, as if she'd been crying.

Celia crossed the room and knelt at her cousin's side. Barbara's eyes were red-rimmed. "What is the matter? Was there bad news in Grace's letter?"

If there had been, surely Jane would've contacted Celia and informed her. Their friendship was as close as that between Barbara and Jane's stepdaughter.

"Not really. It's just . . ." She drew in a breath. "Owen sent Grace a valentine earlier this week. Grace wanted me to know."

"Ah." Owen Cassidy. Someone else who clearly believed in sentimental gestures. "She did not mean to hurt you by sharing the news, Barbara."

Not Grace. She was all that was kind and generous.

Barbara glanced at Grace's letter, tightly folded atop the far corner of the desk. Innocent-looking in the glow of the lamp Barbara had lit. "I know."

"And Owen may wish that Grace would care for him, but she won't—"

"But she does, Cousin! She *does* care for him."

Oh dear. An Irish boy who scraped out a living as best he could—and too often found himself in as much trouble as Celia did, if not more—would never be permitted to court the daughter of a successful, ambitious businessman. "It's impossible, Barbara."

"This is America, Cousin Celia, not England. It *is* possible," she spat. "And now she has Owen, and Addie has Mr. Taylor. Even you have Mr. Greaves. And I . . ."

She dropped her head into her hands and started to cry. A tear dripped onto the sheet of algebra equations she'd been working on.

"You will find someone someday, Barbara." Celia wrapped an arm around her cousin's shoulders and pulled her close.

"I won't. I'm a half-Chinese . . . castoff."

"You are not a castoff, Barbara," Celia said sternly. "In the face of prejudice, your father loved your mother. There will be someone for you. I know it."

She held Barbara until her cousin's tears subsided. In the end, she was strong and resilient; she'd had to learn to be.

"I'm sorry," she said at last.

"No need to be sorry." Celia retrieved a clean handkerchief from Barbara's chest of drawers. "And I will never allow you to be alone. I promise."

Barbara dabbed her damp eyes with the square of linen. "That's what I'm afraid of," she teased and blew her nose. "What did Miss Bremerton want?"

She'd already recovered if she cared to hear about the reason for Miss Bremerton's visit.

Celia went to sit on Barbara's bed. "To tell me that she has to cancel the meeting we'd scheduled for tomorrow," she replied. "I fear Dr.

Schneider was correct about Sebastian Carr. That he won't want Irene Bremerton, his future wife, involved in establishing women's clinics."

Her cousin blew her nose one last time and folded up the handkerchief. "At least she didn't come here to ask you to investigate something."

"We can both be grateful for that."

CHAPTER 3

"Ma'am, you've a visitor already this morning," Addie said, stepping into Celia's bedchamber. "Ma'am?"

Celia was standing in the center of her room wearing only her corset and crinoline, staring at the black bodice and skirt spread across her bed. The same outfit she'd worn yesterday and the day before and the day before that. Black on Valentine's Day. How dreary.

"You've nae need to wear mourning for Patrick Davies, ma'am."

"I want to do what is right, Addie. What is respectable."

"You are always respectable, ma'am."

For heaven's sake, act like a lady, Cecilia. Her aunt's voice, admonishing Celia after she'd returned from an excursion through the woods with her brother, collecting creamy white sorrel flowers and pretty feathers, on the lookout for wild creatures to tend to, finding none but dirtying her shoes and stockings beyond repair. Or the time her aunt had invited the vicar to tea and Celia had managed to spill the entire contents of her teacup onto her new violet dress, a frilly concoction that was tight in all the wrong places and made her irritable. *Act like a lady, Cecilia. Try to be respectable.* Instead of a hoyden.

"And not wearing black for that Patrick Davies, the divil, doesna make you less so," Addie insisted.

Celia looked over at her housekeeper. Addie had taken to wearing a smoke-grey dress since Patrick's death. Not because she cared one whit about that "divil," but because she cared so much for Celia. "Perhaps we should wait until six months' time has passed. Then we can all discard our mourning attire."

"Three months too many," Addie said, clicking her tongue against her teeth. "Here, ma'am, let me help you into your clothes." She picked up the skirt and lowered it over Celia's head.

"Who's my visitor?" Not a patient; Addie would have said so straightaway if it were. Celia's Ellery watch lay open atop the bedside table. Not quite seven o'clock. The sun had only just risen, although she'd been awake for a good hour. Pondering Miss Bremerton and Miss Vanmeter's clinic and the misfortunes of being an independent woman set to marry a domineering man. "A trifle early this morning."

Addie finished tying off the laces of the skirt and retrieved the bodice. "'Tis Miss Vanmeter," she answered. "She's a bit *wees't*, as my mother might say. Like Miss Bremerton yesterday."

"Then I should hurry down to see what she is so anxious about, although I suspect her upset involves her clinic," Celia said. "Show her into the dining room, Addie. She might want breakfast."

After finishing dressing and tidying her hair as best she could, Celia went downstairs. Addie had gone ahead of her and had already provided Miss Vanmeter with coffee and a plate of toast and butter and black currant jam. The food didn't appear to have been touched.

"Miss Vanmeter, good morning," Celia said, selecting a chair opposite the woman.

She'd met Katherine Vanmeter just once before, at a charity event supporting one of the city's orphanages. She had been in the company of Miss Bremerton, who was engaged in introducing her friend to all those in attendance. Miss Vanmeter was plain and short and had dressed in an unpretentious ginger-yellow gown, similar in style to the brown dress she wore today that wafted the odor of camphor off its folds. She'd appeared unremarkable when compared to Miss Bremerton's effervescent, well-to-do beauty. Until she'd smiled, a warm lovely smile that transformed everything about her.

"I apologize for intruding on you at this hour, Mrs. Davies," she said in her strong and clear voice. She'd calmed down since Addie had shown her into the house. She held her hands in her lap, however, and out of sight. Perhaps, beneath the cover of the table, she dug her nails into her palms.

"You are not intruding, Miss Vanmeter. I was already up," Celia said. "I hope you don't mind that I had my housekeeper provide you with some breakfast."

She glanced at the untouched plate. "I appreciate your

thoughtfulness, Mrs. Davies." She smiled that smile. "I didn't eat this morning and do realize that I'm hungry."

"Then please go ahead." Celia considered the woman as she unfolded her napkin. "Miss Bremerton was here yesterday. I presume your visit has to do with the unexpected delay in her plans for the clinic."

"I wasn't sure she'd told you. What am I to do now?"

"Perhaps she'll find a way to convince Mr. Carr to permit her to proceed with funding your clinic, after all," Celia said, stirring milk into her coffee.

"Sebastian is very stubborn, Mrs. Davies," she said. "Very determined to have his way, and that way does not include permitting Irene to do what she wants."

"A typical situation in such a relationship as theirs, Miss Vanmeter."

"I know." She picked up a knife and listlessly spread jam on a slice of toast. "I just thought . . . I hoped for better for Irene."

"She and Mr. Carr are not married yet. She remains free to do what she wishes with her inheritance until then."

"Not with Sebastian insisting she do otherwise. He's like that, you know. Insistent and very persuasive." Miss Vanmeter leaned forward and stretched a hand across the table. Her fingernails had been chewed to nubs. "Is there anything you can do to help me, Mrs. Davies? Perhaps you know of another benefactor who might be willing to assist me financially. I'd hate to give up my clinic when I've found an affordable location to house it."

Celia could barely fund her own clinic with the money Uncle Walford had left her. "I shall see if I can find someone to help you, Miss Vanmeter."

"Thank you, Mrs. Davies." She took a bite of her toast. "This jam is delicious."

"My housekeeper is an excellent cook."

"You're lucky." She daubed her mouth. "Is there any chance you'll be attending the masked ball the Carrs are holding this evening, Mrs.

Davies? If you are, maybe you can speak with Sebastian and explain why the clinic is so critical. He might listen to you."

Celia took a sip of her coffee before setting it down. "I've not been invited, Miss Vanmeter. Besides, I am still in mourning and it would not be proper of me to attend."

"How could I be so thoughtless? Here I've been thinking only of my problems," she said. "I'm sorry."

"Do you plan to attend?"

"Yes, even though Sebastian and I have been at loggerheads over my clinic." Miss Vanmeter dipped a spoon into the floral-painted bowl holding crushed sugar, stirring some of the coarse granules into her coffee, which had probably gone cold. "I have to be there to support Irene. As a friend."

"'Support,' Miss Vanmeter? You make it sound as though she is not excited about the announcement of her engagement this evening." *Don't believe the gossip, Mrs. Davies.*

Miss Vanmeter lowered her spoon to the saucer. It clinked against the porcelain. "I don't mean to suggest that at all, Mrs. Davies. But Irene is understandably upset that he's forbidden her from supporting my women's clinic," she said. "There are times I think he'd rather keep her all to himself, like a precious jeweled bauble no one else is permitted to see or touch."

Or a prize trout.

"Miss Bremerton is a good friend to you."

The comment caused Miss Vanmeter to smile again. "Irene is the best of friends. She has already done so much for me. Has constantly encouraged me."

"I want to help you both and especially you, Miss Vanmeter. You are passionate about a cause which is dear to my own heart," Celia said. "If this opportunity comes to nothing, however, there will be another, I am certain."

"I wish I could be as certain," she said. "I remain convinced that you approaching Sebastian is the best tactic. He *might* listen to you, Mrs.

Davies. He might. Irene has spoken to him about you with great admiration, as did his mother before she passed away. Mrs. Carr was an admirer as well, I've been told."

Celia sighed. The young woman had worn her down. "I shall make an appointment with him early next week and see what I can do, Miss Vanmeter. I'd not get my hopes up, however, if I were you."

"But I have to, Mrs. Davies," she said. "I have to."

• • •

Nick arrived at Celia's house just as a small woman in a dull brown dress hurtled down the front steps, the edges of her short cape flapping. He tipped his hat as she passed him, and she offered a brief nod before rushing off.

Addie Ferguson stood in the doorway and watched the woman hurry along the sidewalk. She greeted Nick as he climbed the stairs, taking them two at a time.

"Is it too early for a visit, Miss Ferguson?"

"Never too early or too late for you, Mr. Greaves," she said and ushered him into the entrance hall.

Taking off his hat, he drew in a breath. The air in the entryway exhaled the aromas he associated with Celia and her home—the lavender scent of her hair, the tang of linseed oil from recently cleaned furniture, the sharp odor of medicines and ointments. A contrast of smells as stimulating as the woman herself.

Addie was eyeing him. "Mr. Greaves?"

Pull yourself together, Greaves. "Is she in her clinic?" The door was open, but the chair in front of her desk, which he could see from where he stood, was unoccupied.

"She's in the dining room. Do you want breakfast?"

"Mrs. Jewett has seen to it that I was fed this morning, but I wouldn't mind some coffee."

Addie nodded and went off to bring him some. He found Celia

seated at the dining room table, staring out the window that overlooked the rear yard.

"Ah, Nicholas, good morning," she said, twisting to glance over her shoulder at him.

He was grateful she didn't add that it had been a good couple of weeks since she'd last seen him. "Hope I'm not disturbing you."

"Not one bit."

She smiled and his pulse jumped like it had the first time he'd seen that smile, nearly a year ago. In his dank, foul-smelling office when she'd shown up to demand he discover who'd murdered a patient of hers, a Chinese girl who'd been a friend. No, later than that. When she'd stood in the parlor of this very house and reminisced about the man who beamed down from a painting on the wall, an uncle whose generosity had allowed her a chance to build a future. He'd fallen hard for her, then. Was still falling.

Nick took the chair across from Celia. A cup of untouched coffee sat off to one side. "Who was your guest, if you don't mind my asking?"

"Miss Katherine Vanmeter." She paused as Addie bustled into the room, removed the cup, and replaced it with a clean, empty one. "A woman who intends to open another free women's clinic, modeled on mine. She's been seeking my expertise and I was all set to help her, except the funds to operate the clinic may have abruptly vanished."

"Sad little creature," said Addie, setting out a plate of warm toast then pouring out coffee for Nick. "To have that Miss Bremerton's fiancé ruin her plans."

"Addie, have you been listening in on my conversations?" Celia asked.

"I'd rather not say, ma'am."

"Miss Bremerton? Irene Bremerton?" Nick asked.

Celia regarded him. "You've heard of her?"

Nick slathered butter onto the toast. He obviously hadn't eaten enough of Mrs. Jewett's breakfast, if he still had an appetite. Out of the corner of his eye, he noticed Addie grin. Also obvious was the fact that he'd spent enough time around these two women for them to know him so well.

"How was your dinner with my assistant last night, Miss Ferguson?" Nick asked.

"Ah . . . quite fine, Mr. Greaves. Quite fine."

He wouldn't be getting much out of her about their rendezvous. One day, Nick supposed, Taylor would simply spring the news that he and Addie were set to get married.

Addie hastily returned to the kitchen. Celia was still waiting for him to explain how he'd heard of Irene Bremerton.

"Here's what I know about Irene Bremerton," he said after swallowing a bite of toast. "She's engaged to a fellow named Sebastian Carr and is wealthy."

The woman across from him lifted one of her softly curved eyebrows. They were darker than the honey gold of her hair. An observation totally irrelevant to their conversation.

"Who mentioned her to you, Mr. Greaves?"

"Are we addressing each other formally now, Mrs. Davies?"

She reached for a piece of toast. "I feel another investigation coming on, which somehow warrants the formality, I suppose."

"Now why would you think you're going to get involved in another one of my investigations?"

She took a bite and chewed for a few seconds before responding. "Because, in the past, the coincidence of us both having recently become acquainted with an individual usually results in that person's involvement in a crime and our subsequent investigation."

"I've gotten too used to you saying 'our' when it comes to my investigations, Mrs. Davies."

"That is assuredly the case, if you have elected to not chide me about my slip," she said. "Tell me about Miss Bremerton's relationship to whomever it was who mentioned her to you. And quickly, before Barbara comes down for breakfast and discovers a fresh cause for more upset."

"Oh?"

"Apparently Owen sent Grace Hutchinson a valentine."

"Ah." Even Owen Cassidy was a romantic. "Celia, I'm sorry. That's why I'm here. I'm sorry that I—"

She stopped him with a wave of her hand. "Don't apologize for not giving me a valentine, Nicholas. We don't need such tokens." The gentle look in her pale clear eyes struck him to the heart. He didn't deserve her. "Addie, however, was starry-eyed when she returned from her dinner outing with Mr. Taylor last evening. I do believe she slept with his card tucked beneath her pillow."

Taylor would be in a rapture of love for days and completely worthless if Nick told him that. "Mrs. Jewett thinks I should've sent you a valentine, anyway."

"She did not used to like me."

"Which was precisely what I said to her when she mentioned it." Mentioned a valentine and that Nick should marry the woman across the table from him.

Ask her, Greaves. Ask her now, even though she's wearing black and you're terrified of how you feel about her. That she makes you forget to breathe. That you would die if you lost her. And he'd already lost so much.

"Nicholas, are you unwell?" she asked.

"Not a problem more breakfast won't cure."

Her brows briefly tucked together, but she accepted his comment and let off discussing tokens of love. "So, back to the reason someone spoke with you about Irene Bremerton."

Nick explained about Louise Ingram and her former affair with Sebastian Carr. That she'd broken off with him when she'd spotted him with Irene Bremerton. How, according to Miss Ingram, his response to her rejection led him to pay a Mexican boy to throw acid on her, leaving her scarred. How that same boy had ended up the only one accused and convicted of a crime, and had died in prison two days ago. The more he explained, the more taut Celia's expression became.

"If Miss Ingram's accusation is true, Miss Bremerton may be making a terrible mistake," she said. "And Miss Vanmeter likely agrees with that opinion. Mr. Carr has forbidden Miss Bremerton from funding her friend's clinic. A cruelty when I suspect the young woman is rich enough to easily do so without harming any of Mr. Carr's plans for her money. Whatever those might be."

Nick finished off the rest of his slice of toast and wiped the butter residue from his fingers. "I haven't even met the fellow and I don't like him."

"Neither do I, but I promised Miss Vanmeter I would attempt to persuade him to permit Miss Bremerton to continue with her planned support for the clinic." Celia got that look in her eye he readily recognized. She had the bit between her teeth and was going to plow forward. "Perhaps while I am meeting with him, I can insert a comment about Miss Ingram. Judge his reaction and his possible guilt."

"Celia, don't do that."

The look in her eye was joined by a wicked grin. "Now, Nicholas, when have you ever been able to stop me?"

Blasted woman.

• • •

Owen wrestled the crate of wine bottles off the bed of the wagon, propping a knee underneath to support it while he wrapped his arms around the wood. A sliver poked him in the arm. *Durn it.* Steadied, he turned to face the house. What a highfalutin place it was, the lace-curtained windows on the first floor glowing golden with lamplight. It was nowhere near where he lived, of course, but on the western flank of Rincon Hill, where all sorts of fine folks were putting up their equally fine houses. He was pretty sure his mouth had flopped open when the wagon he'd hitched a ride on passed the front of the building, which was lit by a whole passel of lanterns. Their glow designed to guide the guests up the wide steps, onto the covered porch, and through the large double doors, inset with cut glass. The whole place was three floors of massive arched windows and some sort of square tower sticking up in the middle. And only one family living in it.

"I heard the place cost ten thousand to build," said another of the fellows hired to bring drink to the partygoers. Angus MacNamara had left his brogue behind in New York City, he liked to joke, but not his gaunt frame. It was almost as if his body couldn't seem to forget growing up during the Great Hunger back in Ireland. He was a rough fellow who favored his left foot when he walked—a gift from the war, he'd told Owen when they'd first met a year or more ago—which didn't stop him from roughly jostling Owen out of the way to reach for one of the remaining crates.

"Ten thousand? No kidding." Owen added a whistle. Some folks had all the luck.

"Yep."

"Hey, you two!" The supervisor who'd come to Owen's boardinghouse looking for men to work tonight pointed at Owen and Angus. "Enough of your gabbing. We're already late with this delivery. And don't nobody drop any crates this time, got it? Don't wanna have to come back yet again with more wine because you oafs are so durned clumsy."

"Yes, sir," Owen called out.

Angus snickered. "Lickspittle."

Wine crate clasped firmly in his arms, Owen headed for the back door, which stood open. It connected to a passage that led to both the kitchen and a set of stairs descending to the cellar below. The kitchen was a hubbub of folks rushing about preparing food, pots clanging against the stove, a woman's hoarse voice shouting orders. Warmth spilled into the corridor along with the smell of cooking so delicious that Owen's mouth instantly took to watering.

As he stood there salivating, the door that connected the passageway to the main part of the house opened, letting in the noise of a small band playing and people talking and laughing. A man in some sort of multicolor checkerboard getup strode through. He wore a matching silk covering over his face, and the gray eyes peering through the holes in the mask flicked over Owen. Nobody important, he must have thought, before turning into the kitchen. He paused in the doorway, as if he was looking for somebody in particular.

"Hey, you again. What are you doing in here? You need to use the outside cellar door, not this one." The fellow who'd hired him had a nasty snarl on his face. "Cassidy, right? That's your name? I'm gonna make sure I never give you a job again, you hear me? Get to it. We're not finished yet."

"Sorry, sir. Yes, sir." He really could use the money; it was never a great idea to upset somebody who might be paying out more in the future.

Down in the cellar, Owen set the crate next to the others lined up against the cold stone wall. Several were already empty. The party had only been going on for an hour or so? These folks must like to drink.

He scurried through the area door—*the one you're supposed to be using, Cassidy*—and up the steps, bumping shoulders against the other men dragging even more wine down the steps. As he turned for the wagon, one of the servants came rushing outside through the back door, her hand clamped over her mouth. She was an awful funny color, sorta green. She stumbled down the stairs and out into the rear yard.

Angus noticed the girl. "Somebody's had too much of the wine they're splashing around here like water."

"I'd be surprised if she could manage to sneak off and drink a bunch of wine without being caught," Owen said.

"You never worked a rich folks' party before, kid? There's always a way to sneak off and get into trouble, if you've got a mind to." He made a sucking noise against his gapped teeth. "Yep."

Folks started shouting in the yard.

"What the tarnation?" one of the men asked.

The girl had sprawled on the ground not far from an outhouse, a trail of sick leading to where she'd fallen.

"What's wrong with her?" Angus didn't wait for Owen to reply and managed to hotfoot it across the yard without his bad foot bothering him, joining the others who were collecting to whisper and point.

"Is she dead?" One of them rudely prodded the girl's legs with the toe of a boot.

"Heck, I hope not!" the boss said, backing away like whatever had felled her might be catching.

Shoot, thought Owen, backing away too. *Shoot.* This was plain not good. Not good at all.

CHAPTER 4

"Sorry about making a fuss yesterday over the valentine Owen sent Grace, Cousin Celia," said Barbara, stepping inside the parlor.

She dropped onto the chair in front of the window. At her back, the evening had descended into deep shadow, the only light the occasional gleam of a lantern at a neighbor's home. Or the flare of the tip of the cigar being smoked by the man across the way who enjoyed sitting on his front steps in the dark.

"It's quite alright, Barbara."

"I shouldn't care that Owen is sweet on Grace," she said, as if trying to convince herself. "He has a right to be happy and she's so pretty."

Celia set aside the book she'd been reading, a well-thumbed copy of *Cranford* that she'd borrowed from Jane Hutchinson. "Valentine's Day can be a very difficult day."

Barbara gazed at her. "Are you upset that Mr. Greaves didn't send you a valentine?"

"Not at all. I do not require gifts of any type from Mr. Greaves."

Patrick had been fond of valentines. Especially when they'd first started courting, her heart stinging from the loss of her beloved brother. She'd let herself believe that Patrick would cure that heartache. Instead, he had caused so much more. Proving, she supposed, that pretty words on lace-covered paper were meaningless when offset by the actions of a fickle man.

Barbara had turned to stare at her father's portrait. "Papa must have loved giving valentines. I found one once in the trunk of my mother's belongings."

"He did." She smiled at that grinning painted face. *How we both miss you, Uncle Walford.*

"Why did Mr. Greaves come by this morning, then, if not to give you a valentine?"

"To apologize," she said. "His landlady had berated him for not sending me one."

Barbara stopped examining her father's painting and resumed studying Celia. "Not to discuss some woman who'd had vitriol thrown onto her? A woman who's somehow acquainted with Miss Bremerton?"

"You were listening to our conversation." Just like Addie tended to do.

"It's pretty easy to hear through the register in my room."

Her cousin's bedchamber was directly above the dining room, and there was an air vent connecting the two spaces to allow downstairs heat to rise.

"I shall keep that in mind in future, Barbara," she said. "We did discuss Miss Bremerton, after Addie mentioned her name in front of Mr. Greaves. Apparently her fiancé was recently accused of hiring a boy to toss vitriol on a former paramour of his, but he himself escaped being held responsible."

Celia wondered if Sebastian Carr had sent Irene Bremerton a valentine, and if his words of love were worth more than the ones Patrick had so casually dispensed. She also wondered how much Miss Bremerton knew about the acid-throwing incident and what the man who planned to marry her had offered by way of explanation.

"He sounds terrible," Barbara declared.

"I've not met him." But she did not disagree with Barbara's assessment.

"So you're not assisting Mr. Greaves with a case?"

"No, I am not."

"Good," her cousin replied with a tight smile.

The doorbell trilled, followed by a fist pounding on the wood. Celia got to her feet as Addie rushed through from the kitchen to answer.

Owen bounded into the entry hall. "Mrs. Davies. Miss Barbara." He grabbed his tattered wool cap from his head and nodded at them.

Barbara perked her chin. "Good evening, Owen," she said stiffly. "I believe I shall retire, Cousin."

She bolted from the parlor, sweeping past him and up the stairs. He stared after her and flinched when she slammed shut the door to her bedchamber.

"Grace informed her about the valentine you sent," Celia said.

"Oh."

"But that's not why you're here at this hour, I presume."

"No, it's not," he said. "I was helping deliver wine to a party at the Carrs' house, Mrs. Davies. I think that's their name. Anyway, one of their kitchen servants has taken sick, ma'am. Really sick."

"They want me to come."

"They do, ma'am. They're afraid she might die, and they've asked for you specifically."

• • •

Celia, the black portmanteau containing her medical supplies clutched in her hand, climbed down from the wagon. The Carrs' house glowed golden from the light cast by torches, tendrils of mist curling off the flame tips into the cool night air. In the rooms beyond the tall arched windows, masked partygoers mingled and danced beneath sparkling crystal chandeliers, their outfits a dizzying display of brightly colored silk and frills and ribbons. A woman in a flamboyant black-and-white gown twirled by in the arms of a man dressed as a Tudor king, her head thrown back with laughter and the tall feathers tucked into her hair quivering.

Owen leaned over the end of the wagon seat. "It's quite the place, isn't it?"

"Quite, Owen."

"You gonna be okay, Mrs. Davies?" he asked. At Owen's side, the man who'd driven the wagon cleared his throat, impatient to be gone. "Want me to stick around, maybe?"

"Your companion appears to be eager to depart and you should go home, too," she replied. "Don't worry. I shall be fine, Owen. Someone here shall provide me a ride later."

His brow puckered. "If you're sure."

"I am."

The wagon wheeled off. Celia strode through the gate in the yard's surrounding fence and climbed the main steps. Irene Bremerton, her mask discarded, flung open the door before Celia could ring the bell. The warmth from the crush of guests inside the house streamed out onto the veranda.

"You were very quick, Mrs. Davies."

She wore a pale yellow dress, its bodice cross-hatched with contrasting lacing, the skirt over-draped with a matching apron and caught up in swags to reveal her ankles. A costume meant to portray a whimsical and highly unrealistic impression of a shepherdess. Somehow, Miss Bremerton also managed to smell of sweet, fresh-mown hay. A fascinating touch, thought Celia.

"I was told that one of the servants is extremely ill, Miss Bremerton," Celia said.

"It's bad." She shut the door, grabbed Celia's elbow, and guided her back across the veranda and down the steps. "I'll take you to her."

Not through the house, though. A widow carrying a black satchel might dampen the mood of the ball.

"Who is she? The girl?" Celia asked, easing her elbow out from Miss Bremerton's grip.

"A hired servant brought in to help prepare the supper planned for later this evening. She's not a usual member of the staff."

Miss Bremerton rounded the corner of the house. The lot alongside had yet to be built upon and a handful of conveyances had parked on the sandy soil, their drivers waiting until the party finished to collect their owners and return them home. A few of the men were huddled together, smoking and muttering.

"Mr. Carr hired the girl through an intelligence office, is my understanding," Miss Bremerton continued. "He feels misled about the quality of the women they provide and is downright furious."

"Why send for me to tend to her, though, Miss Bremerton? Isn't Dr. Schneider here?"

"He left early," she said. "We all agreed that you should be sent for, and I am very happy that you have been."

"The Carrs do not employ a physician who'd be happy to assist?" A temporary servant, however, might not be worthy of the expenses incurred by a doctor.

"You're here because we trust that you will be discreet, Mrs. Davies." She looked over.

"Are physicians not discreet?"

"Not a lot of the ones I know."

"Forgive me for not comprehending why discretion is required, Miss Bremerton." *Forgive me for not comprehending any of this.* "There's nothing shocking about a servant falling ill."

Irene Bremerton came to an abrupt halt. The spot she'd chosen was unfortunately muddy and Celia's heels sank into the muck.

"Her illness is shocking, Mrs. Davies, because the girl fell sick after she drank an entire bottle of Sebastian's vanilla extract, which he uses every day to flavor his coffee."

"She's intoxicated?"

"No. Not that."

Celia peered through the evening gloom at her. "What are you implying?"

"That someone wanted to poison Sebastian," she replied tautly. "Instead, this person sickened a foolish girl who thought she'd see how drunk she could get downing an entire bottle of vanilla extract."

"An attempted poisoning is an alarming allegation, Miss Bremerton."

"Preston, Sebastian's brother, thinks it's laughable," she said. "Personally, I can't decide. It's just too dreadful to contemplate. But who could be to blame?"

The question of the hour.

Miss Bremerton continued onward to a set of white-painted wood stairs that led to a rear door. Another, smaller entrance accessed the cellar, its concrete steps covered with numerous dirty footprints. They climbed the stairs and went inside, where a busy kitchen flooded the flagged passageway with warmth and delicious smells. The party was to go on, despite the presence of a possibly poisoned servant.

"Who suggested that the vanilla extract was poisoned, Miss Bremerton?" Celia asked. "Your fiancé? His father?"

Irene Bremerton glanced at a young woman, wide-eyed and clutching her apron, watching them from the doorway to the kitchen. Another woman's sharp voice summoned her back to her chores.

"The cook, Mrs. Tilden, although she can be pretty emotional at times. Mr. Carr agrees with Preston and refuses to believe her, and Sebastian . . ." She shook her head. "He's seething."

"What has convinced the cook, though?"

"Because, before the girl stopped making any sense and fainted dead away, she was muttering that she shouldn't have drunk the vanilla," she said. "She was crying over how fiercely her throat burned. It was awful to hear, to see."

"Has anyone else fallen ill?"

"No, nobody."

Perhaps the cook was correct that the vanilla had been poisoned. "I can have the bottle the girl drank from tested. In order to be certain." Important evidence, if evidence would be required. "Do you know where it's gone to?"

"It should still be around somewhere. I'll ask the staff."

"Take me up to the patient first, then bring it to me, if you find it."

They headed for the rear servants' stairs, passing a girl scrubbing the passageway flags, cleaning up the remains of the afflicted servant's mess. She scuttled out of their way, her brush dripping soapy water. They climbed to the first floor, where all the bedchambers were located.

"Mrs. Tilden feels terrible," Miss Bremerton said. "She'd only sent the girl upstairs to replenish the vanilla Sebastian keeps in his bedroom because she was underfoot. Gawking at all the guests in their costumes instead of helping in the kitchen, I gather. And then the girl went and drank the contents of the bottle she'd found in his room. All of it."

"Mrs. Tilden shouldn't feel terrible. She could not have anticipated that the girl would do that."

"I told her that, too, but she still feels terrible." Miss Bremerton paused in the gaslit hallway, which was elegantly carpeted by a cream oriental-patterned rug that would get hideously filthy in Celia's house. A water closet was installed at the nearest end of the hall, and the doors to four bedchambers, two on each side, were located along its length. She pointed out a room at the far end, which would overlook the front yard and street. "That's Sebastian's there. Preston is right across the way. Sebastian keeps vanilla and a sugar bowl in his bedroom for his coffee, which he likes to drink while reading the newspapers before coming down for breakfast. He also enjoys a cup after his father hosts social events and the guests have gone home. He'd probably have had some this evening."

They clearly had been courting long enough for her to be aware of such details.

"Here." Miss Bremerton indicated another staircase. "This is how we get to the attic rooms."

Upstairs, the attic ceilings were a good height, due to the home's mansard roof, making the area more spacious and brighter than most below-roof spaces.

"They've put her in the big room. It will become a nursery, if Sebastian and I decide to live here. And are blessed with children."

The room was dark, except for a lantern lit near the cot the girl lay on, and smelled putrid from illness. The young woman was curled in a ball on her side, her soiled clothing bunched around her, her long hair undone and sticking to her face.

"Do you know her name?" Celia asked.

"I don't. Sorry."

"Was she given milk?" Celia set her medical bag on the floor next to the cot and felt for the girl's pulse. Her skin was cool and her pulse was faint but rapid. She stirred and gripped her stomach, groaning from the pain, but didn't fully rouse. "Or an emetic?"

Miss Bremerton stayed in the doorway, her face averted from the sight and the stench. "I don't think so. She was already vomiting so much."

Possibly not enough, however.

"I need a glass and some water." She hunted through her bag for the magnesia she'd packed after hearing Owen's description of the girl's symptoms. The young woman was likely past any help she'd give, though. "And send for the police."

"It *was* poison, then," Miss Bremerton exclaimed. "Not just a gastric fever, like Sebastian's father insists."

"I believe so, Miss Bremerton."

"He won't permit the police being sent for, Mrs. Davies. We have to be discreet. We'd hoped you would be discreet. The gossip . . ."

Celia straightened. "We must send for the police, Miss Bremerton. Immediately," she snapped. "And if you or the Carrs will not, then I shall."

* * *

"Mr. Greaves," Mrs. Jewett called through the closed door to his room and tapped on the wood. "A boy's here wanting to see you. An Irish boy," she added.

Nick sat up on the bed and swung his legs over the side. He'd been trying to compose a letter to his sister in Sacramento to ask what she might know about the photograph he'd been sent, but he'd been struggling to explain why getting it bothered him so much. More importantly, he didn't want to upset her.

Riley trotted over to the door and sniffed around the edges.

"It's only Mrs. Jewett, Riley." He swung open the door. "Does the Irish boy's name happen to be Owen Cassidy?"

She noticed Nick was down to his undershirt and an unbelted pair of pants and hastily glanced away. "Ahem. Well, then you do know him." She looked toward the bottom of the stairs and lowered her voice.

"Scruffy creature."

"He's a good lad. Have him come up while I'm getting dressed."

"Getting dressed?"

"I'd wager Owen's not here for a social call, Mrs. Jewett," he said. "I expect I'll be having to leave the house with the boy, and I don't think I'm properly attired for that."

"And here I thought that, since it wasn't a policeman at the door at this hour, it wasn't going to be a case for once. I should've known better." Sighing heavily, she retreated down the stairs to fetch Owen.

Nick shrugged on a shirt and was hunting for his belt when Owen bounded through the doorway.

"There's trouble at a house off Rincon Hill, Mr. Greaves." He shot a look around the set of rooms. "Hey, this is a nice place, sir."

"Don't go picking up Taylor's habit of calling me 'sir,' Cassidy," he said, sliding his Colt into its holster. "What do you mean by trouble?"

Owen eyed the gun. "Do you carry that everywhere?"

"Yes, Cassidy," he answered. "So . . . 'trouble'?"

"I was working at a masked ball tonight, delivering crates of wine, when one of the servants got really sick." Riley lounged at his feet, and Owen dropped to his haunches to rub the dog's ears. "But what she was, um, throwing up didn't look right at all. It was a funny—"

"I get the idea, Cassidy."

"Anyway, the cook came out to check on the fuss, saw what was happening, and ran off to tell one of the folks who own the house," Owen continued. "A couple of them came out, an older man in a big white wig and a young lady in a yellow dress with her ankles showing."

"Daring," Nick said, finishing with his clothes.

"There was a lot of shouting. The young lady said the servant should be brought back into the house, 'cause it was awful cold outside, but the old man wanted her carted away," he said. "Then they were joined by another fellow in this purply blue coat and yellow knee-pants. He agreed with the young lady about the girl being taken up to the attic, which made the older gentleman—his father, I think—hopping mad."

"You're here because a servant fell sick with a gastric problem?"

"No, because they sent for Mrs. Davies and she told me to fetch you."

Figures. "Mrs. Davies was at this party?"

"She wasn't a guest, Mr. Greaves," he said. "The young lady and the old fellow know her and thought she should come quick. So I offered to bring her to their house."

"Very helpful, Cassidy." Although Celia would've found a way to get to the Carrs' house one way or the other. Not much could keep her from responding to a call of duty.

"Mrs. Davies told me to go home after we dropped her off, but I thought things were mighty fishy, so I didn't. I'm glad I stuck around," he said, giving an appreciative Riley one final scratch behind the ears. "Because it turns out the girl was probably poisoned, Mr. Greaves, and that something funny *is* going on. She's sure to die, Mrs. Davies says."

"Where is this house?"

Owen gave him the address.

"That's not my jurisdiction, Cassidy. One of the other detectives will have to take the case."

"Mrs. Davies thought you'd say that. Which is why she told me to tell you that . . ." He screwed up his face as he tried to recall her exact words. "That the party is at the Carrs' house, and it's possible the poison was intended for Mr. Sebastian Carr."

Damn.

• • •

Celia lowered the nameless servant's head to the cot and set aside the magnesia. She hadn't been able to dribble more than a few ounces down the girl's throat before she had lapsed into a coma. There was nothing more to be done for her, Celia feared. It was too late and the poison—likely arsenic given the symptoms—would finish the destruction it had begun.

A maid, her reddish hair tucked into a cap and a coarse apron tied around her dark dress, stood just inside the doorway. The apron was spotted with grease. She was the girl who'd been peering at her and Miss Bremerton from the doorway into the kitchen, Celia recalled.

"I am finished here for now . . . I apologize, but no one has told me your name," Celia said to her.

"Emma, ma'am."

"Alert me, Emma, should her situation change. That is all you need do."

Emma nodded, but refrained from moving any closer to the girl on the cot. A natural reluctance.

Celia stored away her medical supplies and secured the latch on her portmanteau. "I shall be in the house for a while yet. Possibly overnight, if the Carrs can accommodate me."

She glanced at the girl on the cot. "Is she going to die, ma'am?"

"I have seen patients recover from worse. There is always hope." Not much hope, though, in this instance.

"But she looks so terrible, ma'am. Shaking, and all."

The convulsions had started to occur. "There is always hope," Celia said, patting Emma on the arm as she passed through the doorway.

Miss Bremerton, in her cheery yellow shepherdess costume, hadn't gone far and met Celia near the staircase. Voices and laughter and music drifted up the stairwell, happy sounds utterly at odds with what was underway in the adjacent room. Clearly, no one had alerted the guests to what was going on in the room tucked beneath the eaves.

"How is she, Mrs. Davies?" she asked.

"I've done all I could, Miss Bremerton," she replied. "Someone should send for the girl's family."

"Sebastian tried to contact the manager of the intelligence office who hired her out, but he had no luck. It'll have to wait until the morning."

"She might not last that long."

"That's terrible. Poor thing," she said. "But Sebastian wouldn't drink the entire bottle of vanilla extract in one fell swoop, Mrs. Davies. He only uses a few drops to flavor his coffee, which wouldn't be enough to kill him. Isn't that so? Maybe the poisoner only meant to sicken him a little."

"You are right that he'd not be poisoned immediately, Miss Bremerton, if he was only using a few drops," Celia said. "But over time, the substance added to the extract would accumulate in his body and have the desired effect."

Miss Bremerton shuddered. "This is all really gruesome. To think that somebody would've come to the house with intentions of harming Sebastian is frightening. I can't believe it could be one of the staff, though. However, I don't know them well."

"Detective Greaves will get to the bottom of this matter. Don't worry," Celia assured her.

"Mr. Carr had ordered that he be turned away when he arrives, but Sebastian made him realize he'd have to put up with the intrusion."

Nicholas would have forced his way inside, regardless of the Carrs' opinion on the "intrusion."

"I would like to see Mr. Sebastian Carr's room, if you'd not mind," Celia said. "Before too many people have traipsed through it."

"Of course. Let me show you."

Celia followed her to Sebastian Carr's bedchamber. It was a man's sanctuary, outfitted in shades of lush green and gold. Heavy walnut furniture—a four-poster bed that was too large for the space, a bookcase filled with precisely arranged books, a corner desk, two thickly padded easy chairs, a marble-topped washstand, and a massive wardrobe—crowded the room. Sebastian Carr was a man who appreciated his creature comforts, it seemed. Despite the presence of the wardrobe and the otherwise neat appearance of the space, discarded clothing lay in a pile on the chair set before the fireplace.

Miss Bremerton indicated two chairs and a small table arranged between the room's windows. "This is where Sebastian sits and reads his newspapers in the morning. And here's the vanilla and sugar bowl, like

I told you." An unopened glass bottle sat alongside the ornate crystal-and-silver sugar bowl. "I suppose I should be grateful I didn't take a sip from the poisoned vanilla when I was in here earlier. I saw it sitting there, right there. A nearly full bottle."

"When was this?"

"A little after seven," she said. "I wanted to leave a valentine for Sebastian and I knew he was downstairs with his father and Preston, greeting the guests. I was gone most of today—I had an early luncheon with several of Mr. Carr's friends who weren't going to attend the ball and went for a ride afterward—and didn't return until almost four. Katherine was waiting for me in the library, so I didn't have time then, either. I propped the valentine right here, alongside the sugar bowl, where I was sure he'd spot it. Except it's gone." She hunted around. "Oh, here it is. It fell on the floor."

She retrieved the valentine, decorated with images of pink roses and covered in lace, and gently set it atop Sebastian's desk.

"The girl had been sent up here with a fresh bottle because she'd been gawking at the guests, correct?" Celia asked.

"Yes."

"Any idea of the exact time?"

"Seven fifteen? You'd have to ask Mrs. Tilden."

Indeed she would. "Why might Mrs. Tilden have even bothered to send the girl up with a fresh bottle if the one you propped your valentine against was nearly full, Miss Bremerton?"

Her brows creased as she considered Celia's question. "I have no idea, Mrs. Davies."

"Another question for Mrs. Tilden, it seems." Celia collected the bottle and tucked it into her skirt pocket. "The contents should be tested for poison," she said in response to the questioning expression on the other woman's face.

"The girl didn't drink from that one, though."

"If someone wished to ensure that Mr. Carr consumed some type of poison in his coffee, they may have elected to add it to more than one bottle of vanilla." An idea that implied that a member of the household, someone who had regular and easy access to the food supplies, was responsible.

The door flung open, and a fair-haired man wearing yellow silk knee-breeches and a close-fitted lilac-blue frock coat, like some eighteenth-century dandy, strode into the room. "I thought I heard voices in here. What are you doing, Irene? We have guests downstairs."

"Oh, Sebastian. Ah, this is Mrs. Davies. She's here to tend to the ill servant."

The gaze he turned on Celia was shrewd. "Your patient isn't in my bedroom, Mrs. Davies," he said. "Or are you in my room because of this crazy idea that somebody tried to poison me?"

"I'm sorry, Sebastian," Miss Bremerton apologized. "I shouldn't have brought her here."

"It is my fault we are in your room, Mr. Carr," Celia said. "Miss Bremerton did mention the possibility of poison, which I am curious about. Just as I was also curious to see your bedchamber. Very attractive."

"You know what they say about curiosity, Mrs. Davies," he replied. "And that police officer you summoned has arrived. Maybe you'll want to deal with him before you return to your patient."

"Oh, yes, I suppose I shall. Thank you."

She nodded and stepped around him. But as she exited the room, she could feel his watchful stare burning a hole into her back.

CHAPTER 5

"You're to come around to the back, Officer," said the female servant who'd answered the doorbell. Given the din of loud voices and music inside the Carrs' house, Nick was surprised anybody had been able to hear it ringing. He'd given the knob several strong twists, though.

"*Detective* Greaves."

She had even, pleasant features and nice teeth. The sort of young woman, Nick supposed, that folks like the Carrs would want interacting with visitors. They might prefer, though, that she didn't look so alarmed.

"Sorry, Detective." She held the door open the smallest amount possible, probably to keep the crowd inside from noticing him on the porch. "But you're still to come around to the back."

"Wait, Pru," the voice of a portly middle-aged fellow, outfitted in a long spangled purple coat that reached to the knees of his also purple breeches, boomed. The sound moved her aside. Beneath his curly white wig, sweat shimmered on his broad face, threatening to loosen the black patch he'd stuck on his cheek. "There are guests in my house, Officer."

"There's also a dying girl I need to see about, Mr. . . . . ?"

"Eustace Carr," he replied. "And you can be certain I'll be complaining to the intelligence office tomorrow about sending me a sickly girl. Who knows what disease she has and may have given to me or my family or my staff."

"You don't think a crime has been committed, Mr. Carr?"

"That poisoning nonsense?" He scoffed, the puff of air from his mouth wafting the smell of alcohol Nick's direction. "Ridiculous."

"You don't mind if I ask some questions, though. Just to be sure, Mr. Carr."

"I *do* mind, but you need to go around to the back, if you insist on coming inside."

Before Nick could answer, Eustace Carr shut the door on his face, leaving him to find his way to the rear of the house in semidarkness.

The Carrs hadn't expected any of their guests to be wandering around the side yard and hadn't set up torches like they'd done for the front path. A handful of drivers leaned against carriages parked in the adjacent lot and murmured to each other as Nick passed by.

"Ah, Mr. Greaves," a familiar voice called out from the rear stoop. Celia picked her way down the steps, feebly lit by an undersized lantern. Maybe the servants who used those stairs weren't entitled to more light to see by. "I am glad you are here."

"Looks like there is an investigation after all, Mrs. Davies. Just like you predicted," he said, drawing her away from a curious servant who'd followed her outside. "Cassidy tells me you believe one of the servants has been poisoned."

"The cook proposed the poisoning," she said. "She is convinced that the girl was sickened by consuming an entire bottle of vanilla extract, a supply of which Mr. Sebastian Carr routinely keeps in his bedchamber for use in his morning coffee. The servant confessed regret over drinking it, I gather. According to Miss Bremerton."

"Oh?"

"I cannot confirm the servant's comment for myself because she is now comatose," she said. "However, we have a quandary, Mr. Greaves. Miss Bremerton states that she noticed an opened but nearly full bottle in his room earlier this evening. She was inside her fiancé's bedchamber leaving him a valentine, to answer the question you are dying to ask."

"Thank you for being able to read my expressions."

"I usually cannot," she replied with a fleeting smile. "So why had the girl been sent up with a fresh one at around seven fifteen if a nearly full one was already in his room?"

"I take it you know the answer."

"Yes."

Of course she did.

"Mrs. Tilden, the cook, told me that when she'd made her post-lunchtime rounds of the bedchambers, she had noted that Mr. Sebastian's supply was low. There was *not* a nearly full bottle in his room at that time," she explained.

"So, if we *are* dealing with poisoned vanilla extract, it had been put there between the hour the cook made her rounds and when Miss Bremerton arrived with her valentine."

"Precisely. Which eliminates nearly all the guests from consideration, since Irene Bremerton had gone into Sebastian's room shortly after seven, when everyone was invited to arrive," she continued. "Leaving only an irreproachable reverend and his wife in attendance at that point, according to the head servant, Pru. Along with the hired musicians, the staff, the temporary girls, the Carrs and Irene herself."

"Still makes for plenty of suspects."

"Yes. Sadly." She retrieved a bottle from a pocket in her black dress. "I did collect the unopened bottle in Mr. Carr's bedchamber in case it also contains poison. The one Mrs. Tilden sent up with the girl."

"You do plan to hand that over to the police, right?"

"Would I keep evidence from you, Mr. Greaves?"

"You have before, ma'am."

She smiled without a hint of remorse and tucked the bottle away. "I shall bring it by in the morning."

"What we really need is the one the girl drank from."

"I sent Miss Bremerton to retrieve it from the kitchen." Her brow creased. "That may have been a mistake, if she is a suspect."

An uncharacteristic error for Celia Davies. "Cassidy returned with me and should be around someplace. I'll have him search for it."

The kid had always wanted to be a cop. He'd be thrilled to be given a task Nick would usually assign to Taylor. After this, he'd never hear the end of Cassidy's requests to help more often.

"What a tragic situation, Nicholas." Celia looked up at a window tucked beneath the mansard roof, lit by the glow of a lamp. A shadow moved inside, briefly dimming the light before moving out of the way again. "The girl will likely not survive the night."

"Are you sure she was poisoned?"

"I cannot be positive, of course, but it's likely, given her symptoms," she replied. "Arsenic, most likely. Easily obtained."

A breeze swirled across the empty neighboring lot, and she clutched her mantle tight around her. He would put his arm around her to warm her, but it wouldn't be professional and there were folks watching.

He shoved his hands into his coat pockets to give them something else to do. "Have you had a chance to question anybody else besides the cook?"

She perked an eyebrow. "Treating me like a colleague, Nicholas? My, how far we've come."

Nick frowned. Captain Eagan would be churned into a fury if he found out.

"Here you are, Detective." A young man wearing knee-length trousers and a long coat thundered down the steps. Clean-shaven, his dark blond hair tied back with a ribbon at the nape of his neck, he carried himself—shoulders back, head up, his gaze forceful—as if certain of his self-worth. He stuck out a hand toward Nick. "I'm Sebastian Carr."

I'm not surprised.

The fellow's grip was firm. Nick squeezed just as hard, the man's pinkie ring digging into Nick's fingers. Had to hand it to the fellow for not giving ground, though. "Detective Greaves," he said. "This is Mrs. Davies, Mr. Carr, in case you two haven't already met."

"We have, a few minutes ago. I found Mrs. Davies in my bedchamber accompanied by my fiancée." He looked over at her. "Letting her curiosity got the better of her."

"She does show up in the strangest of places, Mr. Carr."

Celia choked back a response.

"I am sorry if Irene has bothered the both of you tonight," Sebastian Carr said. "There really wasn't a need. I'm sure the girl will be fine."

"I do not comprehend how you can be so certain, Mr. Carr," Celia said.

"Servants get sick all the time, Mrs. Davies," he replied smoothly. "As a nurse, you're probably more aware of that than I am."

"So you don't believe her illness has been caused by poison?" Nick asked. "Poison possibly meant for you, Mr. Carr?"

"Do *you* believe that, Detective?" he countered.

"Mrs. Davies here thinks it's very possible, and I trust her judgment," he replied. "Do you have any enemies who might want to poison you?"

"None that I'd invite to a party at my house."

Nick surveyed the building at Sebastian Carr's back. "So that means Louise Ingram isn't here, for instance?"

Carr's swagger wavered for a moment, briefly dimming like a flame affected by a disruption in the gas supply. "I assure you that she is not, Detective. A woman like her would not be welcome."

"You mean a woman who is scarred from a vitriol attack that you commissioned, Mr. Carr?" Celia asked.

"That is a gross mistruth, Mrs. Davies, and the boy responsible for the attack was found guilty and sent to jail," he said. "Justice has been served."

"Maybe Miss Ingram has sympathetic friends in attendance here tonight, though," Nick said. "Folks who don't believe that justice has been served, as you put it."

"I don't know how anybody could've managed to bring in some poison, take it up to my room, and dump it into the vanilla extract I use in my coffee." Carr scoffed. "Not without being stopped."

"Your fiancée and I made it into your bedchamber without being stopped," Celia pointed out.

He scowled. "I need to get back to my guests. If you have any more questions, Detective—"

"Oh, I will," Nick said. "Especially if that girl dies."

"Good evening to you both." He nodded at Celia and bounded up the back stairs.

Celia watched him go. "Despite my comment to Mr. Carr about easily accessing his bedchamber, it seems we can't suspect any of the guests, Nicholas," she said, her attention fixed on the rear door.

"Although I find it intriguing that Sebastian Carr was very eager to shoo me and his fiancée out of his bedchamber. Why the urgency? What was he afraid I might discover?"

Before he could answer, a servant hurtled through the back door. She scanned the rear yard. "Oh, Mrs. Davies. There you are. Come quick! I think she's died!"

• • •

Celia bent over the cot, the acrid smell of death hanging in the air. She brushed strands of damp hair off the girl's face, her skin cold to the touch. *Poor creature.* Celia looked over her shoulder at Emma, even more pale-faced and trembling than she had been earlier. Perhaps the young woman had never encountered death before. How fortunate for her.

"I'll stay with her until the coroner arrives, Emma," Celia said. "You can go and inform the Carrs."

The servant didn't require further encouragement and sprinted off, her skirts held high to speed her departure. Celia hunted through the chests stored in the room and found a blanket in one. She draped it over the girl's body and said a quick prayer. Downstairs, the musicians who'd been providing the entertainment screeched to a halt. Loud voices replaced the music. Emma had been quick to deliver the news that the girl had died, and not very subtly, based on the occasional shriek echoing up the staircase and into the attic. The Carrs' masked ball would be the gossip of every parlor and men's club in San Francisco by tomorrow afternoon, and not because of the magnificence of the party or how sweetly romantic had been the announcement of Miss Bremerton's engagement to Mr. Sebastian Carr. An announcement that had not occurred, after all.

Outside, someone shouted for the carriages to be brought around front, their owners no doubt hastening to depart. Rather like the proverbial rats fleeing a sinking ship. Celia crossed the length of the attic room to a window that afforded a view of the front yard. She eased the curtain aside. Carriages were rapidly lining up at the gate. The guests in their elaborate costumes, a rainbow of colors, had hurriedly donned cloaks and shawls and scurried along the front path. Was Katherine Vanmeter among them? Or anyone else she might recognize?

An older man wearing a white wig and purple clothing that mimicked *ancien régime* French nobility—the senior Carr, she presumed— took up a spot on the walkway and attempted to speak with guests as they rushed off. More than one of the attendees hastened past him without stopping to give their farewells.

Celia squinted at each of the departing guests as they passed beneath her vantage point. *Blast.* She was too far up to clearly see anyone's face. But what was she hoping to observe? None of them could be suspected—aside from the purportedly unassailable Reverend and his wife—if Miss Bremerton had been honest about when she'd been inside Sebastian's bedchamber, catching sight of the nearly full bottle of vanilla. Celia expected Nicholas was busy interrogating the musicians and the others who had been in the house earlier, though.

A man in a red, yellow, and green harlequin kit came out of the house and stood alongside Mr. Carr. Sebastian's brother Preston, perhaps. Soon after, Miss Bremerton and Sebastian Carr joined him. Carriages rattled off and the flow of departing guests slowed to a trickle. Celia hadn't spotted Miss Vanmeter among them. Perhaps she had changed her mind about attending.

She stepped back from the window. Now what? Perhaps another visit to Sebastian Carr's bedchamber for a more thorough inspection.

"To search for what?" she muttered to herself.

Whatever she might find. Such as a reason for why he'd rushed Celia and Miss Bremerton out of his room.

She hurried across the length of the attic, sparing a quick look at the lifeless form on the cot. *For you. I shall resolve this mystery for you.*

Emma had not bothered to return, so there was no one to notice Celia as she made her way to the staircase. *Please, please, please do not let there be a dawdling guest making use of the water closet. Or let any of the* servants, who might ask embarrassing questions about what Celia was up to, be attending to the family's bedchambers.

Celia tiptoed down the stairs, alert to the telltale creak of anyone coming up them. Perhaps stairs in the Carrs' home did not creak, like they did at her house. Hopefully Sebastian hadn't locked the door to his bedchamber after catching Celia and his fiancée inside it.

She reached the first floor without being discovered. *So far, so good.* But as for the rest of her mission . . .

"Best be quick," she whispered and darted over to Sebastian's room. The door handle turned beneath her hand. She hastened inside, closing the door behind her.

The curtains were pulled back and moonlight streamed through the two windows to offer some light. Not enough to see clearly, though. It was risky to light a lamp and give away her presence in the room, but what if she bumped into a piece of furniture? Or stumbled over an unnoticed object on the floor?

A box of matches sat on the fireplace mantel and she struck one against the surround. It flared to life with a whiff of sulfur. She lit the bronze sinumbra lamp atop Mr. Carr's corner desk and sat. Few papers were stacked on its surface. An unfinished bit of correspondence to an acquaintance. A somewhat wrinkled message congratulating Mr. Carr on his pending engagement. Miss Bremerton's pretty valentine where she'd left it.

Most importantly, Celia did not discover a threatening note promising Mr. Carr's demise. *Had I actually been expecting to conveniently find one?* There was nothing else besides blank stationery, faintly perfumed with a musky scent, and his silver writing implements. She rattled the drawers. Locked. *Blast it.* One day she should have Mr. Taylor give her a lesson on lock-picking. It was a talent of his, apparently.

Celia took the lamp over to the bedside table, which held two books. *The Conduct of Life*, by Ralph Waldo Emerson, was one. An unexpected volume, for a fellow she might categorize as being self-absorbed as opposed to contemplative and thoughtful. *I may have misjudged you, Mr. Carr.* The other—*Two Years Before the Mast*—was somewhat more expected. A folded set of papers had been tucked inside the book. She set down the lamp and extracted them, which actually were a pamphlet entitled *The Handbook and Descriptive Catalogue of the Pacific Museum of Anatomy and Natural Science.*

She'd heard about the exhibits on offer at the museum. Displays meant to titillate the men—for only men were permitted entrance—who wandered through its display cases to gawp at the preserved naked dead bodies, at the disfigured organs and limbs of unfortunate human beings, at the dissected internal wonders of an eye or a heart or a womb. She'd also heard rumors about the doctor who operated the establishment. A fellow who could identify among the men who came to visit those whose curiosity betrayed anxieties about their vigor and strength. A doctor quick to offer dubious cures to restore their manliness.

"Are you concerned about your vigor and strength, Mr. Carr?" she mused aloud.

Reluctantly, she returned the pamphlet to its spot in the book. Its presence in Sebastian Carr's bedchamber was irrelevant to the servant girl's death.

She sighed and scanned the room. Truly, what incriminating evidence had she hoped to find? Her gaze settled on the fireplace and the ashes on the hearth. A servant would normally clear those out every morning, and Celia judged that the Carrs' staff would not be lax in their duties. Which meant someone had set a fire that day. A small one, given the slight amount of debris.

Grabbing up the lamp, Celia carried it over to the fireplace. She jabbed at the ashes with the iron poker and noticed a flash of white among the gray. A bit of paper that had not been fully consumed. She crouched down to retrieve the scrap, shaking off the charred remnants clinging to it.

She squinted at the writing on its surface. "'Must meet. On S . . . ' Blast."

The rest of the message had been burned away. The only clue to the author's identity was the mediocre quality of their penmanship. And where had this person and Mr. Carr planned to meet? She was forced to conclude, however, that the reason to burn the note was to conceal proof of the meeting and its purpose.

Female voices sounded out in the hallway. Celia hastily grabbed a sheet of Mr. Carr's stationery and extinguished the lamp, plunging the room into gloomy shadows. Wrapping the note in the stationery, she stuffed it into her pocket alongside the bottle of vanilla and slowly rose to her feet. She couldn't possibly conjure an excuse for why she was in Mr. Carr's bedchamber again, in the dark, after everyone else had left. She crept toward the desk and restored the lamp to its spot. The voices drew nearer until their owners stopped right outside the door to Mr. Carr's room.

Blast. Blast, blast, blast.

"Mr. Carr senior? He's asked for his heart medicine to be sent up to his bedroom. And Mr. Preston's volunteered to deal with that policeman because Mr. Sebastian has had enough of him," one of them said. "Miss Irene is beside herself upset, and he's taken her into the library and locked the doors so nobody can bother them. He'll be asking for the laudanum for her soon enough."

"Don't blame her for being upset," said the other one, her voice thick with an American accent Celia could not readily place. "Was supposed to be an enjoyable evening celebratin' her engagement to Mr. Sebastian. But look what done gone and happened! That girl goin' and dyin' like that. Puts a curse on a place, you know?"

There was a pause as both of them, Celia imagined, shuddered.

"The marriage is gonna be doomed, starting out like this," said the first woman.

"Maybe she'll back out."

"Might be smart if she did," her companion responded. "Not that she wanted it announced at tonight's masquerade at all. Or Mr. Sebastian, neither. Was supposed to be at a private supper tomorrow."

"Really?"

"Yep! Of course, Mr. Preston was all for having the announcement at this here party and inviting as many folks as they knew," the other one said. "You know how he likes a big shindig."

The woman with the unplaceable accent snorted a laugh.

"Ah, well. Guess we'd best get to it before Mrs. Tilden starts wondering where we've gone to."

The comment was followed by the rattle of keys and the door across the hallway opening then closing. Celia released a breath and darted over to the bedchamber door. She eased it open and peered down the hallway. All clear.

Celia stepped out of the room and quietly shut the door behind her. Setting her shoulders, she strode down the hall as if she had every right to be walking along it. She ascended the attic staircase, praying that the creaking noise below her was simply floorboards settling and not someone trodding upon them, noting her passage.

• • •

"What are you still doing here, Detective?" Eustace Carr had caught Nick in the house's central hallway. He'd removed his white wig, revealing a thatch of hair almost as snowy. His eyes fixed on Nick's face like a hawk's on its prey. "Shouldn't you be gone already?"

"Not finished questioning folks, Mr. Carr," Nick replied. He'd eliminated the musicians from suspicion; their leader had informed him that Mr. Carr had forbidden them from wandering anywhere except to use the outside privy. The fellow had had the look of a man who'd keep a close eye on the lot. "I'm almost done. For now."

"That girl was merely sickly, Detective. That's all there is to it."

"You don't think—"

Nick didn't finish his question, because Carr had turned on his heel and stalked off.

Great.

Just then, Cassidy scuttled through the door that accessed the passageway to the kitchen.

"I found the bottle, Mr. Greaves. Under a table," he whispered. "Or at least, I think it's the bottle. Not that the cook—she's a mean one; meaner than my landlady, I think—was much help. Acted like I was causing trouble, instead of helping the police with an important case."

Yep, he'd be nagging Nick to help all the time after this.

Cassidy fished out the bottle from inside his ill-fitting wool coat and handed it over. Of clear glass and around five inches in height, it was embossed with the words *Burnett's Standard Flavoring Extract.* Its neck was cracked, probably when the bottle had fallen—or been tossed—under that table. Nick sniffed the open end. Definitely vanilla.

"Do you think it's been poisoned, Mr. Greaves?" Cassidy asked.

"We'll test it along with the unopened one Mrs. Davies snatched from Mr. Carr's room." Nick pocketed the bottle. Its contents had been at least eighty proof, guaranteeing that the girl would've gotten tipsy from swigging the whole thing. Maybe she hadn't been able to resist the temptation. She'd come to regret her actions pretty soon afterward, though. "Anybody in the kitchen say anything useful, Cassidy?"

Cassidy glanced toward the door. It was shut, but its wood didn't smother the raised voices beyond it. With that ruckus, no one inside the kitchen was about to overhear what the kid had to say.

"One of the girls got to talking about the other temporary girl who'd been helping out tonight, Mr. Greaves. That she was acting strange. Jumpy all evening," he said. "And then she left straightaway when that girl got sick and Mrs. Davies was sent for and she sent for you. Suspicious, right?"

"Did this other temporary girl have a name?"

"Paulina," he said. "Didn't get much of a description, though. Awful sorry, Mr. Greaves."

"It's okay, Cassidy. You've helped me enough."

"But Mr. Taylor would've gotten a description."

"It's okay."

He looked crestfallen, though. *Yep, being a cop is hard, kid. You might want to rethink the profession.* There were plenty of times Nick wished *he'd* rethought the profession.

A door in the hallway opened, leaking the sound of agitated voices in the paneled room beyond, and a man stepped through. He wore a regular pair of black trousers, but on top he was still dressed in part of his masquerade costume, a tight shirt covered in a pattern of red, yellow, and green triangles. The combination of garments made for an odd match.

"Detective Greaves. You *are* still here. As my father has been grumbling." His smile revealed a set of white, even teeth. His gaze flicked over Cassidy, who was busy eyeing the fellow, before returning to Nick's face. "I'm Preston Carr."

"Cassidy, wait for me outside. I'll make sure you get home."

He gave Carr an odd look before trotting off into the passageway.

"You can help me understand what happened tonight, Mr. Carr?" Nick asked.

He vaguely resembled his brother Sebastian. In his gray eyes and the shape of his face, his dark blond hair. He smelled faintly of alcohol and some woodsy cologne, and shared the other male Carrs' direct gazes.

"I really don't have much to add to whatever my family has told you, Detective." His rich voice reminded Nick of an orator whose speech he'd once sat through.

"Which has been essentially nothing, Mr. Carr."

"Ah. Well, let's see, then." He cleared his throat. "My father hired two girls to assist with preparing the supper and getting the house ready today. Jenny was solely working in the kitchen tonight. The one who fell ill, that is."

"Her name was Jenny."

"You didn't know?"

No, but you did. "Go on."

"Well, she arrived with Paulina. Around three," he said. "Jenny was put to work in the kitchen straightaway, while the other girl helped with the flower arrangements in the house first."

"Paulina went upstairs with those flowers?"

"Yes, Detective, I'm sure she did."

Where was Taylor when Nick needed him? He doubted Cassidy carried a notebook and pencil on him. "Did either of the hired girls know any of the regular servants or any member of your family?"

Preston Carr shook his head. "Not that I could tell."

"You watched them, Mr. Carr?"

"That question makes me sound ungallant, Detective," he replied. "My father tasked me with ensuring that the temporary staff had been assigned their roles and were carrying them out. Which I did when I returned from downtown, where I'd been enjoying a celebratory lunch with Seb. My father doesn't always trust Mrs. Tilden to be thorough, especially on an eventful day like today. Poor Mrs. T, to be so maligned. Although, frankly, most folks don't satisfy my father's idea of thoroughness."

"What time was it that you got home from downtown?"

He made a humming noise as he thought back. "Three fifteen or so? Maybe a trifle bit later."

"And you don't know anything about either of the girls except for their names."

"Sadly, that's all, although they were both pretty, Detective," he said, winking.

Right. "And what about Louise Ingram? Was she here?" Would his reply be different from his brother's?

"What an interesting question. Why mention her?"

"I have my reasons. Was she?"

"She was not invited. Knowing Lou, she wouldn't have shown up even if she had been," Preston Carr said. "She's not prone to melodramatic displays, even if she is convinced Seb was behind that whole vitriol-throwing episode."

He sounded like he admired her. Or felt something more. "You're acquainted with Louise Ingram well enough to call her by a nickname."

"Hard not to be, since she and Seb were together for some time," he replied. "Plus, I've seen her around at the theater, of course."

"Any of her friends here tonight? Anybody who might've been prone to melodramatic displays like revenge, maybe?"

Up to now, Preston Carr had answered smoothly. Like a trained actor performing a rehearsed part, if Nick wanted to draw a comparison. Or maybe the fellow had nothing to hide and was simply comfortable answering police questions, unlike most folks. This time, though, he stumbled. He took a few seconds to collect himself.

"I'll be honest with you, Detective, since you'll find out anyway," he said. "I am friends with her brother, Tony. He's how Seb met Lou, actually."

"I see."

"Tony did ask me for an invitation to the ball tonight. He wanted to deliver a message to my brother from Louise. I was afraid of what that message might be and told him to stay away."

Nick lifted his eyebrows. "Because *he* is prone to melodramatics, unlike his sister?"

"Tony has a temper," he said. "But he never got that invitation he wanted and wasn't here."

It was hard to read the man's expression in the light afforded by the dim output of a nearby gas fixture. "You're sure? Lots of folks in costumes and masks. He might've slipped inside." Although he would've had to arrive before seven, in order to deliver the poisoned vanilla.

"I'm sure I would recognize a friend, Detective, even in a mask."

Maybe he would. "What do you think about Miss Ingram's assertion that your brother was responsible for the vitriol attack?"

"The boy who did it was charged and found guilty. That's all I know."

Nick's old wound took to aching; he wished it would stop one day. "Mr. Carr, you may have already heard, but we suspect poison was added to the bottle of vanilla extract your brother keeps in his bedroom," Nick said. "Jenny was sickened by drinking the vanilla."

He let out a low whistle. "That's what Mrs. Tilden was going on about."

"Did you see anybody head upstairs to your brother's bedroom, maybe?"

"Anybody in the house this afternoon and evening could've gone in Seb's room unobserved, Detective. The place was a buzzing hive of activity, and who'd notice somebody creeping up the stairs to commit a foul deed?" he asked. "I mean I *would* say anybody, except that the bedchamber doors were all locked, per my father's instructions, to prevent any . . ." One corner of his mouth lifted with a crooked grin. "Wanton behavior."

"What time did he give those instructions?"

"Not exactly sure," he said. "Probably before Paulina and Jenny arrived. Mrs. Tilden would know."

Which made Nick wonder whose "wanton behavior" the elder Carr was concerned about—his guests' or the temporary staff's? Or both? "Who has access to the keys to the bedrooms?"

"Mrs. Tilden has a full set, of course," he answered. "We each have one to our individual bedrooms, also. Other than that, no one."

"You mentioned that Paulina was sent upstairs with flower arrangements. Do you know exactly when that might've been?" Before or after the bedroom doors had been locked?

"Let's go ask Mrs. Tilden, shall we?" Preston Carr offered, striding off before Nick had a chance to agree.

Preston Carr threw open the passageway door and strode into the kitchen. "Hullo, Mrs. T. Just me and the police detective."

A tall woman dressed entirely in checked tan, an apron encircling her waist, stood next to the large table in the room's center. She'd been in the middle of whispering with the servant who answered the door—Pru, if he recalled correctly—when Nick and Carr walked in. They broke off their conversation and Pru hurried out of the kitchen, acknowledging Preston Carr with a nod of her head.

Mrs. Tilden peered at them, mostly at Nick. The massive black iron stove still radiated heat, and her forehead glistened with sweat. "We're cleaning up as quick as possible, Mr. Carr."

The aroma of roasting meat hung in the air. Uneaten oysters and a handful of game birds, a rice casserole, green salads and fruits, puddings and decorated cakes were set out in china bowls and on platters, waiting for somebody to decide what to do with it all. A maid, scrubbing dishes in the washroom attached to the kitchen, poked her head through the doorway to gander at Preston Carr and Nick.

"I have no doubt, Mrs. Tilden." He nodded at the other servant in the kitchen, who risked the cook's wrath by smiling in return. "The detective here would like to know when Paulina was upstairs arranging flowers."

"I can ask the questions, Mr. Carr. Thank you," Nick said. "First off, when exactly did you go inspect the bedrooms after lunch?"

"Near to two o'clock, Detective. Before the hired girls got here."

"And when was it that Paulina went upstairs, Mrs. Tilden?" Nick felt his pockets for a scrap of paper and came up empty. *Damn.*

"Not long after three. Isn't that so, Mr. Preston?" she asked.

"As you say, Mrs. T," he replied. "She was already upstairs with the flowers when I got home."

"Was that before or after the bedrooms were locked on Mr. Carr's orders?" Nick asked.

Her mouth fell open. "Before, Detective," she said once it started working again. "And all evening Paulina kept leaving the kitchen and opening the door to the main part of the house. Looking for somebody. No doubt she was hunting for Mr. Sebastian."

"And she took off as soon as word got out about Jenny dying?"

The cook nodded. "She's guilty, Detective. Mark my word."

"Well then, Detective Greaves," Preston Carr exclaimed. "You have found your poisoner!"

CHAPTER 6

Preston Carr's announcement caused a stir. The kitchen maid scuttled over to better hear and Mrs. Tilden shouted at the young woman to get back to her work.

"Thank you again, Mr. Carr, but I'm not quite ready to declare her the poisoner," Nick said. "Mrs. Tilden, did any of the other servants go upstairs this afternoon?"

"Emma set out towels in the water closet," she replied. "When she went up to lock the bedrooms well after three. Later than Mr. Carr had asked it to be done, mind you. But other than that, everyone was in here, helping me get ready."

"I'd like to speak with Emma." *Even if I can't take notes.* "Where do I find her?"

"She doesn't live in the house, Detective. I sent her home, she was near to fainting. No use to me anymore tonight," the cook said. "But I'll have her come by the police station in the morning, if you'd like."

"I'd appreciate that," Nick said. "You told the nurse, Mrs. Davies, that you sent Jenny to Sebastian Carr's room around seven fifteen, correct?"

Her mouth puckered at the mention of Celia's name. "Yes, Detective. Jenny was underfoot in the kitchen," she said. "She was more interested in the guests in their costumes than in doing her work, and I was going to make sure that Mr. Carr heard about it so that he could complain to the intelligence office that hired her out. She returned pretty quickly with the empty bottle to show she'd done what I'd asked. Hmph. Drunk from it, is what she did. And look what happened to her."

"Maybe the bottle Mrs. Tilden gave Jenny to take up to Seb's room was the one with poison in it, Detective," Preston Carr suggested.

"It wasn't any of my supplies that got tainted, I can promise you that, Mr. Preston," Mrs. Tilden huffed. "And the empty bottle Jenny brought back with her wasn't one of ours but an empty Burnett's. We haven't used Burnett's for months, because I've been making my own extracts and bottling them in clear, unmarked bottles."

"Somebody had it in for Seb, then. Luckily for him he didn't get ahold of the one with poison it it," Preston Carr said. "Sorry, Detective. That was unkind to Jenny. God rest her."

"And you didn't notice anybody sneaking through the house who shouldn't have been here, did you, Mrs. Tilden?" Nick asked the woman, who'd located a handkerchief in the pocket of her dress and was using it to mop her forehead.

"No, Detective. But my mind wasn't on monitoring the passageway or the back steps."

"And no one is expecting you to have, Mrs. T.," Preston Carr soothed.

Nick thanked the cook and went through the door into the dining room, indicating that Preston Carr should follow.

"No one would've come through the dining room to get to Seb's bedroom, Detective," he said.

"I just wanted to get out of the kitchen, Mr. Carr," Nick said. "Too many ears."

"Ah."

A fire crackled in the fireplace, warming the room. One of the servants had begun to clear the long mahogany table, dishes stacked at one end, silver forks and knives at the other, but had abandoned her task at some point. Maybe when the news about Jenny's death had circulated.

"I've been told the guests began arriving around seven. Is that right, Mr. Carr?" Nick didn't think he'd been lied to, but it always helped to confirm information.

"Correct, Detective," he said. "The Reverend and his wife were here. Early as usual. He's rather infirm and always wants to be sure his favorite chair is secured for him to sit on."

Not only irreproachable but feeble. And not somebody capable of sneaking upstairs to drop off a poisoned bottle of Burnett's extract.

"The musicians were here about five to set up. Oh, and Miss Vanmeter came early to meet with Irene. As it so happens, she turned up about a half hour before Seb got back from town at four. He dawdled at the office and didn't return when I did," Carr explained. "Miss Vanmeter and Irene are planning to open a women's clinic together, and they often meet to discuss their schemes. It's my understanding, though, that Seb has put the kibosh on that. He wants to enjoy a lengthy honeymoon in Europe and doesn't want to be spending it with a wife who's itching to stay in San Francisco to set up some medical establishment."

What would Celia do if Nick ever attempted to forbid her to operate her clinic? He had a good idea, and it didn't involve her cooperating.

"Was Miss Vanmeter here all day? Until the party began?"

"No, she left after about an hour and didn't return. Even though she'd been invited." He shrugged. "She'd probably had enough of Sebastian for the day."

"What did you do after you got home this afternoon, Mr. Carr?"

"I met with Paulina and Jenny, as I said, stopped in to say hello to my father, and then went upstairs to my room," he answered. "I hid in there until around six, reading and avoiding being asked to help with preparations." He winked. He appeared to enjoy winking. Often. "Before Seb and I were summoned by Papa to hoof it downstairs."

"Is your room near your brother's?"

"Right across from it, Detective."

"So you should've heard anybody going into or out of it while you were in your room."

"I heard Seb for a short while. But after that nothing," he replied. "Not a peep."

Not a peep. Right. "Tell your family and the staff that I'll be back in the morning to question them, Mr. Carr. Nobody's to leave. Understood?"

Preston Carr's eyes twinkled; he was enjoying this. "Yes, sir, Detective."

. . .

"I found the bottle that had the poison in it, Mrs. Davies." Owen looked over at the Carrs' house, the glow from the lamps inside the only source of light along this sparsely developed area of Rincon Hill. His chest puffed with pride. "Just like Mr. Greaves asked me to do."

"It is only conjecture that the vanilla extract is the source of the young woman's illness and subsequent death, Owen." A gust of wind swirled across the lot now empty of carriages, scattering sand and dust. Celia clutched her mantle more tightly about her chest. *If I'd known I would be spending half the evening outside, I would have worn warmer clothes.* "A reasonable guess but we cannot be fully positive as yet."

He screwed up his face. "It's gotta be the cause, don't you think, ma'am?"

"I actually do, Owen, but until we are positive, it is always best to consider other causes."

The rear door opened, and Nicholas exited the house. Slapping his hat onto his head, he strode over to join them. "The coroner hasn't arrived yet?"

"He has not," Celia replied.

"Not as good as Harris, that's for sure," he muttered.

Dr. Harris, a good friend to Nicholas, had lost his position as coroner last December when he'd been replaced by a Dr. Letterman in a wave of anti-Republican sentiment among the voters. "He has only been a few months in his job, Nicholas."

At her use of Mr. Greaves's Christian name, Owen perked his eyebrows. Nicholas scowled at the lad. Clearly, it would require time for him to become comfortable with the new circumstances of their relationship. *Even I will require time to become comfortable with those new circumstances.* She should restrain herself from excessive familiarity in front of his police colleagues, however.

"Have you two solved this case already?" he asked gruffly.

"Wish we could've, Mr. Greaves." Owen wasn't intimidated by

Nicholas's scowls. They adored each other, even if Nicholas was not completely comfortable with that situation, either.

He looked over at Celia. He had the warmest brown eyes, on the rare occasions he allowed himself to be soft or sentimental. Which was not that particular moment. "We may be narrowing down the time of the crime, Mrs. Davies. According to Preston Carr—who I'm amazed hasn't dashed out here after me to continue to offer his opinions—he was in his bedroom between roughly three thirty and six. Preston Carr didn't hear anybody go into his brother's room at that time, aside from Sebastian briefly."

"He might've fallen asleep and didn't hear," Owen suggested.

"Maybe, Cassidy."

Just then, someone extinguished the lamps in the room overlooking the rear yard, plunging the already dark space into even deeper shadows.

"But have we narrowed down the time much at all?" she asked. "The poisoner could have entered Sebastian Carr's room any time prior to three thirty."

"Only if they were able to get in there before the bedroom doors were locked," Nicholas said. "I don't have the precise time yet because the maid responsible, Emma, is not here right now. Likely before three thirty, though."

"The poisoner may instead have entered between six and seven, when Miss Bremerton left a valentine and saw the replaced bottle of vanilla," Celia said. "You said the doors had been secured? Somehow Irene got inside Sebastian's room."

"The culprit must've left the door unlocked," Nicholas said. "I asked the cook when she'd conducted her upstairs inspection and she said it was around two. When she noticed the vanilla in Sebastian Carr's room needed replacing."

"Between two and three thirty, then, or between six and seven," Celia said. "That does put a bracket around the timing, I believe. Although it does not explain how the individual was able to access Mr. Carr's room, unless they had a key."

"The cook is convinced that the hired girl Paulina is responsible," Nicholas said. "Not only was she upstairs around three o'clock handling flower arrangements, but she'd been acting like she was looking for somebody in the house. Plus, she left as soon as she'd heard about Jenny dying. Which the cook confirmed to me, Cassidy. The girl left well before she was supposed to."

"How curious," Celia said.

"She has to be the poisoner, Mr. Greaves," Owen stated, the pitch of his voice rising with excitement. "Who else could it be?"

"Preston Carr would agree with you, Cassidy," Nicholas said. "But who knows if he was telling the truth about when he was in his room and what he might've heard or not heard."

Gad. This was all getting rather complicated. Lies and mistruths and intrigues. "I should inform you, Mr. Greaves, that I discovered an intriguing scrap of burnt stationery among the ashes in Mr. Sebastian's fireplace."

If it were not so dark in the yard, Celia suspected she would observe Nicholas clenching his jaw.

"Mrs. Davies, must you?" he asked, his voice taut. Yes, definitely clenching his jaw.

"Must I what? Search for clues when the time is right? Why, yes, I must."

Owen chuckled under his breath.

"And what was on this intriguing scrap of stationery?" Nicholas asked, the tautness in his voice not softened by Owen's reaction. "That you found while poking around in some fellow's bedroom, meddling in an investigation."

"It was a message arranging a meeting to be held on 'S.' Unclear if that was to be Saturday or Sunday," she said, undaunted by Nicholas's obvious displeasure. He was often displeased with her supposed meddling; he always recovered from the sentiment. "In addition, the location of the meeting and the author's name were burned away. I think we can conclude, though, that Mr. Sebastian Carr did not wish this note to be found lying about and sought to destroy it."

"He didn't do a good job, now, did he, Mrs. Davies?" asked Owen. "We're too clever for him!"

She retrieved the note, wrapped in the piece of Mr. Carr's stationery, from her pocket and handed it over to Nicholas.

Tucking it away, he perked his eyebrows and held out his hand. "And the bottle you collected from his room?"

"All right. Here." She gave him that, too.

Nicholas grumbled under his breath. Something further about interfering meddlers.

"The intriguing note aside, shall we review who was in the house today at the opportune time?" Celia asked before he voiced the grumbling aloud. "Miss Bremerton told me she'd been attending a luncheon with a few of Eustace Carr's friends and then had gone for a ride until shortly before four."

"Eustace Carr and the servants were here all day, of course. The musicians turned up at five, although I've eliminated them. Too closely watched. Aside from a feeble Reverend and his wife, the guests didn't start arriving until after seven," Nicholas said. "Preston Carr back around three fifteen or a few minutes later from lunch with Sebastian, who returned around four. Miss Vanmeter came to visit Miss Bremerton about a half hour before Sebastian showed up, according to Preston Carr. I need to check if she went upstairs for any reason while she was here."

Katherine Vanmeter? A worthy consideration. "A limited number of suspects, then."

"We'd been at the house, too, before the party started. Me and the other fellows delivering wine. But the supervisor kept a close eye on everybody to stop any of us from wandering through the house," Owen said. "Although it was sorta strange that I saw Preston Carr peeking into the kitchen like he needed to talk to somebody."

"Maybe he was looking for Paulina," Nicholas said. "She was apparently searching for someone, too. Although maybe he just wanted a servant to refill his wineglass."

"No, it seemed more suspicious than that."

"How intriguing, do you not agree, Mr. Greaves?" Celia asked.

A comment he answered with a speculative frown.

· · ·

"I hear that Dr. Letterman was in his lab early this morning and has already detected arsenic in the contents of the girl's stomach, Greaves." Harris settled onto the chair opposite Nick's in the detectives' office.

The former coroner had strolled into the station before Taylor had shown up for the day. It went without saying that Detective Briggs wasn't in the office yet, either.

"Our new coroner must be an early riser," Nick said. "Want any coffee?"

Harris shook his head. The right response; the station coffee was terrible.

"Detecting arsenic is accomplished easily enough, though," Harris continued. "Examining the stomach will show that it's inflamed, of course. Further proof comes from an extract of the stomach's contents boiled in hydrochloric acid containing a strip of copper—"

"Thanks, but I don't need the details, Harris," Nick interrupted. He downed the rest of his coffee—burnt-tasting, which was the typical flavor of the sludge boiling away out in the main station room—and leaned back in his chair. "Letterman is positive about the arsenic."

"I'd say he is." Harris peered at him. "Greaves, you know you can go into Letterman's office and ask about his autopsy findings. You don't have to wait for me to inform you what he's found. The man doesn't bite."

Nick lifted his eyebrows. "After all this time working together, Harris, are you finally telling me that you've never enjoyed stopping in the station for our chats?"

He grinned. "I'm here, aren't I?"

Yes, he was. Thankfully.

Nick glanced at a note on his desk. Jenny Bernard. That had been her full name. According to the City Directory, she rented a room at a boardinghouse south of Mission. An area of San Francisco once referred to as Happy Valley, when there were still valleys in that part of town. Before the hills had been leveled to make room for flat lots, which would be more valuable than scrubby piles of sand. He pushed the note aside.

"Poisoned by drinking a bottle of vanilla that Sebastian Carr makes use of in his coffee every day," Nick said.

"The intended victim."

Nick inclined his head.

"What an evening to have this happen, Greaves. Not that there's ever a good time for a tragic death, of course." Harris rearranged his feet to get more comfortable in the chair. "Miss Bremerton's engagement to Sebastian Carr was going to be announced at the ball, wasn't it?"

"It was. Do you know her or the Carrs?"

"My wife and I don't circulate among that crowd, but the pending announcement has been the talk of every tea party my wife has attended in recent weeks," Harris said. "The Carrs have been seeking to improve their social position, and Sebastian's engagement to Miss Bremerton would certainly do that for them."

"Compensating for the scandal he caused by being associated with a vitriol attack," Nick said. "The woman he was accused of injuring was in this office on Thursday. Louise Ingram." Being told that the only person who might've proven that Sebastian Carr had been behind the attack, David Alonso, had just died.

"I expect Miss Ingram didn't attend the ball last night, Greaves."

"I questioned the Carr brothers about her and they both stated she wasn't there," Nick said. "I'll have to tell Mrs. Davies she was right about arsenic causing the girl's death. And why are you grinning at me like that?"

"How is it, Greaves, that Mrs. Davies always ends up involved in one of your murder investigations?"

"Hell if I know," Nick replied frankly. "But in this case, she was called to tend to the victim—Jenny Bernard—because the Carrs sent for her."

"It's also strange that Mrs. Davies is so often acquainted with the relatives of victims or with the criminals themselves."

"I'd say she needs new friends."

Harris chuckled. "Were you able to locate the bottle of vanilla extract that supposedly contained the arsenic?" he asked, rearranging his legs again. The hard-seated chairs in the office hadn't exactly been purchased for their comfort. Make the folks sitting in them—usually suspects—squirm, had been the idea. "Would obviously help your case."

"Cassidy found it in the kitchen." Nick unlocked the drawer to his desk and retrieved the empty Burnett's bottle along with the one Celia had collected from Carr's bedroom. He set them both on the desk. "Mrs. Davies managed to snag the unopened bottle that Jenny had brought up to Sebastian Carr's room. And stop grinning every time I mention her name, will you?"

"I shall try, Greaves."

I bet. "How much arsenic would it have taken to kill her?"

"It's my understanding that two grains could be enough, but I would think ten or twelve would reliably do the trick. But only if it was consumed all at once," he said. "The girl was working in the kitchen at the Carrs' house, correct? Maybe she'd actually ingested some other item that contained the poison."

"I had a chance to question the other staff about that possibility last night before I left, but they don't remember her drinking or eating anything, aside from what they also had. Some tea, at most," Nick replied. "The servants were going to eat after supper had been served to the guests. The girl never got around to being able to enjoy that meal."

Taylor, notebook and pencil in hand, tapped on the office doorframe and stepped inside. "Sorry I'm late, sir." He greeted Harris with a nod then took his usual chair. "Heard that a servant working at the Carrs' soiree last night died. Poison?"

Nick filled him in. "And before you ask, nobody spotted Louise Ingram at the Carrs' house last night."

"She *was* mighty angry the other day."

"We need to head over to the Carrs', Taylor. I haven't had a chance to speak with Irene Bremerton yet. She'd been dosed with laudanum last night before I could talk to her." He wasn't in the mood to wait around until Emma decided to show up so he could interview her, too. Maybe they'd find her at the Carrs' house. "After that, let's try to locate one or both of the Ingrams. Get their stories. Just in case they did succeed in sneaking into the house without being noticed. And tell Mullahey I want him to get whatever information there is from the intelligence office on the other girl that was hired as temporary help last night. Paulina is her Christian name, don't know her last. Maybe she has a reason to poison Sebastian Carr."

"Will do, sir . . . Mr. Greaves." His assistant gestured at the bottles on Nick's desk. "Are those the ones with poison in them?"

"Only one way to find out, Mr. Taylor." Harris stood and took the bottles off the desk. "I'll test any residue myself and let you know."

"Won't Letterman be unhappy if you interfere?" Nick asked. Not that he cared about Dr. Letterman's happiness or unhappiness, frankly.

"He is more than welcome to examine the bottles," Harris replied. "After I'm done with them."

• • •

"Irene sent a message this morning. About a servant dying overnight and that you were there," said Katherine Vanmeter, who'd been pacing the length of Celia's parlor. "Is it true? Is that what happened? She was poisoned?"

"I fear that is indeed what occurred, Miss Vanmeter."

"How awful." She resumed her circuit, beginning at the chair placed before the window. She passed the settee then proceeded to the upright piano in the corner. "How absolutely awful."

She was forced to turn at the closed double doors to the dining room. Her gloved fingers twisted the braided straps of her unadorned and rather simple reticule, which bumped against her skirts as she walked. The entire tour of the room took only a few seconds, and Celia was becoming dizzy watching her as she went back and forth.

"Miss Vanmeter, you will make yourself unwell, walking in circles and fretting like this." *You are making* me *unwell.* "Please, do sit on one of the chairs and allow me to have my housekeeper bring us some tea."

She abruptly stopped, her skirts swinging after the sudden cessation of her forward movement. She was pale, incredibly pale aside from spots of red high on each cheek, and squinted at Celia.

"Tea? How can tea help?" she asked, her tone pleading. "Don't you see? Sebastian is going to blame me! I know he will."

Celia exhaled. She could hear the rustle of clothing on the other side of the closed doors. Addie, waiting to be summoned and eavesdropping while she was at it. Thankfully, Barbara had already been down for breakfast and had returned to her bedchamber to read before Miss Vanmeter rang the bell. Celia was in no hurry to inform Barbara about the servant's death last night. She was grateful she and Miss Vanmeter weren't talking in the dining room, where Barbara could listen to their conversation through the air vent in her room.

"Miss Vanmeter, please. Striding across my parlor will not resolve anything," she said. "You are upset, but why believe that Mr. Carr will accuse you of anything?" Celia asked, an ingenuous question when he might well indeed do so, given their mutual animosity.

"You don't know him like I do, Mrs. Davies." Suddenly, she collapsed onto the chair across from the settee. "He was so angry to find me at the house yesterday, wanting to talk with him again about the clinic."

"You had requested that I speak with Sebastian, Miss Vanmeter. You decided not to wait to see how I might fare?"

"I don't mean to imply I doubted you'd succeed, Mrs. Davies, but Irene had become hopeful that Sebastian was reconsidering his opposition to the clinic, so I went to the house," she replied. "However, Sebastian wasn't there when I arrived. When he finally did show up, he was drunk. After confronting me in the library, he stormed upstairs to avoid me. I went up too and made a bit of a scene. I felt pretty foolish afterward. More foolish to discover that Irene had been wrong."

"So you did not attend the mask, after all."

"No, I didn't." She got to her feet again, too restless to sit, and took to pacing again. "I should have, but I lost my nerve. So I had no idea that a servant had fallen ill and died until I received Irene's message this morning. The police were summoned, she said. Have they decided on a suspect?"

"It is far too early for that, Miss Vanmeter," Celia replied. "I do not understand why you are so upset, though. Did Miss Bremerton's message directly state that her fiancé has blamed you?"

"No, it didn't. I must be reading too much into her brief few words. You're right that I'm being unnecessarily anxious. Thank you for reassuring me."

"Who do you imagine could have been responsible, Miss Vanmeter? You know the Carrs well."

"I can't even begin to think who it could've been, Mrs. Davies," she said. "Someone who hated him."

Like you? "If you remember any detail, any possible clue, please do let me know."

"I shall." She smiled at Celia, the expression holding little warmth. "I should be going now. Good day."

She turned and left. Leaving Celia to wonder what the actual reason for Miss Vanmeter's visit had been.

Chapter 7

"Mr. Sebastian is in the library, Detective." Pru, who'd answered the door again, showed him and Taylor into the front hall. "Miss Bremerton felt unwell and went for a brief ride to try to clear her head. I don't believe she has returned yet. And Mr. Carr has gone into town to speak with the owner of the intelligence office," she informed Nick. "Mr. Preston is . . . I'm not exactly sure where he is, Detective."

So much for the family staying put like he'd requested. "Is Emma here this morning?"

"No. She seems to be running late."

"In that case, Sebastian Carr will do."

"The library door is at the end of the hall," she said and led them down it.

Remnants of last night's party were everywhere, the typical disarray after a crowded affair. Except that after the Carrs' masked ball, the residue didn't include somebody's forgotten cotton handkerchief but a high-quality embroidered linen one. And the dirty glasses scattered about weren't chipped tumblers but stemmed crystal wine goblets assembled on japanned trays. And the aroma of perfume that lingered in the air smelled expensive and French, rather than of common Florida Water.

The girl who'd been scrubbing dishes in the kitchen last night had been assigned the task of cleaning the parlor. She stood in the middle of the room, a dustpan and brush in her hands, staring at the mess as if uncertain where to begin. Traumatized by last night's events, Nick supposed. He understood a little too well how being traumatized felt.

"Looks like folks had a good time at the ball," Taylor observed, his eyes wide at the ostentation on display in the Carrs' house. The gilded mirrors, the heavy mahogany furniture, the thick, colorful Turkey rugs, the ornate fireplace surrounds. The abundance of paintings and portraits suspended from the picture rails. He and Taylor had been inside other rich people's homes before, each time reminding them of just how much some folks were happy to spend on velvet and porcelain and crystal. On wine and food and lavish bouquets of flowers.

"A good time up until a young woman died, Taylor."

"I suppose that's so, sir."

"Taylor, go question the cook and the other staff," Nick said, hanging back so the servant couldn't easily overhear. "Cassidy already talked to a couple of them last night but they might have more to say to you."

"Yes, Mr. Greaves," Taylor said and trotted off.

Pru stopped before she reached the end of the hall and rapped on a door to her left, listened for a response, then opened it.

Sebastian Carr rose from the tufted leather chair he'd been seated in, smoke spiraling off the end of the Havana gripped between his forefinger and thumb. His gold pinkie ring reflected the light coming through the window that faced the side yard.

"I hope you don't mind speaking with me again this morning, Mr. Carr," Nick said, dragging his hat from his head. Not that he would care if Sebastian Carr did mind.

"You have news?" he asked, setting down the cigar to smolder on a carved glass ashtray atop the library's desk. He'd been in the room for a while, because the air was hazy.

"Not much, other than the coroner has confirmed that the hired girl, Jenny, was poisoned with arsenic," Nick replied. "Likely added to the bottle of Burnett's extract she'd drunk. We're still waiting to prove that, though."

"Arsenic poisoning." He shook his head. "I'll be damned."

"Arsenic meant for you, Mr. Carr. Somebody wanted you sickened. Or dead."

"I really can't imagine who'd want to do that, Detective."

"Nobody at all?"

Carr moved aside the ashtray, making room for the hip he propped on the edge of the desk, and folded his arms. A look of casual indifference contradicted by the rapid tapping of his right foot. "Like I said to you last night, not anybody who'd be a guest in this house."

"Why don't you tell me who *wasn't* a guest who might like to poison the vanilla you add to your coffee every morning," Nick suggested. "Somebody, I should add, who not only hates you but is aware of your habit."

For claiming he wasn't able to come up with a name, he didn't take long to produce one. "Tony Ingram. He blames me for what happened to his sister, even though I wasn't responsible," he said. "But Tony was *not* here last night, just like his sister wasn't. I was on the lookout for him. Not unless he snuck in without an invitation and was wearing a costume that fully disguised him. I suppose it could be possible but . . . not likely."

"Was Tony Ingram the person who sent you an urgent message requesting that you meet him?" Nick asked, taking a stab at an explanation for the burned note Celia had found on the fire grate in Carr's bedroom.

Carr drew back. "I don't know what you're talking about."

"You didn't receive a note requesting a meeting?"

"I might have. I don't remember. Folks want to meet with me all the time."

Nick ran the brim of his hat through his fingers. "But do you usually burn those notes after you've received them?"

"Sometimes," he answered. "Sometimes I do."

Right. "What about Miss Vanmeter?" he asked. "According to your brother, she visited Miss Bremerton yesterday. It's my understanding you and she had a falling out over the fact you've forbidden your fiancée from helping Miss Vanmeter with her clinic. Am I right?"

"Katherine . . ." he mused. "It's incomprehensible that she could be capable of a crime like this, Detective. But people can snap, can't they? And she was rather hysterical yesterday."

"So there *had* been a guest in this house who might've wanted to poison you."

"Katherine Vanmeter wouldn't have the nerve," he said. "But you're free to question the staff and ask if any of them noticed her going into or out of my room."

"And you didn't notice anybody else doing anything suspicious."

"I wasn't home much yesterday," he said. "Not before the party. I was downtown at the office and then Preston joined me for lunch."

And some drinks, Nick added to himself when it looked like Carr didn't plan to.

"When I returned, I found out that Miss Vanmeter was here to see me. I argued with her a bit in the library then went upstairs, because any further conversation was not going to be productive," he said. "It was stupid and cowardly to do that, Detective."

"How long were you in your room, Mr. Carr?" The fellow was way more composed than most folks might be in his situation. Or maybe the scrape on the underside of his chin where he'd cut himself shaving was a better indicator of the man's state of mind.

"Hmm . . . until six?"

Which agreed with his brother's account.

"We've also learned that the other hired girl, a young woman named Paulina, had left strangely early last night. Do you know anything about her?" Was Sebastian Carr the one she'd been trying to speak with last night, or was that person his brother? Or somebody else entirely?

"Paulina? Not at all. Didn't know either of them." He retrieved his cigar from the ashtray and resumed smoking, the tip flaring orange with each indrawn breath. "My father was the one who dealt with the intelligence office. Not me."

The library door open and Taylor slipped inside the room. "All finished, Mr. Greaves. Or, as finished as I can be. One of the servants isn't here right now."

"Your man there must be referring to Emma, Detective. Emma Joyce. She doesn't live here—only works a few days a week—and mustn't have arrived yet," Sebastian Carr helpfully explained. "I can make sure she heads to the station to speak with you."

"Mrs. Tilden has already offered to do that," he said. "By the way, until we have some idea who could be responsible for poisoning that bottle of vanilla, Mr. Carr, I'd be very careful, if I were you."

"I plan to be, Detective."

Nick reseated his hat. "We'll see ourselves out."

He strode out of the library, Taylor on his heels. "Learn anything?" he asked his assistant, once they reached the sidewalk in front of the house.

"A few things. First off, I asked about Miss Vanmeter's visit yesterday. The servant who answers the door says she got here around . . ." Taylor consulted his notebook. "Three thirty and waited in the library for Miss Bremerton, because the parlor was being readied for the party."

"Which is what Preston Carr told me."

"Miss Bremerton was out for a ride—she likes her horses, I guess— and Miss Vanmeter waited about twenty minutes before Miss Bremerton arrived, freshened up, and joined her. According to the servant, Miss Vanmeter didn't leave the library the entire time. Not until she went upstairs to try to talk to Mr. Sebastian after he'd come home. She left right after that."

"He didn't mention that she'd come upstairs to try to talk with him. I wonder why."

"He didn't want you to know." Taylor brightened. "Or maybe he'd fallen asleep and she got inside his room without him being aware."

"You and Cassidy should compare notes."

His assistant frowned.

"Don't mind me, Taylor," Nick said apologetically.

"Everybody seems to think that the other hired girl, Paulina Lyons, is guilty," he said, trotting alongside Nick, whose strides were longer. "The kitchen maid—her name's Sally—only saw one other person head upstairs before seven, and that was Emma when she went to lock the bedrooms."

"Maybe Emma poisoned Mr. Carr's vanilla." She'd had the opportunity, apparently.

"Could be, sir," he said. "But why yesterday, if she's been working for the Carrs for a while?"

"Maybe she'll grace us with a visit to the station and we'll find out," Nick said. "Go on."

"Sally also told me that Paulina acted like she'd never worked in a kitchen or a fine house before. Didn't know the first thing about how to plate food, for instance," he said. "Sure hope Mullahey discovers something about her."

Nick stopped and stared back at the house. Noticed a twitch of a curtain in the window of the leftmost bedroom. Whose was it, he wondered. "Have we reduced the number of suspects, Taylor?"

Taylor scratched at his neck with the edge of his notebook. "I suppose not really, sir."

The curtain fell back into place. "Let's get that to change, Taylor."

• • •

"I have another appointment with Dr. Schneider," Celia said to the woman who'd intercepted her before she had taken three steps inside the man's surgery. She'd gone to the police station only to find Nicholas and Mr. Taylor away. The officer who'd informed her of their absence refused to tell her where they'd gone. So she'd taken advantage of the police station's proximity to Dr. Schneider's office to stop in and ask some questions. "I am expected."

The other woman screwed up her eyes, drawing together the wrinkles at the corners of them. "I keep track of his appointments and no, you are not. He only schedules a few on Saturdays, and you are not on the list."

"I am certain that was the agreement I had with Dr. Schneider." Celia crossed to the appointment book, open upon a small table, and peered at the entries. "Oh, I see. My error. However, I shall only be a moment, and as it appears he is not presently occupied . . ."

She charged over to the closed surgery door, leaving the woman spluttering, and flung it open. Dr. Schneider, seated at his desk, looked up from the paperwork he was reviewing and scowled.

"Mrs. Davies." He adjusted his spectacles and glanced past her to the entrance area beyond the open door. Looking for the woman who'd allowed Celia to breach her redoubt. "My wife didn't inform me that you'd requested an appointment today. Furthermore, after Thursday, I presumed our business was concluded."

"I am not here to discuss my cousin Barbara," she said, taking the consultation chair against the wall even though she'd not been invited to sit. Would he grab her by the arm and drag her out of his surgery office? He should be too polite for such a display, although he did appear to be mulling the idea. "I am here to ask your professional opinion on the distressing event that occurred last evening at the Carrs' masquerade ball. About the servant who died."

"I did hear of the girl's great misfortune."

Revealing the speed at which gossip winged its way around town. It was barely ten in the morning, after all.

"Frankly, I was surprised that the Carrs did not request you to attend to her, Dr. Schneider, as you were already at their house for the mask," Celia said. "Perhaps they thought it ill-mannered to ask you to break away from the festivities to attend to a servant."

"I only stayed long enough to congratulate the happy couple on their pending nuptials, Mrs. Davies. Ten or fifteen minutes at most."

Blast. He had left very early, and likely hadn't been at the house long enough to have witnessed anything worth witnessing.

"It is my understanding that the police believe the girl was poisoned." Celia wasn't revealing any information Dr. Schneider wouldn't soon learn; the news would be in the papers as soon as the coroner released his autopsy results. "And that one of the Carrs was actually the intended target. Can you imagine?"

The scowl he'd been wearing for the past few minutes became two deep furrows around his mouth. "Where did you hear such a rumor?"

"You believe it must be a rumor with no truth to it? That no one would wish to endanger any of the Carrs in such a fashion?" she asked.

"You have to comprehend my concern for Miss Bremerton, Dr. Schneider. I would hate to see her come to any harm."

"You shouldn't pay attention to tittle-tattle, Mrs. Davies."

"I have heard that the senior Mr. Carr was quite distressed last night."

"He has nothing to worry about. But his sons, especially that Preston Carr and the theater crowd he associates with . . . utter riffraff." He tutted. "I've said too much."

An intriguing observation. "Do you have any idea who may have been responsible?"

"I don't have time for gossip, Mrs. Davies."

"The police are looking for any clues, any bit of information that might help," Celia said. "They are quite stumped and even questioned me."

"Hunting for clues, eh?" He sucked air through his teeth. "They should speak with me, Mrs. Davies, because I may have noticed a suspicious individual last evening."

"Oh?" she asked, leaning forward. "What did they look like?"

"I can't precisely describe them. There were so many people in attendance, all of them in their elaborate costumes. Quite a whirlwind of color." He narrowed his eyes. "But I am quite certain I caught a glimpse of an individual lurking outside. A very strange fellow in the garb of an Oriental."

"Not one of the guests?"

"Oh, no," he said. "A person clearly up to no good."

• • •

"Heard the captain is going to let you investigate that attempted poisoning of Sebastian Carr, Greaves." Briggs exhaled a plume of smoke from the stub of the cigar he'd been smoking. He didn't put much effort into directing the plume away from Nick's face. Typical Briggs. And just when Nick had fancied they were starting to get along so well.

He tossed his hat onto his desk. How was Briggs so deep in the captain's pocket that he'd heard information like this? The servant had only died last night. "Oh?"

"It's the new guy's jurisdiction," Briggs said. "But Eagan is having him help the customs officers with an opium smuggling case and doesn't want him distracted by some dead-end case that's going to end up being a servant dying from eating spoiled fish."

New guy? Since when was there a new guy? Nick hadn't noticed this new guy in the detectives' office. Making him a second Briggs. Unless he had an office upstairs near the captain. That would figure. "I'll make sure to tell Eagan I appreciate his confidence in me."

Briggs stubbed out the remnant of his cigar in the brass ashtray atop his desk. "Right, Greaves," he said, locked his desk, and clomped out of the office in his heavy boots. He bumped into Taylor on his way in.

Nick sat down at his desk. "What did the Ingrams have to say for themselves?"

"They weren't at home, Mr. Greaves. The neighbor told me he'd seen them leave together. They usually do go off someplace on a Saturday morning, I gather." Taylor took his usual chair up against the wall. "You know, I always thought theater folks were late risers."

The few Nick knew were. "They didn't have luggage with them, did they?"

"I did ask that question, which made the neighbor stare at me funny. The answer was no, sir."

Nick glanced at the clock ticking on the office wall. "Let's head to the Ingrams' in a little while. Give them some time to return to their house after their morning jaunt."

"I wonder what Miss Ingram's reaction to the attempted poisoning of Sebastian Carr is going to be."

Glee? Satisfaction? "Disappointed the wrong person died, probably."

"Probably, sir. Oh, I ran into Mullahey outside," he said. "He went to the intelligence office—a Mr. Finnemore's place—but the blinds were drawn on the windows and the door locked tight, Mr. Greaves."

"Probably closed down for the day after having the elder Mr. Carr shout at him about Jenny Bernard."

One of the station officers rapped on the office door. "Detective Greaves, a young woman's here to see you."

He ushered inside an ashen-faced young woman wearing a faded rust-colored dress. Nick recognized her from last night. Taylor, always polite, got to his feet. She didn't appear to notice.

"I'm Emma Joyce, sir." She clutched a satchel to her chest like a protective shield. "Mrs. Tilden said you'd spoken with the staff and wanted to talk to me."

"We do. Thank you for coming in." Nick indicated she should sit in the chair opposite him. Taylor pulled out his notebook.

"It's terrible, what happened," she sniffled. "I was with that girl and the nurse last night . . ."

Taylor hunted around in his pockets for a clean handkerchief, produced one, and handed it to her. He must have an endless supply, thought Nick.

She quietly blew her nose before continuing. "In all the time I've been working for the Carr family, nothing like this has ever happened. Poor Jenny."

"Have you been with the Carrs long?"

"Almost two years, Detective. Ever since my brother and I moved to San Francisco from Illinois. Found a job with them straightaway," she said. "My brother didn't stick around long, though. Headed off to Nevada City, even though I've heard that there's not much money to be made from the mines anymore. Not for regular folks."

"I'm from Ohio," he said. "We had a farm there." Maybe she'd find it comforting to be in a room with somebody who hailed from her part of the country.

She smiled in response; he'd been correct. "My family has a farm, too. One hundred sixty acres," she said. "San Francisco is awful different from back home, don't you agree, Detective?"

"In many ways, miss." Many, many ways.

A memory of the family farm, of Ellie and Meg and him so much younger, rose unbidden, like a persistent ghost. The sound of Meg's giggles, the sweet smell of alfalfa, the image of them in a photographic studio. An image somebody wanted to remind him of . . . Nick pushed aside the thoughts.

"How do you like working for the Carrs?" he asked, shooting a look at Taylor, who was watching him, concern creasing his forehead. Leery of Nick's moods. "Are they good employers?"

She shrank at the question. Was she afraid to speak the truth? Afraid that Nick might draw out any criticisms she had, when criticizing the Carrs might forfeit the position she'd held since she'd arrived in a bustling port city, a world apart from an Illinois farm? Or afraid he might discover she had a reason to hate Sebastian Carr?

"They don't mistreat any of us," she replied.

"So you like working there." Which was not what her answer had implied.

"It's a good position in a fine house. Plus, they pay well."

He propped his elbows on his desk and folded his hands together, tapping them against his chin while he stared at her. "What about Mr. Sebastian Carr?"

She glanced over at Taylor, taking notes. "Mr. Sebastian is fine. I don't see him all that much, actually," she said. "He sticks to his room in the mornings and then goes off to work at his father's office. He doesn't come home until late, most evenings."

"What is he like, though?"

"I don't have an opinion, Detective, other than to say he's not mean."

Not a particularly positive assessment of the man. "What about the others? What do you think of them? Preston Carr, for instance."

"He's okay. He laughs a lot and likes to sing. I used to hear him when he'd convince his mother to play the piano, when she was still alive," she said. "I've been told he enjoys acting on the stage, too."

"Does his family approve of his hobby?"

"I can't say, Detective. I don't help in the dining room."

Where she might overhear family arguments. "Was there any talk among the staff when Mr. Sebastian was accused of playing a part in the assault on a young woman recently?"

"Nothing, Detective."

Hmm. "As far as you know, Miss Joyce, has the family or Miss Bremerton been worried about Mr. Sebastian's safety?"

"All I've heard is talk about the engagement and Mr. Sebastian's marriage to Miss Bremerton. Mr. Carr is very pleased," she replied. "That's all, sir."

Which would make the Carr household the household with the least gossipy servants in all of San Francisco. "Who was aware that it was Mr. Sebastian's habit to keep a bottle of vanilla extract in his room and add it to his coffee every morning?"

Emma gasped. "It's true, then. That there was poison or something awful in it, and that's why Jenny died from drinking Mr. Sebastian's vanilla."

"We can't be completely certain, Miss Joyce."

"But you're not denying it, so it must be," she observed. Smartly. "One of the girls told me she'd seen Jenny coming back into the kitchen with the bottle. After she'd polished off the contents."

"Who all knew of Mr. Sebastian's habit, Miss Joyce?"

"Everybody, I'd guess." She shifted in her chair and attempted to return Taylor's handkerchief to him

"You keep it, miss."

She stuffed the used handkerchief inside her satchel. "Sally—she helps Mrs. Tilden in the kitchen—thinks it's peculiar, but then she doesn't like coffee at all. Maybe adding some vanilla does help the taste."

Nick wondered if vanilla would help the station coffee. As if anything could. "Is it possible that Jenny ate or drank something else last night that might've made her sick?" They'd already asked, but he had to make sure.

"Oh, no. Mrs. Tilden never lets us have even a nibble when the

Carrs are entertaining," she said. "She did let us have a sip of tea, but that was it."

"And Jenny drank tea with you all."

"She did, even though the temporary girls aren't supposed to." She glanced at Taylor again before turning back to Nick. "Are you thinking that one of the household poisoned that vanilla? Are we in danger?"

"Don't worry, Miss Joyce," Taylor soothed. "You and the other girls should be fine."

So long as none of you drink or eat anything meant for Sebastian Carr. "Had you ever met Jenny Bernard before?"

"No. Never seen her before, and the Carrs have never hired her to work at their house before, neither," she said. "Mrs. Tilden wasn't happy with her one bit. Or the other girl. Said Jenny'd never be coming back to the Carrs', if she had anything to say about it. 'Course, Jenny won't be ever working there or anyplace again, will she? God rest her."

"And you didn't know Paulina, either," Nick said.

"Not at all," she stated. "Both of them were strangers. Hiring them was very last-minute. When Mr. Carr realized there wouldn't be enough help for the party."

Two strangers. One of them dead, the other yet to be located. "I was told you locked the upstairs doors at three thirty. On Mr. Carr's orders. Is that right?"

Her eyes widened with alarm. "Has Mr. Carr complained that I was late locking them?"

"Not to me, Miss Joyce."

"That's good." She released her breath. "It wasn't quite that late, actually. More like quarter after."

"Did you see anybody upstairs while you were locking the doors?" Nick asked.

"I saw Paulina," she replied. "She had just finished with the flowers for the alcove on the landing and was coming down the steps as I was going up."

"What about any of the family?" Nick asked. "Was Preston Carr in his room at that time, for instance?"

"He wasn't in his room when I locked his door, Detective."

Behind her, Taylor scribbled notes as fast as he could push his pencil.

"He had been in the house most of the day, though," Nick said, prodding for holes in what he'd been told so far.

"I don't think so. Gone until after three. Oh, that's why he wasn't in his room. Anyway, he and Mr. Sebastian had been in town together celebrating the upcoming engagement announcement, is what Pru told me," she said. "Apparently when Mr. Sebastian got back at four and heard that Miss Vanmeter was in the house, he hotfooted it upstairs quick as a wink. Didn't leave his room until after six. Mr. Carr wasn't happy."

Carr's unhappiness was irrelevant. Her version of events did match the others', though. "And what about Preston Carr? Where was he after he returned?"

"Mr. Preston spent some time with the temporary girls, I heard."

"Making sure they were doing their duties properly, is what he told me."

She didn't confirm or deny Nick's comment. In fact, her face didn't move at all.

"Is that all, then, Miss Joyce?" he asked.

"Oh, I almost forgot that I noticed Miss Irene heading upstairs with her lovely valentine for Mr. Sebastian. Right when the Reverend and his wife arrived."

At seven, like she'd told Celia. "Do you have any idea who might've wanted to poison Mr. Sebastian's vanilla, Miss Joyce? Does he have any enemies that you're aware of?"

She clutched her satchel to her chest. "None at all, Detective. None at all."

Nick drew in a long breath. His stomach hurt; that was new. A change from his old wound aching. "So it wasn't you who put poison in his vanilla extract."

She blinked a few times. "What?"

"Did you put poison in Mr. Carr's supply of vanilla extract, Miss Joyce?"

Her face went a shade of white he rarely saw on somebody who wasn't dead. "Who's accused me? Has somebody accused me?"

"You had the opportunity, Miss Joyce," Nick said. "One of the few people in the house who did."

"But I didn't. I swear on my mother's Bible that I didn't."

Nick got to his feet. "Thank you, Miss Joyce," he said and she stumbled from the room.

• • •

Should I have sent that valentine to Miss Grace?

Owen's cleaning rag made large, streaky circles on the window at Roesler's Confectionery—even though the dust and muck from the street somehow always reappeared on the glass in short order, ruining his efforts—as he pondered the question. Maybe he'd been too forward. After all, Grace Hutchinson was the daughter of a businessman and went away to a ladies' college. And Owen was . . .

He frowned. "A nobody whose parents ditched him."

I shouldn't have sent it. But it was too late to get it back.

He was so lost in thought that he didn't hear the approaching thud of a man's boot heels until they—and the fellow—were right on him.

Owen dropped his rag in the bucket of murky, soapy water. His first thought was that he was going to find it was Caleb Griffin breathing down his neck. But Caleb liked to sneak up on folks and wouldn't be clomping up the street. More importantly, Caleb was dead. Murdered. There were other folks, though, he might owe favors to. It was hard to keep track sometimes.

"Oh, it's you, Angus." Relief drained from Owen like somebody had opened a tap on his body to let it out.

"Here is what you're owed for Friday, Cassidy." Angus fished around in his pants pocket, coins jingling. He scanned the street for anybody who might jump out of the shadows before handing them over. "One dollar. Like you were promised."

Owen gawped at the coins. He'd never been given that much money at one time. Well, aside from when his pa had handed him five dollars along with his fare-thee-well before disappearing from Owen's life forever.

Deciding that Owen was satisfied with the money, Angus grunted and turned on his heel.

Owen tucked away the coins. "Hold on, Angus," he called out. "I got . . . I've got a question for you. Did you happen to see anybody funny on Friday night at the Carrs' place? You know, creeping around the house like they were up to no good?"

"Plenty of folks were lookin' funny at that party, Cassidy." He snorted over his commentary on odd rich people doing odd rich people things.

"No, I mean some fellow on the servants' staircase, maybe." That would be the only way somebody might get upstairs in the Carrs' house without being noticed by the rest of the guests. They sure wouldn't have taken the main staircase if they meant to creep up to Mr. Sebastian Carr's room and poison that bottle of vanilla. Unless nobody thought it was weird that they were taking the main staircase. Wasn't there some kind of a toilet room up on the second floor? Guests would've been allowed to go up there to make use of that. *Shoot. I'm no good at this stuff.*

"Didn't you notice?" Angus was saying.

Owen had been so busy beating himself up over his dismal detective skills that he wasn't sure he'd heard Angus right. "Who?"

"The person on the rear servants' staircase. The one you just asked about." Angus rolled his eyes. "Are you not so smart, Cassidy? You are making me wonder, you know."

Out of the corner of his eye, Owen noticed that Mr. Roesler stood on the other side of the store window, peering through it to figure out why Owen had stopped cleaning the glass. "What was this person doing?"

Angus released a long, hard sigh. "Creeping about on the servants' staircase," he said. "One of the servants was talking with them. Asking what they were doing. I noticed them together when I was bringin' some wine to the pantry."

"They let you into the pantry?"

"What are you sayin', Cassidy?" Angus swelled his chest and glowered. He might be scrawny, but his expression was so mean that he scared off a pair of women coming up the sidewalk, even though he hadn't been glowering at them. They steered clear by choosing a path out in the street. "Are you thinkin' I'd not be good enough to be walkin' through the Carrs' kitchen and into their pantry?" he asked, rediscovering his Irish brogue.

Well, yes, matter of fact. But Owen knew better than to say that aloud.

"Was it a man or a woman?" They *had* to be the person who'd tried to kill Mr. Carr. Just about had to be.

"Can't say." Angus shrugged. "Just saw the maid up on the landing. Fit to be tied to run into . . . Whoever it was."

"Which maid, Angus?" Owen asked, excitement making his voice squeak. He thought it had stopped squeaking years ago. *Shoot.* "The one who died?"

"No, not her. The one with the red hair."

He'd noticed her but he couldn't remember her name. Mrs. Davies would, though.

"Why are you so interested, Cassidy?"

"I'm . . . I'm just . . ." Owen stuttered, his tongue sticking to the roof of his gone-dry mouth. Heck, maybe he should tell Angus the truth. At least part of it. "The person might be a killer, Angus."

Angus's thick eyebrows did a jig up his forehead. "Are the cops offerin' a reward?"

Were they? "I'm not sure."

Angus grinned. "Well, in case they are, how about *I* tell them about what I saw?"

"Um, maybe you should tell the cops, Angus. Maybe you should." And *he* needed to tell Mrs. Davies. As quick as he could.

Owen patted his pocket to make sure the coins were still in there before collecting the wash bucket and scooting back inside Roesler's, leaving a bewildered Angus staring after him.

"Miss Ingram is upstairs in her studio," said the black-haired girl who'd answered the door to the house Louise Ingram and her brother rented. Her large eyes went wide at the sight of Taylor in his policeman's uniform.

"What about Mr. Ingram?" Nick asked.

"Not at home, sir. He's gone to the theater."

"Then can you take us to Miss Ingram?" Nick asked when it started to look like her awe over Taylor's sewn-on badge had glued her feet to the threshold.

"Oh. Yes, sir. Of course."

She showed them in, hurrying down the narrow hallway that passed a scantily furnished parlor and dining room before scrambling up the staircase at the end. The house was chilly and damp, and the glimpse Nick had of the fireplace looked as if it hadn't been lit in a while.

"She does her pictures in the front room. Mr. Ingram, her brother, gave her the best and biggest bedroom in the house for her painting, which I think was really nice," the girl said as they climbed to the second floor, where the bedrooms were located. "She's awfully good at painting. Even with her, you know . . ."

"The injury to her arm and hand," Nick supplied.

"Mighty rough. It's just not right."

They turned at the top of the steps. Four doors led off the hallway. The one at the street-facing end stood ajar.

The maid tapped on the door before pushing it wide. "Miss Ingram, these police officers are here to see you."

It was a large, airy room that spanned the entire width of the house. The curtains on the windows were open all the way, admitting as much light as a February day had to offer. A collection of empty frames and blank canvases crowded one wall. Large canvases were stacked against the other, scenery Miss Ingram had completed. On a table in the corner, she'd left a vase of wilting flowers. Maybe she couldn't afford to replace them with fresh. A clean palette and a sectioned box holding cubes of dried paint sat on another table, which was so scratched and stained it looked as if she'd found it in a thirdhand store. All that was missing was a sofa for a half-dressed woman to recline on. Nick supposed, though, that Miss Ingram wasn't that kind of a painter. Overall, the space was tidy and well kept, aside from the wilting flowers. She and her brother might be low on funds, but they both had their pride.

Miss Ingram stood with her back to the windows and frowned at a canvas propped on an easel, a paintbrush in her right hand. She'd removed the bandages she'd had on when she had visited the station, exposing her healing wounds. They were raw and angry-looking. She held the brush awkwardly, like she meant to stab the canvas rather than paint on it.

"Miss Ingram," the maid repeated.

She looked over at Nick and Taylor and exhaled sharply. "Detective Greaves."

Nick dragged his hat from his head. "Sorry to bother you."

"I just wasn't expecting to see you so soon. Or ever again, actually," she said. "Thank you, Truda. And once you're finished with the laundry, you can leave for the day."

The girl scampered off, and Louise Ingram dropped the paintbrush into a jar of turpentine sitting at her side. She had a smear of yellow paint across her forehead and on her fingers. "It's pointless. I can't grip a brush properly with the damage to my hand."

Taylor crossed the room to look at what she'd been working on. "It's really good, miss."

"That's kind of you, but the painting doesn't meet my standards. Or those of anybody I might try to sell it to." She glanced at the door Truda had left open. "We'll probably have to let Truda go if I can't find employment or find buyers for my work. The manager of the Metropolitan lets us use her a couple days a week when she's not cleaning at the theater, but even that's going to be more than we can afford. I've already inquired at several different theaters if they had a job for me—anything at all, not just painting—and to a man they took one look at my arm and pushed me out the door."

"I'm sorry, miss," Taylor said.

"So am I," she said, stripping off the paint-splattered holland apron tied around her waist. "I presume you're not here to discuss my painting, Detective Greaves. Have you come to tell me that you're interested in re-examining the case against Sebastian Carr, after all?"

Hoping that her pleas on Thursday had convinced them? She was going to be disappointed. "We're here to ask where you were last night, Miss Ingram," Nick said. "You and your brother."

"Why? What's happened?"

"Where were you last night?" Nick asked again.

She draped the apron over the back of a nearby chair. "I was here."

"Here in your studio?" Even though the sun set not long after five and it would be too dark in the room, equipped with only a solitary gas jet and a glass kerosene lamp with very little kerosene in it, to paint.

"I finished up around five, prepared a light meal for Tony and myself, did some mending and read by the fire in the kitchen stove, then went to bed," she said. "So, here. In the house."

She reached for the linen bandages, which she'd tossed aside on the table, and started to wrap them around her hand and wrist. They didn't look particularly clean.

"You should have somebody look at that, miss," said Taylor.

"I know I should, but I can't afford a doctor. Not without a job."

"Mrs. Celia Davies could help you, miss," Taylor offered. "She's a good nurse."

"Taylor," Nick warned. He didn't need to be sending suspects over to Celia's house for her to interrogate; she managed to track them down well enough on her own.

His assistant either didn't hear the reprimand in Nick's voice or chose to ignore it. Which wasn't like Taylor to do. Maybe he was too dazzled by Miss Ingram's looks to be listening, or the turpentine fumes were getting to his head.

"She doesn't charge ladies, Miss Ingram," Taylor added.

"Taylor!" Nick repeated.

"Oh. Yes, sir." He took out his notebook and bent over it.

"What about your brother, Miss Ingram? Was he here with you last night?"

Her gaze took in both Nick and Taylor. "You haven't explained why you're asking these questions, Detective."

Nick turned the brim of his hat through his fingers. "I will once you answer, Miss Ingram."

"All right." She used her teeth to help tie off the bandage. They were white against the grungy ivory of the cloth. "Tony wasn't here all night with me. He's taken a temporary job playing for the California Minstrels' show at the American Theater. The usual trumpet player fell ill with a fever a few days back, so Tony has stepped in for him while he recovers. Tony doesn't have much to play, since the minstrels perform most of the music with their tambourines and pigs' bones, but he didn't have another engagement this week, so he took the job."

"What time did your brother leave for the theater?"

"What is Tony supposed to have done that makes you want to know where he was?"

Nick exhaled. "Answer my questions, miss. Please," he said. "You don't want to lose the good light you've got and things will go faster if you do."

She frowned at the canvas she'd been working on before continuing. "Six, I think. He had a quick bite with me, like I said, and then headed out."

"Shows usually start at eight, don't they, miss?" Taylor asked.

"Tony likes to get to the theater early to warm up." She took to fiddling with the bandage tie. "Before when the others typically arrive."

He'd have to verify when the musicians in this particular case had been asked to be at the theater. "So, he left here around six, spent the night playing the trumpet for a minstrel show, then returned home . . . when?"

Not that her answer mattered much, as far as his alibi was concerned. The poisoned vanilla had been delivered to Sebastian Carr's room long before a minstrel show would have finished.

"Eleven, I believe."

"You stayed up for him? Is that how you know the time he came in last night?"

"I can't sleep until I know he's safely back."

Meg would've done the same with him, if she'd been alive long enough to worry about Nick and where he was. Celia would likely care that much, too.

He considered Miss Ingram, who was still nervously toying with the bandage ties. "Can anybody vouch for your whereabouts between when your brother left for the theater around six and when he got home around eleven, Miss Ingram?"

Her gaze jumped between Nick's face and Taylor's. "Why do I need someone to vouch for me, Detective? What is going on?"

"Somebody attempted to poison Sebastian Carr last night."

She stiffened, her breathing kicking up a notch. "Is he all right?" For a woman who'd been furious with Sebastian Carr only the other day, she sure sounded concerned.

"I'm surprised you're worried about Mr. Carr, Miss Ingram. I got the impression you hated him because of the vitriol attack," Nick said, pointedly eyeing her bandaged hand. "You were ready to blame him for it when you were in the station Thursday."

"I . . ." She drew in a breath. "I am still concerned about him, whether or not it's wise. Is he all right?"

"He is, but the servant who drank the poisoned vanilla didn't fare so well," Nick said. "She died."

"Vanilla? You mean the vanilla he adds to his coffee?" she asked. "Seb and his ridiculous habit."

"Who all knows that he likes to do this?"

"Everyone in the house would know, certainly," she said. "Any anyone who is acquainted with him, even passingly. He extols the virtues of supplementing coffee with vanilla to anybody who'll listen. You'd think he owns stock in Burnett's." She scanned them both again. "Did someone claim that I was at the ball last night, Detective? That I'm responsible?"

"No one has suggested that, miss," said Taylor, looking up from his notebook.

Not yet. "However, you're telling me you don't have anybody who can vouch for your whereabouts, Miss Ingram."

"I was here all night. Ask my neighbor. He's always spying on everyone who lives on this street. He would've noticed if I'd left the house," she said. "I was here all night, Detective. I swear it."

On your mother's Bible, maybe?

Nick reseated his hat. "One final question and then we'll let you get back to your painting," he said. "Who do you think could be responsible for attempting to poison your former beau? If not you."

She flashed a wry smile. "Sebastian has plenty of enemies, Detective. Although maybe the woman who was set to become engaged to him last night can best answer your question."

"You think Irene Bremerton could be responsible?"

"I'm not the only woman Sebastian Carr has dallied with over the years, Detective," she replied, her expression flat, her tone biting. "And I expect I won't be the last. No matter that he's marrying the wealthy and lovely Miss Irene Bremerton. Who might already be tired of his philandering."

• • •

"Is Miss Bremerton here?" Celia asked the servant who'd responded to the summoning of the Carrs' doorbell.

"She is, but I don't know if she's available, ma'am," the young woman replied. She had an efficient and succinct air about her, as if she were used to being brusque with the people who rang the bell. *No, Mr. Carr is busy with a business associate. No, Mr. Sebastian is at his office downtown. No, we do not purchase such items from people like you who should* be knocking *at the service entrance and not the front door.* Or perhaps she was merely exhausted from last evening's unfortunate excitement and wished that people would cease ringing the front bell.

"I am the nurse who attended the girl who died last night. Mrs. Celia Davies. I shall only be a few minutes." She smiled, having applied the full extent of her English accent. In the few years she'd lived in America, she'd found that most of its residents were invariably charmed by it. The Carrs' servant did not appear to be greatly impressed. "I do not mean to disturb the household at such a distressing time. I merely wish to see how Miss Bremerton is doing and if there is any way I may be able to assist."

"The doctor has been here, and Miss Irene does not need your medical support."

"Perhaps you could enquire with Miss Bremerton if I might simply speak with her," Celia said, unyielding. "Only a moment. I promise. None of the Carrs need be aware that I am in the house."

"We won't be able to prevent that, ma'am, but I'll ask her," she said and shut the door.

Blast. Celia looked around—no one to notice—and moved the edge of her bonnet aside. Right ear freed, she pressed it to the wood. All she could hear was a man's raised voice, too muffled to make sense of what he was saying. A woman answered him, her tone distressed. They sounded as though they were in the dining room to her right. Celia checked again to confirm that no one was nearby and tiptoed over to the windows that let onto the porch. She peered around the window frame, but the curtains were closed, preventing her from seeing inside. But she could better hear. Somewhat.

"The police are already asking too many questions. Bothering us," the man huffed. Sebastian Carr? Preston? The senior Carr?

The woman gave a quiet reply, which was followed by furious whispering. Celia hiked her skirts and hurried down the steps. Maybe she could peek through the side dining room window to better follow their conversation.

"Blast," she muttered. The shutters were closed, thwarting her attempt. She needed to head back to the front door before she was discovered.

As she turned, a flash of magenta fabric, snagged on one of the evergreen shrubs that bordered both sides of the house, caught her eye. She plucked the item free from the branch. It was a scrap of ribbon or trim off a piece of clothing. How had it come to be stuck there, though?

She realized the voices had stopped and, tucking the bit of trim into her reticule, rushed up to the front door just as it flung open again.

"Miss Bremerton will see you in the library, Mrs. Davies." She scowled. Likely to prevent Celia from developing the mistaken impression that her visit was welcomed and not merely tolerated.

Celia stepped inside before the offer was rescinded and followed the young woman into the parlor. The pieces of furniture—settees and armchairs covered in sapphire-colored velvet, heavy mahogany tables, a piano, marble-topped plant stands—had been restored to their original locations after having been pushed aside to make room for last evening's dancing. On a side table lay a discarded needle and pink thread, which had undoubtedly been used to mend a woman's costume after a round of boisterous dancing had torn it. A servant swept up petals that had fallen from the many groupings of hyacinths and crocuses, vases of cut daffodils and white lilies, that decorated the room. The girl looked over, her broom's movement stilling, as she watched Celia and the other servant pass.

"Has anyone heard from Paulina?" Celia asked. "The other temporary servant hired for the mask."

"Not a peep. She's probably hopped a boat to someplace far away by now."

"Not a peep? That does make it seem as though she was involved in what happened last night."

"Yes, it does." She halted at a set of doors at the far end of the parlor, sliding them open. "Here you are, Mrs. Davies."

Beyond was the library. Walnut bookcases climbed the walls, and a tasteful arrangement of comfortable chairs and settees had been supplied, where one could sit and read beneath the glow of gaslight shed by etched glass fixtures. The room smelled of sweet pipe smoke and leather and books. So many books. Celia itched to pull one down from the shelves. It had been too long since she'd been in a well-stocked private library. Not since she'd lived in Hertfordshire, where she'd often crept inside her uncle's library late at night to sneak one of his books to read.

Irene Bremerton was seated in a chair by the window. Around her drooping shoulders, she clutched a fringed cashmere shawl, a swath of crimson and cream paisley so lovely it could be an artwork. She did not seem to care that the shawl dragged on the floor. "Oh, Mrs. Davies, I am glad you're here," she said with scant energy behind the words. Her face was ashen, and circles darkened her eyes.

"Miss Bremerton, how are you this morning? Were you able to sleep at all last night?" Celia asked.

"I borrowed some of Mr. Carr's laudanum. I slept, but it's caused me to have a headache," she said. "This morning, Mrs. Tilden gave me a dose of bitters to help that. I went for a ride earlier, hoping some outside air would help me feel better, but it didn't. I feel rather awful."

Outside air in San Francisco was as likely to make you feel worse as better, especially this near to the gas works and a brass foundry. "Oil of camphor rubbed on your forehead might offer some relief, Miss Bremerton."

The other women smiled feebly. "Thank you," she said. "The police were here earlier. To see Sebastian. Apparently it is true that the girl died from arsenic poisoning."

"So it has been confirmed."

Miss Bremerton clutched her shawl against her chest. "Yes."

Celia took a nearby chair. "Miss Bremerton, I have to ask—did you notice anyone going upstairs to the bedchambers who may have been acting strangely yesterday? Guiltily, perhaps."

"The house was in chaos with preparations for the ball, Mrs. Davies.

A whole troop of people could've gone upstairs without my notice," she said, sounding a trifle annoyed at having to point out the obvious difficulty.

"Completely understandable. I was simply hoping for clues that might uncover the identity of the poisoner, Miss Bremerton," she said. "Miss Vanmeter visited me this morning. After receiving a message from you about the poisoning. She is afraid Sebastian is going to accuse *her* of the attempt."

"I can understand why she'd think that," she said. "She was so upset and angry with him. She chose the wrong time to speak with Sebastian by coming here yesterday afternoon."

"She told me that you'd informed her Mr. Carr had changed his mind about her clinic and was now inclined to allow you to help her. Which was why she came to the house."

"Yes, well . . ." She ran her hand over the shawl where it draped across her arms. "I thought he might've changed his mind, but I was wrong. I can so often be wrong about Sebastian."

Something Celia might have said, might have felt, when she and Patrick had first been together. Should she offer Miss Bremerton advice about trusting her heart in such matters? Would she listen? *Would I have listened?*

"I recently learned of a suspicious individual spotted outside last night in the garb of an Oriental. Were any of the guests dressed like that, Miss Bremerton?" Celia hadn't observed anyone in such a costume, but perhaps they had left early, like Dr. Schneider.

Miss Bremerton's fingers closed around her forearm. "You mean somebody wearing a caftan and turban?"

"I might. Did you see them too?"

"Yes." She nodded. "I did. I should've told you last night, but in the middle of all that was going on, I'd completely forgotten."

"Can you describe them?"

"They had on a turquoise-colored caftan and white turban. I spotted them through the parlor window. Outside," she said. "Do you think they're the person responsible for the arsenic, Mrs. Davies?"

"Possibly."

Miss Bremerton's fingers relaxed and she smoothed the wrinkles her grip had created in the shawl. "It had to have been that woman who's been harassing Sebastian. The one who accused him of hiring a boy to assault her with vitriol."

"You know about the incident."

"I do read the newspapers, Mrs. Davies," she replied.

"What has your fiancé had to say?"

"I've chosen to not discuss it with him."

Probably wise. "I should point out, Miss Bremerton, that the person was described to me as being a man."

She cocked her head. "How difficult is it to conceal one's gender in a costume, Mrs. Davies? Especially one like that. Not so difficult at all, I'd say."

• • •

"Guess we shouldn't be too surprised that Miss Ingram has accused Miss Bremerton, should we, sir?" Taylor asked, turning into an alleyway near Montgomery that accessed the rear of the buildings facing the street, one of which was the American Theater.

"My thoughts exactly, Taylor."

"And we can eliminate Miss Vanmeter, right, sir?" he asked. "She arrived at the Carrs' house after the doors had been locked. Plus, she was in the library with Miss Bremerton."

"Sounds like she's not a suspect, Taylor, but I'd like to hear what she has to say for herself. Especially concerning her little visit upstairs to confront Carr, which he didn't tell me about," Nick said. "Once we're finished with Mr. Ingram."

A number of businesses lined either side of the alley, a lane so narrow that Nick might've been able to touch the brick walls on either side if he stretched out his arms. The alley reeked, as though a cleansing rain never succeeded in squeezing through the gap to wash away the slime underfoot. They passed a hat manufacturer and a fur dealer. An attorney's office and a costumer's.

"This should be it, sir." Taylor stopped at an entrance marked *Stage Door*, a broken chunk of brick wedging it open. Inside, the chair where the fellow assigned to keep folks out was abandoned, along with a mostly finished cup of coffee. The former occupant had stubbed out a cigarette in the sludge coating the bottom. "Looks like folks are here now."

The door opened onto a narrow unlit hallway, down which came the muffled sound of a banjo twanging. After a few yards, they passed a set of dressing rooms, locked until the performers arrived later in the day to get ready for their show. The hall ended in a room stacked with crates and the paraphernalia of a theater—coiled ropes, unused lamps and lanterns, a few pieces of furniture haphazardly stacked, a row of pegs for hanging up coats and hats, numerous large black trunks that were heavily strapped and secured, the name of their owner painted on the surface in bold, white letters. A pot of *Meyer's Grease Paint, No. 3*, sat atop one of the trunks.

"Must be pretty valuable, whatever is inside," Taylor observed.

"Costumes," Nick said. "Wigs and paste jewelry and makeup. Like that greasepaint, there." He'd been in the back rooms of a theater before, and not always while investigating a crime. "All of it *is* valuable, to the owner."

The room led onto the rear of the stage, the floor covered in various chalk marks and bits of painted scenery pushed to one side. Heavy drapery formed the far wall. From the other side of the curtain came the sound of voices and one of the musicians tuning a violin. The banjo playing had stopped.

Nick found the opening in the curtain and walked through, Taylor following. "I'm looking for Anthony Ingram. Is he here?"

A handful of men seated on chairs arranged in a semicircle, their instruments on their laps, had been chatting. The talking halted and several turned to face Nick.

"We're rehearsing. You need to get out," said a stout fellow from behind a stand covered in sheets of music. He had heavy whiskers, which compensated, Nick supposed, for the lack of hair atop his head.

"I'm Detective Greaves, and this is my assistant, Mr. Taylor."

He glanced at Taylor. Despite the profusion of facial hair, Nick could readily make out the downturn of the fellow's mouth. "I don't know what you want, but we are busy here, Officers. Come back later when we're finished."

One of the seats out in the darkness of the theater creaked, and a man in a dark suit strode down the center aisle. "What's going on? We had to call this extra rehearsal this morning, after the mess everyone made of last night's opening, and we don't have time for interruptions."

A criticism of last night's opening that didn't sit well with the musicians, who grumbled.

"It can't be helped," Nick replied. "Which of you is Mr. Ingram?"

A fellow who'd been clearing accumulated spit from his trumpet through the water key met Nick's gaze. "That'd be me."

Tony Ingram had angular features that were handsome in their evenness, and longish thick, dark hair that he kept having to sweep back from his face. Nick could imagine that the ladies enjoyed running their fingers through it. He could imagine that Mr. Anthony Ingram, charming theater musician, enjoyed having them run their fingers through it.

"What've you been doing now, Tony, that's got you in trouble with the law?" one of the men asked, causing the trombone player at his side to snigger.

"I haven't done anything. I don't know what they want." Tony Ingram set down his trumpet and stood. "Let's talk outside, Officers." He scanned the other musicians. "And don't any of you touch my trumpet."

One of the men rolled his eyes in response.

Ingram sidestepped Taylor, shoving aside the curtain and letting it fall shut before either Nick or his assistant could pass through.

"Guess he doesn't like us, sir," said Taylor.

"Guess I don't care, Taylor."

Ingram hadn't waited for Nick and Taylor, striding in long-legged steps across the stage and into the side storage room. Taylor trotted after him.

"No need to hurry, Taylor. Mr. Ingram isn't going anywhere without his beloved trumpet."

The man was outside in the back alley, just beyond the stage door, fishing a cheroot out of his coat pocket.

"What is this about, Detective?" Ingram located a match and struck it against one of the building's bricks. He lit his cheroot and tossed the spent match aside.

"I have a few questions for you about the Carrs' masquerade ball last night."

"Why?"

Taylor retrieved his notebook and pencil.

"Preston Carr told me that you'd requested an invitation to the party, Mr. Ingram," Nick said. "Why were you so keen to attend?"

Tony Ingram pulled on his cheroot, the tip flaring orange. Pondering, Nick presumed, exactly what his friend Preston Carr had said to the police.

He plucked the cheroot from his mouth, rolling it between his thumb and forefinger. "I wanted to talk with Sebastian last night," he said. "But I didn't go. I was here, playing for the minstrels. Ask anybody."

"Taylor, go do that."

Taylor went back inside the theater.

"You wanted to confront Mr. Carr about the attack on your sister, Louise. At a public event," Nick said. "Isn't that so?"

"I've already spoken with Sebastian about my sister, Detective," he said. "He's managed to convince everybody that he wasn't behind the assault, however."

"But not you, maybe?"

Tony Ingram frowned. "That poor kid. Convicted then dying in prison."

"You don't think David Alonso was guilty," Nick said.

"David Alonso was a dupe, Detective. Deceived into tossing that acid on Lou," he said. "He was so scared at the trial. Barely spoke any English. I wonder now if the boy even understood what was happening to him. The jury looked like they'd made up their minds from the start that he was guilty, though. Some pitiful Mexican kid. Easy scapegoat."

Justice not always being all that just.

Taylor returned. "He's right, sir. Here last night. They were called to rehearsal at seven."

"Seven? Your sister told us you left the house at six," Nick said.

"You've already questioned her."

"We have," he answered. "And she told us you left the house at six. Doesn't take an hour to get to this theater, Mr. Ingram."

"I wanted to get here early."

"Ah," Nick replied. "So if you've already confronted Sebastian Carr about the attack on your sister, what else was left to say to him that required trying to obtain an invitation to that party, Mr. Ingram?"

Ingram tapped his cheroot with his middle finger, dribbling ash onto the ground. "I wanted to convince Sebastian to call off his engagement to Irene Bremerton before they publicly announced their plans to marry."

"Oh? Why?"

He stared Nick in the face. "Because Sebastian Carr is an ass, Detective, and Irene Bremerton deserves better than to be saddled with him for the rest of her life."

"That's very noble, Mr. Ingram. But why are you so concerned about the happiness of a woman you don't even know?"

"She seems decent, and I don't want anybody else suffering like Lou has suffered. That's not hard to understand, is it?"

"So you went to the Carrs' to . . . to what? Threaten Sebastian Carr of what you'd do if he hurt another woman?"

"I told you I didn't go to the Carrs', Detective. You both have been listening, haven't you?" He shot a look at Taylor, whose face was expressionless. Aside from eyeing Ingram's cheroot as if he were craving a smoke.

"Just have to be sure, Mr. Ingram," Nick said.

"Preston convinced me my showing up would be pointless." He took another quick puff on his cheroot then stubbed it out. "Sebastian wouldn't have been cowed by any threats I might make. An ass with no fear."

"You sound like you don't like him, Mr. Ingram."

"I don't," he replied. "But I'm not in the habit of trying to kill people I don't like. Besides, how could I have? When I wasn't there."

"Anybody else hate Sebastian Carr enough to want to harm him?"

He gave a sarcastic smile and brushed back the wave of hair that had flopped over his forehead. "What other enemies does Sebastian have aside from me? That is what's behind all your questions, right?"

"Perhaps."

"I really can't say, Detective. But before you decide to suspect Lou, don't," he said. "She's still upset, angry. Of course she would be. She might never paint again. But she's not so stupid as to take out her revenge on Sebastian Carr."

"Do you happen to know where your sister was last night?" Nick asked.

"Leave her alone. Lou has suffered enough."

"She asked us to question your neighbor, and I did," Taylor said. "He didn't catch sight of her leaving the house, but that doesn't make for much of an alibi, Mr. Ingram. He might've simply not noticed."

"Leave her alone. The both of you. Please." Ingram tested the heat at the end of his cheroot before returning it to his coat pocket. "I have to get back to rehearsal before I'm dismissed. Good day."

He kicked aside the broken brick propping open the stage door and let the door slam shut behind him.

"You know what I find interesting, Taylor?" Nick asked. "That Ingram knew that somebody attempted to seriously harm Sebastian Carr last night."

Taylor tucked his brows together. "But I don't see . . . oh! Because Mr. Ingram mentioned not wanting to kill Mr. Carr."

Nick inclined his head. "The information hasn't been in the newspapers yet, and the only folks who are aware of our suspicions are some members of the Carrs' staff, Miss Bremerton, and the Carrs themselves," he said. "Which leaves us with the question—which of them made sure to hurry up and inform Anthony Ingram that somebody had died? Somebody who was the wrong victim."

CHAPTER 9

Mrs. Tilden grumbled about having meal preparations interrupted but eventually supplied Celia with the name of the intelligence office that had hired out Paulina and Jenny. Although the mysterious individual in the oriental outfit—more familiarly referred to as a Turk costume— seemed the most likely suspect, she still wanted to understand why Paulina had fled the Carrs' house last night. Perhaps she and this person had worked together to poison Mr. Carr's vanilla. First, however, she would have to locate the young woman.

The intelligence office was in a part of town suitably located to serve those most in need of its services. A less salubrious neighborhood than the location of the Carrs' impressive home, and where the stench of dung wafted like a miasma over lanes that did not enjoy the services of a street cleaner as often as those in the wealthier parts of town. Celia scanned the street numbers marked above the doors of the businesses lining the road. Two-ten. Two-twelve. *Ah, here we are.* She tucked away the scrap of stationery on which she'd written the name of the hiring agency and contemplated the sign painted upon the window glass: *Finnemore's Intelligence Office. G. Finnemore, owner.* Simple enough and requiring no further explanation.

Mr. Finnemore's establishment was grubby around the edges, although the window frames appeared to have been recently painted with a fresh coat of white. The sound of someone tuning a piano drifted into the road from a musical instrument dealer across the way. Next to Mr. Finnemore's, a man stumbled out of a dentist's establishment, his aching jaw cradled in his hand. He nodded to Celia before staggering up the street.

The bell above the door, its clapper missing, failed to ring when she stepped inside. The office was presently empty of customers and no one stood behind the high oak counter stretched across the back. Perhaps people did not usually apply for work or request hired help on a Saturday. Or perhaps Mr. Finnemore's intelligence office was not all that popular with those seeking employment.

"Hullo?" Celia called.

There was no immediate response. Someone would eventually arrive to assist. The iron stove in the corner was unlit, leaving the space damp and chilly. Numerous bills and advertisements were attached to a wall. *Wanted–a good cook. $60 per month. A good seamstress, $30 per month.* Worth less than a good cook, apparently. *Ten good miners for Sierra County. $60 per month and board. Steady employment for six or eight months.* And then what? wondered Celia. More unemployed men to stream into San Francisco, desperate for a job. Although they'd not find one, unless they were *good*, whatever that word actually implied. Requests for more help, ones yet to be posted, littered the top of the counter.

At last, the bluish brown fabric curtaining a rear entry parted and a clerk stepped through.

"Ma'am?" he asked somewhat timorously, his expression pinched, as if anticipating criticism of one of the company's hired-out help. The newspapers had been extremely critical lately of the quality of women—no comments about the quality of the men—which intelligence offices such as this one offered for employment. Calls for a Woman's Labor Exchange were growing by the day. What had one of the papers recently claimed? That the "insolent servant might learn better manners" if she were properly vetted, rather than permitting women to obtain positions because the owners of intelligence offices were more interested in collecting their fees than in guaranteeing a supply of quality servants.

Celia couldn't help but wonder if the women were truly insolent or simply insufficiently docile and biddable. It often was of no benefit for a female to hold opinions. Even less beneficial to express them. *Lord knows.*

The clerk's expression became more pained the longer Celia took to respond to his greeting. He settled behind the counter, one finger dragging nervously at the collar of his shirt. "How might I help you today?"

She smiled, which relaxed his shoulders and dropped his finger. "I am seeking information about a young woman I observed working at a fete I attended last evening. The ball at Mr. Eustace Carr's home. It is my understanding that she was hired out of this intelligence office."

"The Carrs' masquerade ball."

"From the tone of your voice I gather you have already heard about the unfortunate incident that took place last evening."

The pinch returned to his face. "We were notified by the coroner that one of our girls had suffered an accident."

"Dreadful, is it not? That wretched girl falling so disastrously ill. No doubt your employer is most upset by the entire affair." Jenny's suspicious death would cast a pall upon his agency that could easily shutter it.

"Mr. Carr arrived in our office early this morning to speak with Mr. Finnemore," the clerk said. "The conversation distressed Mr. Finnemore so greatly that we only opened the office ten minutes ago. Can't have the women we hire to the upstanding citizens of San Francisco getting sick and dying."

Indeed. "I expect Mr. Carr will not hold Mr. Finnemore responsible for the girl's death. He is a generous and understanding man, from my experience of him."

The clerk failed to prevent his unfavorable opinion of the senior Mr. Carr from showing. He wisely pivoted the conversation to Celia's original request. "You wanted to know something about the other girl Mr. Carr employed?"

"Yes," she said. "This particular girl looked very familiar to me and I am concerned about her. You see, I am a nurse and I . . . well, this is very delicate. Can I trust you to keep a confidence?"

He stuck out his spindly chest. "Certainly, ma'am. I can absolutely be trusted."

But can I be trusted? Celia drew in a breath and affixed a concerned look to her face. "This young woman required my medical help some months ago. She didn't supply me with more than her Christian name and my services don't require that I have more information than that," she said. "However, her illness was so alarming that I was worried about her for some time after."

His gaze narrowed. "What was wrong with her?"

"She did not have some shameful disease. Please do not think that." Celia would ruin the girl's chances of ever being employed again if the fellow came to believe she had syphilis or the like. "It was an illness that nearly took her to death's door, though. She never returned to my clinic, however, and I would very much like to ensure that she is completely well. She did appear quite healthy last night, but I wish to make certain. You understand."

"Mr. Finnemore—"

"Will not blame you for assisting a nurse who wishes to confirm that one of the girls you hire out is healthy. As healthy as she needs to be to fulfill the requirements of her employment." She clasped her hands at her chest. "Please. I merely wish to speak with her and reassure myself that she is better. I have lost sleep worrying about the young woman, not knowing how to contact her. I would have questioned her last evening, but the opportunity never presented itself and I did not wish to make a scene."

He ran his tongue over his teeth as he considered what to do. At last, he released a sigh.

"Of course, ma'am. Let's see what I can find." He reached for a ledger book off to one side, sliding it toward him and flipping through the pages to find the date that Mr. Carr's request was fulfilled.

Celia snuck a peek at the names written on the ledger. Whoever had recorded them had terrible penmanship, making it all the more difficult to read the entries upside down.

"Here's the entry for the two women Mr. Carr requested." The clerk squinted at the book. "Miss Jenny Bernard and a Miss Paulina Lyons were sent. Is the latter your former patient?"

"Paulina, yes. That is her."

"Pretty sure this was the first time she's made use of our services, ma'am. Just another Irish girl looking for a job." His brow furrowed.

"She was mighty set on working the Carrs' party. When she saw the posting, she pestered Mr. Finnemore to get sent to the masquerade ball. Claimed she'd always wanted to work at the Carrs' grand party, which they hold every year at this time," he said. "Mr. Carr left the hiring of the girls to Mr. Finnemore, and he sent Miss Lyons along with Miss Bernard."

"Where can I find her?" she asked. "And do not worry that I am surreptitiously attempting to hire the girl on my own in order to cheat you out of your fee."

The clerk stepped back, as if ruffled by the possibility that she could read his mind. If he knew that her true goal was to locate a possible murderer—or a young woman who might possess information about a murder—he'd be even more alarmed.

He ran a finger around the edge of his collar, again, and cleared his throat. "Here's her information, ma'am. She's on Battery Street." He gave her the precise address. "Hope you find out she's okay."

"As do I."

• • •

"Sebastian *has* accused me of trying to poison him, hasn't he, Detective Greaves?" Miss Vanmeter asked. To most folks, she might appear small and wan and inconsequential—she even dressed like she didn't want anybody to notice her, wearing a bland flax-colored dress that was poorly fitted and caused her to blend into her surroundings—but she was full of fire at the moment.

"You already know about the attempt?" Nick asked.

"Irene sent a note," she replied. "He has accused me, hasn't he, Detective? Just like I told Mrs. Davies he would do."

Surprisingly, Taylor didn't chuckle over the fact that Celia had spoken with Miss Vanmeter before them.

Nick could've said no, not exactly, but instead he opted not to answer as she strode through the empty storefront. Every so often she slowed to glare at him, standing near the door turning the brim of his hat through his hands. He was trying to picture the space turned into a women's clinic. Dust coated the floor, the skim of dirt broken by the trail of her footprints, and faded wallpaper peeled in the corner. It was also too close to the racket of Market Street and would never be as quiet as Celia's. It might never be as clean and tidy as her examination room, either. Or maybe he was simply prejudiced in Celia's favor.

"Now, Miss Vanmeter, there's no need to get ruffled," Taylor said, hating to see a female—anybody, actually—upset. Even if they might've committed a crime and deserved to be upset. "We're here to ask a few questions. We need to find who's responsible and are hoping you can help, that's all."

"You make it sound as if the police interrogating me is as trivial as inquiring after the time of day."

"We are not interrogating you, Miss Vanmeter," Nick said, unperturbed by her sharp tone. "We just want to ask a few questions."

"That is pretty much the same thing, isn't it?"

Maybe he was splitting hairs. "Tell us about your visit to the Carrs' yesterday."

"You suspect *me*."

"Since you're aware of what I'm investigating, Miss Vanmeter, perhaps you understand why I'm questioning you and everyone else who was in the house during the hours we believe a poisoned bottle of vanilla was put in Sebastian Carr's room."

"I was in the library the whole time, waiting for Irene to join me."

"Not the whole time."

She stopped to stare out the window, which needed a good scrubbing. Everything in the storefront needed a good scrubbing and some repairs. She'd have to replace the stove that, based on the short section of flue protruding through the ceiling, had once occupied the nearest corner. Along with all the fixtures that used to cover the gas taps. She also needed to finish installing the barriers that divided what had once been a large single room into multiple spaces for examining and treating patients. Would she have the funds to do all that and pay the rent? Funds that might be hard to come by, now that Sebastian Carr had forbidden Irene Bremerton from subsidizing her clinic?

Miss Vanmeter listlessly drew a finger across one of the muntins holding the window's glass panes. It came up black. "The situation is humiliating, Detective."

"Somebody attempted to poison Sebastian Carr, Miss Vanmeter. Succeeded in poisoning an innocent young woman," he said. "Forgive me if I'm not too concerned about your humiliation."

She futilely wiped her fingers together to clean them. Taylor noticed and pulled out one of his handkerchiefs, handing it over. Nick needed to reimburse his assistant for all the handkerchiefs he ended up giving to suspects and witnesses.

"I'd gone upstairs, after Sebastian and I had argued in the library, in one final attempt to convince him about the merits of this clinic."

She looked around her, at the dirty floor, the stained ceiling, the broken chair in the corner that the prior occupant had left when they'd taken the stove. Not exactly a fair exchange. Maybe she was envisioning what it could become one day. Nick doubted she was seeing the space for what it actually was—an empty room in need of endless repairs, the din of traffic invading the space, dust sifting through the gaps in the door and the windows. He expected that when it rained, the ceiling leaked.

"Why go upstairs to talk with him?" Nick asked. "To his bedroom? Might not appear proper, if anybody found out you'd been in there."

"I am past concern for my reputation, Detective Greaves. All that matters is this clinic," she said. "He wasn't in his room, though. Or at least he didn't want me to think he was in his room. I pounded on the door but he didn't respond."

"He didn't respond, miss?" Taylor asked, jotting a note.

"No, he didn't. I even rattled the door, but it was locked," she said. "Preston heard me and came out of his room to see what was going on. He had quite the laugh at my expense."

"Preston Carr didn't tell me that he'd spoken with you in the hallway," Nick said.

"He laughed at me and I ran off, mortified. Not much of a conversation, Detective, and, knowing him, not something he'd think was important enough to mention. Maybe he was trying to protect my reputation," she said sarcastically. "So you see, I did not slip inside Sebastian Carr's room and leave him a poisoned bottle of vanilla extract. Somebody else did."

"Any idea who, Miss Vanmeter?"

Her demeanor shifted, her tense shoulders dropping, the taut muscles in her throat, visible above the lace trimming her neckline, easing. Relieved that suspicion might be shifting off her and onto somebody—anybody—else.

"The Carrs had invited so many people to the masquerade ball last night," she said. "It had to be one of them. Not all of those in attendance are affectionate friends of the Carrs', Detective."

"Anybody particularly not affectionate?"

She turned to stare out the window again. "After I received Irene's message and spoke with Mrs. Davies about what had happened, I went to the Carrs'. Irene told me Mrs. Davies had come by," she said. "And that she'd told Mrs. Davies about spotting a fellow in a turquoise-colored caftan and white turban outside last night."

Celia, collecting clues before he had a chance to. "What exactly was this fellow doing?"

"Running away from the house. Not the actions of a guest." She folded Taylor's dirtied handkerchief into a neat square. "You know, it's odd. I saw Preston wear a very similar costume once. Onstage, performing in an amateur theatrical."

"That wasn't what he had on when I spoke with him last night, Miss Vanmeter." He'd been wearing a harlequin outfit. Or at least the top half of one.

"Maybe he changed out of it," she suggested. "It would be easy to quickly remove a turban and caftan, Detective."

"I'll check and see what I might find at the Carrs', sir," Taylor murmured to him.

Nick nodded at him. "Thank you, Miss Vanmeter. But don't leave town. Do you understand?"

She smiled grimly. "Yes, Detective. I understand."

. . .

Paulina Lyons had supplied an address on Battery to Finnemore's Intelligence Office. Not far from the main post office and the brand-new Merchants' Exchange building, a popular locale for men of consequence to read newspapers or to discuss stocks and plot business dealings. Celia strode past numerous businesses selling the necessities for everyday life, but what she could not readily find were boardinghouses. And certainly none for a proper young lady. It was not a quiet area for residing in, anyway. The din of barrels rattling down wagon ramps merged with the clatter of horses' hooves on cobbles and the ding of ships' bells out in the harbor, a scant few blocks distant. A cacophony of sounds.

"Well, Miss Lyons, do you actually live on this road?" she murmured, drawing the attention of a passing delivery boy, his arms laden with parcels.

He slowed. "Ma'am? Are you speaking to me?"

"Ah, no. My apologies. A habit of mine."

He mumbled a comment about loony women and continued on his way.

Celia hurried across the intersection and paused at the address the clerk had provided. The number belonged to the office of a small newspaper printing office. She retreated to the edge of the pavement, nimbly evading a paperboy scuttling past who was headed for the corner to hawk newspapers, and surveyed the road. She was positive this was the number the clerk had given her. Unless Miss Lyons lived above the office. Or behind it. As she'd already observed, there were scant few lodging houses and no hotels on Battery.

The door opened, discharging the steady clatter and clank of a printing press in operation, and a man stepped outside. He was dark-skinned, with a severe side part in the tight curls of his hair and a neatly trimmed goatee. He also had a most penetrating gaze.

"Can I help you, ma'am?" he asked. "You've been staring at the window of my newspaper office for a while now." The edge to his deep voice suggested he mistrusted the reason for her surveillance.

"Forgive me. I was given this address as belonging to a woman I am looking for, and clearly it does not," she said.

"Is she a colored woman?" he asked flatly.

"She has been described to me as being Irish, actually," Celia replied. "Her name is Paulina Lyons. Have you ever heard of her?"

"I haven't, ma'am, and I can assure you she does not live here." He considered her. "Might I ask why you are looking for this woman? I am a newspaperman and by nature curious about such things."

"It involves the sudden death of a servant at a party last evening," she said. "Miss Lyons was hired to also work at the party and may have information relevant to what took place. I would like to speak with her about the event, but it appears that she misled the intelligence office about where she lives."

"You are sure the intelligence office itself didn't make a mistake."

"I have reason to believe that is not the case." It was far more likely that Miss Lyons had provided Mr. Finnemore a false address. Possibly even a false identity. A masquerade all her own.

The man glanced at the address painted on the window above the door. There was a crack emanating from a pit in the glass as though it had been struck by a stone. The crack extended through the name of the newspaper—*The Elevator*—immediately below the number.

"Why might the young woman have chosen my address, I wonder?" he said.

"I would also like an answer to that question."

His gaze returned to Celia's face. "Why are you so concerned about this young woman and the sudden death of a servant, ma'am? Is that not a matter for the coroner?"

"Yes, indeed it is, and he has been notified. I am merely . . ." *For pity's sake, Celia, be honest with the man.* "I am assisting the police. The servant's death is suspicious."

His lips slowly curled with a broad smile. "You must be Mrs. Davies."

"You have heard about me?"

"As I said, I am a newspaperman. It is my business to hear about people," he said. "You are also known for helping the poor women in this part of town, Mrs. Davies. Aid given out of charity, not because it makes you feel superior, I'm told."

People spoke about her, and not merely to gossip about her role as a "female detective"? "I had no idea I was so well-known."

"You are." He inclined his head. "And I am Mr. Philip Alexander Bell, ma'am."

"I am aware of your efforts to advance suffrage and fight for equality, Mr. Bell, " she replied, astonishing him by extending her hand so that he might shake it. Which he did. He was man who craved justice. A man she could easily admire. "You are far more famous than I am."

He shot a look at the crack in the glass. "Not always in ways that bring me accolades, Mrs. Davies."

Two stout men in gray suits, their faces smug above their thin silk cravats and white collars, eyed Mr. Bell and Celia. A black man and a respectably attired white woman in mourning chatting on the pavement. Shocking. They scowled, the one appearing ready to hurl an insult when the other pulled his companion away and out into the street where they could avoid close contact.

"Do not mind them, ma'am."

"My cousin and ward is half-Chinese, Mr. Bell. I often encounter such reactions when I am in her company," she said. "As for my search for Miss Lyons, I feel she must have had a reason for using this particular address."

"Her selection could have been made at random, ma'am. Or she might've done so as a joke."

"Both possibilities make my search for her that much more difficult."

"How about I ask around? See if I can find anybody who might've heard of Miss Lyons, or who might know where she actually lives."

"I would appreciate any help, Mr. Bell," she replied. "Again, the name she gave to the intelligence office that hired her out was Paulina Lyons. I cannot, however, vouch for the veracity of the name."

"Paulina is not a common name. Maybe it actually is her Christian name," he said. "Might be easier to locate her, if that's the case."

"You have my deepest appreciation, Mr. Bell," Celia said. "But I confess I do not comprehend why you are willing to help me."

"You're a kindred spirit, ma'am. Despite our . . . differences."

She smiled. "Thank you for saying so. This is where I may be reached." She found one of her cards in the depths of her reticule and handed it to him.

He bid her farewell and returned to his office. Celia turned to face the road. Now what? Wait for Mr. Bell to uncover answers? Stop in every warehouse and manufactory to inquire about Paulina Lyons, whose name was increasingly likely to be as false as the address she'd supplied?

Or head home, where she undoubtedly would have a patient waiting for her? She was neglecting her clinic, again.

She headed up Battery toward home, pausing as a buckboard wagon trundled by before crossing the street. She stood there long enough to notice the name of the business she'd stopped in front of. *Carr and Co.'s Express. Eustace Carr and sons, owners.* The blinds on the windows were closed tight against inquisitive eyes, and a sign suspended on the door declared the office was *Closed.* But it was not the fact that the Carrs had elected to shut their express office the day after a suspicious death had occurred at their masquerade ball that Celia found so very interesting, but the address of their business. 642 Battery.

She looked down the road. Mr. Bell and the *Elevator* were at 624 Battery. Perhaps Miss Lyons had not intended to use Mr. Bell's address as her own, but had meant to use the address for Carr and Co.'s Express, where the Carrs shipped parcels and freight to other parts of California. Which suggested the address she'd supplied had not been chosen at random or on a lark but rather as an attempt to link her existence to that of the Carrs. An attempt that had gone slightly awry because she'd unintentionally mistaken the precise number.

The question remained, though—why link herself to the Carrs at all?

• • •

"Mr. Greaves! Nicholas! Wait, please!"

The woman shouting out on the street in front of City Hall, where everybody could hear, dashed across the road, zigzagging between a pair of hackney carriages that were pulling up to collect a lawyer Nick recognized. The lawyer was accompanied by a woman Nick also recognized, although she was usually found in one of the Barbary's alleyway doorways, the hem of her brightly colored skirt short enough to show off her petticoats and shapely ankles.

"Looks like Mrs. Davies wants to talk to you, Mr. Greaves," Taylor said, failing at keeping his amusement out of his voice.

"I think I can see that, Taylor."

"Mr. Greaves, do wait." Celia Davies startled one of the hackney carriage horses, drawing an angry shout from the driver. She made an apology and deftly jumped over a freshly deposited pile of manure left at the curb.

"I'm not going anywhere," he said.

"Good." She nodded at Taylor, who'd tipped his hat at her. Her color was high, the outward sign of her inward exhilaration at the challenge of another case. "What a day and it is not even . . ." She glanced at the watch pinned at her waist. "Not even one. Addie will be wondering where I've gotten to."

"And where have you been, Mrs. Davies?" Nick asked. "Although I have an idea, based on my conversation with Miss Vanmeter."

"She came to see me. Very early," Celia gasped as she struggled against the confines of a corset preventing her from catching her breath. He had a sudden thought about what her corset might look like, might feel like beneath his hands. A thought he'd better put out of his mind—quickly—if he was going to focus. "She is worried that Sebastian Carr will accuse her of poisoning his vanilla."

"Since they aren't exactly friends, I'm surprised he hasn't," Nick said. "She also mentioned that Miss Bremerton told you about a stranger wearing some sort of caftan and turban. Whatever those are."

"A caftan is a sort of loose outer tunic-like garment that Eastern men wear," she explained. "And a turban is a long strip of cloth that is wound around the head to cover the hair. Often referred to as a Turk costume."

"Seems a little late to be bringing up this fellow, doesn't it?"

"Better late than never, as they say. Dr. Schneider was where I first learned of this individual, though," she said. "Not one of the guests but a man lurking on the property."

How did she do it? How did she manage to find out so much so quickly? "Who's Schneider?"

"A physician I consulted Thursday morning—was it so recent?—about surgery to repair Barbara's foot. He attended the Carrs' mask last evening," she answered. "How did Miss Vanmeter already hear?"

"She stopped in to see Miss Bremerton right after you'd been there."

"Ah. Well, Miss Bremerton has accused Miss Ingram of being the person in the costume," she continued. "She is aware of Sebastian's assault on Miss Ingram and their prior relationship."

"On her part, Miss Ingram has suggested Irene Bremerton. Revenge for his dalliances," Nick said. "The Ingrams' neighbor, who makes it his business to keep the street under surveillance, told Taylor he didn't notice Louise Ingram leave the house last night. But how reliable is his word? Her brother has provided an alibi, but I'm not sure it's as solid as he wants us to think. However, he did admit that he'd wanted to go to the mask because he's hoping to stop the engagement. We'll say he thinks Sebastian Carr is a scoundrel." Rather than use the word Ingram had chosen.

"Well, the attempt on Mr. Carr's life may have already succeeded in that regard, Mr. Greaves," Celia said. "When I made to leave Miss Bremerton this morning, she informed me that, after last evening's shocking events, she has requested that the engagement be postponed. Until the uproar passes."

Whenever that might be.

"Maybe Miss Bremerton is right and one of the Ingrams was this person in the caftan and turban, sir," Taylor said, jotting a note in his book.

"Miss Vanmeter told us she'd seen Preston Carr wear a costume like that onstage once, Mrs. Davies."

"What an intriguing comment," she said. "Dr. Schneider does not hold a high opinion of Mr. Preston Carr. His association with the theatrical crowd has tarnished his reputation."

If associating with the theatrical crowd or singers in *lagerbier* saloons tarnished a person's reputation, Nick's was probably thoroughly corroded.

"I should also inform you that I have been on the hunt for Paulina Lyons," she continued. "The hired servant who ran off early last night. I have discovered that she provided the intelligence office a false address. I suspect even a false name."

"Which is going to make finding her pretty difficult, Mrs. Davies."

"As I am aware, Mr. Greaves."

At her back, a gust of wind rustled the scrubby trees on Portsmouth Square, blew across the road to stir the black ribbons of her bonnet, fluttering one against her cheek. He'd draw it aside with a fingertip just to have an excuse to brush her skin, but it wasn't just Taylor who'd notice. Or who'd be tattling in the station, he thought, eyeing one of the officers exiting through the alleyway door and catching sight of Nick standing close to Celia. He smirked before turning to jog across the road.

Nick took a step back. Felt idiotic for taking a step back and having Celia stiffen because his retreat bothered her.

"There appear to have been several individuals sneaking around before and during the Carrs' ball, Mr. Greaves," Celia replied, brushing aside the bonnet ribbon herself. "Paulina. The fellow in the Turk costume."

"Maybe even Miss Joyce," Taylor added.

"And yourself, ma'am," Nick said.

"Including myself."

Taylor's pencil tip snapped and he let out an uncustomary curse. "Sorry, ma'am."

"Quite all right, Mr. Taylor."

She hunted around in her reticule and pulled out a fresh pencil, which she gave to Taylor, along with a scrap of red cloth.

"You both will be interested in this. I found it in the shrubs off the Carrs' veranda." She handed the scrap to Nick. It was of velvet and very soft, and smelled faintly of a floral perfume. A woman's scent. "It appears to be a length of trim torn away from an item of clothing. Torn while possibly attempting to enter the house through a side window."

Nick exhaled. "Celia . . ."

"Retrieving this bit of material was not dangerous, Nicholas, and nobody observed me."

For some reason, Taylor didn't snicker. Maybe he was tired of Nick glaring at him.

He pocketed it. "Thank you, Mrs. Davies. I'll hold on to the bit of trim until we know if it's important at all."

"It's too rich a color for a servant, someone who may have been gardening, to have worn, Mr. Greaves," she observed. "So who was out amongst the shrubbery tearing their clothes if not an individual at the masquerade attempting to sneak into the house?"

"The Turk costume, as Miss Vanmeter described it, was not red."

"Magenta would be more precise," she retorted. "But you are correct about that."

She sounded reluctant to admit it.

"There you are, Greaves. Mr. Taylor. Mrs. Davies," Harris called out as he climbed down from a hired cab stopped at the curb. "A fine day, don't you agree?"

He tipped his hat at Celia, who smiled back at him.

"Since you're looking pleased with yourself, Harris, I'd wager you've had a chance to test the vanilla extract bottles," Nick said.

Like a magician pulling a pair of rabbits from a hat, he produced them from his coat pocket. "I have."

"And?" Nick asked impatiently.

It wasn't like Harris to be intentionally coy. Maybe he was enjoying life away from his former duties as coroner. He was far more relaxed than the man who used to mourn every suicide and murder victim, his shoulders sagging from the senseless loss of life.

"Definitely traces of arsenic in the empty bottle." Harris raised the hand holding the cracked Burnett's bottle.

"Which verifies that it was through the vanilla that Jenny was poisoned," Celia said.

"What about the full one containing the extract made up by the Carrs' cook?" Nick asked.

"None detectable."

"There's our answer, sir." Taylor stowed his notebook and collected both bottles from Harris. "Somebody *outside* the family is definitely responsible for the poisoning that caused Jenny Bernard's death."

"Or that's what somebody *inside* the household wants us to think, Taylor."

☙ CHAPTER 10 ❧

"I was wondering when you might visit, Celia. To ask about the Carrs," Jane Hutchinson said. "Bring tea, please, Hetty," she ordered her servant then slid closed the parlor doors.

"You have heard the news." Celia perched on the edge of one of the stuffed armchairs in the room, her skirt dusty from the morning's expedition, which had dragged into the afternoon. She did not want to dirty Jane's furniture. "That a servant died."

"I did hear. Not many details, though." Jane sank gracefully onto the sofa, covered in a silk fabric of pastel blue in a room of blues and golds and scarlets that was pristine and peaceful. Celia often envied the hush; it was impossible to predict when the quiet at her own home might be disrupted by the boisterous shouts of neighbors' children, the whoops of laborers playing cards on a nearby porch, or the boom of the Point Bonita fog gun on a misty night. Perhaps, though, she did not truly envy Jane and Frank their more tranquil existence away from the world she had come to love.

"I was out this morning and happened to run into one of the Carrs' guests," Jane continued. "She told me that a police detective was sent for, disrupting the party and sending everybody scurrying for home. I take it the servant's death was suspicious, if the police were called in."

"It was. Poison, in fact."

"Goodness, Celia," her friend said. "I presume you've become involved, or else you wouldn't be here, looking for my help."

"Frank will not appreciate you assisting in one of my misadventures again, Jane." She had previously proven to be extremely useful and extremely brave, however.

"He is not at home at the moment, and you're here simply to visit."

"Well, please do not get in trouble with your husband for my sake." Frank's threats to forbid his wife from even speaking with Celia had become more insistent with every incident.

"Tell me what happened."

Celia relayed the evening's events. "By all measures, the poison was intended for Sebastian Carr."

"So you would like me to discover who his enemies might be?" Jane asked.

"Precisely," she replied. "I am surprised, though, that you and Frank were not at the masquerade ball. You must be acquainted with them."

Jane drew in a breath. "We were invited, but we had to decline. I haven't been feeling well lately."

"Jane! You should have told me. What is the matter? How can I help?"

It was then she noticed Jane's hand resting on her stomach, her fingers stroking the fabric of her dress where it covered her middle. *She is pregnant.* A chill spread. *I should be happy for her.* Jane had wished for a child for so long. A child that could be hers and Frank's. Not one she was sharing with the memory of his dead wife.

"You are with child," Celia said, wondering if her voice sounded as hollow to Jane as it did to her own ears. *I should be happy for her rather than envious.*

"Not any longer, Celia."

Celia went to sit next to Jane and clasped her friend's hands in her own. They were cold. "Why did you not tell me? I might have been able to help. You should have told me, Jane. You know I understand."

Patrick had wanted children. Celia had wanted children, too. Desperately. But her own attempts to have a child, undertaken when their marriage had still seemed salvageable, had all come to nothing. The pain had dwindled but she'd not forgotten it. Jane would not either, no matter how brief the pregnancy.

"I wanted to be positive before I said anything, Celia," Jane replied, her eyes dry. Perhaps she had exhausted her supply of tears. "I was barely certain I was with child when I . . . well, it's been over a month now, but Frank insists that I refrain from too much excitement until we're sure I've recovered. That is why we did not attend the ball last night, even though we'd received an invitation."

"I should leave. I am being selfish and inconsiderate to burden you with talk about my silly escapades."

"They are far from silly!" Jane countered. "And please stay. I always enjoy your company. And your escapades."

"Only if you promise me you will rest as soon as I leave," Celia said, squeezing her friend's fingers. "I will not allow you to fall ill."

"Oh, Celia." Jane leaned over and pecked her on the cheek. "I will be fine. In fact, it was because I felt well that I went out this morning for the first time in weeks."

"In future, I insist that you let me know if you need anything. Anything at all. I'll be here in two twos, as Addie might say."

"I will, I will! I promise!" she said, smiling so that Celia would relinquish the crushing grip on her hands. "And I will rest, but not until after you share the details of what happened last night at the Carrs'."

Celia retook her chair. "What did the friend you encountered this morning have to say?"

"Not much of use. I ran into her outside my milliner's," she replied. "I nearly literally ran into her. She does have a tendency to charge along the sidewalk. Like you," she teased.

"You are definitely feeling well if you went hat shopping." A task Celia had no fondness for.

"Frank thought a new bonnet would lift my spirits. I didn't have the heart to tell him no," she said. "My friend was also surprised that Frank and I hadn't attended the party and had to post me up on the details. Mention who was there and what they wore and who'd been roaring drunk and had embarrassed themselves. A typical society evening. Aside from the need to leave early."

"Dr. Schneider—do you know him?—told me that Sebastian Carr is as pleased as Punch to have captured Miss Bremerton."

"I do know Dr. Schneider and I'm not surprised one bit by his opinion about the engagement," she said, glancing over at the doors when they slid open and Hetty reappeared, bearing the tea things and a small tray of cold chicken sandwiches. She placed the items on the marble-topped table at Jane's knee and departed, closing the doors once more. "The Carrs want to establish their bona fides in San Francisco society by marrying into an established California family like the Bremertons'."

"Irene has requested that they delay the engagement because of last night's tragedy."

"I'm astonished that the Bremertons ever encouraged Irene to accept Sebastian Carr. They mustn't know about the scandal surrounding him. About his involvement in that assault upon a theater girl his name was linked to," Jane said, pouring out a cup of tea for Celia. "Or maybe they did hear but chose to discount the gossip, since a connection to the Carrs offers financial advantages that are hard to pass up."

Marriage as a mere business transaction.

Celia accepted the teacup, delicate china painted with cerulean roses that matched the color of the sofa. "Irene knows about the attack, and the woman is not exactly a theater girl but rather a scenery painter."

"Sebastian has his supporters who are positive he wasn't responsible," said Jane. "One or two have blamed Preston, just because they don't like him. Others accuse Eustace Carr, keen to have a troublesome woman removed from his elder son's life. I've even heard a theory that Irene paid the boy."

"'There is no fire without smoke,' Jane, as they say," Celia replied. "Perhaps the situation is more complicated than we've been led to believe, and there is truth in the gossip."

"I'll ask around and see if there's more than smoke to the story, Celia," she said and sipped from her tea. "And do not worry about me. I will be fine. Besides, I could use the distraction."

"If you feel the least unwell, you will rest, correct?"

"I haven't forgotten, Celia!" Jane said. "It won't be easy to avoid alerting Frank, though. He is watching me like a hawk these days. Hetty is sure to report to him that you were here."

"Oh?" Celia set down her tea and got to her feet. She put a finger to her lips to keep Jane quiet, hurried over to the doors on tiptoes, and pulled them open. The hallway beyond was empty.

"What are you up to, Celia?" Jane asked.

"I was ascertaining whether Hetty might go further than simply informing Frank about my visit," said Celia, closing the doors and returning to her chair. "Apparently, your maid is not as inclined to eavesdrop as Addie."

"Both Addie and Hetty mean well."

"I know they do." Nonetheless, she lowered her voice. "The woman who was attacked by vitriol is named Louise Ingram. Also, if you can, discover if anyone has ever heard of a Paulina Lyons. She was hired to assist at the Carrs' party last evening, and had gone upstairs at an hour that may have afforded her an opportunity to place an arsenic-laced bottle of vanilla in Sebastian Carr's bedchamber."

Jane lifted an eyebrow. "Poisoned vanilla. What a choice of murder weapon."

"Murder or a lengthy illness. Arsenic is easily obtained and too often used, Jane, based on the reports in the newspapers." Just last week, there was an article in the *Daily Alta* about a mother using the chemical to poison her children. "I attempted to locate Miss Lyons, but she gave the intelligence office a false address. I wonder if her name is even accurate. You must recall that we've encountered this situation before." *Masquerades* . . .

"Is she the main suspect?" Jane asked, slipping a sandwich onto a plate. It was good to see that she had an appetite.

"I wish I could say for certain." Celia helped herself to a sandwich also. "There is also a mysterious fellow in a caftan and turban, observed by both Dr. Schneider and Irene Bremerton."

"How appropriate to wear a costume as a disguise to a masquerade."

"This individual does not eliminate others from suspicion, including Miss Katherine Vanmeter and even Miss Bremerton," she said. "Preston Carr cannot be removed from consideration, either."

"I don't know Preston or his brother well enough to judge their relationship, but I will make sure to ask about that, as well," Jane said. "Your forehead is creasing again, Celia. I will be okay."

"I cannot help worrying about you." Celia tapped her fingernail against the brim of the teacup, the china offering up a genteel ping. "I should also tell you about an intriguing item I found in Sebastian Carr's room last night, Jane. A pamphlet from the Pacific Museum of Anatomy. Perhaps Mr. Carr is concerned about his virility."

Jane laughed. "You searched his room?"

"The commotion after the girl died made for a perfect distraction," she said. "I also found a mostly burned note requesting a meeting between him and an unknown person. He is hiding something, Jane. A situation or a fact that might explain why someone attempted to murder him."

"Do you think this person will try again?"

Celia contemplated the question, which she hadn't before had time enough to consider. But having Jane ask it now forced her to.

"They very well might, Jane."

• • •

The rear door to the American wasn't propped open like it had been earlier. In fact, none of the doors to the theater were open. Rehearsal must be finished for the day. Which made it difficult to confirm information sent to the station after Nick and Taylor had visited that morning. A note from one of the musicians stating that Ingram was late showing up Friday night. Maybe the man had been afraid to tell Taylor when he'd questioned the musicians about Ingram's alibi. Maybe Ingram's temper was worse than Preston Carr's offhand comment had implied.

Nick rattled the rear door to the American Theater one more time, just to prove to himself it was locked. He scanned the length of the alley, his gaze settling on the back entrance of a costumer's across the way. Maybe a visit to learn if they'd rented a Turk costume to a suspect in a poisoning would be worthwhile. The business's alley door was locked, so he went around to the front.

Inside, a suffocating quantity of clothing hung from hooks and filled shelves. If Nick wanted a pair of breeches, they could supply them, along with a long vest in orange. A parson's getup too. Tricorn hats were plentiful, as were plumes for decorating ladies' hair. A flimsy white costume equipped with a bow and garlands of silk flowers had been spread across a table. Cupid, maybe? Perfumes must be a key part of folks' costumes as well, given the sweet, musky smell of the place.

In the corner by the front window, a man was busy hemming a forest-green skirt. His long fingers moved swiftly as he squinted through the wire-rimmed spectacles poised on the end of his nose. He looked over from his needlework.

"Sorry I didn't hear you come in, sir." He set down his needle and removed the skirt from his lap, climbing off the stool he'd been seated on. "Are you here to collect a masquerade ball costume?"

"I'm Detective Greaves," Nick replied, fingering a velvet mask on display with others in every color a customer might want. Including magenta. "I'd like to ask you about a costume you may have supplied to an individual connected to an investigation I'm conducting. Attempted murder."

He recoiled so sharply his glasses fell off his face. He bent to retrieve them. "I . . . I . . . how can I help, Officer?"

"The person was wearing a Turk costume. That's how it was described to me," Nick said, examining the contents of the small storefront and not spotting anything that might fit his idea of a "Turk costume." "A turban and a caftan with a sash. Do you offer costumes like that?"

"We haven't had a call for an 'Oriental Potentate' or Turk costume in several months," the fellow said. "I don't even have any currently in stock. But there are other costumers in San Francisco who might've rented to the individual you're looking for."

None as conveniently close as this one was to the American Theater, though. "But you used to carry a costume like that."

"I did, but the production that rented one from me never returned it," he said. "The manager skipped town without paying the bill or returning the clothes. The sash was figured red silk! Expensive to replace."

"Red or magenta?"

His brow creased. "Cherry red."

Not magenta. *I guess.* "Do you have a record of who the manager was and where the performance had taken place?"

"I should. Let me fetch my books." He went to a large desk against the back wall and rifled through a stack of ledgers stacked atop it. "Ah, here we are. As I said, the manager left town the evening the production folded. Scathing reviews."

He showed Nick the entry. Not a name he recognized. "Where is this theater?" He didn't recognize its name, either.

"It was a small venue that used to host amateur performances on occasion, among other entertainments. It is no longer open," the costumer answered. "If folks want to put on amateur productions now, they usually rent one of the halls in town."

"An amateur production?"

"Yes." The fellow peered at him. "Sorry that I couldn't help you more, Officer."

"Don't worry about that," Nick replied. "You've helped me enough."

• • •

"I am back at last, Addie," Celia announced to the entry hall, stripping off her gloves as she peeked into the parlor then her examination room. Both were empty. "Hopefully no patients showed up while I was away."

Addie pushed through the door at the end of the hallway, the delicious smell of baking bread gusting down the narrow passageway. Celia's stomach gave an unladylike rumble. The case clock in the entryway chimed four; she'd been gone much of the day and had neglected to eat anything, aside from tea at Jane's, since breakfast that morning.

"Weel, there you are." Addie brushed her palms across her apron and bustled over to help Celia with her mantle and bonnet. "After rushing off without telling me where you'd gone or how long you'd be."

"I went to the Carrs' to see how Miss Bremerton is faring after last evening's upsetting events," she said. Which was the truth if not the entirety of it. She'd not mention the visit to Dr. Schneider or the hunt for Paulina Lyons just yet; she would save Addie's upset over Celia's participation in one of Nick's cases for later.

Addie gestured toward the open door of Celia's examination room and the black portmanteau visible on the floor alongside her desk. "You went to visit Miss Bremerton without your medical bag?"

"I am not her attending physician, Addie. I merely visited as a friend," Celia said, bending to clean dust from her skirt in order to evade her housekeeper's observant gaze. "Then I stopped in to visit Jane. It has been so long since I've seen her."

"And how was Mrs. Hutchinson?"

"Well. She was well." Jane would not wish her sharing the news that she'd lost a pregnancy, not even with Addie. "The visit was so pleasant that I completely lost track of the time. I do apologize. Did I have any patients while I was gone? None were scheduled."

"No patients, ma'am, and I ken what you're up to." She was wearing a scowl nearly as fierce as the ones Nicholas was fond of displaying. "A young lass perished last night, suspiciously, and you sent for Mr. Greaves to investigate. I've come to expect that you'll be asking questions, too."

"How did you hear that I'd sent for Nicholas?"

She had offered Addie only the merest of details when she'd returned home last night, explaining that the servant had died and the Carrs' masquerade ball had come to a sudden, distressing end.

"Owen is here, ma'am," she replied, folding Celia's mantle over her arm. "He told me."

So much for not informing Addie.

"Should Owen not be at Roesler's? Or has he been let go again?"

"Mr. Roesler allowed him to leave early. The fellow is attending a mask this evening, it seems." She glanced the direction of the dining room. "The laddie needs to talk to you. Which means he's caught up in this, too. The both of you should know better."

Dearest Addie. Always worried. And rightfully so, given Celia's—and Owen's—histories.

"Where is Barbara?" Might she be lingering nearby? Or was her cousin upstairs in her room, her ear pressed to the warm-air register in the floor?

"In her room, ma'am."

The register, then. *Blast.*

Addie lowered her voice. "She's still upset with Owen about the valentine he sent to Miss Grace and ran upstairs when she saw it was him at the door and not one of your patients."

"I see." *For love, thou know'st, if full of jealousy.* More wisdom from Mr. Shakespeare. What could she do for her cousin, though, since she rarely listened to any advice Celia might offer? What was the advice from a woman who herself had failed at love worth, anyway? "Thank you, Addie."

She found Owen at the dining room table, slurping from a bowl of beef soup Addie had hastily prepared for him. Celia always suspected Owen's visits were prompted as much by a desire for one of her housekeeper's meals as any other reason.

"Mrs. Davies." He downed the remainder of the soup and wiped his mouth with a napkin. "I'm glad to see you."

She took the chair across from him. "Addie said you wanted to speak with me, Owen. I hope you are not in trouble."

"Not this time," he said, reaching for a slice of bread and slathering butter on it. "But I wanted to tell you about something I learned from Angus MacNamara."

Overhead, the floor creaked under the weight of Barbara's feet. Celia glanced up at the grate recessed into the ceiling, sure that a shadow was visible through the loops and curves of the iron. She sighed. There'd be no keeping the news about the servant's death or whatever Owen had to relay from her cousin.

"Who is Angus MacNamara?" Celia asked. Aside from obviously being an Irishman. Owen's life in San Francisco had never taken him far from his heritage and those who shared it.

"I worked with him last night, both of us stocking the Carrs' cellar with wine and whiskey." He stuffed the bread into his mouth and rapidly chewed, swallowing so quickly Celia feared he might choke. "He came by Roesler's today to give me my pay. I asked if he saw anything funny last night, and he sure did, Mrs. Davies. He saw one of the maids talking with somebody who wasn't supposed to be in the house."

She leaned forward as much as her blasted corset and the edge of the table allowed. "Where? Exactly when?"

"On the stairs. You know, the back ones that lead upstairs from that passageway next to the kitchen."

"Yes. I do know which stairs you mean." The same ones Irene Bremerton had led Celia up, rather than risk having a woman with a medical bag spotted by the partygoers.

"I can't say exactly when, though, but it was before I showed up to help with the second delivery of wine," he said, snatching the last slice of bread. "Seven, maybe?"

Everything seemed to have taken place at seven. "What was it the maid said to this individual?"

He scrunched up his face as he thought back, the wrinkles across his nose causing his freckles to stand out in relief. At times, he could still look like a boy.

"Angus told me she said 'what are you doing?' That was it, ma'am," he said. "Doesn't sound like it could've been one of the guests or family, because they'd use the main stairs to reach the upper floors. Wouldn't they?"

He sounded a trifle uncertain about what was properly done in the homes of the upper crust. The nicest house Owen Cassidy had likely ever been in, aside from the cellar and back passageway of the Carrs', was this one.

"Yes, they would, Owen. Unless they wished to pass unnoticed to an upper floor."

"Which they didn't manage to do. Angus couldn't see the person because they were up on the steps beyond the landing, though," he said and popped the bread into his mouth.

"Does your friend Angus know which maid it was who recognized this person?"

More furious chewing and swallowing ensued. "He said she had red hair. Do you know which of the maids that is, ma'am?"

"Yes, I do. Her name is Emma Joyce."

She'd appeared so timid and frightened last night. Had Celia mistaken the reason for the girl's unrest, assuming her behavior had been caused by standing in that airless attic room while Jenny lay sweating on a cot, her life ebbing away? When instead her unease may have been caused by seeing a person utterly out of place on the back stairs of the Carrs' home?

A person who may have attempted murder and might be willing to try again? Just as Celia had said to Jane.

• • •

Nick returned to the station after visiting the costumer. He hung around until he learned from Taylor what his search had uncovered at the Carrs' house. Which was precisely nothing. No caftan and turban hidden away. Nobody confessing to having crept about in the bushes outside and torn a piece of their clothing. Furthermore, Mullahey hadn't had any luck tracking down Paulina Lyons either. Although, at the rate Celia was unearthing information, she'd probably locate the girl first.

He dragged the soles of his boots across the iron scraper at Mrs. Jewett's front door, mud dislodging in clumps. He was tired and he was hungry, and he wondered if there'd be much to eat. Knowing there would be, because Mrs. Jewett would never let Nick starve. Especially now, with the anniversary of Meg's death approaching. His landlady was as faithful about remembering the date as she was in commemorating her son's death. When she would drape his photograph in its ornate frame—a brave young man in his uniform, his gun at his side—in black crepe and fix his favorite meal for dinner.

"Evenin', sir," said the lamplighter passing on the street. The fellow's ladder thudded against the pole and he scrambled up the rungs and set the gas ablaze, throwing a pool of light wide enough to reach Mrs. Jewett's front steps.

Nick roused himself. "Evening."

Riley heard him and took to barking in Nick's room above the street. He went inside. Mrs. Jewett bustled out of the dining room with her usual haste, indicating she'd been waiting close by for Nick to come home.

"There you are, Mr. Greaves. Finally."

"I'm not that late, Mrs. Jewett," he said, pulling his hat from his head.

She took it from him, wiping dust from the brim, and hung it on the peg by the door. "I worry."

"No reason to worry." She would anyway.

"I kept the stew warm for you." She glanced toward the commotion Riley was making. "I'll tend to him. You sit and eat."

"I'll deal with Riley."

"I insist that you sit and eat," she said, giving him a gentle shove toward the table, set with a bowl and plate and a spoon. She hurried off and returned with her stew, ladling it out. "Oh, I almost forgot. This came for you today. Looks like it's from the same person as the other one, Mr. Greaves."

Brows tucking together, she set down the stewpot and withdrew an envelope from her skirt pocket. It was from the same person as the last letter, the loops of their handwriting distinctive, the purplish black iron gall ink not quite dark enough, as if they'd bungled the recipe they'd used to make it.

"I can tell you I didn't like the look of the fellow who dropped it off," his landlady said, eyeing the envelope.

"Why is that?"

"He was a grimy character. Unpleasant," she said. "He kept trying to peer into the house like he was looking for you."

"Thank you for letting me know about him, Mrs. Jewett. But he's probably harmless," he said, aiming to sound like he wasn't concerned about either the grimy character or what the envelope might contain.

She pursed her lips. "Since when are folks poking around in your business harmless, Mr. Greaves?"

Since never. "If you're concerned, I'll have the policeman who walks this beat keep an eye out."

"Now I really am worried," she replied, although his response seemed to have appeased her somewhat.

As soon as he heard her climbing the stairs, Nick pulled out a chair and sat, breaking open the wafer sealing the flap. No studio daguerreotype this time. Just a note.

I hope you got the photograph.

Nothing else.

"Take six grains of Dover's Powder in the evening, Mary," Celia instructed her patient, hunched and weak, her skin creased, her eyes dull. She might never have been described as a beauty, but she'd been fairer once. Before the consumption had begun to destroy her body. "And a spoonful of cod liver oil twice a day."

"Yes, ma'am."

Celia handed the woman the powder, carefully wrapped in brown paper, and hoped she had sounded reassuring. It was difficult to sound reassuring when the woman's condition was serious and there was so little Celia could do.

"Can I take White Pine Compound, too?" Mary asked, her hand trembling as she took the packet and tucked it away. "I've run out of prayers to recite that I get better. My little ones need me. My husband needs me. But I know what happens with the consumption."

Her gaze was pleading, hopeful that Celia would say that she'd not have to worry. That the Dover's Powder and White Pine Compound and cod liver oil would change that outcome and she would be cured. Celia could not lie, however, and the reality Mary faced was grim.

"Feel free to take White Pine Compound, if you wish," Celia said, gently squeezing the other woman's thin arm. "Rest and try to stay warm." An ill-considered thing to say to someone who likely could not afford enough coal or wood to keep her rooms heated. And it was so damp and cool this morning after an overnight rain.

Mary coughed into the handkerchief she'd balled in her fist. Celia did not need to examine the cloth to know that blood would be mingled with the phlegm. "I'll do what I can to stay warm, ma'am."

Celia showed her out and glanced at the case clock in the entry hall. Nearly nine. Blast, it was late. Far later than she'd intended to get to the Carrs' in order to question Emma. She would have gone immediately after learning Owen's news last night, but a patient with a serious nosebleed had shown up and then another with bronchitis.

Appointments that had kept her in the clinic until it was too late to convince any of the usual neighbor boys to take a message with Owen's information to Nicholas while she went out to the Carrs'. She'd visit the station once she was finished.

Addie and Barbara were still at church services, so Celia was able to leave without explanation. The same brusque young woman who'd answered the Carrs' door yesterday did so again.

"Mrs. Davies. Miss Bremerton is not back from services yet, and will not be receiving visitors when she is," she added, scotching any chance for Celia to volunteer to wait for Miss Bremerton. "She intends to return to her parents' home tomorrow and will be busy packing."

Her return home indicated the seriousness of her plan to postpone the engagement. "Mr. Sebastian must be distressed by her pending departure."

Not a flicker of an opinion about his possible emotions—good or bad—crossed the woman's face. "Is there anything else, Mrs. Davies?"

"Are the police aware Miss Bremerton means to depart?"

"Do they need to be aware?" the servant asked, her hand sliding up the door and her fingers gripping the edge, readying to slam it shut. Although the young woman seemed far too self-controlled to actually slam doors.

"She is a possible witness to a suspicious death," Celia said. "They will not be pleased if she leaves the city before their case has been resolved."

"I will inform Miss Bremerton when she and the others get home from church," she replied. "Now, if there is nothing else—"

"I am not actually here to speak with Miss Bremerton. I would like to talk to Emma Joyce," Celia said. "I would like to present her with a token of appreciation for assisting me with Jenny Bernard. If that would be possible. I meant to appropriately thank her yesterday, but it slipped my mind."

The servant glanced at Celia's reticule, perhaps wondering what this "token"—which did not in actuality exist—might consist of.

"Emma doesn't work on Sundays—she is a part-time girl—and isn't here," she said. "She will be in early tomorrow, though, even though Monday is not one of her usual days either. Because of the mask on Friday, and the unfortunate event that occurred, there is a great deal of laundry that needs to be done, so she'll return in the morning. Hopefully, that is. If she's not poorly again."

"What do you mean? Has Emma been unwell?"

Realizing she'd been oversharing information, the servant scowled. "It doesn't matter. She's gotten better, with Miss Vanmeter's help." The woman stuck out her hand. "I can take whatever it is you want to give Emma, Mrs. Davies. Make sure she gets it tomorrow."

"I would rather deliver my thanks in person. Where can I find her?" she asked. "If you do not mind telling me, that is."

"Let me fetch her address."

She closed the door to discourage Celia from wandering about inside the house. After a length of time that made Celia wonder if she'd been very cleverly brushed off, the door opened again.

"She lives with her friend." The servant thrust a folded note into Celia's extended hand.

Celia tucked it into her reticule. "Oh, perhaps you can help me with another question. Which I also forgot to ask yesterday. I noticed a particular guest here on Friday. A man wearing a head wrapping and a loose turquoise-blue tunic. I do believe he is the husband of an old friend of mine, but I might be mistaken. Do you know who he was?"

"We didn't have a guest wearing a costume like that, Mrs. Davies," she replied. There was nothing in her manner to suggest she was being dishonest.

"Oh. How odd." The fellow had certainly not been a guest then, but that did not mean he'd not gained access to the house. "Perhaps I could ask one of the Carrs about him." Irene Bremerton had already told Celia all she knew about the person.

"As I said, Mrs. Davies, the Carrs and Miss Bremerton have gone to church and are not home."

Celia rose on her tiptoes to scan the entry hall behind the servant. "Even Mr. Preston and Mr. Sebastian have gone to church?"

The servant heaved a weary sigh. "They are not home, Mrs. Davies. So, if you're finished, I need to wish you a good day," she said.

And slammed the door.

• • •

"I wasn't expecting you to show up at the station on a Sunday morning, Mr. Carr," Nick said. He hadn't been planning on being here himself. "But thank you for responding to my request that you come and speak with me again as soon as possible."

Preston Carr bowed, theatrically, over the arm bent at his waist. "You sent for me and I obeyed, Detective," he said in his deep, rich voice. "Besides, there's nothing else to do on Sunday. Might as well, since I didn't have any plans."

For not having any plans, he was smartly dressed. Spiffy, as Mrs. Jewett might describe Preston Carr in his fine clothing—black cassimere pants, gray brocade double-breasted vest under his charcoal frock coat, striped cream silk cravat with a coordinating pocket handkerchief. Not a spot on any of it, either, which wasn't easily achieved in San Francisco. His woodsy cologne had been slathered on even more thoroughly than it had on Friday.

Nick retook his seat and indicated that Carr should take a chair too.

"I am grateful you sent for me, Mr. Greaves, because a summons to the police station made for a nice excuse to not attend services with my family this morning."

"You're not a churchgoer, Mr. Carr?"

He gave Nick a pointed look. "You don't seem to be either, Mr. Greaves. Since you're here on a Sunday morning." He gestured at the detectives' room, empty aside from them. "Unless the police station is your church and the law is your god," he said and winked. Naturally.

A lot of folks would consider his comment blasphemous. However,

God had abandoned Nick on a battlefield in the Wilderness, set ablaze by a fusillade of bullets, the stench of charred bodies as strong as the acrid smell of burning brush. Maybe he did worship the law instead, even though it could prove to be just as fickle.

"Your father didn't come with you." He'd been part of the "summons."

"He does fully believe in the good Lord and never misses a church service."

"And your brother?"

The right corner of Preston Carr's mouth twitched with a grin. "He never misses a church service," he replied. "Your man was at the house last night, looking for an article of clothing. What was that about?"

"A person wearing a turquoise-blue tunic and a white turban was observed creeping around outside your house during the masquerade ball, Mr. Carr," Nick replied. "We have reason to believe this fellow was not one of the invited guests. We'd like to figure out who it was."

"You want to figure that out by hunting through our wardrobes for the clothing he wore?" Carr asked. "I don't understand . . . oh, wait. Yes, I do. You think it was one of *us* in that costume."

"I've been told it's an outfit you've been known to wear onstage," Nick said. "In fact, I spoke with the costumer who may have lent it to you. Only to never have the outfit returned."

"I may have donned something similar once in one of my many performances, but I was not responsible for ensuring the wardrobe made it back to the costumer, Detective," he said. "Unfortunately for your investigation—although fortunately for me, I suppose—Mr. Taylor didn't find the ensemble inside our house. And why would I have been wearing that outfit on Friday night, Detective? I was dressed as a harlequin that evening, as you know. Furthermore, I don't have any need to prowl about in the yard."

"Unless you went outside, wrapped in a tunic, because you wanted people to catch sight of a suspicious stranger. A stranger who might then be suspected of poisoning your brother's supply of vanilla."

Carr lowered his eyebrows. "I don't appreciate being a suspect, Detective."

"Everybody is for now, Mr. Carr."

"Even my father? What a thought," he said. "However, it wasn't me outside the house dressed like an oriental potentate. Who was it, though? Have any ideas? And how could they have gotten inside without being noticed and snuck up to Sebastian's room? They must have, though. I'm amazed they pulled it off—"

Nick cut him off with a loud exhalation. "Remind me how long you were in your room on Friday, Mr. Carr."

"We've covered this already, Detective."

"I always like to be sure, Mr. Carr."

He cleared his throat and pursed his lips while he pondered. "Let's see. Downtown with Seb for lunch. Returned home a bit after three. Fuss already underway. Irene in a *tête montée*. Spoke with the hired girls and Papa and retreated shortly after. Back downstairs near to six, because the old man was roaring for everybody to be in the parlor before the guests arrived." He rolled his eyes. "An entire hour too early, but then Father always likes to be prepared."

"When was it again that you heard Sebastian in his room?"

"After four. He rustled about for a bit and then went quiet," he said. "Content to hide in his lair just as I'd done. Keep away from Miss Vanmeter, attempting to corner him over her clinic, as well as stay out from under Mrs. Tilden's feet, you know." He winked, because that's what he did. "She's had a time of it ever since Mama died. Trying to keep the household in order."

"And that was all you did that afternoon, Mr. Carr?" Nick tented his fingers and peered at Carr over their tips. "You didn't interact with Katherine Vanmeter, for instance."

He chuckled quietly. "She told you."

"She said she went upstairs to try to get Sebastian out of his room, in order to talk to him, and started pounding on the door. But he didn't respond." The long-healed wound in Nick's arm took to aching.

"You heard her. I know you did, even though you just omitted that from your account. Just like you've also neglected to tell me that not only did you hear her but you came out of your bedroom in order to laugh at her. Right?"

"Right, Detective," he replied. "I didn't want to embarrass her by telling you about the event, and I didn't think it was relevant to your case."

"I decide what's relevant to my cases, Mr. Carr."

He inclined his head, not a strand of his hair shifting with the movement. He must use pomade to keep it in place. "My apologies, Detective."

"Why did you laugh at her?"

His brow furrowed. "Did I? Maybe I did, which I shouldn't have. Not very gentlemanly."

No. "What did she do after that?"

"She ran off, her face as red as an apple."

"And your brother never came to the door to see what was going on?" Nick asked.

"No."

Nick leaned back in his chair, slowly enough that it didn't creak. "Do you get along well with your brother, Mr. Carr?"

The question appeared to take Preston Carr aback, and a few moments passed before he came up with a response. "Everybody might be a suspect to you, Detective Greaves, but I wouldn't try to poison Seb."

"It would be natural to be jealous of him," Nick said, watching the other man's face. "The older brother. The heir to the family business. Set to become engaged to a very lovely and wealthy woman. He seems to have everything a man could want."

A muscle flexed in Preston Carr's jaw. "It does seem that way, doesn't it?" he asked innocently, as though he'd only just realized his brother's good fortune.

"I've heard gossip that he's had plenty of other lovely women, too.

Whoever he might want, I assume."

"Louise Ingram is not the only woman Seb has had dalliances with, Detective." An honest answer.

"Her brother wanted to attend the mask in order to convince Irene Bremerton she was making a mistake," Nick said. "That's the reason he gave me."

"But Tony didn't come to the ball, Detective. As I've said over and over."

"He might not have attended the ball, Mr. Carr, but one of his fellow musicians at the American has told us he was late getting to the theater Friday evening. After seven, when he was supposed to arrive."

Preston Carr tilted his head to one side. "How interesting. How very, very interesting," he said. "I do hate to accuse Tony—he's a good friend—but maybe he did show up without my knowledge. Maybe *he* was that fellow in the oriental potentate costume. Damn, poor Lou. First the vitriol attack and now the possibility that her brother attempted to poison Seb. It's shocking to think you know people well, only to discover they might not be who you believe them to be."

Was Carr still referring to Tony Ingram, or to somebody else?

Out in the station behind him, a policeman crossed the room. Unfortunately, it wasn't Taylor. Hadn't he mentioned taking Addie Ferguson somewhere nice today? Nick couldn't remember; he should be paying more attention.

"Do *you* think Irene Bremerton is making a mistake with your brother, Mr. Carr?" Nick asked. "Given that Sebastian is susceptible to unwise liaisons. A tendency that might continue after they're married."

He released a short bark of a laugh. "Detective, a lot of married men are susceptible to unwise liaisons."

Not married men Nick cared to be associated with. He'd had his own share of romances, it was true, but he wasn't a married man. And now that he'd found Celia, he could not imagine ever wanting another woman. Ever.

"Do you think Miss Bremerton will accept Sebastian having liaisons,

Mr. Carr?"

"Are you now trying to get me to accuse Irene of attempting to poison him, Detective?"

"I'm just trying to get your opinion of Irene Bremerton."

"She's lovely. Smart. Even-tempered." He smiled. "And is good at winning bezique, which she has taught us all how to play."

"Would you let her provide financial help to Miss Vanmeter's clinic?" Unlike Sebastian.

"Probably." He chuckled. He liked to laugh as much as he enjoyed winking. "It's hard to say no to her, which is why we've been playing bezique since she came to stay, even though the old man doesn't like card games."

Nick cocked an eyebrow. "Sounds like you're in love with her yourself, Mr. Carr." In love enough, maybe, to want his brother out of the way.

Carr sobered. "Don't be ridiculous, Detective."

• • •

The address the Carrs' servant had provided Celia took her to the streets around the Barbary. An unexpected part of the city to live, if one was a quiet, diminutive girl like Emma Joyce. Unless she'd not been aware just how dangerous the area could prove to be when she'd decided to share a room with her friend. It might have been advisable to have stopped at Mrs. Jewett's and notified Nicholas of her plans that morning. Or perhaps ask him to accompany her. Too late now to change her course of action. Not that she was greatly concerned; she had wandered these streets on many occasions and knew how to be careful.

Furthermore, it was Sunday, and the neighborhood was more peaceful than it would be at any other time. The saloons and places of entertainment were closed by law, and the street vendors were forbidden from hawking their wares because of the din of their shouting. The roads weren't completely empty, though, and Celia drew an uncomfortable glance from a man exiting a barbershop, curious why a nicely dressed widow lady was wandering about in the Barbary. The apothecary on the corner stepped out of his shop and nodded, recognizing Celia. She'd visited patients in the Barbary before, as well as a few women in the nearby Chinese quarter, back when she'd been more free to walk those streets. Before a Chinese girl she'd befriended had tragically died and her presence became unwelcome.

She stepped aside to let a porter jog down the pavement, the bar across his shoulders sagging under the weight of the sacks attached at each end, his tunic a flash of aquamarine as he passed. Not everyone had Sunday off from their labors. If she continued on another block, she would encounter shops selling brightly colored Chinese and Japanese goods. Items like slippers or cigars. Most of those would be shuttered, too, despite the presence of the porter on the road. But the tantalizing smells from a Chinese restaurant drifted along the road. And from the temple on the corner, paper lanterns suspended beneath the balcony leaning over the road, came the sound of gongs and chimes, the pungent aroma of incense burning. She'd ventured inside the temple once, the interior a riot of ornate woodwork awash in reds and golds, to marvel over the seated bearded figures placed on an altar lit with lanterns and draped in silks. Patrick had accompanied her and had muttered an unkind comment about heathens, even though the only time she'd known him to enter a church had been for Uncle Walford's funeral, and then only reluctantly.

Celia waited for an Omnibus Railroad horsecar, half empty, to rattle past before crossing the road. Miss Joyce's address belonged to a narrow wood building, partitioned into apartments, that was adjacent to a coffeehouse. The coffeehouse was open and doing a brisk business for a damp, gray day. Or perhaps because it was a damp, gray day. She searched for a door that would allow her access and found it between the coffeehouse and the closed carpet-beating establishment on the other side. Unsurprisingly, the door was locked.

She went inside the restaurant, the pleasingly bitter aroma of coffee filling the air. The majority of the patrons were men, the tang of their cigarette and cheroot smoke hanging heavy in the room. Between sips, they were reading newspapers and discussing politics and other topics, some of which a respectable woman like Celia wasn't supposed to overhear. Somewhere was a separate space for ladies, according to a sign in the window. The powerfully built proprietor—perhaps he had worked at the docks before turning his hand to selling coffee—hurried over to greet her, ready to escort her to the ladies' dining room, Celia presumed.

"You can follow me, ma'am," he said. He had a broad smile and a voice tinged with the accents of an Eastern European homeland.

"I am not here for coffee, regrettably." It did smell heavenly, even though she favored tea. "I am wondering how I might be able to speak with Emma Joyce. She has a room in the building next to your coffeehouse, I believe, that she shares with another young lady. Do you know her?"

His affability faded and his eyes studied her. In the Barbary, it paid to be apprehensive of strangers asking questions. "Yes."

"I am a nurse and she assisted me with a patient the other day," Celia said. "Quite beyond her normal line of work, of course."

"She is a servant."

"Which is why I was so grateful for her assistance," she said. "I went to her place of employment and was told she does not work on Sundays, but that I could find her here. I would like to offer her a small token of appreciation for her help."

He hesitated. A few of the closest customers had stopped drinking their coffee to stare.

"Do you have a key to the street door, by any chance? Or know how I might access the door to her rooms?" Celia asked. "You may accompany me, if you doubt that I know Miss Joyce and have only honest intentions."

His eyes completed another scan before he turned to a rangy fellow in an apron, cleaning one of the empty tables. "Peter, show this woman next door to Miss Joyce's room. Peter lives on the ground floor," he explained.

"Thank you."

Peter tucked his damp rag in the waist of his apron and sauntered over. He squinted at Celia before indicating with a jerk of his head that she should follow him back outside.

He produced a key to the street door and opened it. With another jerk of his head, he climbed the stairs ahead of her. The bawling of a young child echoed in the stairwell. The sound of a woman singing did too. Peter paused at the landing to wait while her eyes adjusted to the darkness of the stairwell, insufficiently lit by the meager quantity of daylight coming through the transom window. She wished someone had opened the transom after the rain in order to allow some fresh air into the space.

"She and her friend rent this room here," Peter said, just when she was beginning to wonder if he could speak.

"I do appreciate your help," she said, squeezing past him when he did not step aside to make room for her and her skirts.

He grunted a reply and retreated down the stairs and back outside.

"Miss Joyce?" Celia rapped on the door. "Miss Joyce, it's Mrs. Davies."

Beneath the pressure of her knuckles, the door squeaked open a few inches. Celia's pulse quickened and she eased the door open the rest of the way. The window was ajar and the muslin curtain fluttered in the current of morning air. Weak daylight lit the room. Fell across a pair of beds and an oak chest of drawers. Across a washstand and its porcelain basin, a green cloak hanging off a hook alongside.

Across the pool of dark red spilled upon the scratched floorboards, Emma Joyce's hair a tangle about her face and head, an unwound skein of pale auburn mingling with the blood.

☙ Chapter 12 ❧

"What is going on in here—" The woman who'd stormed into Emma Joyce's room did not finish her sentence. Instead, she chose to scream. "You've killed her!" she exclaimed, once her screams concluded.

Celia stared at the pool of blood at her feet, dark and beginning to cake around the edges. Not recently spilled, by the looks of it. "Please alert the police."

"I'll not be taking orders from a murderer!"

"You are free to ask Peter"—*wherever he'd gone*—"if Miss Joyce was or was not already deceased when I stepped into the room. He will inform you that she was. Sadly."

"You can be sure I will."

"And on your way out, please close the door." Several individuals, including a child of around ten years, were standing, mouths agape, on the narrow landing just outside the room.

The woman muttered a prayer, shouted at the boy to go back to their apartment, and closed the door with a firm click. A noise that suggested the latch still worked. Emma had allowed her killer access. Or the person had possessed a key.

Celia drew in a breath, the pungent smells of death ameliorated by the open window. Emma had been murdered by a slice to her throat, likely delivered from behind, and she lay crumpled on the floor where she'd fallen. She'd not dressed to greet her visitor—if the killer could be described as such—and still wore a plain cotton nightdress and dressing gown, stained with her blood. Celia drew off a blanket from the nearest bed and laid it over her prone body, covering the skin turning blue, concealing the gash to her neck that had severed any chance of her crying out in horror.

She opened the window all the way and leaned out. Steep wood stairs descended from a rear door immediately adjacent to Emma's rented room. The door and the steps provided the residents on this floor with access to the privy in the yard. Had the killer gained entry to the building through that door instead of the street-facing door, which required a key to unlock? Or, had Emma left the window open overnight for the killer to climb through? A quick inspection of the sill and the floor beneath the window showed that the wood was dry, meaning the window had not been open during that morning's early rain. Furthermore, clambering over the back stair railing and leaping inside would have entailed a significant feat of agility. The window, however, might have been the avenue of escape for the killer. Why not simply retreat down the rear steps? Perhaps a sound out in the hallway had startled them. Celia squinted at the mud beneath the window. It was too churned up from the recent passage of feet to determine if it held the footprint of someone who'd dropped to the ground.

Heavy boots clomped up the interior staircase and the police officer they were attached to flung open the door. "All right, all right there, ma'am. You need to be explainin' what you'd be doing in here."

"Oh. Officer." She brushed dirt off her gloved hands and smiled politely. "Please do have someone send for Detective Greaves. I hope he is at the station, although if not, I have his home address."

The man's thick eyebrows rose up his ruddy forehead. "You do, do you, now?"

"This young woman may have been murdered because of what she knew about a case he is presently investigating," she replied. "He will want to be alerted about her death immediately. And, knowing his temper as I do, if he is not notified immediately, he will . . . well, let us not discover what he might do."

"Detective Greaves, is it," he said. "All right, then. And *you* stay right where you are. Do not touch anything, do not take anything, or we'll find out what *I* mean to do," he threatened before retreating and reshutting the door.

"Well, Celia, now what?" While she waited for Nicholas and his reportedly fierce and vengeful temper.

Hunt for any clues, was the answer to her question.

The rented room was not large—only around twelve by twelve—and was furnished with the two beds, the washstand, the chest of drawers, and the hooks on the wall she'd already taken notice of. It contained not much more. A pair of chamber pots. A lovely framed piece of needlework. An old flat-topped wood trunk at the foot of the nearest bed. Celia got down on her hands and knees and searched under the beds. No discarded bloody weapon. And nothing behind the other furniture. The murderer had taken it with him—or her. Perhaps a quick search inside the chest and the trunk would be of use.

The chest produced only neatly stacked clothing—all of which looked to belong to a woman larger than Emma—a stash of poorly concealed dollar bills, and some personal items of no particular value. The trunk held Emma's things. Spare underclothing and stockings, a Bible, a box with a hinged lid holding trinkets and a pair of earrings. And at the very bottom, a letter, the edges worn from frequent handling. A letter addressed to "Beloved E."

• • •

No undertaker's wagon was parked outside the coffeehouse on Dupont, leading Nick to hope its absence meant that he'd managed to arrive at Emma Joyce's room before the coroner. Several of the customers had exited the restaurant to gawk at the sight of the neighborhood policeman outside the door to the adjacent rented rooms. Their gawking encouraged others to do the same. People were always ready to goggle at other folks' misfortunes, counting their blessings that it wasn't them needing a cop to stand guard.

Nick showed his badge to the policeman and introduced himself. "I take it the coroner isn't here yet."

"Not yet, he isn't," the fellow said with an Irish lilt, like many of the cops on the force. Maybe Cassidy should pursue the job; he'd fit in perfectly. *Don't be thinking of encouraging him, Greaves.*

"Glad you're here, though, Detective. It's a bad one, it is," the officer continued. "The colleen had her throat slit clear across." He embellished his description with a quick flick of his thumb across his neck.

"I didn't need the demonstration, Officer, but thank you." Nick gestured at the folks clogging the sidewalk, pressing closer to overhear the conversation. "Learn anything useful from her neighbors or the coffeehouse customers?"

"I'm just tryin' to keep the sightseers from going inside and having a peek for themselves, Detective." An answer clarifying that questioning potential witnesses was Nick's job and not his. Right then, the officer shooed off a couple of boys sauntering past to demonstrate how serious he was about his task. "Although I couldn't pry that woman out of the room. Told her she'd better not touch anything."

"Woman?"

"She said she knew you."

"Ah." He could only mean one particular woman.

Nick took the stairs two at a time. The cop might have kept random sightseers from nosing around, but he hadn't prevented the other residents of the building from clustering outside Emma Joyce's door. Fortunately, there were only a handful.

"You! You need to keep back," Nick shouted, startling an elderly fellow at the edge of the group. He jumped clear out of the way, proving to be more spry than his stooped frame suggested.

"Now, did any of you know Miss Joyce?" He retrieved a crumpled piece of paper from his pocket and a stub of a pencil, annoyed that he hadn't been able to locate Taylor. Did he intend to spend the entire day with Miss Ferguson?

A woman wearing her Sunday best shook her head. "She's only been here a few weeks, Officer. Moved in with Leona, who used to rent the room alone," she said. "None of us have gotten to know the girl. She keeps to herself, you see, but is polite. *Was* polite. Always wishing you a good day."

"Leona hasn't been around for the past few days, so you can't ask her any questions," said a tall fellow with a port-wine stain on his forehead. "Went to visit her sister, who's sickly. In Portland, I think."

He looked at the others, who nodded to confirm what he'd been told.

"Did any of you see anybody or hear anybody with Miss Joyce this morning?" Nick asked. "Hear an argument, maybe? Or a struggle?"

"That girl was murdered!" the elderly gentleman screeched, as loud as he was spry. "This place ain't safe anymore. Not since all those Orientals started moving in nearby."

Nick let the man's sour opinion of Chinese people go. There was nothing to be gained by arguing with witnesses.

"I'm pretty sure I heard her talking to somebody out here on the landing," said the woman in her Sunday attire. "I'm in the rooms at the other end of the hall. With my two children. My youngest wanted to use the . . . the necessary house. I heard her talking with somebody when I got up with him."

"A man or a woman?" Nick asked.

"Not sure, Officer."

"What time did you hear them?"

She wrinkled her nose while she considered. "It had just started to get light out, I'd say."

A few hours ago. "Was she still out here on the landing when your youngest went down to the outhouse?"

"No, she wasn't," she said. "I'd heard her door close when I'd got up with him, but by the time were were both set to go down to the yard, it was quiet in her room here."

"Anybody else hear or see Miss Joyce this morning?" Nick asked.

"I heard a thud upstairs around then, too," the fellow with the birthmark piped up. "I live right below. I wasn't quite awake yet—I like to get my sleep on Sunday mornings. Don't have a chance other days—so I didn't get up to see what was going on." His face brightened. "And I heard tromping on the outside steps, Detective."

"That was my youngest going out to the necessary."

"I shoulda figured it'd be him, Dora."

The woman scowled at the fellow.

"Then nothing else important, Detective," he said, turning to Nick. "I guess killers are pretty sneaky."

"That's it, then? Nobody saw anyone running away, for instance?"

The old man shook his head and muttered about the Chinese again.

"It was peaceful before that woman started pounding on the door," said Dora.

Time to go talk to "that woman."

He pushed open the door. Celia sat on a chair between the two narrow beds in the room, her spine stiff.

She looked over. "There you are, Mr. Greaves. It appears that Emma Joyce has had her throat—"

"Cut," Nick said, finishing her sentence and causing the folks assembled out on the landing to gasp. He shut the door on their faces. "The street cop told me. Are you positive that it's her?"

Celia had pulled a blanket off one of the beds and draped it over the body. The woven cotton was stained red in the area of Emma Joyce's neck. It would be simple to peel back the blanket and look at the body himself, be sure it was her, but Nick couldn't always rely on his ability to keep down the contents of his stomach when examining murder victims. Some days, he was just as bad as Taylor.

"I am positive it is Emma Joyce, Mr. Greaves. I suspect she has been dead for several hours, based on the condition of the drying blood," she said. "But we will leave that for the coroner to confirm."

"The woman at the end of the hall heard her talking with somebody a little before sunrise," he said. "Nobody saw or heard the killer fleeing the scene, though."

"The crime occurring at sunrise would agree with the condition of the drying blood," she said, rearranging the blanket to better conceal the young woman's corpse.

"You know, Celia, I've got to ask how you've managed, yet again, to discover a dead body. I doubt you were simply wandering past and decided to pop in for a visit," he said. "Furthermore, how did you even get in here?"

"The door was unlocked. Whoever killed her left it that way, I suppose. Additionally, the door was not forced, suggesting Emma admitted the individual or they had a key." She sighed and got to her feet. "As for what brought me here, I wished to question Emma about a person she was observed speaking with on the Carrs' back staircase not long after the mask got underway. Emma appeared to be upset and wanted to know what this person was doing. According to an acquaintance of Owen's who was also delivering wine that night."

"Cassidy came to *you* with that information?" He was trying to not get angry with her, but it wasn't easy. He was also angry at Cassidy, playing at detective, but he couldn't yell at him at the moment.

"He only learned it late yesterday, Mr. Greaves. He is not attempting to keep clues from you."

"Right."

"Honestly, Nicholas. There is no need to be upset." She nodded at the scrap of paper crushed in his fist. "And do you mean to write any of this down, or do you merely intend to glower at me?"

At least she'd stop calling him Mr. Greaves. "If glowering worked with you, I'd keep at it," he said, stuffing the scrap and pencil back into his pocket. "And I'm not good at taking notes. That's what I need Taylor for, but nobody can seem to locate him."

"That is because he is at Swain's with Addie, as I believe you know, along with a neighbor's daughter. To keep everything proper," she replied. "Do you expect him to be always at your beck and call, even on a Sunday?"

Before Addie Ferguson had entered Taylor's life, he always *had* been at Nick's beck and call. "They went out again?"

"Honestly, Nicholas. So, as I was saying, after learning Owen's news, I went to the Carrs' this morning to speak with Emma. They informed me that she lived here with a friend, who is not presently in town," she said. "One of the workers at the coffeehouse who lives downstairs let me into the building. As I mentioned, the door to this room was unlocked, so I came inside, saw Emma, and sent for you."

"While you were waiting for me, did you find anything of interest in here?"

"You do not trust that I would wait for the police to conduct a search?"

"I know better." There wasn't much to look through in the room, and he was positive Celia wouldn't have wasted the opportunity to do some looking.

"I did indeed make good use of my time while I waited for you." she said. "I searched the room for a murder weapon, and did not find one."

"The killer took it with him."

"Or her," Celia said. "Although a leap from the window to make their escape would not be so easily achieved in the confines of a crinoline, I assure you."

"Unless she'd removed it," he said, squatting next to the blood splattering the room's braided rag rug and the wood floor beyond its edge. The blood was smeared as though somebody had stepped in it.

"I noticed the smudge as well, Nicholas. The owner's shoe should be dirtied as a result," Celia said. "There should also be bloodstains on the killer's sleeve, at the very least. It would be very difficult, I think, to cut someone's throat and not get blood on your arm."

Nick stood. "I agree."

"I also took the opportunity to inspect the contents of the chest of drawers and the trunk. The latter appears to have belonged to Emma, based on a note I found inside that is addressed to her." She stood, withdrew a folded paper from her skirt pocket, and handed it to him. "It appears to be a love letter. The signature of the author is particularly interesting."

"'Tony,'" he said, reading it off.

"Is it possible that 'Tony' could be Mr. Ingram?" she asked. "It's not clear from the contents of the letter, but I must wonder."

"Funny that Preston Carr is now willing to consider his good friend a possible suspect in his brother's poisoning. Which makes me wonder if Emma could've been somehow involved. If she'd assisted Ingram." Nick pocketed the letter. "Only one way to find out."

"He'll not tell you the truth about being the author of that note, Nicholas."

"Why would he have a reason to lie, if he's not aware that Emma Joyce has been murdered?"

She frowned in response. "Please be careful."

• • •

"Jane, I was not expecting to see you today." Celia had arrived home to find Jane picking out a tune on the parlor piano. Her stepdaughter and Barbara had once played a duet on the instrument. How long ago that day seemed. "Did Barbara let you in?"

"Yes, she did."

Celia stripped off her gloves. One of the fingertips was discolored from Emma Joyce's blood. She set them aside on the hall table for Addie to find and fret over.

Barbara strolled through the dining room and into the parlor, carrying a tray of tea things. She banged the tray down on the settee table, the china clinking together. "There you are, Cousin. Finally. I had to let Mrs. Hutchinson in, since Addie isn't here. You were gone an awfully long time," she added.

"Thank you, Barbara, for making tea for Jane."

"I didn't mind, especially since we haven't seen her in ages." Barbara shot an accusatory glance at Celia. Apparently she'd decided that Jane's absence was her fault. It was not Celia's place, however, to inform Barbara that Jane's miscarriage had been the cause.

"I'm sorry for that, Barbara. Frank and I have been so busy lately," Jane replied, smiling so that Celia's cousin might not notice the pain in her eyes. "But I am here now. And of course Grace sends her affection."

"Has she sent her affection to Owen, too?"

"Barbara, that is enough," Celia scolded.

"You know how she feels about Owen, Barbara," Jane said calmly. "They are friends, nothing more."

"Unfortunately, I also know how Owen feels about Grace, Mrs. Hutchinson."

She stalked off, climbing the stairs as fast as her upset and her aching foot would allow.

Celia sighed. "I never, ever know what to do for her, Jane."

"She'll get over her heartbreak. Trust me," she said, closing the piano's fallboard and getting to her feet. "Where is Addie, though?"

"Out for a light lunch at Swain's with Mr. Taylor and one of our neighbor's daughters." A rendezvous Nicholas had not been pleased to learn about. Evidently Mr. Taylor had not informed him.

"Their relationship must be getting serious," Jane said.

"A development Barbara is nearly as upset about as the valentine Owen sent to Grace," Celia said, hearing her cousin stomp across the floor above her head.

Jane peered at her. "Are you all right, Celia? You look pale."

Dearest Jane. Always caring about others, even in the midst of her own heartache. "I discovered one of the Carrs' servants murdered this morning. At her lodgings in the city."

"Should I come back later?"

"If you have learned something important, which I presume is why you are here, then we cannot wait until later."

"In that case . . ." Jane lowered herself onto the settee. "I had a lengthy conversation with an acquaintance—not the woman I met outside my milliner's yesterday—at church this morning. A place where I can talk to anybody without Frank getting suspicious."

Celia gestured at the teapot and cups. "I am forgetting myself. I should serve you tea before you get started."

"There's no need to bother. I am floating on the amount of tea I consumed after the service today. My acquaintance is not the quickest of talkers."

Celia took the chair across from her friend. "What did she have to say?"

"I learned nothing about Paulina Lyons, but there was plenty of other gossip about the tragedy at the Carrs' masquerade ball," she said. "The universal consensus among the gossipers being that they were all glad they hadn't received invitations to the event because you could've guessed something terrible might happen. Given the scandalous whispers swirling around Sebastian Carr."

"I expect *before* Friday evening that they felt differently about not being invited."

"They'll be doubly happy they didn't go when they learn about this servant's murder," Jane said. "Any suspects yet?"

"Nicholas and I wonder if Anthony Ingram is responsible," she answered. "I found a love letter from a 'Tony' addressed to her."

"If he loved this girl, why kill her?"

"Love does not prevent a person from striking out, Jane, especially if the victim had evidence you'd committed another crime," Celia said. "Nicholas went to question him."

"Mentioning Tony Ingram brings me to why I'm here." Jane scooted forward to the edge of the settee. "According to my acquaintance, Preston Carr has cause to hate Sebastian too, and it involves Louise Ingram. They had been romantically attached beginning as long as a year ago."

"Louise Ingram was with Preston Carr? But at some point she became involved with Sebastian."

"Let's see if I can explain," Jane said. "Apparently, one evening Preston invited his brother to attend an amateur theatrical production he was acting in. It was then that Sebastian noticed Miss Ingram, who'd painted the scenery of the show and was in attendance in the audience that night. She is very striking, from what my friend told me."

"Your very useful friends who do seem to know a great deal, Jane."

"Mostly gossip, Celia."

"In this instance, as in all the others, gossip is precisely what I am looking for," she said.

"It was 'love at first sight,' as they say. Desire might be a better description. Maybe as much to possess Louise Ingram as an impulse to take something valuable from Preston," Jane said. "It seems that Sebastian and his brother have been rivals since they were children. A not uncommon story, of course."

Had she and Harry ever been rivals? Celia could not recall a time when she had fought with her brother. At least, not over anything more consequential than who'd get the last ratafia cake or who would be first in completing their arithmetic assignments.

"So Sebastian Carr set about winning Miss Ingram's affections." A trophy to be captured like when he'd later "snagged" Miss Bremerton.

"He developed a sudden urge to attend every theatrical production and musical event she was a part of," Jane said. "It wasn't long before Sebastian Carr and Miss Ingram were seen together. Not in polite society, as my friend put it, but at taverns and the occasional less-respectable restaurant where young unmarried women might enjoy the company of young unmarried men. They were reportedly most fond of Bishop's."

"A locale, I take it, that does not refuse its business to young unmarried ladies dining with young unmarried gentlemen." A restaurant unlike Swain's, which pointedly catered to families. "A place that acquaintances of your friend also somehow managed to find themselves in, if they observed Louise Ingram and Sebastian Carr together."

"Pecksniffs, as Frank likes to call the sanctimonious and hypocritical," Jane said. "Unsurprisingly, Preston was extremely jealous of his brother's blossoming relationship with Louise Ingram. My friend's husband is a member of the Pacific Cricket Club, which Preston Carr also belongs to, and heard Preston grumbling about his brother's *affaire de coeur*."

Cricket, amateur theatrics, and a keen interest in throwing parties? Preston Carr had a fascinating array of hobbies. "But their affair did not last long, because Irene Bremerton came along and Sebastian Carr abandoned Miss Ingram.”

“Irene’s name became linked to Sebastian’s around Christmastime,” Jane said, distractedly reaching for the teapot to pour herself some tea even though she’d declared that she’d already had too much. “Not too long after she’d arrived in San Francisco for a brief visit with a distant relative that turned into a long-term stay at the Carrs’ more spacious and comfortable house. With her parents’ blessings.”

Marriage as a business transaction, after all. “Preston Carr must have assumed that he could resume his relationship with Miss Ingram at that point.”

“Except that two things stood in his way—it seems that Sebastian Carr did not want to completely relinquish Miss Ingram, and Louise Ingram was not interested in resuming her relationship with Preston.”

“Your friend’s husband learned this at the cricket club, as well?” Celia asked, realizing she hadn’t heard Barbara moving about upstairs for some time and wondering where her cousin was listening in from.

“He witnessed a disturbance at one of their meetings. Preston had shown up drunk and belligerent, babbling on and on about Sebastian and Miss Ingram. He was removed from the premises to sober up.” Jane sipped her tea. “You know that there’s as much gossip to be had at men’s clubs as there is at church socials, Celia.”

She very well did. “When was this, Jane? This disturbance. Did your friend say?”

“In the middle of January.”

“Not long before a Mexican boy named David Alonso was hired to toss vitriol onto Miss Ingram . . .”

“Could it be that Preston *is* responsible for the attack, Celia? Angry that he didn’t win Louise Ingram back?”

“Perhaps Preston is also responsible for adding arsenic to his brother’s supply of vanilla extract,” Celia said. “Angered by not only losing Louise Ingram to Sebastian but by also having to endure the humiliation of his brother’s pending engagement and marriage to the sought-after Irene Bremerton.” A reprisal that had resulted in the wrong victim.

"Preston wouldn't have needed the commotion of a party to access his brother's room and poison the vanilla, though," Jane countered. "He could've gone in there anytime."

"However, a large party does provide numerous other suspects, Jane."

"Would he have also killed his family's servant today?"

Celia perked her brows. "He might have done, Jane, if Emma had witnessed him on the servants' staircase, at an hour he should have been elsewhere, while acting in a manner that was highly suspicious."

• • •

Nick had been forced to wait for the coroner to arrive in order to give his report to the man. Precious time that might be permitting a killer to conceal his tracks. Might be allowing him to dispose of a weapon and bloody clothing.

When Nick arrived at the Ingrams', the curtains to the upstairs room Miss Ingram used for her studio were closed, as were the ones at the parlor window. They might not even be home. He pounded on their door anyway. Nobody came to answer.

A neighbor slid open a side window—the area snoop, Nick assumed—and fixed an eye on Nick. "What's the racket on a Sunday about?"

"Do you know where the Ingrams are?" Nick asked, showing his badge to encourage the fellow to answer.

"Should be around, Officer. Neither of them are much for church-going. Theater types, you know."

The door to the Ingrams' house flung open. Louise Ingram stood on the other side, clothed in a simple indigo-blue dress, the top buttons unfastened and her hair down.

She coiled a thick hank of it against her head and stabbed a hairpin into the twist to secure it. "Detective Greaves. What do you want?"

Had she only recently gotten out of bed or had she spent the past few hours attempting to scrub blood out of her clothes? Or maybe her brother's clothes.

Nick stepped over the threshold, forcing her to retreat. "Is your brother here?"

"No. He isn't."

She finished fussing with her hair and held her bandaged hand against her waist. The daylight did nothing to diminish Louise Ingram's beauty. It was easy to see why Sebastian Carr had been attracted to her. Maybe his opinion of Carr was a harsh one, but Nick doubted the source of the man's admiration had been the young woman's talent and courage.

He strode into the entry hall, scanning the parlor to his left, steeped in shadows. "Where can I find him, then?"

"He's probably at the oyster saloon down the street. He likes to have a meal there on Sundays," she replied. "Are you still trying to blame him for the poisoning? Is that what this is about?"

He looked over at her. "Is he acquainted with a young woman named Emma Joyce?"

"No. Not Emma. Something hasn't happened to Emma."

"She was murdered this morning, I'm afraid."

"Dear God. And you want to accuse Tony of that, too?" she asked. "They were in love with each other, Detective."

"Which you think means he couldn't have killed her."

"He couldn't have," she insisted.

"However, their love might explain how he managed to get inside Sebastian Carr's room on Friday, which had been locked," Nick said. "Did Emma help him? Is that what happened?"

"My brother is innocent, Detective Greaves."

"Since he's innocent, I suppose you won't mind if I search his bedroom." If he didn't find anything right away, he'd have Taylor and Mullahey come back and turn the place over.

She retreated until she bumped into the wall at her back. "Go ahead. His is the room at the top of the stairs."

Thankfully, she hadn't demanded that he produce a warrant. Not that he needed one now that she'd given him permission to hunt around.

The door to Tony Ingram's bedroom stood open, and Nick went inside. It was as sparsely furnished as the downstairs rooms. Pretty much just a plain rosewood wardrobe, a small chest of drawers, a bed topped with a brightly colored quilt, and an old rocking chair somebody had passed down to him and Louise. The walls were hung with several paintings. His sister's work, Nick presumed.

Nick searched the chest first. No bloody shirtsleeves. No handkerchief used to wipe off a knife. No knife inside it or on the washstand next to his bed, either. But there was shaving soap, a brush, and a strop. Where, though, was his razor?

"Maybe I'm not looking for a knife," Nick muttered aloud. None of the supplies looked like they'd been used recently, though. Maybe he'd needed to replace his razor and hadn't gotten around to it.

A pair of shoes were tucked beneath the bed. There wasn't any dried blood on the soles or the heels. Nick replaced them and turned to the wardrobe. It didn't give when he tried to open the door. Locked.

Louise had tired of waiting downstairs and strode into the room. Nick hadn't heard her footfalls on the stairs. Uncle Asa—the best cop, the best detective Nick had ever known—would've been disappointed in him. He'd have to be more careful in future.

She stopped in the center of the bedroom, her back plank-straight, and scowled. "You haven't found anything, have you?"

"Do you have the key to this wardrobe, Miss Ingram? I'd like to have a look inside."

"Tony has the only key. He doesn't trust Truda, so he keeps it locked."

"Guess he doesn't trust you, either." Good thing he'd brought his bowie knife with him.

"You'll ruin the wardrobe!" she cried.

He applied the knife blade to the gap between the two doors and pried, cracking the wood and popping them open.

Three shelves, the bottommost one empty except for a hat. Two pairs of pants, a vest, and a carefully folded jacket on the others. Along with a case containing a nice silver belt buckle and a watch. The items he must not want Truda to steal. Most interesting was what was on the topmost shelf. Nick pulled it down. A length of white silk that had been pinned together to form a wrapped bowl of cloth, which would fit over the head like a helmet. A turban, he supposed. He set it on the bed and retrieved the piece of clothing that had been stashed alongside.

"I don't know what you think those pieces of clothing prove, Detective," she said. "Because Tony didn't kill Emma. He was here this morning."

Nick glanced at the coiled length of silk. "And you're still certain that he didn't go to the Carrs' on Friday evening, either."

"He did not. He left the house at six, as I've already told you, on his way to the theater in the clothes he wears when he's playing. Not to the Carrs' house."

"Are you willing to testify to that?"

She reddened. "You need to leave, Detective Greaves. I shouldn't have let you come inside the house to begin with."

Probably not.

He unfurled the folded piece of clothing he'd tucked under his arm. A greenish blue tunic-like garment Celia had called a caftan. "Well, you might be convinced your brother isn't guilty, but *this* is pretty damning proof he *was* at the Carrs' party, Miss Ingram."

✍ CHAPTER 13 ✎

Nick stood on the sidewalk outside Tony Ingram's favored oyster saloon, people bustling in and out with sacks of oysters in hand. He repositioned the bundled caftan under his arm, feeling in his bones that he'd found a killer. What had Uncle Asa said about trusting feelings and intuition? Nick couldn't remember and it bothered him.

He went inside. Like every other oyster saloon he'd been in, the air smelled like the sea. The briny odor came from the large grate-topped range against the far wall, where a pair of men hunkered over the flames with long-handled pans. Nick was partial to oysters himself, but he wasn't here to eat. He scanned the crowd looking for Tony Ingram. The place was packed, folks elbowing for space at the bar, where they could both get a meal and a drink, or casting around for an empty seat. Tony Ingram had found a table by the window.

Nick scraped back the chair opposite him and sat.

"Hey!" Ingram exclaimed, looking up from his fried oysters. "Oh. It's you, Detective." He'd been in the saloon long enough to have smoked through a cheroot, which he'd stubbed out on a plate. His food, though, had barely been touched. Guilt had a way of dampening the appetite. "What do you want now?"

Nick set the bundled costume on his lap and retrieved Emma Joyce's letter from his inner pocket. "I found this note"—*Apologies, Celia*— "addressed to one of the Carrs' maids, and I was wondering if you'd written it. A fellow named Tony signed it." He cleared a space on the table and spread it flat so that Ingram could have a look. "The girl who got this letter is Emma Joyce, by the way. Know her?"

Ingram stared at the letter, his fork clutched in his fist, an oyster dangling off the tines.

"Your sister thinks you know her," Nick prompted when an answer wasn't forthcoming. "How long have you been courting Miss Joyce?"

"A while. It's no secret." He lowered his fork. "It's not a crime to be walking out with one of the Carrs' servants, Detective Greaves."

Nick refolded the note and tucked it away. "I'd like you to describe your relationship with her."

"What's it matter?"

A fellow in a checked apron strode up to the table. "You can't sit here and not order food," he said to Nick, his body tensed like he was anticipating a quarrel. "We're busy and we can't afford to have folks occupying seats when we've got paying customers."

"I'll have a half dozen fried," he said, simply to get the fellow to go away.

"Mr. Ingram?" the waiter asked.

"I'll just finish these."

Nick waited for the man to depart before continuing. "Your relationship with Miss Joyce matters because I have to wonder if she might've helped you attempt to poison Sebastian Carr, Mr. Ingram. Maybe she gave you access to his room."

"I didn't try to poison him, Detective."

"Even though he deserves it."

"You know my feelings about him."

Sebastian Carr, the cad. And Tony Ingram, the valiant savior of Miss Bremerton's future happiness.

"I should inform you that Emma Joyce was found this morning in the room she's been sharing with one of her friends, Mr. Ingram," he said, lowering his voice. "Dead."

He turned a bit green. "Emma. You're sure."

"I saw the body." Letterman had made him look, sending Nick's stomach swimming. "And I've met Miss Joyce. I'm sure it was her."

The waiter chose then to return with Nick's fried oysters. He squinted at Ingram, shaking and pale. "You okay, sir?"

"He's fine," Nick said, even though Ingram looked like he was going to get sick all over the table. Nick paid the waiter and shooed him away.

"Miss Joyce noticed somebody Friday at the masquerade ball who shouldn't have been where they were when they were," Nick said, pushing aside the freshly delivered plate of oysters. "And now she's dead. Murdered."

"Are you accusing me, Detective?" Ingram asked. "I didn't kill her. I loved Emma."

Had years of playing his trumpet in theaters given Tony Ingram insight into how to be an actor? Or was his display of distress genuine? Nick's search of the Ingrams' house hadn't unearthed any bloody clothes or a discarded weapon. Just an old costume that might've been rented from a store behind the American Theater and never returned.

"Where were you this morning around sunrise?" he asked. The coroner had confirmed Celia's estimate that Miss Joyce had been dead for several hours, meaning she'd likely been killed not long after her neighbor had overheard her speaking with somebody.

"In bed," he replied. "I wouldn't have killed Emma. I cared about her. I really did."

"This love note is a couple of months old," Nick said, tapping his coat where the inner pocket was. "Were you still in a relationship with her or had it ended, Mr. Ingram?"

"I did not kill Emma," Ingram replied, each word distinct and forceful.

"Was she having an affair with Sebastian Carr, just like your sister once had?" Nick was taking a shot at a motive, but it was a reasonable shot. Servants and their masters? Happened all too often. "Maybe you'd had enough of the way he treats women. Especially women you love."

Ingram's expression was stony.

"Preston Carr, your supposed friend, has suggested that you could be responsible for attempting to poison his brother."

"He what?"

Nick was positive Celia, if she were here, would be able to produce a quote appropriate for traitorous friends. "Have you ever played the trumpet for one of Preston's amateur theatrical performances, Mr. Ingram?"

Ingram was taken aback by the sudden change in direction of Nick's questions. So he answered honestly. "Yes. What's that got to do with anything?"

"Well, it might explain why I found this in your bedroom, Mr. Ingram." He set the bundle atop the table. "A caftan and a turban. An outfit worn by a suspicious man spotted by two different individuals on Friday evening outside the Carrs' house."

"I . . . I don't understand."

Nick shoved back his chair and stood. "Well, maybe by the time we get to the police station, you'll have figured it out."

• • •

Where might Preston Carr have gone to after speaking with Nicholas at the police station this morning? As a woman, Celia would not be allowed to enter whichever assembly room the Pacific Cricket Club used for their meetings—which would not occur on a Sunday, anyway—and it seemed rather pointless to go back to the Carrs' home in search of him. He might not have returned there yet and even if he had, Celia expected that the redoubtable servant who guarded the front entrance would not permit her to pass. Ever again, probably.

She could look for him at one particular location, though. If she were lucky, he would be there. Bishop's Restaurant, often frequented by his brother in the company of Louise Ingram and possibly a favorite spot for Preston as well. Perhaps he had even dined there with Louise himself, before he'd lost her to the brother he envied. And might have attempted to poison.

After Jane had departed with promises to go home and rest, Celia had dug out her copy of the city directory and found the address of Bishop's. It was on Kearny, two blocks south of Portsmouth Square and the police station. More importantly, it was one block east of a coffeehouse next to which a timid servant had bled out her life. She should not read too much into the proximity, however.

Celia paused on the corner across from the restaurant, staring uncertainly at the patrons entering the establishment. She found that she was rubbing her thumb over the bump her wedding ring made in her left-hand glove. It felt strange to be wearing the ring again, but the gold band provided her a shield of sorts. The mourning widow unwilling to accept her new status, a more respectable woman than an unwed one visiting a restaurant without a female companion. She'd been standing there long enough that a trio of male customers departing Bishop's gave her dubious looks before moving off down the pavement together.

Get on with it, Celia.

Hiking her skirts, she dashed across the road, her speed more habitual than born of any need to evade traffic. The door to Bishop's restaurant stood open, even though the weather was chilly, to welcome the passing pedestrian in need of a warm meal. Its large windows were curtained with white lace and the pleasant aroma of cooking meat wafted through the doorway. For a place that welcomed unmarried men and women dining together, it did not at all appear disreputable. In fact, Bishop's looked to be quite nice. Perhaps Jane's acquaintance was merely snobbish.

A friendly fellow greeted her, his smile shifting the whiskers bracketing his face. His smile had the unfortunate consequence, however, of revealing several missing teeth.

"Can I help you, ma'am?" His eyes scanned her outfit, pausing briefly on her left hand as she prematurely peeled off her gloves. If she was going to go through the bother of wearing a wedding ring, she may as well make sure it was on display. Did the ring help, though, or make her appear to be a married woman plotting a liaison with a man who wasn't her husband?

Gad, Celia.

She was here; she'd not turn back. As the saying went—in for a penny, in for a pound.

"I was wondering if Mr. Preston Carr was here," she said, clasping her folded gloves in her hand. "I believe this is one of his popular haunts."

The restaurant was not large, merely a single wide room, and she scanned it for Mr. Carr. She should recognize him, even though the only time she'd seen him was from an attic window.

"Mr. Carr?" the fellow who'd greeted her asked.

He shot a glance at a man halfway down the length of the room, his back to them. He had dark blond hair, and the set of his shoulders reminded Celia of Sebastian Carr. Thankfully, he was alone. She would have had to come up with a far better approach to questioning him if he'd not been.

"Is he expecting you?" The door greeter gave her a speculative look. Even proper British widows sporting wedding rings were not above suspicion of being disreputable. A liaison, indeed.

"No, he is not," she said. "But I am a close friend of his future sister-in-law and wish to speak with him about a fete I am planning for Miss Bremerton. I would so like to have his assistance. He is very skilled at hosting parties, I am told."

"Uh-huh."

"I do not wish her to learn about my plans, which is why I have come here to speak with him," Celia continued. "This is not a restaurant Miss Bremerton might happen upon."

The fellow did not appreciate what sounded like a veiled insult and his smile dropped off his face. "Can I get your name?"

"Mrs. Davies." She wondered if Preston Carr had heard that she'd come to tend to Jenny Bernard Friday evening and would recognize her name as a result.

"Let me go ask Mr. Carr if he's in the mood for company, ma'am."

He crossed the room, snaking between the tables and their occupants. He bent down to whisper in Preston Carr's ear. Mr. Carr turned to look at Celia, smiling generously until he observed that she was wearing black. He gestured for her to join him. Perhaps he was as curious about her as she was about him.

"Mrs. Davies, I wasn't sure that was you at first. This is unexpected." He politely rose from his chair and indicated she should take the empty one across from him.

"I was not aware that you knew me, Mr. Carr."

"I saw you arrive to attend to that girl who so tragically died on Friday," he said, sitting again. "I asked Irene who you were."

She had not walked through the house and the thought that he'd been watching her from one of the windows was unnerving. "Ah. Of course."

"To what do I owe the pleasure?"

"I told the maître d' that I wanted your advice on a fete I am planning for Miss Bremerton."

He chuckled; he had a warm voice that was quite appealing. If he sang, he'd be a baritone. A good voice for the stage.

"Maître d'? A rather grand term for that fellow." He glanced the direction of the man, lifting his hand in order to signal to him. "Would you care for some lunch, Mrs. Davies? They're still serving."

"Thank you, no. I have already eaten." Which she'd not done—she was always missing meals in the midst of an investigation—but she did not wish to be seen dining with Preston Carr. Sitting here with him would generate enough gossip, should any of her acquaintances enter the restaurant.

"Are you actually here to discuss your plans for a fete for Miss Bremerton, Mrs. Davies? I didn't realize that you two were close friends."

"I've known her for some time through various charitable organizations," she replied. "And I would have been pleased to attend or even host a fete for Miss Bremerton, but the shocking events of Friday evening do make a party now inappropriate. Furthermore, it is my understanding that she intends to imminently depart San Francisco."

"She does? Well, that's news."

Indeed. "You must be pleased for your brother, Mr. Carr. Miss Bremerton is quite the catch."

Beneath his frock coat, his shoulders stiffened. If she could see through the striped cravat he'd tied around his collar, past to where his tendons corded his neck, she expected they would be tensing, too.

"My apologies, Mr. Carr. I appear to have upset you," she said, fixing a penitent expression upon her face. "Are you displeased about your brother's pending engagement?"

He laughed, forcing himself to relax. "You haven't come here to discuss some congratulatory party for Irene that you're planning, have you? Not at all. No, my guess is that you want to gather some gossip." He leaned forward. "Do tell me what they're saying. I am dying to know. Or maybe I'm not dying to know, if people are claiming I'm jealous of Seb."

He smiled; such lovely teeth he had. They rather brought to mind the tale of "Little Red Riding Hood." Was Preston Carr about to eat her?

"You are correct, Mr. Carr. I am not interested in soliciting your help with a fete." Celia briefly surveyed their surroundings in search of eavesdroppers. No one appeared to be paying them any mind, and the hum of other diners talking, flatware clinking against plates and bowls, chairs sliding across the wood floor, provided an adequate screen for their conversation. "I am here because I would like your opinion on what took place Friday night."

"Do the police hire nurses to ask questions these days?" he asked. "Detective Greaves has very thoroughly interrogated me, I assure you."

"You have no specific idea about the identity of the perpetrator, then." Not Tony Ingram, for instance. He had been willing to lay the blame at his friend's feet earlier that day, according to Nicholas. "An identity you might not have wished to share with Mr. Greaves but might be willing to share with me, a concerned friend of Miss Bremerton's."

"I can't believe that a member of the San Francisco police force would've sent you here to play detective. Although it is delightful." He winked. For a potential wolf, he was quite charming. Although the wolf must have been charming, too. "Oh, I remember now! You're the one they've written about in the newspapers."

She felt a spark of irritation. She should be used to the comment by now, but she obviously wasn't. "Mr. Greaves is not aware I am here."

"Of course he isn't. I don't know why I imagined you might be acting on behalf of the police, Mrs. Davies," he said. "You are merely inquisitive."

A better choice of word than *nosy*, she thought.

"Sadly, you're rather late with your questions," he continued. "As I mentioned, I was at the station this morning, talking with Mr. Greaves."

Now she was feeling utterly foolish, being chastised by a suspect for retreading the same ground. Except that Nicholas had spoken with Preston Carr *before* Celia had discovered Emma's dead body.

She studied his clothing as surreptitiously as possible while he drank from his cup of coffee. He appeared perfectly neat and orderly. If he'd ever been spattered by blood, not an obvious drop remained on his pristine clothing.

"Are you admiring the monogram on my cuffs, Mrs. Davies?" he asked, setting down his cup in order to shoot his cuffs so that the letter C, embroidered with lilac-colored silk, was clearly visible in the light cast by the restaurant's suspended gas lamps. "Or am I misinterpreting your intense gaze?"

Her cheeks flushed hot. Who was doing the interrogating here—her or Preston Carr? And clearly her attempts to search for bloodstains had not been surreptitious in the least.

"I do not believe I have ever seen embroidered cuffs before, Mr. Carr, and am allowing my fascination with them to distract me."

"Is that it? Or are you trying to figure out how to get me to confess to attempting to poison my brother?" he asked and grinned.

Actually, she was attempting to figure out how to get him to confess he'd sliced Emma's throat. "If you *would* confess," she said, "I could conclude my supposed 'detective' tasks and resume the work at my clinic that I have been neglecting."

He laughed, a boisterous guffaw that caught the attention of everyone within earshot. Essentially, the entire restaurant. "You are much more amusing than Detective Greaves, Mrs. Davies."

Amusing him was not what she sought to do, but she found she was being drawn into his lighthearted charm, forgetting the gravity of the situation. Then the raw memory of Emma Joyce's slit neck surfaced, returning her firmly to earth.

"There were two curious people at your house on Friday, Mr. Carr," she said.

"Only two?" He winked again.

"Only two that I—and the police—are concerned about."

"Detective Greaves questioned me about the fellow wearing a caftan and turban—I assured him it wasn't me. What's more, the outfit wasn't found inside our house, despite the best efforts of his assistant. Although I did once convince Seb to wear a similar outfit onstage in a small part. A lark I quickly regretted when I witnessed his acting," he said, clicking his tongue against his teeth. "Who was the other 'curious' person, Mrs. Davies?"

"A person observed on the back staircase of your house around the hour the mask had gotten underway."

"Have you told Detective Greaves about this individual? Because he didn't ask me any questions about them."

"I have, but I would like to ask you if you noticed them, since I am here in Bishop's being inquisitive," she said.

"I did not notice anyone on our back staircase, Mrs. Davies. I was too busy greeting our guests," he said. "But are you sure this individual is different from the person in the Turk costume? In my opinion, they must be the same fellow. Who was the person who noticed them, by the way?"

"Emma Joyce," Celia replied. "She was apparently alarmed to find them on the stairs."

Preston Carr didn't flinch at the mention of Emma's name. "Detective Greaves urgently needs to question her about their identity."

"He has spoken with her, but for some reason she did not mention this person to him," Celia said. "You must know Emma very well, since she is one of the few servants in your house. Why didn't she inform the police, do you think?"

"She hasn't been with us all that long," he replied, his voice tight. "I don't really know her. She's so quiet."

"So it was not Emma you were attempting to speak with in the kitchen on Friday evening?" Celia asked. "Forgive me, but a friend of mine who attended the masquerade mentioned that they noticed you in the passageway in search of someone."

He scowled. "I'm free to walk about my house when I please, Mrs. Davies, and I'd like to know who this friend of yours is. Because you can be sure they won't be invited to any more of our parties," he said, all of his charm gone. "Acquaintances of ours should not be telling tales to strangers."

Not that Owen qualified as someone who'd been invited to the Carrs' masquerade ball or who was an acquaintance of theirs.

"You are right to be angry. I do apologize."

He inclined his head, all graciousness restored. "To answer your earlier question, I have no idea why Emma didn't tell Detective Greaves." His eyebrows jerked up his forehead. "Oh, no. Could this person have been Louise Ingram? Emma has been in a romantic relationship with Tony and would recognize his sister."

And why had you not told Mr. Greaves you were aware of their affair? "It is my understanding that *you* were once involved with Miss Ingram yourself."

"A brief interlude with a lovely theater girl. That's all."

What a casual dismissal of a romance. "Were you jealous when she took up with Sebastian?"

He sighed wistfully. "I'm not made of stone."

"Would Miss Ingram have wanted to poison your brother?"

"You've heard about the attack on her, haven't you, Mrs. Davies? She has a strong motive to want revenge on my brother," he said. "Really, though, you shouldn't be wasting your time speaking with me. You should be talking with Emma."

"It is no longer possible to question Miss Joyce, Mr. Carr," she replied. "Because when I went to the room she rents not far from here, I discovered that she is dead."

He sucked in a quick breath, his nostrils flaring. If she had been watching him in hopes that his reaction would be incriminating, she was let down. "How? Murder?"

"Yes," she said. "And I am forced to conclude that her death is connected to the attempt upon your brother."

He sat, very still, as he absorbed what she'd said. "The person on the staircase killed her."

"That would be my first guess," she replied. "Might Tony Ingram have sought to protect Louise, if *she* was that person and Emma had spotted her?"

"Tony. I was right to suggest him to Detective Greaves. I thought I understood my friend, but I must have been mistaken," he mused. "'Most friendship is feigning—'"

"'Most loving is folly,'" she completed the quote.

"You know Shakespeare, Mrs. Davies."

"Some," she replied. "But is love folly in this situation, Mr. Carr? Or are you suggesting he chose his sister over the woman he loved?"

He began to rub his right thumb over the knuckles of his opposite hand. "Emma and Tony . . . there were problems between them lately."

"What sort of problems, Mr. Carr?"

He leveled his gaze at her. "They involved Sebastian."

"Oh?"

"He'd gotten her with child, Mrs. Davies," he replied.

She gasped; his comment had caught her totally by surprise. Was he being honest, though? She could not tell, she was too dizzied by Preston Carr's accusation. Perhaps he intended to confuse her, manipulate her. The coroner would discover, however, if she had been pregnant. So it must be the truth.

"If Emma was with child, how can you be sure it was not Tony's, Mr. Carr?"

"Seb admitted to me what he'd done." His tone was flat and hard. How changeable he was, she thought. Chameleon-like, shifting and blending depending on the need for cover. "You have to be wondering just like I am, Mrs. Davies, if Sebastian killed her. He'd have no intention of being trapped into a marriage with one of the servants when he has Miss Bremerton on the hook."

"But he was at church services with your father and Miss Bremerton this morning, according to the servant who answers your door."

"I'd wager, Mrs. Davies, if I were a gambling man, that he wasn't with them all morning."

CHAPTER 14

"These pieces of clothing are yours, aren't they, Mr. Ingram?" Nick threw the tunic onto his desk, where it landed atop the coiled length of white cloth. "They were inside the wardrobe in your bedroom."

"They are," said Ingram, slumped in the chair across from Nick. "I've had them for so long I don't remember where I got them from. Something to do with Preston, probably."

"A convenient lapse of memory, Mr. Ingram."

Nick heard the alley-side station door slam open. A few seconds later, Taylor came into view. Nick gestured for him to wait outside the detectives' office and joined him.

"Sorry to be just getting here, sir," Taylor said.

"How was Swain's?"

Taylor flushed a bright red. "It was nice, sir. Mr. Greaves. They're not serving their ice cream right now, because it's too cold, but their food is . . . umm, never mind."

"Good." *Great.*

"I heard about Miss Joyce, sir," he said. "I also heard that one of the men is headed over to the Ingrams' house to search it for evidence."

As Nick had instructed the first officer he'd come across at the station. "Tony Ingram is in my office, Taylor, because I found the costume we've been looking for inside a locked wardrobe in his bedroom."

Taylor whistled. "He *was* at the Carrs' house on Friday night. Explains why he was late to the theater."

"His sister insists that she saw him leave their house on Friday in his performance clothes. But the tunic I found could easily have covered them."

"Maybe Mr. Ingram hid the costume someplace and changed into it," Taylor suggested. "But what about this morning?"

"Snoozing away in bed, according to both him and Louise Ingram." *A meager alibi.* "I did look through the house for a weapon or bloodied clothes and didn't find either. Maybe a more thorough search will turn them up."

Taylor went inside the office and Nick followed. He was too restless to sit, though.

"Mr. Ingram, you've claimed that you were not the person seen wearing this outfit on Friday." Nick prodded the tunic with his forefinger.

"It wasn't me. I was at the theater," he said wearily. "We've already been over this. You've spoken with the others there that night, haven't you?"

"We have," he replied. "But there's a gap between when you left your house and when you arrived at the American. Apparently you were late. Didn't get there at seven, like you were supposed to. Like you've wanted us to believe."

"All right, I was late. But I didn't use that time to go to the Carrs' house and attempt to poison Sebastian, Detective," he said. "I walked rather than take the omnibus. I think better when I walk. That's all."

Nick strolled over to the window and leaned back against the windowsill. He should've made sure it wasn't coated in grime that had blown in off the street before risking the cleanliness of his coat. "And that made you late?"

"I lost track of time."

"What did you want to think about that required all that walking, Mr. Ingram?"

He pulled in a breath. "Emma wanted to move away," he said. "She wanted us to get married and leave San Francisco. I told her I wasn't ready. That I couldn't leave Lou behind. Emma wasn't keen on having my sister go with us. Lou wants to stick it out here, though. Try to work her way back into painting theater scenery. Even if her chances seem slim."

"Did you and Emma fight about the move?"

"Not like that, Detective. Just a quarrel." He dropped his chin to his chest and scrubbed his hands through his hair. "I told her I'd think about it. About what to do."

"Did Emma spot you at the house Friday night?" Nick asked. "You didn't need to kill her. She'd kept your secret and hadn't said a word to us when she was here yesterday, sitting in that same chair."

Still alive. Still vibrant, if frightened and small. Like a quivering mouse before the cat strikes.

Ingram didn't respond.

Nick looked over at Taylor, scratching away in his notebook. "But now Miss Joyce is dead. Murdered this morning, her throat slit. Killed, maybe, for noticing you someplace you weren't supposed to be," Nick said. "Where did you toss your bloody clothes, Mr. Ingram? Slicing her throat had to have ruined the sleeve of your coat."

"Like I told you, I was in bed and didn't even get up until after Lou left for church," he said. "Did you ask her? You were at my house this morning, poking around, finding clothes that somehow implicate me in the poisoning. You must've asked Lou."

"I did question her," Nick said. "You know, your neighbor doesn't judge you two to be churchgoers."

"She decided to this morning," he said. "I was not out . . . what kind of a monster do you think I am, Detective? I'd never hurt Emma. Never."

Even though all the clues they had pointed Ingram's direction, Nick felt his certainty about the man's guilt beginning to slip. If he faltered now, he might never learn the truth. *Intuition is a good thing, Nick, but don't let it cloud your judgment. In the end, you always have to think with your brains, if you want to be a good detective. Always.* That's what Uncle Asa had told him once about trusting intuition. Maybe he wasn't thinking. Maybe he was putting more faith in a feeling in his bones than in logic.

"Do you shave yourself, Mr. Ingram?" he asked, pressing on. Nick had searched Ingram for a knife and hadn't discovered one on him. Not finding a bloodied weapon didn't eliminate the man from suspicion, though.

The man's forehead furrowed. "Yes."

"That's what I thought, because I noticed your shaving supplies in your bedroom," Nick said. "Except you're missing your razor. Where is it?"

"My razor?" Ingram swallowed. He'd reasoned out why Nick was asking the question. "It broke where the blade joins the handle. I haven't gotten around to buying a new one yet. I've been visiting a barber on the street one over from ours instead."

"Ah. I see."

"I didn't use it on Emma . . . dear God."

"Why *were* you at the Carrs' house on Friday, Mr. Ingram? Preston Carr wanted you to stay away because he was afraid of what you might do. How you might act," Nick said. "He told me you've got a bad temper."

"I'm not going to respond to these comments and questions any longer, Detective. If you don't believe me, repeating myself isn't going to change that."

True.

"Then who *was* it wearing this costume on Friday?" Nick tapped the caftan. "Who was it our witnesses saw? Who was it Miss Joyce noticed on the Carrs' rear staircase, alarmed that they were there, if it wasn't you?"

"I have absolutely no idea," he responded, despite his intention not to. "There's probably another costume just like this one at the American. And it could've been anybody on those stairs."

Nick would have Taylor or Mullahey follow up on the quantity of caftans and turbans in storage at the theater.

"I can understand why you'd want to get revenge on Sebastian Carr," Nick said. "I had a sister once and I might've retaliated against someone who'd harmed her, if there'd been a need."

Taylor glanced up from his notebook, confusion—or maybe it was worry—creasing his face. Nick rarely ever talked about his sister and never while interrogating a suspect.

"I admit that I hate Sebastian, Detective, but I'm either too stupid or too cautious to have concocted the idea of poisoning him," Ingram replied. "Just like you don't have any proof that I murdered Emma, you don't have any proof that I got into the Carrs' house and tried to poison him."

"Maybe not yet, but I'm only just getting started." Nick got to his feet. "Taylor, take him out to the sergeant and have him booked for the murder of Emma Joyce. Along with the attempted murder of Sebastian Carr, which resulted in the death of Jenny Bernard."

• • •

"Detective Greaves might be a while, ma'am." The sergeant who processed incoming residents of the station's jail cells eyed her. He wasn't the usual officer who occupied the desk adjacent to the heavily barred door. Celia must not come into the station on Sunday all that often if she wasn't acquainted with him. "Are you sure you want to keep waiting?"

"Quite certain."

Celia rearranged her hands on her lap—she'd removed her wedding ring and stashed it in her reticule—and squared her shoulders, emphasizing her commitment to remaining affixed to the chair until Nicholas Greaves concluded the interview in progress inside his office. She did wish he would hurry, though. The stench inside the room was no nicer on a Sunday than it was on any other day of the week.

"It could be another hour," the sergeant said as though she were daft. Celia was surprised he hadn't crossed the room to sniff her to determine if she was drunk and might need some time inside the jail cells he guarded. "Might be better for you to go home."

"I have never known Mr. Greaves to require an hour to conduct an interrogation, Sergeant," she replied. "And I am content to wait as long as is required."

The door to the detectives' office opened, rescuing her from a continued argument with the officer, and Mr. Taylor stepped through. His hand was clamped around the elbow of a dark-haired fellow resisting every attempt to drag him away.

"Mrs. Davies." Mr. Taylor nodded at her. "Come on, Mr. Ingram."

So this was Anthony Ingram. "Is Mr. Greaves available?" she asked Taylor just as Nicholas exited his office.

"Ce . . . Mrs. Davies," he said, shooting a look at the sergeant, who was watching them both. "How long have you been out here?"

"Long enough."

"I kept telling her you'd be awhile, Detective," the sergeant said. "But she wouldn't listen."

"She rarely does. You may as well come in, Mrs. Davies." He returned to his office.

Celia took the chair in front of his desk. It was still warm from having been recently occupied. "You have found proof that Tony Ingram murdered Emma."

"No proof yet but his alibi—asleep in bed, according to his sister—is pretty weak, so I'm having him jailed for the crime. It doesn't help his cause that I found something rather incriminating in a locked wardrobe in his bedroom." He pointed at the pile of clothes on his desk. "Evidence that he was the fellow Miss Bremerton and Dr. Schneider saw Friday night. He claims the reason he left his house at six on Friday, an hour before he was required to show up at the American, was because he wanted to walk and do some thinking. Might've been enough time to head to the Carrs', though. We have heard from one of his fellow musicians that he was late arriving."

"Is that so?" She fingered a corner of the tunic. The material was both supple and oily and a trifle sticky, that strange tactile sensation only provided by silk. The theater it had come from did not stint on its costumes. "Given this development, Preston Carr may have to reconsider his accusation against Sebastian. Insofar as Miss Joyce's horrible murder is concerned, that is."

"When did you talk to him?"

"I came directly here from Bishop's restaurant, where I located Mr. Carr."

Nicholas dropped onto his chair. "He didn't happen to mention having spoken with a very upset Katherine Vanmeter Friday afternoon, who'd been banging on Sebastian's locked door, did he?"

"He did not, but she alluded to it. Yesterday morning when she came to speak with me so urgently. She said she'd caused a scene by storming upstairs to confront Sebastian, although she neglected to mention that she'd interacted with Preston." How curious. "I informed him of Emma's murder, by the way. I hope you do not mind too much."

"I doubt it would stop you if I did mind."

He was teasing. At least, that was what she thought he was doing. It was so difficult to tell some days.

"Preston Carr wants me to believe that Sebastian is responsible for killing Emma Joyce, Nicholas. Because Sebastian had gotten her with child and wanted her out of the way." The words were hideous to speak aloud.

Nicholas's expression darkened. "Neither of the Ingrams mentioned anything like that."

"Such a situation is humiliating for the woman involved," she replied. "It is possible Louise Ingram was not aware. Perhaps Emma had not even informed Tony of her condition."

"She was pressuring him to marry her and move away, and he was resisting," he said. "Maybe after failing to convince Ingram to marry her, she tried to get Sebastian Carr to do what was honorable."

"Emma could hardly bear the child and raise it on her own, without employment, without support." A woman of her station, dependent upon a good reputation to secure a respectable position, would face an impossible future with an illegitimate child. Celia's heart ached for all the women who had ever found themselves in such an untenable situation. Some of those women had visited her clinic, and there would be more. "My impression of Sebastian Carr, however, is that he'd be nearly impossible to persuade to 'do what was honorable' by her."

"More reason to believe Tony Ingram is the murderer," Nicholas said. "Maybe he'd figured out why she was so eager to get married.

Maybe he'd figured out who the father was, as well."

He shifted in his chair, and the low afternoon light coming through the window at his back burnished the brown of his hair. The strands were soft and thick; she'd run her fingers through them once, a rare moment when they had been alone together. If she leaned across the desk, she could reach out and stroke his hair again, straighten the lock that sagged crookedly across his forehead. He'd left the door open, though, and the sergeant would undoubtedly notice. Besides, this was no time for tenderhearted touches.

"Celia?" He was watching her and she wondered how long she'd been sitting there, staring.

Her cheeks warmed. "Woolgathering. Excuse me," she said. "Where was I? Oh, yes. In support of Preston Carr's claim that his brother killed Emma, he suggested that, if we questioned his father or Miss Bremerton, we'd discover that Sebastian had not accompanied them to church this morning but rather met them there. Although I've not the faintest idea how he would be aware of that, since he'd not attended services either."

"I need to head over to the Carrs' house and ask a few questions, it sounds like."

"While you are there, you might wish to speak with Miss Bremerton about her plans to depart San Francisco," Celia said. "I was told this morning by the young woman who answers the door that she is packing and means to leave tomorrow morning. Preston Carr was rather surprised, genuinely so, to hear the news when I told him of her intentions. A sudden change of her plans, is how I read his reaction."

"We'll stop her from doing that, Celia."

"I should have informed you earlier. But after finding Emma . . ."

"An understandable lapse," he generously said. "As it stands, Celia, we only have Preston Carr's word for it that Emma Joyce had become pregnant and that his brother had admitted to being responsible. I wouldn't call Preston Carr the most trustworthy source."

"I can well imagine, though, Sebastian bragging to his brother about such an accomplishment," she said bitterly.

"If only we had the blasted coroner's report." He started hunting through the papers on his desk. "He should be done with it by now."

"Unless Dr. Letterman does not work on Sunday, Nicholas."

"Harris did."

She feared he would be longing for Dr. Harris for the rest of his days as a police detective.

"Greaves?" a voice called out in the station. "Oh, there you are."

"Dr. Harris, we were just talking about you," Celia said.

"Mrs. Davies, I'm never surprised to find you here." He took the hand she extended and squeezed her fingers. "I've got news from Dr. Letterman, Greaves."

"He's finished the autopsy on Emma Joyce?" Nicholas said.

"Yes. He did confirm, I hear, that the wound was definitely not self-inflicted," Dr. Harris said. "Any suspects?"

"We have a man in custody," Nicholas answered. "Her former lover and a man who is also a suspect in the attempted poisoning of Sebastian Carr. Anthony Ingram, the brother of the woman who was the victim of that vitriol attack in January."

"Her brother? I can understand why he'd want to retaliate against Sebastian Carr, but why kill his sweetheart?" Harris asked.

"I have learned from Preston Carr that Sebastian may have forced himself on Emma, Dr. Harris. Perhaps, though, Mr. Ingram misunderstood the relationship between them and struck out in jealousy," Celia replied. "During the autopsy, did the coroner discover that she was with child, by any chance?"

"He did, Mrs. Davies," the doctor replied. "But she'd recently lost the baby."

"One of the Carrs' servants had mentioned to me that Emma had been feeling unwell lately but had recovered." Had pregnancy been the cause of her illness? Likely so, it now appeared.

"So Ingram no longer had her pregnancy as a reason to get back at Carr," Nicholas said.

"He still may have wished to, even though she'd lost the child, Mr. Greaves," she said. "He would remain angry with Sebastian Carr for what he'd done to her."

"But the loss of the baby *does* eliminate the need for Sebastian Carr to kill Emma. His problems had been resolved," Nicholas said. "Unless she hadn't told him yet."

"The note, Nicholas!" Celia noticed Dr. Harris grin at the use of his Christian name. "The note about a meeting that I found in Sebastian Carr's room, burned. What if that message had been from Emma? Attempting to arrange a meeting to inform him that she was no longer pregnant," she said. "And this morning, Sebastian Carr misunderstood the reason for the meeting and went to deal with the problem—which no longer existed—striking her down before giving her a chance to speak." How utterly cruel.

"Maybe her murder isn't resolved, Greaves, and Mr. Ingram is not guilty," Dr. Harris said.

"Thanks for pointing that out, Harris."

• • •

"Detective?" The servant who'd answered the door at the Carrs'—not Pru—blinked at Nick.

"I need you to assemble the Carrs so that I can speak with them."

"Miss Bremerton has gone for an afternoon carriage ride with Mr. Sebastian, Detective," she said, looking every bit like she regretted answering the bell and finding a policeman on the porch. She glanced behind her for rescue, which only confirmed Nick's assumption. "It's been her habit ever since she came to stay with us. Early in the morning and every day before dinner. Even when it's chilly like it is today."

"Did she go out this morning before heading to church?" he asked, pushing his way into the entry hall, where it was warmer than on the porch. She'd made the mistake of leaving the door open wide.

"Yes. Miss Irene went out for a short ride as soon as the sky started to get light," she said, moving aside. "Surprised there was anybody at the livery stable to help her with the horse, but maybe she'd arranged for them to always be ready, no matter the day or the weather."

"She goes alone at that hour?" He didn't know of any other women who'd take a risk like that. Except for Celia. But the risk might've been worth it if your goal was to murder a rival.

"She doesn't seem to think it's dangerous," she replied. "If Mrs. Carr were still alive, she'd be screaming down the house about how improper it is for a genteel young lady to go off on her own. But Mr. Carr and Mr. Sebastian don't seem to mind so much."

"I've heard she intends to return home tomorrow. Do you know if those are still her plans?"

"Her luggage has been brought up to her room but without Pru here—she's off to visit her mother in Oakland and took the ferry over before lunch—she doesn't have anyone to help her pack."

Miss Bremerton couldn't pack without the help of a servant? "Did anybody else leave the house early this morning before heading off to church?"

"Not that I saw, sir. Pru could have told you that too. Sorry she's not here," she said. Nick could imagine exactly how much she was sorry. If Pru had been in the house, *she'd* be answering his questions instead. "I've been in the kitchen most of the day. And doing some tidying, since Emma doesn't come in on Sundays, even though it would've been a help if she had today. We haven't finished cleaning up after the party. There will still be plenty to do tomorrow when she does get here."

The household obviously hadn't heard the news that Emma would never be returning. "You're positive, then, that you didn't notice any of the Carrs sneaking out of the house before dawn."

Her forehead creased. "Sneaking?"

"Leaving. I meant leaving."

"I don't think so, Detective. Mr. Carr and Mr. Sebastian and Miss Irene went to church together. That's what Mrs. Tilden said," she replied. "Well, not Mr. Sebastian, I think. He came back with them, though, in time for the light Sunday lunch we serve. Does that help?"

Yes and no. "What about Mr. Preston?" he asked, even though when Preston Carr had been in the station he hadn't looked like he'd recently slit a young woman's throat.

"He's been out most of the day. He doesn't attend church services." She looked disappointed in Preston Carr. "He was back for a little bit, but then a police officer came for some reason and he went off with him. So it's just Mr. Carr here right now."

Taylor trotted up the front walkway. "Got news from the officer who did the search, sir. Completed and nothing found."

Damn. No arsenic, no bloody clothes, no weapon at the Ingrams'. But a few hours had passed between Emma's murder and when Nick and then the officer had searched their house. Too many hours.

"Thank you." Nick nodded toward the gravy-stained apron tied around the servant's waist. "Looks like you're preparing dinner. Are you expecting Miss Bremerton and Mr. Sebastian to be back in time to eat?"

"I suppose we are."

"And when is that?"

She peered at the dial of the long-case clock in the hallway. "A half hour or so, Detective. Mr. Carr likes to eat early on Sunday evening."

Nick pulled his hat off his head. "Then I'll wait. The parlor's right over here, correct?"

"But—"

"Sorry, miss," Taylor said, trailing after him.

The pocket doors at the far end of the parlor slid open. Eustace Carr marched into the room.

The maid had scurried into the parlor behind Nick. "I'm sorry, Mr. Carr. He barged in."

"Go back to work, Sally. It's almost time for dinner," he ordered.

Nick looked over at his assistant. "Taylor, have her take you upstairs to the bedrooms. You know what you're looking for."

"Yes, sir," Taylor said, jogging off.

"Detective Greaves, your assistant has already been poking around our house and asking questions. Along with that woman, the nurse who think she's a detective," Carr said, so red-faced that Nick feared he might collapse from a heart attack. "You don't need to disturb our Sunday by having him look around again."

"We shouldn't be too long," Nick said. "You've been notified, I assume, that we did find arsenic in the bottle of vanilla Jenny Bernard drank from, Mr. Carr."

"I have heard. A dose meant for my son," he said. "But I don't see how the information justifies another intrusion on our peace." The man stepped nearer. He was almost as tall as Nick and obviously used to intimidating people with his size. Nick didn't budge. "The household has suffered a terrible shock and the constant presence of the police in upsetting."

"You wouldn't want us to rush the investigation, would you, Mr. Carr?"

"Most certainly I would not, Detective," he retorted. "But that shouldn't require you to be crawling all over our house every day."

"To shorten the time we spend crawling all over your house, Mr. Carr, maybe you can confirm where you and the other members of your household were this morning. Around sunrise," Nick said. "Sally told me that Miss Bremerton had gone out for a ride. Is that correct?"

"I believe so."

"What about Sebastian? He didn't go with her."

"He didn't? I thought that was why he didn't take the carriage with us to church but met us there later."

Interesting. "And Preston?"

"He told me he was going into town. More important than attending services," he said scornfully. "But not at sunrise. Preston never rises that early."

"I've learned that one of your guests was seen milling about outside around the time that the party got underway on Friday," he said. "The folks who noticed him, which includes Miss Bremerton, thought this fellow looked a bit shifty. A man wearing a turquoise-blue tunic sort of outer garment and a length of white fabric wrapped around his head. Sound familiar?"

He drew back an inch or so. "None of my guests wore that costume on Friday night, which is rather astounding, actually," he said. "The 'Turk' is a popular choice at masquerades."

"You've seen it before."

"Yes."

"On anybody in particular?" Tony Ingram, for instance. Although it was far-fetched to imagine that Eustace Carr and Ingram might've ever attended the same masquerade ball.

His gaze turned inward and he frowned, as if he was plumbing recollections that weren't all that pleasant. "My wife wore the costume once on a lark," he said. "Years ago. Preston mentions that night every so often, but for me it is a painful memory, Detective Greaves."

"I'm sorry."

"Is there anything else? Sebastian and Irene should be back soon from their drive and I don't want to keep dinner waiting much past then."

"Not much longer, Mr. Carr. Oh, one more thing. Inform Miss Bremerton that her plans to leave San Francisco need to be canceled," Nick said. "One of your maids, Emma Joyce, was killed this morning and nobody who's a suspect should be contemplating leaving town."

"Emma . . . That's why the officer was here."

He did sound shocked. "To collect one of you to go to the coroner's and confirm her identity," he said. "Were you aware of a relationship between Miss Joyce and Sebastian, Mr. Carr?"

Eustace Carr scowled. "Such things like that do not occur in my house, Detective."

"Of course not."

"You're not suggesting that Irene is to be suspected in the girl's death because she was jealous, are you?" he asked. "Miss Bremerton is above reproach."

"I don't close down any avenue of an investigation, including an avenue that might lead to one of your houseguest, until I'm sure it's a dead end, sir."

"Is that so? And your pursuit of this particular avenue is why you sent your man upstairs to search. Which is ludicrous. Absolutely ludicrous," Carr wheezed. "And you can be sure I'll speak to your superior about your baseless accusations."

Great.

cb CHAPTER 15 bc

"Bloody . . ." Celia muttered aloud, closing the drawer to the desk in her examination room. She needed to write down her thoughts on who may have murdered Emma Joyce and poisoned Sebastian Carr's vanilla, but the nib for her favorite pen was dull and the supplies in her office had run out.

She went up to her bedchamber and sat at her dressing table, where she kept her rosewood and brass writing box alongside her brush and comb and hairpins. She unfolded the box, setting aside sheets of paper embossed with her initial, and rummaged among the pens and pencils in the bottom. She found a nib that would work. She also found at the back of the box a white ivory paper knife, the handle carved with a pattern of vines that revealed their twists and turns to the pressure of a fingertip.

Addie rapped on the bedchamber door. "I've been waiting for you in the parlor, ma'am. You dinna mean to have tea this evening?"

"I do, but I was hunting for a sharp pen nib and found this, which has distracted me." She held up the paper knife, its lovely handle cool to the touch. She rarely made use of it, since she could no longer afford to purchase hand-made books whose pages might need splitting or received letters whose seals were not easily broken by a fingernail. "Do you remember when Patrick gave this to me, Addie?"

Her housekeeper set the cup of tea she'd brought on Celia's dressing table and scowled at the slim knife as though it were Patrick himself. "Aye, I do, ma'am. It was his gift for your first Valentine's Day together after we'd moved into that drafty old house in London."

"I had thought him romantic to give me a gift so practical and thoughtful. A gift 'that would not fade like flowers or be consumed like candies,' was what he'd said."

She truly had been touched by Patrick's gift. *Perhaps I do mind that Nicholas did not give me anything for Valentine's Day.* He'd been strangely aloof lately, although there were moments still when he would look at her and make her blush. But today, he'd permitted Dr. Harris to show her home rather than take the opportunity to accompany her himself. Perhaps she misunderstood the depth of Nicholas's feelings for her, blind to the reality.

"Romantic? Mr. Davies? Humph," Addie grumbled, resisting the urge to call her deceased husband the "divil," as she so often did.

"I did misunderstand Patrick for so many years." Perhaps she could never trust her heart.

"You were suffering, ma'am, after your brother died. Anyone might make a mistake in those circumstances."

In truth, it had not been Patrick who'd healed Celia's heart after Harry's death. It had been Addie's constant and devoted friendship.

"A mistake I do wish I could forget." Celia returned the paper knife to the bottom of the writing box and restored her stationery, burying the knife beneath the sheets of cream linen paper. "But mementos insist on cropping up to remind me of him."

"Perhaps we should search the house, find all those mementos, and toss them out," Addie said. "Just like we did with the landscape he painted that used to hang in the entry hall."

Celia closed up the box. "It is an excellent and elegant paper knife, however."

"Then why did you bury it where you'd nae see it?"

"Another astute observation, Addie." She gathered up the fresh pen nib and a few sheets of blank paper. The table book in which she'd compiled her thoughts for the last murder she'd investigated with Nicholas had been put to use for other purposes since then. "Bring the tea down to the dining room. I have to summarize my suspects."

Addie followed her downstairs. "Hasna Mr. Greaves put a fellow in jail, though?" she whispered, so that her voice didn't echo up the staircase and Barbara, in her chamber reading before she went to bed, would hear.

Celia had told Addie about the arrest of Tony Ingram. "Yes, but too many of the individuals involved have motives. Furthermore, their supposed alibis contain as many holes as a coal sieve. It is time I collect my thoughts, Addie, and figure out what the truth might be."

• • •

Nick sat at the table in his room, his pencil poised above the words he'd written, the lantern overhead casting the shadow of his fingers across the paper. He'd given up on sending a letter to Ellie and had settled on a short telegram, which he'd found equally difficult to compose, dreading her response. That she hadn't sent the copy of the studio portrait. That an unknown enemy had. Because he had to think the person responsible was an enemy. No friend would torture him like this.

Riley, his head draped over Nick's feet, let out a whimper. Nick's right foot had fallen asleep. He didn't want to disturb the dog, though. And maybe he didn't mind the prickling in his toes because he needed Riley's comforting.

Ellie. Did you send portrait of us and Meg? Came in unsigned envelope. If not you, who? N.

The more he looked at the words, the more certain he was that her reply wouldn't be good. It wasn't her handwriting on the outside of that envelope. And she wouldn't have sent the photograph to mark the anniversary of Meg's death as some sort of surprise. Not Ellie. She was too solemn, too sensible.

He glanced at the daguerreotype, sitting out of reach on the table. The photographer had produced four copies, one for each of the people captured in the image and one for his parents to display on their mantel at home. He was pretty sure the latter was still on that mantel in the house in Sacramento. Nick had his in a silver frame atop his chest of drawers. And as far as he knew, Ellie still had hers. What he didn't know was where Meg's had gotten to. It hadn't been with the few personal effects the coroner had collected and had given to Nick. At the time, he'd been too shaken by Meg's death to notice it was missing from her belongings. All that sweetness and laughter snuffed like a candle flame, taking every bit of the light in the world with her. Plunging Nick into a darkness so deep he thought he'd never climb out. He hadn't cared about a missing photograph. He hadn't cared about much of anything afterward except his job.

Nick reread the note and folded it. He'd take it to the telegraph office in the morning, even though he'd probably written more words than he wanted to pay for. Because somebody was trying to send him a message and he needed to know who.

• • •

"Ma'am, your tea's gone cold again," Addie said, turning up the gas light in the dining room.

"I am finding it difficult to settle into my task."

"I'll bring you fresh hot water. Might help," she said, going off to fetch some.

Celia stared at the empty sheet of stationery. She'd not a clue why she was so stuck. She simply needed to start at the beginning. The poisoning of Sebastian Carr's vanilla.

She wrote *Poisoning* on the topmost blank page.

When had the poisoned bottle been placed in his room? After Mrs. Tilden had done her post-lunchtime rounds of the house—at two—and noticed the vanilla needed to be replaced. But before Irene had gone inside to deliver a valentine at around seven in the evening and propped it against the almost full bottle on his table.

The doors were locked around three fifteen, which further limited the time. Along with Sebastian's presence in his room between four and six and Preston's claim that he did not hear anyone go in or out. Between two and three fifteen and six to seven, the latter stretch of time assuming that when Sebastian had departed his bedchamber he'd accidentally left the door unlocked. Celia and Irene had been able to get inside the room without a key.

Next item, then, a review of who'd been inside the house during those few hours.

The temporary staff, Jenny Bernard and Paulina Lyons, showed up around three to help prepare for the evening's festivities. Paulina to first help with the flowers—a task that sent her upstairs—and Jenny straight off to the kitchen. Not long after, Emma did a scan of the upstairs to ensure everything was in readiness for any guests who might use the water closet and to lock the doors. Irene was away from the house until approximately three forty-five or so. Preston Carr returned from downtown after three, followed by his brother at four. Eustace Carr was in the house the entire day, although Nicholas must not consider him a serious suspect. Why poison the goose that had laid the golden egg by securing Miss Bremerton's promise to wed that goose? Over the course of several hours, Owen and his fellow workers arrived at the house to deliver wine and other liquor. A short time after the mask was underway, Angus MacNamara observed Emma speaking with an unseen individual on the back stairs. She never informed the police about the encounter, although she'd been alarmed to encounter them.

Celia contemplated the young woman's name, the ink drying on the paper, and wondered how long it would be before her family in Illinois came to fetch her body. To return her to the soil of her home. Would they even be able to afford to do so?

She re-inked her pen and continued. Miss Vanmeter came to the house around three thirty, one final attempt to convince Sebastian to permit Miss Bremerton to support her clinic.

"Even though she had asked for my help in convincing him." Impatient, Celia supposed.

A servant attested that Miss Vanmeter was in the library with Irene until she went upstairs to confront Sebastian, who had refused to speak with her about the clinic. According to Nicholas, Preston Carr interacted with her at that time. She left the house after their brief altercation. Owen observed Preston searching for someone in the area of the kitchen, which he refused to explain when Celia had questioned him. *Very odd.*

The remainder of the guests arrived at approximately seven, including Dr. Schneider, who spotted the man in the Turk costume. A fellow Irene Bremerton had also observed, although she had neglected to tell Celia about him on Friday. Had she recognized them, perhaps? Sought to protect them?

An intriguing thought, Celia.

All of this left next to no time for a guest to sneak into the house, slip upstairs, and swap out the bottle of vanilla before Irene deposited her valentine around seven. Meaning the Carrs, Miss Bremerton, the staff, the temporary help, and Miss Vanmeter were the only viable suspects.

"Scratch that. *Not* Miss Vanmeter." Katherine had arrived after the bedchamber doors had been secured. Also, Katherine had left the house before six.

The mysterious person in the Turk costume, found in Mr. Ingram's locked wardrobe, had to be added. Mr. Ingram was reportedly late to arrive at the theater on Friday. In addition, someone had been lurking at the perimeter of the house, someone wearing magenta, if the torn piece of fabric Celia had found in the bushes was any evidence. Who had that been? Not the tunic-wearing individual.

Jenny, underfoot in the kitchen, was sent upstairs by Mrs. Tilden around quarter after seven with a fresh supply of vanilla extract. She consumed the entire contents of the bottle she found in Sebastian's room and returned to the kitchen with it. Approximately an hour later, she fell ill and the Carrs sent for Celia, whom they viewed as being reliably discreet.

Celia sipped from her teacup and considered what she'd written so far. One last item. Shortly after the news spread through the house that Jenny had died, the young woman calling herself Paulina Lyons fled.

Now to consider each suspect in the attempt on Sebastian Carr's life. Which, to be fair, might only have been an attempt to gravely sicken him.

"Here, ma'am." Addie, worry creasing her forehead, placed a hot pot of water on the table along with a fresh cup. "As much as I admire what you've done to help Mr. Greaves in the past, I always fret over you. Whenever you get involved in one of his investigations, you get hurt."

"Addie, I promise I will be careful," Celia said. "To be frank, though, I do not feel that I am in danger."

Her housekeeper's expression shifted from worry to skepticism. "So you say, but you've been attacked nearly every other time."

Perhaps it would be kinder to everyone to focus solely on my clinic. But the simple act of the Carrs sending for Celia to tend to Jenny had drawn her into this case, and she could not walk away from it so easily. Not when another young woman had died. And not when the possibility existed that the killer might not be finished with his—or her—crimes.

"But not so far in this investigation," Celia replied.

"Weel, luckily for all of us, ma'am," Addie said. "Och. What am I to do with you?"

She huffed and stomped back into the kitchen.

Celia smiled, even though she should not, and returned to her list and her thoughts. Suspects, then. For all of them, the choice of using arsenic was not unusual, as the substance was frightfully easy to obtain. Addie kept a box of rat poison in their house, even.

Anthony Ingram. Motive—revenge for the vitriol attack on his sister, Louise, which Sebastian was suspected of arranging but never formally accused of executing. Also, hatred of the man who may have impregnated his sweetheart, Emma Joyce. A friend of Preston Carr's, he was told to stay away from the party for fear of a scene. The caftan and turban found in his bedchamber supported the idea that he'd been the stranger observed outside the house. Uncertain how he'd known about the supply of vanilla in Sebastian's room or how he'd managed to enter the bedchamber unobserved. Had Emma somehow helped? Or was he the person she'd seen on the staircase?

Blast. Why not just have *Emma* poison the bloody vanilla rather than sneak about the house himself?

"Perhaps she had done, Celia," she whispered, tapping the end of her pen against her teeth. She'd had access to Sebastian's bedchamber before she had locked it.

Lastly, Tony Ingram left his house an hour before the musicians were required for the evening minstrel show at the American Theater, and was reportedly late.

Preston Carr. Motive—jealousy of his brother. Relationship with Louise Ingram collapsed when she took up with Sebastian, who then discarded Louise in favor of Irene Bremerton. It was Preston's idea to celebrate the pending engagement at the masquerade ball and invite a large crowd, an event that would provide enough clamor and confusion to conceal his plans to poison Sebastian. Would have known about his brother's predilection for vanilla-flavored coffee. Could come and go upstairs without anyone remarking.

Strange, though, that he'd insisted that Tony Ingram not attend the party. His presence in the house would have made the perfect cover for Preston's planned actions and provided the obvious scapegoat. Unless, of course, Preston was not responsible. Initially failed to mention that Katherine had come upstairs to confront Sebastian. Why?

Irene Bremerton. Motive—jealousy. Aware of Sebastian's rumored role in Miss Ingram's assault. May have discovered that Sebastian had forced himself on Emma Joyce. Also upset that he'd forbidden her from helping her good friend, Miss Vanmeter, with her clinic. May not have thought the arsenic—which he would've consumed in small doses over a long period of time—would kill him but only make him ill. A small portion of vengeful punishment. Out at a luncheon and enjoying a ride that afternoon before returning to find Katherine waiting for her in the library. Purportedly delivered a valentine to Sebastian's room around seven, noticing the nearly full bottle of vanilla—the poisoned one—at that time.

If Irene had known about Emma's pregnancy, who might have apprised her? Not Emma herself, who would have risked dismissal. And certainly not Sebastian.

Celia's gaze traveled up the sheet of paper to the name immediately above Irene's. Preston Carr. Who may have enjoyed the disruption to his brother's connubial happiness.

I do keep returning to him, do I not?

Celia gathered a fresh blank sheet of paper, re-inked her pen, and moved on to the next suspect.

Katherine Vanmeter. Motive—distressed over Sebastian Carr's interference with Irene's support of the clinic. Irene may have told her about Sebastian's vanilla habit. Removed from suspicion, though, because she was not in the house when the door to Sebastian's room was unlocked? Interesting that she came to visit Celia Saturday morning, afraid Sebastian would blame her for the poisoning attempt. Why would she do so if she was not guilty in some fashion?

Louise Ingram. Motive—revenge for Sebastian paying a boy to toss vitriol on her. May have also learned about Sebastian and Emma. Aware of upcoming party and engagement announcement, which would explain the timing of her revenge. Was she the person in the Turk costume or the unknown individual Emma had confronted on the staircase? Was that why Emma, possibly sympathetic to Louise's ordeal at the hands of Sebastian Carr, had not informed the police of seeing the person? Would very likely know about Sebastian's love of vanilla-flavored coffee. Her neighbor maintained that she'd not left the house Friday evening.

Paulina Lyons. Motive—unknown. Helped with the flower arrangements, among other tasks, taking one upstairs, which gave her access to the bedchambers. Left abruptly once the news of Jenny Bernard's death spread through the household. Provided false address to intelligence office and possibly a false name, as well. Clearly intended some sort of wrongdoing. If that included poisoning Sebastian was unclear.

Celia wished she knew anything at all about the young woman. She sincerely hoped Mr. Bell would provide an answer or two. And soon.

Man in Oriental or Turk costume. Motive—unknown. If not Tony Ingram, found with the costume, who could it have been? Louise Ingram? Dr. Schneider noticed the individual when he arrived, *after* seven. Seemingly too late to deliver a bottle of poisoned vanilla to Sebastian's room, which Irene had propped her valentine against close to seven o'clock. Unless they'd been there for a while, hiding in the house and waiting for the optimal opportunity to sneak back out.

Emma Joyce. Motive—retaliation. Strike back at the man who'd assaulted her. Although by the time of the masquerade ball, she was no longer pregnant. Perhaps Sebastian was still making unwanted advances. She was responsible for locking the bedchamber doors, which meant she could have easily gone inside Sebastian's room. Did not kill herself, though.

So, on to her murder.

For all of the other suspects in Sebastian's attempted killing, they held one likely motive in wanting Emma dead—Emma had evidence they'd poisoned the vanilla. Or at least had been upstairs at a time that would have allowed them to do so. But she'd not provided any such evidence to the police. Why? Either because she actually had no evidence or she had sought to protect the person. Emma would only choose to protect one of the Carrs or Miss Bremerton if she feared for her position in the house. She'd not likely be motivated to protect Miss Vanmeter. However, Emma *would* want to safeguard the Ingrams. Both of whom she would have willingly admitted to her rented room. Nicholas had implied that both of their alibis were not particularly strong for this morning.

As far as Celia knew, the bloody clothes and the weapon used on Emma had not been found. Which meant only the thinnest thread could connect any of them to the crime. However, Miss Bremerton had been out very early that morning. And where had Sebastian Carr been before joining his father and fiancée at church?

A question that segued to the other motive to kill Emma. Her pregnancy. Preston Carr had implicated his brother rather than the obvious father, Tony Ingram. Could Sebastian Carr be responsible? Celia recalled the pamphlet she'd found in his room. *The Handbook and Descriptive Catalogue of the Pacific Museum of Anatomy and Natural Science,* a brochure that told a different story. It was a place men might visit to obtain help with their . . .

"Manliness," she whispered to herself.

At the bottom of the page she wrote *The Pacific Museum of Anatomy* and circled it. She'd never been inside the museum herself—women were not permitted to enter—but she had always been curious about the items on display. Since the likelihood was essentially nil that she'd be able to get even a toe past the threshold of the museum's front doors, she would need to send a male to inquire in her stead. While she set about questioning a young woman who might be intimately familiar with Sebastian Carr's virility.

· · ·

"Tell me about Emma and Sebastian Carr, Mr. Ingram." Nick leaned an elbow against the crossbar in the cell door. After Taylor's search of the Carrs' house yesterday had been unproductive, he'd sent both him and Mullahey back to the Ingrams' to tear up floorboards, if necessary. They'd finally found the proof Nick needed to show that Tony Ingram had murdered Emma. A shoe tucked behind a large, heavy trunk that had eluded Nick's hasty search, and the other officer's, too. A shoe with an incriminating trace of dried blood on its sole. "About the attention he'd paid to her."

Ingram sat up on the cell's cot. A piece of straw had worked its way through the mattress cover seams and clung to his trouser leg. "What do you mean?"

"You know what I mean."

Ingram glanced at the fellow in the cell across from his. The drunk—a regular—was dead asleep and snoring loudly, oblivious to the world and whatever Ingram might have to say. It was early morning, so the snoring could be forgiven. Although Nick suspected the fellow would still be snoring this afternoon.

"I didn't try to poison Sebastian because of how he was treating Emma, Detective Greaves," Ingram insisted. Spending the night in the miserably dank jail cell hadn't softened him up any.

"No, you tried to poison him because he'd gotten her pregnant. Isn't that so?"

Ingram jumped to his feet and slammed a hand against the bars. "Don't say that! Don't say that about her!"

The thud had startled the drunk out of his sleep. "What in tarnation?" he muttered, coughed a few times, and resumed snoring.

"You didn't know she was pregnant, Mr. Ingram?"

Ingram pushed away from the cell door. "I did suspect. She'd been unwell recently and I recognized the signs. I remember my mother's many pregnancies. But Emma never admitted that she was and I hadn't gotten her with child," he said. "I dismissed my concerns."

"But the child could've been Sebastian Carr's?" Nick asked.

"I doubt it."

The warden at the end of the aisle slurped noisily from his cup of coffee, his attention pinned on Nick. Monday morning's entertainment. He snickered in response to Nick's scowl.

"Your story is you left your house at six on Friday in order to get to the theater by seven. Except you arrived late," Nick said. "It doesn't take an hour to get from your house to the theater, Mr. Ingram, not even if you're walking slowly, lost in thought. I know because I had a policeman check. And it definitely doesn't take *more* than an hour."

Ingram collapsed onto the cot, causing more straw to poke through the mattress seams. It would not be comfortable in the least, but then discomfort was the point. "Okay, I'll admit it, Detective. I did head to the Carrs' house that evening."

At last, thought Nick. *Intuition, Uncle Asa. It does work.*

"Made it as far as Market Street before turning back. I realized I couldn't accomplish anything by going there. Nothing except trouble,"

Ingram continued. "Anything I said to Sebastian Carr or did to him wouldn't heal the scars on my sister's hand. Would only make things worse."

"Your aborted trip to the Carrs' house is the reason you were late to the theater. That's what you want me to believe?"

"Yes, and I nearly got sacked because of it," he said. "It wasn't me in that costume, Detective, as I keep telling you. Those items of clothing never left my house. They've been collecting dust on that shelf in my wardrobe for months."

"Maybe Louise put it on, out for revenge when it looked like she was never going to get the justice she sought."

"The wardrobe is always locked and she doesn't have a key. There's only one. No spare." He ran his hands through his hair and looked up at Nick. "It was somebody else in an identical costume, Detective. Or the whole episode has been created. Have you considered that? That this person doesn't even exist? That the real perpetrator made them up?"

"Two different people saw him, Mr. Ingram."

"Who are these people? I think I have a right to know."

Nick drew in a breath, grateful that somebody had strewn fresh sawdust in the cells—beneficial when the occupants weren't always willing to make use of the slop bucket—and it didn't stink as much as usual. Aside from the tang of the ever-present damp and mold and outside sewage. "Irene Bremerton, for one."

"Irene?"

"Why would she lie, Mr. Ingram? Plus one of the guests saw the fellow too. A Dr. Schneider." Nick doubted Schneider had a reason to lie about spotting the fellow, either.

"I can't explain how he could've."

And that was the problem.

"Were you angry with Emma about the pregnancy?" Nick asked. "Is that why you didn't want to marry her? Because you didn't want to be responsible for some other man's child?"

"Angry with Emma? Whatever had happened, it wouldn't have been her fault," he said. "But you know what's ironic, Detective Greaves? I'd decided I did want to marry her, after all. That we could leave San Francisco and find a way to make it work."

"You know what's actually ironic, Mr. Ingram? Emma lost the child recently. She didn't need anybody to marry her out of pity any longer."

Ingram exhaled, his breath misting in the cold, damp air of the jail. "That's why she'd been acting so strangely lately. Distant. Irritable."

Nick leaned into the cell door. "And it dawned on you that she must be pregnant, which is why you went to see her yesterday morning. My assistant, Mr. Taylor, found one of your shoes with blood on it. Emma's blood," he said. "You hid it pretty well but we found the shoe eventually."

"What does any of this matter now? You think I tried to poison Sebastian and killed her, and you don't want to listen to anything I have to say."

"So you're denying you were in her room yesterday. Despite the bloodied shoe we found."

Ingram had run out of lies and didn't respond.

"Did you go to her apartment to ask if she'd seen you at the Carrs' house on Friday?" Nick asked. "Did she reply that she had, so you had to shut her up? Or maybe you murdered her out of jealousy. Sebastian Carr is a handsome man."

Ingram slumped against the cell wall. "I did go to see Emma yesterday, Detective. I was worried about her," he said. "She wasn't alive when I got to her place."

Nick waited for the thrill that usually came when a suspect started to talk, but he didn't feel it. "If you're so innocent of her murder, Mr. Ingram, why didn't you contact the police after finding her body?"

"I panicked. I was afraid one of her neighbors might've seen me going into her room. They'd think I was the murderer."

They would. "So instead of summoning the cops, you went to the oyster saloon and calmly sat down to a meal."

"I wasn't thinking. I was just acting out of habit," he replied, a tremor in his voice. "I didn't want to believe it was Emma. I'd almost convinced myself the body belonged to somebody else."

"How did you get inside her room if she didn't let you in?"

"It's easy. I took the rear steps—she never wanted the woman who lives at the other end of the hall to see her admitting a man to her room. The back door is usually unlocked. The kids forget to refasten it after they've been down to the outhouse. It was open, as usual. Just like the door to her room. That wasn't usual." He paused, his breathing unsteady, swallowing before he started talking again. "She was sprawled there on the floor, already dead. I crouched next to her . . . I stepped in the blood . . . There was so much . . ."

He squeezed his eyes shut, hoping to blot out the memory. Nick could tell him the attempt never worked; the memories, the sights got stuck inside your brain, and no amount of closing your eyes helped.

"And then I heard voices out in the stairwell. Emma's neighbor with one of her kids. Returning from church, I think," Ingram continued. "I threw open the window and jumped out. I'm lucky I didn't break my ankle."

Nick stared at him, letting the silence—what there was of it inside the jail, noisy with the clatter of horses' hooves and wagon wheels, the dripping of unseen water, the drunk snoring—stretch, hoping it might rattle Ingram, encourage him to confess. It didn't.

"If you didn't kill Emma Joyce, who did?"

"I don't know. Preston, maybe. Preston." He dragged the thin plaid blanket off the cot and wrapped it around his shoulders. "He wanted Emma for himself. Couldn't stand that Sebastian had gotten to her first. Just like he had with Louise. Just like he had with Irene Bremerton."

This was a twist. A believable one. "But Eustace Carr has always intended for Miss Bremerton to marry his elder son, hasn't he?"

"That might be so, Detective, but that doesn't mean Preston hadn't hoped she might choose him instead," he said. "And you know? He might've tried to poison Sebastian, too. I've always thought they were a bit like Cain and Abel. But I never thought it might go that far."

Her morning patient dispensed with—a woman who'd required a quick consultation on an ankle sprain caused by awkwardly stepping off a curb —and with the address of the Ingrams' house in hand, Celia ventured out for the day. Before visiting Louise Ingram, she needed to stop at Roesler's and collect Owen in order to recruit him for a trip to the Pacific Museum of Anatomy. Hopefully he wouldn't prove to be too squeamish while visiting there.

The shop's bell chimed merrily as she walked through the door. Mr. Roesler had applied his usual welcoming expression upon hearing the bell, only to observe that the entering customer was her. He'd not been fond of Celia ever since she had utilized Owen to search the man's customer logs for clues in a prior case. He'd not be any more pleased if he discovered what she intended for Owen today.

"Owen Cassidy is busy, ma'am." Mr. Roesler's brows lowered over his black eyes. Owen had once described his employer's eyes as resembling a beetle's. She did grasp the comparison, especially at that moment.

"I would like to purchase a pound of your best chocolates, Mr. Roesler, and I need Owen to deliver them to a friend. Immediately," she replied as pleasantly as she could. "So if you would put together a selection, I would be most grateful."

Upon hearing her voice, Owen popped through the curtain blocking off the back room.

"Mrs. Davies!" he said, eyebrows perked. He knew Celia only showed up at Roesler's Confectionery when she needed him for some sleuthing.

Mr. Roesler shot him a look before retreating to the rear of the rightmost glass case, sets of which lined both sides of his shop. He pulled out an empty decorated tin—which would cost more than a simple paper packet—and proceeded to fill it with candy.

"What is it you need, ma'am?" Owen asked her, his voice low.

"A pound of Roesler's best chocolates, Owen," she replied, smiling.

"Oh." He glanced over at his boss. "Of course."

Finished, Mr. Roesler held out the tin. "That'll be fifty cents, ma'am."

Gad. She fished the money from her reticule, took the candy in one hand and Owen's elbow in the other.

"Who are we delivering the candy to, Mrs. Davies?" he asked once they were out on the street.

"No one, Owen. I merely needed to acquire your services and it was the only scheme I could come up with." An expensive one. She would have to delay replacing her pair of gloves that had a tear in them. "Please drop the chocolates off at my house. I am headed for the Ingrams' for an overdue visit with Miss Ingram."

She handed Owen the tin. The container was too large to stash inside her reticule.

"You think one of them tried to poison the Carr fellow?" he asked, tucking the tin under his arm.

"Mr. Greaves has arrested Anthony Ingram for the crime. He found an incriminating piece of evidence inside his house," she said, setting out at a quick pace. "Mr. Ingram may also have murdered one of the Carrs' servants yesterday morning, Owen. The maid, Emma, who saw the unknown intruder on the back stairs that Mr. MacNamara told you about."

Owen whistled. "That's awful, ma'am. Just because she saw him," he said. "But what's that got to do with why you want to talk to Miss Ingram?"

"She may possess information concerning Sebastian Carr. I've not dropped him from consideration, you see, as it seems he may have gotten Emma with child. Another scandal for him, and his engagement to Miss Bremerton not yet finalized," she said. "Irene may have dismissed the rumors about the vitriol attack on Miss Ingram, but she might not overlook this indiscretion."

"But he could just deny he was the father, right?" he asked as he trotted alongside. "Nobody'd believe a servant over a rich fellow like him. And he wouldn't have tried to poison himself, would he?"

"Two stumpers that suggest he is not guilty," she replied. "However, to be quite certain Mr. Carr had no part in Emma's condition, I need you to go to the Pacific Museum of Anatomy for me."

"Wait, ma'am." Owen came to a dead stop in the middle of the pavement, forcing her to lurch out of the way of a clerk hurrying along with a parcel in his arms. "Isn't that where fellows go to speak with the doctor who runs the place to get help with their . . ." He blushed a red that nearly swamped his freckles. "You know, their, ahem . . ."

"Their virility," she supplied. "Do I want to know how you're aware of such matters, Owen?"

"I'm not a little kid, ma'am!"

"No. You are a young man." One who sends valentines to Grace Hutchinson and breaks Barbara's heart in the process. "A very handsome young man."

"Aww, you don't need to say that, ma'am," he replied, abashed. "But how am I gonna find out what you want to learn? Don't think folks there will be open to gossiping about private stuff like that."

"I have complete faith in your abilities, Owen."

His chest noticeably swelled. "I can do it, ma'am. Count on me. I'm learning how to handle this detective business."

Oh dear. "If you finish quickly, meet me at the Ingrams' house." She gave him the address along with enough coins to pay the museum's entrance fee. "In case I require your assistance there."

"You're not expecting trouble, are you?"

She smiled to reassure him, although by this point in their relationship, Owen would not be easily fooled by smiles. "I am not expecting trouble, but it never hurts to be prepared."

• • •

"What did Mr. Ingram have to say, sir?" Taylor asked, standing just inside the door to the detectives' office. He'd missed Briggs, who'd been in the office only long enough to smirk that Nick hadn't resolved the case yet. Briggs had wisely left before Nick punched him. "Did he confess to killing Miss Joyce?"

"He's decided to blame Preston Carr instead." Nick bundled together the caftan and length of white silk and stuffed them inside his lower desk drawer. It jammed on the material when he tried to close it. "Envy, supposedly. Wanted Emma for himself."

"But we found that bloodied shoe in Mr. Ingram's room."

Nick gave the drawer another shove, finally getting it to shut. "Ingram had an explanation for it. Said he went to visit Emma because she'd been acting strangely lately and he was worried about her. Showed up after she was killed. He stepped in the blood."

"Do you believe him?"

Instinct, Greaves? Or thinking with your brain? "He's all we've got right now, Taylor, and the evidence against him is pretty damning."

"I suppose so."

Nick hated when his assistant didn't sound convinced.

"I've got the final report from the coroner on Emma Joyce, sir." Taylor handed Nick a sheet of paper, a few lines written in a tidy hand marching across its surface. "Nothing different than what Dr. Harris told you, Mr. Greaves. And Dr. Letterman agrees that she was probably dead several hours before Mrs. Davies found her body. Although you'll hear all this at the inquest this afternoon."

"Why don't you attend for me, Taylor. Tell the coroner's jury what you've found."

"Yes, sir," he replied, exhaling. "So that's it, then. Mr. Ingram wanted revenge against Sebastian Carr, but ended up killing the wrong person. And innocent Emma Joyce paid the price for what she'd seen Friday evening."

"That or jealousy."

"Pretty terrible."

"It is, Taylor." Nick kicked at the drawer, even though it hadn't inched open again. "It is."

• • •

I'm gonna get fired. I'm gonna get fired. I might be doing this to help Mrs. Davies, but shoot.

"I'm gonna get fired," Owen muttered aloud.

He'd stopped at Mrs. Davies's house to hand off the tin of chocolate to Addie, who was mighty confused by it, and had needed to come all the way back down Montgomery to the museum. Meaning he'd been gone from the store way longer than Mr. Roesler's patience would allow.

Fired, for sure.

Sighing, he stared up at the building housing the Pacific Museum of Anatomy. On the corner of Pine and Montgomery, it occupied a section of Eureka Hall. The building's tall street-level windows overlooked the wagons and horsecars and folks passing by in one of the busiest parts of town. Should draw all sorts of curiosity seekers through its doors. In fact, right then a hunched fellow was peering at the front door, probably debating if he should go in and see the sights. He didn't debate for long and charged inside.

Owen swallowed, his tongue sticking like it always did when he was nervous. Not just about getting fired—he was pretty certain Mr. Roesler wasn't going to forgive him this time like he did last time Owen skipped out on work in order to help Mrs. Davies—but about going into the museum himself. He'd heard about the weird objects they had on display. The insides of ladies. All sorts of dissected parts of people, including a brain. An entire room dedicated to the effect of diseases like syphilis on folks, meant just for medical men to examine. Although one of his mates had been able to visit the room and he wasn't a doctor. Not by any stretch. Skeletons from executed criminals. The foot from an Irish giant. Owen didn't know whether to believe the foot was real, since if there'd ever been giants in Ireland, he was sure his pa would've told him. Pretty sure, at least.

To gather courage, Owen sucked in a long, deep breath. Not a good idea, since the street hadn't been recently cleaned of manure and there was a foul stink from a nearby butcher's. Coughing, he hurried across the road and charged straight into the museum like the hunched fellow had done.

Along the walls and in the middle of the room stood glass cases, lots and lots of glass cases filled with all those body parts he'd been told about, and a goodly quantity of bell jars with more oddities inside them. The cases were covered in fingerprints like folks had tried to touch the contents, only to be stopped by the glass. Mr. Roesler would be horrified to see so many smudges on a display case. But these cases weren't filled with tempting chocolates and sugared almonds. No sir, not at all. He wasn't even sure he should be looking at the nearby models of naked women. His landlady would say the exhibits were obscene. Although Owen thought they were sorta fascinating, too.

"Twenty-five cents," said a man who'd appeared out of nowhere, making Owen jump.

"What?"

The fellow, in a dark checked suit that was too small for him, stuck out his hand. His fingers were spindly and freakishly long. Maybe when the fellow died, the proprietor would cut off *his* hand and put it on display. "The admission fee. Twenty-five cents."

Owen rooted through the pocket where he'd stashed Mrs. Davies's money and handed him a quarter. Twenty-five cents was an awful lot.

"Would you like a copy of our descriptive catalog?"

Not if it cost more money. "I'm just here because, well, you see, I work for the Carrs. And I overheard Mr. Sebastian talking about this place. I had to come and see for myself." Owen fixed a wide-eyed look on his face. Which wasn't difficult.

The fellow with the spindly fingers grinned. "Dr. Jordan has collected the most amazing specimens for the education and edification of the good citizens of San Francisco."

The good male citizens, that was.

"Perhaps you are here to gaze upon our cyclops child," the fellow continued, guiding Owen over to the nearest display. An arm that had been taken apart, all its insides exposed, and was making Owen nauseated. "Or the exquisite dissection showing twins in the womb. Our many fetal preparations cannot be compared to any others', Dr. Jordan declares."

Owen was curious about one thing. "Is it true about the foot of the Irish giant?"

He guffawed. "Why, yes. It is in the corner over there."

Maybe he should have a peek before he left. "And is it also true what they say?" he asked. "That the doctor, you know, can help a fellow?"

"Aren't you a little young to be worried about having problems like that?" the man asked, screwing up his eyes to scan Owen.

Owen's cheeks got as hot as if he'd been plunged into a fire. "I'm not asking for myself, of course. I'm not worried." He chuckled. Not that he'd ever had a chance to test his, umm, manliness. "I'm asking for my older brother. He's been having trouble with his wife and he's too shy to come here. I thought I'd help him out."

"Ah. I see. Marital difficulties." The man nodded. "The doctor frequently consults with gentlemen about such issues."

"So he can help?" Owen asked. "I didn't know whether or not to believe Mr. Sebastian, because I couldn't imagine him coming here. He seems healthy enough to me."

The fellow sniggered coarsely. Owen didn't like the sound. "You can't tell by looking at a man if he's going to have such problems."

"So he *has* been in here to speak with Dr. Jordan. I never would've reckoned it." Owen shook his head. "Mr. Sebastian is going to be married soon. Bet he's troubled about that."

"About the wedding night, you mean."

"Yeah. Exactly."

"Well, Dr. Jordan set him up, so he should be fine enough," the man replied. "If he isn't, Dr. Jordan will be happy to provide more treatment in total confidence."

"I'll tell Mr. Sebastian that. Thank you," Owen said, turning and heading back out.

"Wait! What about your brother? Wasn't he why you came in here?" the fellow called after him.

Owen was out on the street before he remembered that he'd wanted to see the giant's foot.

Shoot.

• • •

The curtains on the upper floor windows of the Ingrams' house were thrown wide, admitting the sunshine that made a pleasant change from the recent dreariness and rain. The house had a nice southerly exposure on a stretch of the road that was not quite as busy as other sections of it. It would likely have sun-lit rooms perfect for painting in. Only one way to find out. Celia waited for a lumber delivery wagon to lurch up the street, and dashed across.

A young woman—slim, petite, her straight chestnut-colored hair worn parted in the middle and bound in what the Americans called a waterfall chignon at the nape of her neck—answered the bell. A trace of purple paint was smeared along her jaw where she'd rubbed at it. She was strikingly lovely.

"Can I help you?" she asked, taking in Celia's widow's weeds as though assessing how well she and her black gown might appear on canvas.

"I am Mrs. Walford." Barbara's last name and Celia's maiden name. As was abundantly clear, she was becoming too well known by her real name. Infuriating newspaper articles. "Are you Miss Louise Ingram?"

"Yes."

"Oh, good. I was hoping I had the correct address," she said. "I came by on Friday, after I'd attended a lengthy afternoon tea in memoriam of my recently departed husband, to see if you were in, but no one answered my knock. Around six, I believe. Or perhaps a trifle later."

Miss Ingram's fingers—also paint-spattered—gripped the edge of the door. She kept her right hand out of view in the pocket of her apron.

"You did? I didn't hear your knock and Truda wasn't here then. I'm sorry I missed you," she said. "Why did you wish to speak with me?"

Celia inched forward across the threshold, forcing Miss Ingram to step back in order to avoid getting crushed by Celia's encroaching skirts. "You were highly recommended to me as someone whom I could commission to do a painting. For my parlor."

Brilliant, Celia. What do you do if she agrees? She could not afford fifty cents' worth of chocolates. She could hardly afford a painting.

Louise Ingram's grip on the door tightened. "I am not painting for commission at the moment, Mrs. Walford."

"The work can wait a few weeks. Or months. Whichever suits you best, Miss Ingram." Celia took another step into the hallway until she was entirely inside the house. "I would like to see some of your work first, however, before I decide whether or not to employ you."

"I . . . who gave you my name?"

"A friend. I do not recall precisely who." Celia looked around her. "This is a lovely home. Do you live here alone?" What an intrusive question. Surprisingly, Miss Ingram answered.

"No, I don't. My brother lives here with me."

When he was not in jail accused of multiple crimes. "How comforting for you, I am sure."

"Yes." Miss Ingram struggled to close the door, which jammed on the threshold. "This door. Tony keeps forgetting to repair it."

The space was very tidy, and if the rest of the house was like the parlor, the Ingrams appeared to have few furnishings or bits of bric-a-brac. Siblings living in straightened circumstances, was how Celia read the situation. Their household economy no doubt impacted by the damage to Louise Ingram's painting hand.

Celia strolled over to a landscape hung above the settee in the parlor. It was a watercolor depicting a river and mountains, a more sedate rendering than the grand paintings of Yosemite that crowded every city art gallery. Celia found that she liked it. "Is this one of your pieces?"

"Yes, back when I did paintings like that as opposed to the theater scenery I paint now. That I used to paint," she corrected.

"My friend did tell me that you'd had an unfortunate accident, resulting in a temporary cessation of your work with the local theaters." Celia smiled sympathetically. "I am so sorry to hear that, as it appears you are quite talented."

Miss Ingram removed her damaged hand from where she had been hiding it in the depths of her apron pocket. The scars from the vitriol attack were red and ugly, and Celia wondered why it wasn't wrapped. Perhaps bandaging felt uncomfortable. Celia had to stop herself from recommending a poultice that might offer some relief. She was not here as a nurse.

"I doubt I'll ever again be able to paint backdrops at the theaters with the damage to my hand, Mrs. Walford."

"I'd not be so quick to dismiss the prospect, Miss Ingram," Celia said. "I have an acquaintance who had burned her hand upon a hot poker and who despaired of ever being able to engage in the correspondence she was so fond of. Despite her distress, she did heal and was back to composing letters as frequently as before." She had no such acquaintance, but she had long ago learned that a patient's faith in a cure could be as important as the cure itself, if not more important. "You must at least feel some relief from seeing the perpetrator behind bars."

"The boy who was accused and convicted died in prison just the other day, Mrs. Walford. I am convinced he was not guilty, though," she said. "I don't mean to suggest that he didn't toss the contents of that bottle on me, because he did. I saw him clearly. But I firmly believe he had no idea what was in that bottle." Miss Ingram frowned. "How scared he looked when I screamed from the pain. The judge, the jury, though . . . They wouldn't listen to my testimony. I tried to save David Alonso. I truly did."

"My apologies, Miss Ingram. I did not mean to remind you of such a traumatic event."

She clenched her damaged hand, the stretching of the unhealed scars making her wince. Could she have gripped a sharp weapon and sliced Emma Joyce's throat with it? Not easily.

"I can't forget the event, Mrs. Walford. I live with the scars and the pain every moment of every day."

"Still."

"Maybe I'll be like your acquaintance and recover fully," she said. "I do keep trying to paint. Some days are better than others, even though I can't keep a good grip on the brushes most of the time."

"Hope, then."

Miss Ingram considered her hand for a moment before using it to gesture in the direction of the staircase. "Let me show you what other work I have completed. I can't promise that I would be able to paint as well for several months, though. If I do recover like your friend."

"That timeline is perfectly acceptable, Miss Ingram."

She led Celia upstairs. Morning sunshine slanted into her studio. The space smelled of handmade pine frames and vinegar, a bowl of which had been set out to absorb the sulfurous aroma of egg tempera paints. Paintings in various stages of completion leaned against walls and covered nearly every open surface. It had been years since Celia had been inside a painter's atelier. Not since her aunt had concocted the idea that Celia should receive painting lessons, thereby enhancing her limited womanly talents, and had taken her to a nearby artist's studio for an introduction. Celia had not been opposed to the notion, she'd merely been horribly incompetent and her instructor had given up after a handful of classes. Her aunt had never again suggested artistic endeavors.

"These are so lovely," Celia commented, flipping through a stack of paintings of a fanciful Italian village.

"Renderings of backdrops I'd been hired to provide. The attack occurred before I could start work on the full-sized canvases." She tucked her damaged hand inside her apron pocket again.

Sympathy tugged at Celia's heart. Of all the wrongs that could have been done to Louise Ingram, taking away her ability to paint was the most wounding. Perhaps that had been what the perpetrator had intended. If she or her brother had plotted to poison Sebastian Carr, Celia was no longer certain she could blame them. In fact, she was beginning to feel guilty about asking the young woman any questions at all.

"You must really despise him, whomever it is you think was actually responsible for the attack," she said softly.

"I've given the police his name. They haven't done anything about my suspicions."

"I have had encounters with the local constabulary once or twice, Miss Ingram, and I find that they do try their best."

"Their best has not been good enough, Mrs. Walford."

"Perhaps they merely require more time." Celia wandered over to the easel propped in front of the window. "Is this what you are currently working on?"

"Trying to work on. Yes."

"What an unusual subject for a painting, Miss Ingram," Celia said. "A street scene of San Francisco. I do not believe I have ever noticed a painting like this in an art gallery before."

"My wilderness paintings used to sell well, Mrs. Walford, but I can no longer afford to travel and create new ones. Nor will I be able to find the necessary funds to travel in future, it seems."

Louise Ingram had planted herself in the center of the room, as if she didn't wish to look at the painting on the easel. At *any* of the paintings in her studio. Sad memories of better days.

"Unless you heal, which I believe you shall."

"As you keep saying."

Yes. "You know, Miss Ingram, the longer I am in your presence, the more I am convinced that I have met you before," Celia said. "Were you at a masquerade ball on Friday given by the Carrs, by any chance?"

She stiffened. "The Carrs would never invite me to a masquerade. You've confused me for somebody else."

Celia released a gasp, raising her fingers to her mouth. "I now recall who you accused of having that boy toss the vitriol on you, Miss Ingram. You accused Sebastian Carr. It was in the newspapers. How silly of me to have forgotten. And it was *he* who someone attempted to poison at that party on Friday. Dreadful."

She narrowed her eyes. "Who are you? Why are you asking all these questions? What do you want? Not a painting, I think."

"I need to know about your relationship with Sebastian Carr," Celia answered, dropping all pretense of being a slightly daft well-off young widow in need of an artist.

"Did the police send you? Is that why you're here questioning me? Pretending that you want to buy one of my paintings?" She leaned close to Celia, the smell of turpentine lifting off her clothing. "Who the hell are you?"

"Celia Davies."

"The woman the newspapers have written about," she said. "Don't you know that the police have arrested Tony for trying to poison him? For murdering Emma? You are too late with your questions, Miss Davies."

"Emma Joyce had been pregnant, Miss Ingram. Were you aware of that?" Celia asked.

"She was?"

"You were not aware."

"No." She retreated from Celia, ending up in the doorway to her atelier, her face obscured by the shadows cast by the doorframe. It was dark and quiet out in the staircase, the light that streamed into her studio not reaching the depths. An empty house seemingly filled with sorrows and regrets. "But that explains . . . so much."

"Who was the father, Miss Ingram? Your brother denies it was his child."

"Of course it wasn't Tony's child."

"Sebastian, then. Is that why you went to the Carrs' on Friday, Miss Ingram?" Celia asked softly. "To confront the man you still love about a woman he may have gotten with child? The same man who'd paid a gullible Mexican boy to scar you with vitriol?"

"It couldn't have been Sebastian. It couldn't . . ." She paled. "She knew. Dammit, she knew."

The other woman bolted for the hallway, taking Celia by surprise. She was halfway down the stairs by the time Celia had collected herself and chased after her.

"Stop, Miss Ingram!" Celia grappled with her skirts, more cumbersome than the lighter dress that Louise Ingram was wearing. "Stop!"

Louise had reached the front door but struggled to free it, the bottom catching on the threshold.

Celia stumbled down the last steps and caught up to her. "Louise—"

The other woman delivered a well-placed kick to Celia's knee, staggering her. Louise yanked the door open and hurtled out into the street.

Celia's knee protested as she scrambled to her feet and lurched outside. Owen stood across the street, his mouth agape.

"Owen! Stop her!"

"Ma'am!" He dashed across the street, nearly colliding with a horse and rider. "Ma'am, are you okay?"

"I will be fine. We need to stop Louise Ingram."

"Shoot." He took off running. Louise Ingram had already disappeared around the corner.

Celia gave her knee a hasty massage and limped after him. She only made it about a dozen yards, her halting progress having been noted by everyone she passed—only one of whom asked if she required assistance—when Owen returned.

He shook his head. "She got away, ma'am. Sorry."

"Owen, please close the Ingrams' front door, which I left open, and hail me a cab," she said. "We need to go to the police station."

☙ Chapter 17 ❧

Knuckles rapped on the door to the detectives' office and Mullahey poked his head around the corner. "Some fellow claimin' to be a friend of Owen Cassidy's is here to talk to you, Mr. Greaves. Angus MacNamara."

Taylor scuttled into the office behind him. "He wouldn't tell me what he wanted, sir."

"Show him in, Mullahey."

A short, gaunt fellow sauntered into the room. "I've got information about that crime on Friday at the Carrs' place, Officer. The poisoning."

"Oh?" Nick asked.

"I was helping deliver wine to the Carrs' party and saw one of the servants talking with a mysterious person on the back stairs. She was upset to find them there." He waggled his eyebrows for effect. "They must've been the poisoner, Officer."

"We're already aware of her and what she saw, Mr. MacNamara," Nick said.

"Bloody Cassidy," he hissed, adding a few more choice curse words.

"Mr. MacNamara, while you are in my office, maybe you can answer a question." Nick retrieved the Turk costume from his drawer. "You appear to have been very observant on Friday. Did you notice a fellow wearing this outfit that night? Others noticed, but from a distance. No chance to get a look at the man's face. You might've been closer, since you were outside."

He held it up for MacNamara to examine.

"That? No. Can't say that I did," he answered. "Lots of strange getups but nobody wearing that."

"Thank you, Mr. MacNamara."

He stuck out his hand. "So, can I have the reward, Officer?"

"There's no reward, Mr. MacNamara," Taylor said.

He cursed again, in both Irish and in English this time. "Cassidy lied to me."

"Did he tell you there was one?" Nick asked, doubting the kid had.

Grumbling, the man stomped off.

"Would've been useful to find a witness able to identify Mr. Ingram in that costume, wouldn't it, sir?"

"Yes, Taylor," he said, stuffing the costume back into his desk drawer.

"Good day, Mrs. Davies," Mullahey called out in the main station room.

Now what?

Taylor chuckled. Celia claimed that she never could read Nick's facial expressions, but his assistant never seemed to have any trouble.

"Ah, Mr. Greaves. Mr. Taylor," she said, hobbling into the office.

"What have you done to your leg, Mrs. Davies?" Nick asked.

"A minor accident." Taylor pulled out the chair in front of Nick's desk and helped her sit. "I have news for you."

Of course she did. The only thing that kept Captain Eagan from regularly complaining about her involvement in Nick's cases was the fact that the police department was getting so much work for free. If her name continued to turn up in the *California Police Gazette*, though, Nick expected his boss's benevolence would finally run dry.

"Two items," she said once he'd retaken his chair. "Firstly, based on questioning conducted by Owen at the Pacific Museum of Anatomy, it appears unlikely that Sebastian Carr was capable of fathering Emma Joyce's child. Not impossible but unlikely. The doctor there has "treated" him for, shall we say, inadequate male vigor."

Taylor blushed; he might never get used to Celia's blunt talk.

"You have to stop roping Cassidy into your schemes, Mrs. Davies."

"Do I?" Her pale eyes sparkled defiantly. "Owen is very helpful, Mr. Greaves. I need not inform you of that fact. Although, you will undoubtedly have to vouch for him with Mr. Roesler again, I am sorry to say."

It wouldn't be helpful to be angry with either of them, Nick reminded himself. "And secondly?"

"In case Owen did not succeed, I approached Miss Ingram on the topic of Sebastian Carr's virility," she said. "I also desired to question her about our crimes. I'd not had an opportunity as yet."

"Celia—"

"However, in the course of questioning Miss Ingram, she became very upset," she said. "She cried out 'she knew' and ran off. She eluded Owen's attempts to catch her."

"Does her getaway have something to do with why you're limping, Mrs. Davies?"

"Miss Ingram delivers a sturdy kick, and apparently my skirt and crinoline are not thick enough to provide my knees protection."

"You're fortunate she was only wielding her foot, Mrs. Davies, and not a weapon."

"An unnecessary reminder, Mr. Greaves."

"Who was Miss Ingram talking about, though, Mrs. Davies?" Taylor asked.

"I wish I could say."

"Taylor, find out from Tony Ingram where his sister might have gone. Who the woman might be who 'knew,'" Nick said. "And get Mullahey and a few of the boys to start searching for her."

"She was wearing a dark gray dress, Mr. Taylor. No cloak or bonnet," Celia explained.

Taylor tucked away his notebook and sprinted from the office.

"By the way, Tony Ingram has explained blood on the bottom of one of his shoes by admitting that he went to visit Emma yesterday morning, but only because he was worried about her," Nick said. "He claims he arrived there after she'd been murdered. He was the one who left the window open in her room."

"I see."

"He's trying to cover for killing her, of course," he said. "And his sister running off doesn't help his case."

"I do not believe we can be certain what Miss Ingram's actions mean, Nicholas. Furthermore, I have a question that has been bothering me ever since you found the caftan and turban," she said. "If Mr.

Ingram had worn those items on Friday, why did he leave them where you could easily discover them?"

"He wasn't expecting us to come and search his house," Nick said, instantly wanting to retract the words.

"I can see from your face that you do not believe he would be so careless."

She *was* getting better at reading his expressions.

Celia leaned forward. "What if it was *not* him at the Carrs' on Friday dressed in a Turk costume?" she asked. "I am aware that he was late to the theater that evening. I am aware that you found the costume in his bedchamber. But, still."

"We haven't found any other costumes like it, Celia," Nick said. "Taylor asked at the American Theater and a few other ones. It has to be the one and he has to have been the person wearing it."

"Worth noting." She primly folded her hands in her lap. "However, I have begun to question Dr. Schneider's reliability as a witness."

This was going to be good. "I can't wait to hear why you've changed your mind about him."

"I shall explain," she said. "The way that I prodded him for clues may have encouraged him to invent the fellow. Furthermore, the doctor may have attired this individual in an Oriental outfit simply because he does not like Orientals. He certainly did not treat Barbara with much respect."

"But Miss Bremerton confirmed what he saw."

"She may have seized on this suspicious stranger in order to protect the person she believes is actually responsible, Nicholas. Perhaps, for instance, she is acquainted with Paulina Lyons, comprehends the young woman's motive, and seeks to deflect attention from her. Or there is another person she wished to protect. Emma, for instance," she suggested. "I should inform you that Dr. Schneider wears spectacles. I wonder if he is vain enough to have left them at home the evening of the masquerade. Or if he could not comfortably wear his glasses and a mask at the same time."

"I wish you'd thought of this earlier, Celia," he said testily and got to his feet. Her information might explain, though, why Angus MacNamara hadn't noticed anybody in the caftan and turban that night. Because there hadn't been anybody wearing a Turk costume that night.

"As do I, I can assure you." She rose as well. "How might I assist?"

"You can go home and stay there, that's how."

She perked her chin; she wouldn't be staying home if she found a reason to leave.

"Might I ask where are you off to, Mr. Greaves?"

Back to formalities. Sighing, Nick grabbed his hat off his desk. "To test Dr. Schneider's eyesight."

. . .

Where might Louise Ingram have gone? To confront the person, the "she," about her supposed knowledge was all that Celia could logically conclude. She lifted her skirts out of the way and climbed the steps of her house. But who was that woman? There were several candidates—Miss Bremerton, Miss Vanmeter, the mysterious Paulina Lyons. Perhaps even Mrs. Tilden or one of the Carrs' maids—and some Celia might not even be aware of. Hopefully Mr. Taylor or another of the officers located Miss Ingram before she found that individual and . . .

"And harmed her," Celia murmured as she reached the front door.

Addie flung it open before Celia could turn the handle. "A fellow calling himself Mr. Bell is waiting for you in your examination room, ma'am."

"No need to look so alarmed, Addie. He has located Paulina Lyons." At last.

She handed off her mantle and bonnet, corrected a few loosened strands of hair, and strode into the room.

"Mr. Bell. Good afternoon."

He turned away from his inspection of her medical supply cabinet.

"Mrs. Davies," he greeted. "I was just admiring your clinic here. Most commendable."

"Nursing is my first and highest calling, Mr. Bell. Not that of being some sort of detective, even though I regularly find myself in that role," she said. "I take it you are here because you know where I might find Miss Lyons."

"I have the young woman's address," he said, patting the left breast of his coat, the location of an inside pocket. "But I need to understand your intentions toward her."

"Are you wondering if I mean to hand her over to the police?"

He inclined his head.

"I will if I firmly suspect she is guilty of a crime, Mr. Bell," she said. "At the moment, however, I merely intend to question Miss Lyons about what took place on Friday at the Carrs' masquerade ball. Specifically, why she fled that night without explanation. Many people suspect her of complicity in a crime."

He cocked his head to one side. "Why might she speak to you, Mrs. Davies, if she's not been willing to share what she knows with the police?"

"I have had surprising success with witnesses in the past, Mr. Bell, that is all I can say," she replied. "Where might I find her?"

"Here." He withdrew a folded piece of paper from the inner pocket and handed it to her. "And her name isn't Miss Lyons. It's Paulina Alonso."

"Alonso?" The same last name as that of the Mexican boy who'd tossed vitriol on Louise Ingram.

"Yes, ma'am. Alonso."

It couldn't be a coincidence. Neither could it be mere chance that she had carefully planned to be inside the Carrs' house on Friday, assisting with the ball. *Well now, Miss Alonso, are you a witness or a criminal?*

"It's my understanding she works at the North Cosmopolitan School," he said.

"As a teacher?"

Celia must have sounded as though she was taken aback, because Mr. Bell scowled. "Just because she is not a white woman of British descent doesn't mean she can't teach, Mrs. Davies."

"I did not mean to suggest that, Mr. Bell, but you must admit the situation is unusual for a female of her background." Although Miss Alonso would be more likely to be employed by a school dedicated to instructing the children of French and German immigrants in their own language, among others, and which might welcome a non-British female. "Especially when you take into account that she hired herself out as a kitchen servant to work at the Carrs' on Friday. Not the usual actions of a teacher."

"I can't disagree, ma'am."

She'd have to take the North Beach horsecar to Greenwich and walk the rest of the way to get to the North Cosmopolitan School. *Hobble* the rest of the way. Perhaps she should spend the money and hire a cab. Two in one day. The expenses were piling up.

"Thank you, Mr. Bell, for helping me find her," she said with a grateful smile. "How can I repay you?"

"Not with money, if that is what you're considering."

"Then would you like an exclusive interview, should helping me locate Miss Alonso prove crucial to solving the crime?"

"Not usually what I publish in the *Elevator*, ma'am, but I'll let you know," he said. "And I'm sure you'll be able to return the favor to me someday."

"I am in your debt."

He tapped his fingertips to his forehead and exited the house.

Addie darted from the kitchen into the examination room the instant the front door closed behind him. "Weel?"

"He has located Miss Lyons, whose real name is Miss Alonso. She has to be the sister of the boy hired to toss vitriol on Miss Ingram. The last name is far from common," Celia replied. "Mr. Bell was concerned that my sole purpose in attempting to locate the woman is to hand her over to the police. The use of a false name and her likely relationship with David Alonso does not predispose me to think that she is completely innocent, however."

Addie peered at her. "But that *is* your sole purpose, ma'am. To find her and hand her over to the police so that Mr. Greaves can question her."

Celia exhaled. "Yes, Addie. If I am honest with myself, it is."

• • •

"Excuse me, Detective, but can you explain again why you are here?" Dr. Schneider peered at Nick through his spectacles.

Schneider's examination room was stuffed with more forceps and syringes and knives and labeled glass medicine bottles than Celia's. The overfilled cabinets pressed in from all sides and made Nick twitchy. It didn't help that the smells—the faint tang of decay along with the sharp bite of medical compounds—reminded Nick of the hospital he'd been sent to after the war. A memory he'd prefer to not have.

"You attended the Carrs' masquerade on Friday, correct?" he asked.

"I should've guessed that is why you're here. What a horrible incident." The doctor shook his head. "To think that someone would try to poison Mr. Carr. Do you need my medical opinion in the matter?"

"You told a colleague that you'd noticed a suspicious fellow wearing a tunic and turban that evening."

"I told Mrs. Davies that I observed a mysterious fellow in an oriental costume, yes. Is she a colleague?"

Schneider didn't even try to pretend that was a serious question. "It was dark out, though, by the time you'd observed this person."

He stretched to his full height. "I know what I saw."

Nick gestured at his spectacles. "Were you wearing your glasses that evening, Dr. Schneider?"

"What sort of a question is that?"

"Were you or were you not?"

"No, I was not," he said. "My mask didn't fit over them."

"Ah," said Nick, staring at the doctor long enough to make a bead of sweat pop on the doctor's forehead. "Maybe you won't mind participating in a little test, Doctor. If you'd take off your glasses and come over to the window with me."

He'd stationed one of the neighborhood kids, excited by the prospect of earning some money, on the sidewalk across the street. Approximately the same distance as the space between the Carrs' porch and the side yard of their house, according to Nick's best estimation.

Reluctantly, Schneider got to his feet and joined him at the window.

"Now, Dr. Schneider. Can you tell me if that person across the street is a male or a female? An adult or a child?"

The kid was standing sideways so it wasn't obvious if they were wearing a dress or a pair of wide canvas pants, and Nick had asked the girl—who'd tied up her hair and was tall and skinny—to pull her unadorned brimmed hat low on her face. But it wasn't hard to tell it was a girl. Not in daylight. And not if you had decent eyesight.

Schneider cleared his throat and peered out the window. "It is, well . . . anyone can see that it is a young man."

Nick waved at the girl and she ran off, her skirts kicking wide.

"A simple mistake, Detective," he said, scowling. "And I do not comprehend what you mean to prove by this exercise."

"Shall I explain, Dr. Schneider?" Nick asked, turning to face him. "You didn't actually see a man wearing a tunic and turban outside the Carrs' house on Friday night. Did you?"

Jutting his chin, Schneider grabbed his spectacles and put them back on. "I may have mistaken that girl out there for a boy, but I know what I saw Friday evening."

"Lying to the police isn't advisable, Doctor." Even though folks did it all the time.

"I . . . I . . ." He harrumphed. "All right. Mrs. Davies asked me if I had any important clues concerning the crime. I believed I had seen a shady character. I may have been mistaken."

What you actually may have done is want to seem more informed and useful than you really are.

"Thank you, Dr. Schneider. I'll see myself out."

Nick exited the examination room, striding past the fellow's wife, who was frantically yelping that somebody needed to explain what was going on, and out onto the street. He slapped his hat onto his head. Now to speak to Irene Bremerton.

• • •

Celia was grimy and tired by the time she arrived at the North Cosmopolitan School, a substantial brick building with tall narrow windows situated on the northern downslope of Russian Hill. The school was run by the renowned Miss Kate Kennedy, who campaigned—unsuccessfully, so far—for equal pay for female teachers. If Celia wasn't preoccupied with locating Miss Alonso and questioning her, she would have loved to meet Miss Kennedy.

Her aching knee rebelling, Celia climbed the steps to the front doors. Her heels clicked across the encaustic-tiled entry space, intersected at a right angle by a wide corridor. The school had been erected only last year, and it seemed to retain the aroma of fresh paint and sawn wood. A low hum of voices echoed out of the four large classrooms arrayed on either side of the corridor. From one of the rooms came the sound of children singing, some off-key. Straight ahead stood a waiting area, and Celia entered.

A woman with broad shoulders, the part in her dark hair so perfectly straight it could have been formed with the assistance of a ruler, sat at the desk guarding the principal's office at her back.

She looked up from her paperwork. "Are you here to collect Thomas? He's with Miss Chapuis. He's been very sick."

"I am sorry to hear that, but I'm not here for Thomas. I am here to speak with Miss Alonso," Celia said. "I am her cousin and I only recently received news of her brother's funeral."

"She took Friday off work," the woman said. "I believe that was when the funeral was held. You've missed it, ma'am."

Which confirmed that Paulina Alonso was David's sister, because how many other Alonso boys would have so recently died?

"Yes, of course. Truly terrible." Celia sadly shook her head. "I merely wish to have a brief conversation with her about a donation I would like to make in the boy's honor."

The woman raised her eyebrows, which simultaneously shifted her hairline. "Why interrupt Miss Alonso at work rather than visit her at her home?"

"If I may be honest, I was afraid she'd not answer my knock," Celia replied. "You see, my side of the family has been out of touch with her and David for so long. But then this does happen in families, does it not? Estrangements. However, I wish to make it up to her and to his memory."

"Maybe you didn't hear how he died," the woman said, her voice tinged with the malice that accompanied censorious gossip. "From a sickness while he was in prison for assaulting a woman with acid."

Celia gasped. "How dreadful! I remember him as a young child. He was such a good boy."

The other woman clicked her tongue against her teeth.

"Nonetheless, might you direct me to Miss Alonso's classroom?" Celia asked. "If it is convenient and I will not disturb her and her pupils."

"She's been excused from drilling the students on their penmanship today—she does have a lovely hand—due to her grief over her brother's death. Miss Kennedy is very generous," she said. "You'll find Miss Alonso in the presently empty classroom next to us, grading compositions."

Celia thanked her and turned the direction the woman had indicated. Through the glass inserted in the classroom door to Celia's left, she spied numerous children leaning over their work, at least forty or more. A few were reciting lessons in German. The room opposite was empty, save for a young woman at the desk situated atop a small, raised platform.

Celia stepped inside without knocking. "Miss Alonso?"

Young—younger than Celia was, she'd guess—Paulina Alonso wore a simple green dress that brought out the warmth of her pretty face, which was framed by thick reddish hair tied back in a chignon. Her prettiness was marred, however, by her bloodshot eyes. She had been crying.

"Yes. Who are you?"

"I am sorry to disturb you," Celia said, closing the door behind her. Miss Alonso's gaze flicked at the door before returning to Celia's face.

"I am very busy, as you can see." Her tone was calm yet firm, perfect for a teacher, and her voice held no perceptible accent indicating her heritage. Could it be the voice of a murderer? "What do you want?"

"I am Mrs. Celia Davies and I have been searching for you, Miss Alonso," she answered. "Or I should say Miss Lyons?"

CHAPTER 18

Paulina Alonso blanched. She had to admit her real identity; Celia had caught her out.

"You have confused me with someone else," the young woman replied.

"I am afraid I have not, Miss Alonso. I know that you worked at the Carrs' masquerade ball on Friday under the name of Paulina Lyons," Celia responded. "I also know that you are David Alonso's sister, and have every reason to wish to harm Sebastian Carr because of your brother's death."

Miss Alonso got to her feet. She was shaking and clasped her hands tightly to halt their trembling. "How did you find me?"

"I'd rather not say. The person told me in confidence. I hope you understand."

"I do *not* understand. I also do not understand what you want."

"I want your help," Celia said. "I *need* your help. A man is in jail for attempting to poison Sebastian Carr on Friday at the masquerade ball, but I believe he is not guilty."

"Does being innocent keep a person from being accused, Mrs. Davies? Does being innocent mean there will be justice?" she asked bitterly. "Or maybe this man isn't a Mexican boy who has no hope for either."

"I am aware how unevenly justice can be meted out, Miss Alonso, but allowing an innocent man to be convicted for attempting to poison Mr. Carr will not bring back your brother."

"Are you wanting me to confess instead?"

Celia stepped closer to her. "Tell my why you were at that party, Miss Alonso. Tell me what you intended that night."

"That *is* what you want. My confession," she said. "Let the man who has been jailed prove his innocence without forcing me to admit to something I didn't do."

"Did you go to the Carrs' in order to confront Sebastian, hoping he might feel remorse about David?" Celia persisted. "Or did you go there to obtain revenge for your brother's death, Miss Alonso? So you slipped inside Sebastian Carr's room and added arsenic to the vanilla he uses for his coffee. Who told you about his habit?"

The other woman narrowed her dark eyes. "I don't know anything about Sebastian Carr's habits. I don't know anything about the Carrs at all, aside from their cruelty. Aside from their willingness to let my brother stand accused of a terrible crime and then die in jail."

"Paulina, please. Please tell me why you were at the Carrs' house on Friday."

"I needed the work."

"Which does not explain why you picked that particular event and used a false name while you were at it," she said. "I'm also aware that you were hunting for someone that evening, Miss Alonso. I've been told that you repeatedly went into the passageway outside the kitchen as though searching for that individual. Sebastian Carr, correct?"

"People were spying on me?"

"Not intentionally."

Miss Alonso rolled her lips between her teeth and studied Celia, the distant hum of children's voices seeping into the room. And then her shoulders eased; she had decided to be honest.

"I'll tell you what happened, Mrs. Davies, but I'd like to know why you even care."

"Because justice matters to me, Miss Alonso. A great deal," she replied. "And the police listen to me."

"Do they? You must not be Mexican," she said cynically. "And do not suppose I don't suffer prejudice because I look Irish, courtesy of my mother. I witnessed what my father endured. As well as as what happened to David. Who was my half brother."

"I see."

"Do you? I wonder." She turned to look out the window, which had a view of Filbert Street and the crowd of houses beyond it that tumbled toward the Golden Gate. "I was so angry the day David died. I went to the Carrs' business, wanting to yell at someone. Anyone. They threw me out." She paused to draw in a long breath before continuing. "That same day, I learned that the Carrs were seeking temporary help for the masquerade ball. It felt as though God had ordained that I would have my chance to confront Sebastian Carr. I never managed to."

"You took a great risk going to the Carrs' house, Miss Alonso. Any one of them could have recognized you from your attendance at your brother's trial."

"I did not go to his trial, Mrs. Davies," she said, sounding regretful. "I did not live in San Francisco yet. I moved here only a couple of weeks ago, when Miss Kennedy took me on."

"Did David ever tell you who'd paid him to toss vitriol onto Miss Ingram?" Celia asked. "He never informed the police, which is why Sebastian Carr was never formally accused."

"It was dark and the person tried to conceal their identity. David was scared to tell me that much. They must have threatened him," she said. "But the janitress working here gave me Sebastian Carr's name, Mrs. Davies. The story was in all the newspapers. A scandal involving a rich man. The type of story people enjoy talking about."

"Was David the sort of person who'd accept money from a complete stranger to toss an unknown liquid onto someone else as a prank?"

She looked at Celia over her shoulder. "Not the David I thought I knew, but a hard life can change people."

Hadn't Owen said as much so often?

Celia considered her, a young woman for whom the promise of a new life with her brother in San Francisco had come to nothing. However, Miss Alonso appeared to be someone not readily shattered by her misfortunes.

"Did you plan to only confront Sebastian Carr that evening or to poison him, Miss Alonso?"

"Why would I ever dream I could find a way to poison him, even if I wished to?" she asked. "You are right, Mrs. Davies, that I cannot bring back my brother. So why attempt revenge, something so stupid and so unlikely to succeed and which would only bring more trouble?"

"If you'd done nothing wrong, though, why flee when Jenny Bernard died?"

"I *knew* I'd be suspected, once people found out my real name. And see? Here you are, questioning me," she said. "I was in the kitchen when I heard that Jenny had been in Sebastian Carr's room. That she'd drunk an entire bottle of the vanilla extract he kept there and had fallen sick. Mrs. Tilden immediately assumed the vanilla had been poisoned and told everyone in the kitchen that. The cook must think he has enemies to have jumped to that conclusion. Obviously, he does."

"Running away only succeeded in making you look guilty, Miss Alonso."

"Would it have been better for me to stay, be questioned, and then get thrown in jail? Wait and pray for justice like David?" Along the hall, a bell clanged. Miss Alonso bent to gather her things off the desk. "The students will be returning to this classroom soon. I need to leave."

"Mrs. Tilden could have been mistaken about the bottle being poisoned, Miss Alonso," Celia hastily said. "Yet you were also quick to suspect that the vanilla had been tampered with. Why?"

She paused, her papers haphazardly clutched in her arms. "Because I saw a person outside Sebastian Carr's room that afternoon, when I was upstairs with the flowers. A person with a bottle in their hand who did not want to be seen."

Celia tried the recall the timing of that afternoon's events. "At three, you mean."

"Not then. Three thirty. I went up with a handful of lilies that had been forgotten," she answered. "I know the time because one of the bedroom clocks chimed the half hour, and I turned to look down the hall to discover where the sound had come from. It was very pretty."

"But I'd been told that all the bedchambers were locked at three fifteen."

"I knew you would not believe me." Miss Alonso tried to push past Celia.

Celia grabbed her elbow to stop her. "Somehow this person got inside his room. We will figure out how later," she said. "For now, just tell me who it was you saw. What they looked like."

"It was a woman. She was short, very short, and wearing a dull brown dress," she answered. "I had only a glimpse, because I was returning down the stairs, since I had finished with the flowers on that floor."

"Katherine Vanmeter," Celia murmured.

"She called out to me, except she called me Emma."

Gad. "You should have stayed, Miss Alonso. You should have told the police what you saw."

"The half sister of a convicted assailant? The police would never have believed me," she stated. "And they will never believe you, either. No matter what you say, I will stand accused."

• • •

"The fellow in the caftan and turban doesn't exist, does he, Miss Bremerton?"

Nick had forced his way past Pru and upstairs to Miss Bremerton's bedroom, where she'd been huddled over a trunk, packing even though she'd been told to not leave town. Apparently, a desperate urge to depart had taught her how to stow her clothes without the help of a maid.

She finished folding a pink bodice and laid it in the trunk. "I did see him, Detective Greaves, just as the guest Mrs. Davies interviewed did."

"That guest was Dr. Schneider, Miss Bremerton, and he is as blind as a bat without his glasses. Which he has admitted to not wearing to the masquerade on Friday," Nick said. "He invented this suspicious stranger in some puffed-up attempt to seem important. And so have you. Why? Who are you protecting? Yourself?"

She straightened. "I didn't try to kill Sebastian, Detective. If that's what you're accusing me of."

"Why lie about the stranger dressed like an Oriental, if not to protect yourself or the person you suspect of putting poison in Sebastian's vanilla?" he asked. "So, which is it?"

"Anyone I name is just a guess because I have no proof," she said. "No more proof than that supposedly held by those who've accused Tony Ingram."

Who'd been nothing more than a scapegoat, now that it was beginning to look like there hadn't been any fellow skulking about in a Turk costume Friday night.

"Where did your very specific description of a turquoise-blue caftan and white turban come from, Miss Bremerton?"

"I *did* see a suspicious stranger outside, Detective Greaves, but I may have allowed Mrs. Davies's questions about the fellow confuse me."

"Were you aware that Tony Ingram had a costume exactly like that in his possession?"

"I didn't," she replied, retrieving a pair of knit stockings from a chest of drawers against the wall. "How strange."

"So you weren't trying to incriminate him with your very specific description," Nick said.

"Of course I wasn't. I have nothing against Tony Ingram. I've only met him once or twice."

Nick slowly turned the brim of his hat through his fingers; the movement stopped him from rubbing the ache in his arm. "Louise Ingram, based on a comment she made to one of my associates, believes there is a woman who knows something important about Emma Joyce. Is that woman you, by any chance?"

"I don't know anything about Emma, other than in her capacity as a servant here," she replied. "A very good servant, I might add."

"She was pregnant, Miss Bremerton."

Irene's hands, which had been occupied with folding the stockings, stilled. She looked over at Nick. "Was it Sebastian's?"

Interesting that she didn't presume the child had been Tony

Ingram's. "We're not certain yet, but we don't think so," he replied. "Who might've known the father's identity, though? Other than the man himself." If Emma had even told him.

Irene tossed the stockings into the trunk. "Katherine, Detective," she said. "She would've known. Katherine would've known."

• • •

"Katherine is not here." The landlady at Miss Vanmeter's lodging house folded her arms and scowled. The sleeves of her dress were rolled up, revealing chapped hands and forearms toughened by hard work. "Like I told that other woman who was here looking for her not fifteen minutes ago."

"Was that woman's name Louise Ingram, by any chance?" Celia asked.

"She didn't offer her name and I didn't ask," she replied. "I don't have time for conversations with folks looking for my residents. We're in the middle of laundry right now."

"Of course. My apologies," she said. "Where did you tell her to find Miss Vanmeter?"

The landlady exhaled. "At her clinic probably. Where else would she be?"

"Thank you. I'll not keep you from your—"

The woman banged shut the door before Celia could finish her sentence.

"Well, then."

Celia had once before visited the empty storefront where Miss Vanmeter sought to operate her clinic, so she knew its location. Unfortunately, that location was a good five blocks distant and Celia's knee was throbbing even more than it had been after Miss Ingram had kicked it. Another cab and a further outlay of cash was required.

A hired carriage was easily located and the ride brief. Celia had the driver stop a few doors shy of the clinic's address. Perhaps she was being overly cautious, but she could not be certain what Miss Ingram intended. Nor how Miss Vanmeter—now the likely person behind the poisoning of Sebastian's vanilla—might respond. Unfortunately, she had not anticipated she might require a weapon when she'd left her house to confront Paulina. One would have come in handy right then.

She approached the storefront and peered around the edge of the nearest window frame. The front room was empty. Perhaps Miss Vanmeter was not at her clinic and Miss Ingram had been forced to go searching for her elsewhere. Celia tested the front door. It was unlocked and Celia eased it open. She was immediately greeted by the sound of raised voices emanating from one of the smaller enclosed rooms partitioned out of the main space.

"It was Preston's baby, wasn't it?" a woman was shouting. Celia could not be positive, but she thought the voice belonged to Louise Ingram. "How could you have ever let Tony think it was Sebastian's?"

Preston Carr was the father?

"I never told your brother it was Sebastian's child." Katherine Vanmeter's voice now. "I didn't tell him anything after I had examined Emma and determined that she was pregnant. She didn't want Tony to know."

"But he suspected anyway."

Celia crept forward, praying none of the uneven floorboards would creak and give her away.

"I can't help that, Louise," Katherine replied. "Besides, how would I have known who'd fathered the child?"

"You would've known because she had confided in you, Katherine," she snapped. "She trusted you. You were going to help her."

"I did help her."

Dear God.

Skirts rustled and feet moved across the floor. One of the two women moving nearer the other, Celia presumed.

"Were you hoping that Tony would do something?" Louise hissed. "Would retaliate against Sebastian, maybe? Kill him, maybe? Except he didn't because my brother would never go that far. As much as he hates Sebastian, he'd never try to kill him."

"I don't understand why he didn't, Louise. Honestly."

"If Tony didn't confront Sebastian after he'd paid that boy to throw acid on me, he is never going to take revenge."

"You really believe that Sebastian was responsible for that incident." Celia could hear the incredulity in Katherine Vanmeter's voice. "Why would he have needed or wanted to scar you, Louise? He has Irene. That's all he's ever wanted, really. Someone rich and pretty."

A mere flicker of a pause met Katherine's statement. "It was Preston. It was Preston, wasn't it? Not Sebastian," Louise said, sounding horrified. "And you've known all along that he was responsible for that attack on me just like you've known all along that he'd gotten Emma with child. How could you, Katherine? How could you keep that secret from me?"

"I had no proof Preston had paid the Mexican boy, Louise," she replied. "Nothing solid, at least."

"But you were happy to tell me, tell Tony, tell anyone who would listen, that Sebastian was behind it. Because accusing him suited your plans," Louise said, spinning out a logical explanation. "You *were* hoping Tony would hurt Sebastian, weren't you? A man you so thoroughly despise. Hurt him or worse. But you got tired of waiting for him to act. Or for me to act. So you decided to take advantage of the masquerade ball in order to see Sebastian punished for having crushed your dream."

It all made sense. It all made so much sense. Celia could feel her heart pounding in her chest, the heaviness of her own breathing. *Calm, Celia. Do not give yourself away yet.*

"That boy died in prison because of your dishonesty, Katherine," Louise continued.

"He did toss the vitriol on you, Louise. He didn't have to do that."

"He didn't know that the liquid wasn't a harmless dye. He thought it was a joke!" Louise cried. "To think that I ever admired you for what you planned to do with this clinic.”

“I’m sorry for what happened to him. I truly am.”

“How did you find out that Preston had hired the boy?” Louise asked, more quietly than before. She had gained control over her justifiable anger.

“I overheard him arguing with Sebastian not long after it happened,” she replied matter-of-factly. “I came to the house to visit Irene and they were having a terrible row in the library.”

“Are you telling me Irene knew the truth, too?”

“No, she was away on one of her rides and I was waiting for her in the parlor,” she said. “Sebastian and Preston must not have been aware I was in the room right next to them.”

“So you *did* have proof.”

“My word against theirs, Louise. Who would’ve believed me?”

“You could’ve spread rumors that it was Preston and not Sebastian responsible, but then again, you were motivated otherwise.” Louise paused. “How did you get inside Sebastian’s room? The detective told me the bedrooms had been locked.”

A question Celia would definitely love to know the answer to. She shifted to hear better, the change in position also offering a clearer view of a cloak hanging on a hook nearby. A cloak with an interestingly colored lining. She reached for it, the sudden movement buckling her injured knee. Unable to steady herself, she slammed the wall with her arm. *Blast.*

“Who’s out there?” Katherine shouted.

“Katherine, what are you doing? Put that away!” Louise shrieked.

Katherine Vanmeter rushed into the narrow passageway between the divided rooms, a knife in her hand. “Mrs. Davies.”

“Is that the weapon you used to slice Emma Joyce’s throat, Miss Vanmeter?” Celia asked with as much composure as she could muster. “Because you believed she had noticed you exiting Sebastian’s room with a bottle of vanilla extract in your hand, and she had to be silenced?”

"She did see me, but I didn't hurt her, Mrs. Davies. I didn't."

Louise had stepped into the passageway behind her. "Katherine, put that knife down. This is ludicrous."

Katherine spun about, the knife extended. She'd misjudged how close Louise was and sliced through her arm.

Screaming, Louise collapsed to the ground, red blooming on her sleeve.

"Louise!" Celia tried to rush to the woman's side.

Katherine, caught between Celia and Louise, hurled herself against Celia. The jolting impact dislodged the knife from her grip, sending it skittering across the floor. Celia stumbled and fell, taking Katherine to the ground with her. Celia's head hit with a thud, dizzying her. Katherine scrambled to her feet and lurched for the storefront's door.

She grabbed for the handle just as Owen threw open the door and burst into the room.

CHAPTER 19

"Bet you were surprised to see me, Mrs. Davies." Owen's grin could not have possibly filled up more of his face.

Celia lent a hand to the hastily bandaged Miss Ingram as she climbed into a waiting cab. "Very surprised, Owen, considering that you should be at work." She smiled reassuringly at Louise. "Here is the address for my clinic, Miss Ingram. My cousin Barbara can tend to your wound." Which was, thankfully, not deep.

Louise grabbed Celia's hand. "Did she kill Emma, Mrs. Davies?" She shot a glance in the direction of the wagon parked a short distance up the road. Nicholas was wrestling an obstinate Miss Vanmeter onto the bed of the vehicle with Officer Mullahey's assistance. "Did she try to poison Sebastian too?"

"Mr. Greaves will ascertain her guilt, Miss Ingram," she said. "Rest assured, though, that your brother will be released as soon as Mr. Greaves returns to the station."

"Thank you." With a grateful nod, Miss Ingram released Celia's hand.

Celia stepped back and signaled for the driver to depart. At her side, Owen danced on the balls of his feet. "Now perhaps you can explain what you are doing here, Owen, if you will," she said. "Mr. Roesler has let you go again, hasn't he?"

"Not exactly."

"It is my fault if he has," she said, folding Miss Vanmeter's cloak with the magenta lining over her arm. A quick inspection had revealed a rip along its hem. Celia anticipated that the piece she had found snagged in the shrubs at the Carrs' house would match the tear. "I should not have asked you to go to the anatomy museum and neglect your job."

"Oh, I didn't mind doing that, ma'am. It was pretty interesting. If sorta odd," he said. "And I don't expect Mr. Roesler will be mad for long, since I was responsible for capturing a dangerous criminal."

"Which gets me back to asking how it was that you arrived so fortuitously."

He screwed up his face. "Oh! You mean how I managed to arrive here in the nick of time," he said. "Well, I was considering where Miss Ingram might have run off to. The question was bothering me something fierce, and I couldn't concentrate on selling candies while I was pondering. When I measured out five chocolate pralines instead of six for a customer, Mr. Roesler told me to get out. So I thought I'd go look for Miss Ingram. And I figured that the smart place to start would be at the theaters, where she'd have friends who might take her in."

The wagon holding Miss Vanmeter and Mr. Mullahey wheeled off. "Very smart, Owen."

He grinned. "It was outside the Bella Union that I ran into Mr. Mullahey. He told me that Mr. Greaves had sent a message asking him to come here," he said. "Mr. Mullahey didn't mind if I tagged after him. When I saw what was going on inside, I had to jump in and help."

She leaned forward and pecked him on the cheek. He blushed nearly as brilliant a color as Mr. Taylor tended to do. "Thank you, Owen, for coming to my aid once again."

Nicholas strode up to them. "How did you know about Katherine Vanmeter?" he asked Celia.

"I located Miss Lyons, who is actually Miss Alonso," she said.

"Of course you did."

Before *he* had, he did not want to admit aloud. "She informed me that she'd noticed Miss Vanmeter leaving Sebastian's room with a bottle in her hand. Katherine confused her for Emma, however. From behind, they have features in common. Namely their general size and hair color."

"Miss Alonso should've informed me of that."

"As I also said to her, but she insists you would not have believed her. After all, she is David Alonso's sister."

"She should've told me, anyway." He looked over at Owen. "Thank you, Cassidy, you can go back to work now."

Owen hesitated, scuffing his toe against the pavement.

"You've been fired again, haven't you?"

"Maybe I should get going," he replied and scampered off.

Nicholas groaned. "Did you learn anything else useful while you were solving the crime, Celia? Might make my report writing easier if you just sum it all up for me."

He could be so irritable when she bested him in gathering clues. "I learned that Preston Carr needs to be brought into the station, Nicholas, and questioned for having Louise Ingram attacked with vitriol. He may also have been the father of Emma Joyce's child."

• • •

"Tell me exactly what happened on Friday, Miss Vanmeter." Nick rested his elbows on his desk. Taylor opened his notebook. Mullahey had been sent off to round up Preston Carr. And Celia stood in the corner near Briggs's desk, her gazed fixed on the woman seated across from Nick. "It's easy enough."

Miss Vanmeter pinched her lips together and returned Nick's stare.

"All right, so you don't want to talk to us. Fine." He sat back again. "How about I outline what took place. You went to the Carrs' house that afternoon around three thirty, angry that Sebastian had refused to allow Miss Bremerton to support your clinic," he said. "You wanted to punish him, so you snuck upstairs with a bottle of poisoned vanilla before he'd returned from downtown. You'd probably learned from Miss Bremerton about his habit. We were told you waited in the library until she joined you, at approximately four o'clock, but it wouldn't have been too difficult to get up to his room without being noticed. The household was preoccupied with preparations for the ball."

Out of Miss Vanmeter's line of sight, Taylor was mimicking trying to open a locked door and shrugging. That was a problem. Nick didn't figure Miss Vanmeter to be a picklock. The door must have been left unsecured. Or maybe she'd managed to snag a key.

"I did not sneak upstairs, Detective."

"Despite your insistence otherwise, you were spotted upstairs at a most curious hour, Miss Vanmeter," Celia said. "Paulina Lyons, one of the temporary servants hired for that evening, observed you outside Sebastian Carr's bedchamber with a bottle in your hand, acting suspiciously. Only a few moments after you had arrived at the Carrs'."

"Obviously she's lying," she said. "She would've given you this information earlier, Detective Greaves, if it was the truth and not recently concocted to hide her own guilt."

Miss Vanmeter had a point.

Celia pressed ahead. "You hate Sebastian Carr a great deal, don't you, Katherine?" she asked. "The man who has disrupted your close friendship with Irene Bremerton. The man who was going to quash your dreams."

Nick exhaled. "Mrs. Davies, can you let me conduct the interrogations that take place in my office?"

Taylor bit the inside of his cheek rather than laugh out loud.

"Apologies, Mr. Greaves, but perhaps you will indulge me for a few more moments," she said.

He gestured for her to continue. She'd keep interrupting, anyway.

"You fiercely hate Sebastian, do you not?" Celia asked again.

"I can't pretend to like Sebastian, but I did not try to poison him. No matter what Paulina Lyons claims to have seen."

"I overheard your argument with Louise Ingram, Miss Vanmeter, where you informed her that Preston Carr was responsible for hiring David Alonso. That he was the father of Emma's child, as well," Celia said. "Miss Ingram proposed that, upon discovering Preston's secrets, you realized how handy it might be to have Sebastian blamed for them. Offenses that might encourage one of the Ingrams to take revenge on the man you despise."

Interesting. "Is that true, Miss Vanmeter?" Nick asked. "What Mrs. Davies has said."

"No," she snapped.

"She also proposed that you'd grown tired of waiting for Tony or Louise to act, so you decided to," Celia said. "She is correct, isn't she?"

"This is ridiculous. I didn't try to poison Sebastian."

"Why should we believe you?" Celia asked. "For instance, you have stated that you'd not returned to the Carrs' house Friday evening, yet I see that the lining of your cloak is torn and a fragment of material is missing." Celia held up the garment, which she'd draped over Briggs's chair, and pointed out the rip. "Possibly the fragment I found in the shrubs outside the Carrs' dining room window. Mr. Greaves?"

Nick obediently retrieved the scrap of magenta fabric from his desk drawer and handed it over to Celia. The piece matched up perfectly.

"Why tell us you'd not returned? You had an invitation that would have justified your presence," Celia said. "Unless you knew we would learn you'd not attended the mask. Instead, you'd been peering through the windows, wanting to spy on Sebastian as he added the poisoned vanilla to his coffee later, another of his habits after a social event at the house."

"Spy on him and gloat," Nick added.

"I ripped the hem of my cloak at another time."

"You're in the habit of creeping around outside the Carrs' house? Sounds like a strange thing to do to me," Nick said.

She had no reply.

"Perhaps while you were at the Carrs' you attempted to speak with Emma—on the back staircase—and explain what you'd been doing upstairs with that bottle of vanilla," Celia said. "Try to convince her you had an innocent reason for your actions, even though she actually wasn't the servant who'd seen you."

"That wasn't what happened at all, Mrs. Davies."

"Stop pretending you didn't try to poison Sebastian, Miss Vanmeter," Nick said. "You'd gotten tired of waiting for the Ingrams to act and went ahead yourself."

Tears welled in her eyes and slipped down her cheeks. Taylor mustn't have noticed them, because he didn't produce a handkerchief.

"It wasn't them I'd hoped would act," Miss Vanmeter said, so quietly it was hard to hear her voice over the din from the street outside the office window and the usual clamor in the main station room. "It was Irene. I'd hoped she would come to hate him and break off the engagement. But that's not what she did. She did something so much worse."

• • •

A lengthy silence followed Katherine Vanmeter's statement, as though her words had sucked the air from the office and left them all gasping.

"Oh, dear," Celia said, dropping onto the nearest chair, which happened to be Detective Briggs's. Perhaps she should have inspected it for crumbs before sitting. "Irene Bremerton. But she was the first person to mention poison to me, Miss Vanmeter. Why would she do that if she were responsible?" She had acted so pleased to see Celia when she'd arrived at the house to tend to Jenny.

"Attack can be the best form of defense, Mrs. Davies," Nicholas said. "If Miss Vanmeter is now telling us the truth."

"I am," she protested. "And I did try to stop Irene, but I failed."

"How long have you known she intended to poison him?" Celia asked.

"I'd only figured it out on Friday, Mrs. Davies," she said, swiping a tear off her face. "She did occasionally tease about doing something vile to him, like adding poison to his vanilla. His 'stupid vanilla,' as she referred to it. I once even caught her reading a treatise I owned that discussed a strychnine poisoning case. But it wasn't until I received her message asking me to urgently visit that afternoon, promising a 'surprise,' that I feared she was actually going to proceed."

"That was your reason to go to the Carrs' Friday afternoon," Celia said. "Not to try to persuade Sebastian about the clinic one last time."

"I wouldn't have been able to persuade him even if that had been my intention. He hid from me, the coward," she said. "I'm sorry I lied to you, Mrs. Davies."

Was she sorry? Celia found the woman's blank expression devilishly hard to decipher. Almost as inscrutable as Nicholas's could be.

"Why the sudden change of heart about Sebastian, Miss Vanmeter?" he asked. "Irene Bremerton was going to eliminate the obstacle interfering with your plans. Seems like you should've been pretty happy."

"I did *not* want her to try to sicken him with arsenic, Detective. I didn't. I wanted her to realize what a swine he is by showing her the newspaper reports about the attack on Miss Ingram. By hinting that Emma was with child and that Sebastian might be responsible," she said, sniffling back tears. "I wanted her to refuse the engagement and leave him, not try to poison him."

"You had to have been terrified when you heard that Jenny had died," Celia said, unmoved by the idea of Miss Vanmeter's terror. "You came to me to learn if Sebastian had accused you yet. Afraid that Emma had told him she'd spotted you upstairs with a bottle, even though it was not her who'd seen you."

"That's true," she replied. "I also wanted to know if you suspected Irene, Detective."

"Why *were* you outside Sebastian's room around three thirty with a bottle of vanilla, Miss Vanmeter, if not to poison him?" he asked.

Mr. Taylor flipped to a fresh page in his notebook.

"To interfere with Irene's plans," she explained. "I went up to his room as soon as I arrived, snuck inside to retrieve the vanilla there. If she intended to poison him, that was how she would go about it. And if that was not what she'd meant in her message, then the worst that had happened was that I'd stolen a bottle from his room."

"You had a key?" Nicholas asked.

"I didn't need one. It wasn't locked," she said. "So I went in, found a bottle of vanilla on his desk, an almost empty one, and took it. The bottle Paulina Lyons saw me with."

Nicholas had a bored look on his face as though he found her story completely far-fetched.

"I thought I'd taken care of the problem, except that when Irene finally joined me in the library, I learned she'd been gone from the house most of the day," Katherine continued. "It was unlikely she'd been able to poison the vanilla yet, and I'd retrieved the wrong bottle. Imagine my frustration. I tried to convince myself she didn't mean to harm him, but then I observed her behavior. She was so agitated, so excited. Not like her at all. So I went back upstairs to try again."

"When Preston came out of his room to laugh at you," Nicholas said.

"I think he somehow suspected what was going on. He thought it was all very funny." She drew in a breath. "I wanted to warn Sebastian, but he refused to come to the door. I did try. And tried again, one final time that night."

"It was *you* on the back staircase whom Emma saw," Celia said.

Nicholas leaned back in his chair and folded his arms, content to let her proceed. Or giving up on conducting his interrogation.

"I don't know who that was," she said. "When I returned, I skirted the outside of the house, not wanting Sebastian to spot me inside. He would've made a scene. I looked through the windows, hoping I might find Irene alone in one of the rooms. I wanted to get her attention so I could persuade her to collect the bottle I believed she'd poisoned before it was too late." Her expression darkened. "But then I saw Sebastian in the dining room with her, his hand around her waist. Clutching Irene like she was his property. She was trying to get out of his grasp, but the harder she resisted, the more he tightened his grip. I don't think I could've hated him more than I did at that moment. So I left. And now an innocent girl is dead."

Upset flared, the image of a lovely young woman's slit throat surfacing in Celia's mind. "Two women are dead, Katherine, and if you had told us what you suspected earlier, Emma might not be one of them."

"I had no idea that Emma might be in danger, Mrs. Davies," she said defensively. "It's true I thought she'd spotted me, but *I* didn't intend to hurt her."

"But Irene might have."

"No. She had no reason to murder Emma."

"Are you sure, Miss Vanmeter?" Nicholas asked.

"Maybe I'm not," she replied quietly.

"Irene embellished a guest's story about a stranger in a Turk costume lurking outside in order to protect herself, didn't she, Miss Vanmeter?" Celia asked. "To protect you both, perhaps."

"That ridiculous costume. The one Preston had worn for one of his amateur theatricals," Katherine replied. "She must've remembered it, Mrs. Davies, when you mentioned the guest's story to her. She may have found it amusing to have the suspicious stranger dressed in that outfit."

Gad.

"She didn't accuse Preston, though. She accused Louise Ingram of wearing it," Nicholas said. "Only for her brother to end up being accused of a crime he didn't commit because of that costume."

"I'm sorry for that."

"Did she ever admit to you that she was responsible for the poisoned vanilla, Miss Vanmeter?" Celia asked.

She drew in a breath. "No."

Nicholas scowled. "Taylor, see her out. And have her charged as an accessory."

She jumped to her feet. "What? What do you mean?"

"Taylor, if you will."

"Come along, miss." He took Miss Vanmeter's elbow and escorted her from the room.

"I'm having her charged for protecting Irene, Celia," Nicholas said. How tired he sounded at that moment. "Even if she won't admit Miss Bremerton confessed to her."

"'A friend in need is a friend indeed,'" she replied. "Or 'in deed.' Either."

"Nothing from Shakespeare, Mrs. Davies? Just an old proverb?"

"Mr. Shakespeare could be rather cynical about friendship, Mr.

Greaves," she said. "Irene had to have also killed Emma Joyce. She was away from the house Sunday morning, quite early. She must've believed Emma had some sort of evidence."

"She'd seen Miss Bremerton taking the valentine up to Carr's room, but that was all she'd told us concerning her," he said. "I doubt Irene Bremerton will confess to that crime, either."

"But you shall release Tony Ingram, won't you? I told Louise you would."

"That was premature, Celia."

"But you shall, correct?"

Nicholas rubbed his arm where his old wound ached. "He had Emma's blood on his shoe," he reminded her.

"He is not responsible, though." How could Nicholas think he was? *Mexican boys are not the only ones who do not receive justice, Miss Alonso.*

"I'm just telling you the sort of evidence that might be presented in order to defend Irene, Celia, if we charged her with killing Emma Joyce along with the poisoning attempt on her fiancé. We have no proof she murdered Miss Joyce. None."

Celia sighed. "I know."

There was a commotion out in the main station room and Mr. Taylor dashed into the detectives' office. "We've found the clothes worn by the killer, sir. Or I should say one of the boys living at Miss Joyce's place found it. A bloodied men's jacket stuffed into the pit in the outhouse."

Nicholas got to his feet. "Where is it?"

Mr. Taylor's brow creased. "You didn't want me to bring the jacket in here, did you, sir? It's been in the latrine."

"No, you're right, Taylor. I didn't."

"This was in one of the pockets, Mr. Greaves." He pulled out a linen handkerchief, relatively unstained, with a distinctive C embroidered upon it in lilac silk. "He must've forgotten it was in there and might identify him."

"I recognize that embroidered initial, Mr. Greaves," Celia said. "I observed an identical one on Preston Carr's cuffs yesterday morning, in the same thread."

Nicholas looked over at her. "Well, that solves that problem."

CHAPTER 20

"I hear you've bailed out your fiancée, Mr. Carr. Your *former* fiancée, I suppose I should call her now." Nick leaned against the windowsill in his office and studied the folks passing on the road. A man in striped pants and a sack coat that had seen better days stumbled into the street, a sheet or so in the wind. It took nerve to wander drunkenly past the police station.

Sebastian Carr shifted in the chair he occupied. "I have."

"And here I thought you might be ready to get rid of her," Nick said. "She almost helped you out by trying to flee the city. One of the officers who works down by the wharves stopped her, though, before she boarded a ferry." No longer able to trust that Katherine Vanmeter would keep silent about her plots.

"It hasn't been proven yet that Irene is the one who put poison in that vanilla, Detective, and she cannot be left to rot in one of your jail cells while we wait to find out."

Plenty of folks were left to rot in jail cells, but not a Bremerton, Nick supposed. Maybe she had a sister Sebastian Carr was now pinning his hopes on.

"Oh, I think we'll discover she's guilty, Mr. Carr," he said, turning to face him. Carr looked uncomfortable to find himself in the detectives' office, less smug. "You didn't bail out your brother, though."

"*He* can rot for a while, Detective," he said. "But are you certain he killed Emma?"

"We found an item of his clothing with blood on it stuffed into the pit of an outhouse behind her rented room, along with the knife he'd used." Finding the weapon had required digging around in the pit. He didn't envy the cop who'd had to do that job. "Also, the girl who works in your kitchen told one of my officers that she saw Preston speaking with Emma the evening of the party, and that Emma was upset afterward."

He'd been the unidentified person on the staircase, but Sally, who'd observed the interaction, hadn't thought to tell the police. They'd been asking about suspicious people and to her way of thinking, Preston wasn't one.

"You *are* certain." Sebastian Carr shook his head. "I can't believe he killed her."

Nick had been fooled, too. Preston Carr had been completely calm when he'd been in the station Sunday morning. Not a hint that he'd slit Emma's throat less than an hour earlier. An actor through and through.

"And for what? Emma had lost the child, Mr. Carr," Nick said. "She wasn't going to cause your brother any more trouble."

"Emma was only looking for some financial support from him, but even the small amount she'd asked for was more than he could spare. Preston has debts that Father doesn't want to cover any longer."

Nick pulled out his chair and sat. "You're probably not surprised about Katherine Vanmeter's role in all this."

"Only that she wasn't actually behind trying to poison me," he said. "I do have to give her credit for trying to foil Irene's plot."

"She ended up happy to see you potentially sickened, though."

"She'll be charged for not sharing what she knew with the police, won't she?" he asked.

Nick would love to say no just to irritate him. "She already has been."

"Good."

"I have a few remaining questions, Mr. Carr," Nick said. "Such as how Miss Vanmeter managed to get inside your room after the doors had been locked. She told us she doesn't have a key."

"That was probably Preston's fault. He has a key to my room and likely wanted to get his hands on the note I'd found addressed to him from Emma."

That note. "Why does your brother have a key to your room?"

"He's always liked to play pranks on me. Short-sheeting my bed or swapping out one of my magazines for a *Godey's Lady's Book*. Childish, really," Carr said. "I took to locking the door, but he'd find a way in. I now have to resort to regularly changing the lock, even though he always manages to get a fresh copy of my key made."

"What was in that note?" Preston Carr hadn't said, although Celia had proposed it was Emma requesting a meeting with the father of her child to inform him she'd lost the baby. A very reasonable proposal.

"Just a request that they meet on Sunday morning, urgently," he said. "I told Preston I'd intercepted it, and he was furious. He probably came into my room looking for the note—he wouldn't have wanted Father to read it—before I'd returned from downtown on Friday. Too late, because I'd burned it."

"Your brother left your door unlocked after his fruitless search."

"I'd say so," he said. "I did lock it before Katherine came up to hammer on my door. I presumed she wanted to continue to argue with me about her clinic, so I acted like I wasn't inside my room."

Preston wasn't the only childish person in their family.

"I must've forgotten to lock up again when I went downstairs to greet our guests," Carr added.

"Which allowed Irene to get in."

"To leave me a valentine and another lovely gift," he said. "If we believe she's guilty, that is, Detective."

Nick inclined his head. It was always possible she'd be found innocent, as he'd said to Celia. Folks with more evidence stacked against them than the limited amount Nick had on Irene Bremerton got off all the time. Although aiming to board that ferry didn't work in her favor.

"Preston has come up with a story that he and Emma had planned a tryst on Sunday morning, which erupted into a heated argument." Manslaughter instead of murder.

"Is that the angle he's trying?" Carr asked, scoffing. "Well, that was not what she wrote. She wasn't planning a tryst. And I went to meet her instead, at the coffeehouse she'd indicated. To find out exactly what she wanted from Preston this time," he said. "She never showed up, obviously, and I was late to church. I wish I'd never told him about that note."

Preston might not have killed her in a desperate rage if Sebastian had kept quiet.

"The fact that he'd stashed a clean change of clothes nearby—we haven't figured out exactly where yet—refutes his story about a planned tryst, Mr. Carr."

"Preston is creative," he replied. "All those years on the stage."

Nick leaned back. Slowly, so that the blasted chair didn't creak. "You'd discovered that your brother had hired David Alonso to toss acid onto Louise Ingram but you were willing to risk being accused in his place," he said. "Why?"

Sebastian Carr narrowed his eyes. "Whoever told you that I knew Preston was responsible is lying."

It would be up to a jury whether or not to believe Katherine Vanmeter.

"Once you found out, maybe you thought you'd let sleeping dogs lie. It was only a Mexican kid, after all," Nick continued because it felt good to vent his anger, his disgust at the way the Carrs had acted. "And since the boy never provided us with a description of the man who hired him—we suspect that Preston had threatened David Alonso to keep him quiet—you pretty quickly realized that neither of you were going to be formally accused. Let the boy rot in jail. Or die, as it turned out. Isn't that so?"

Sebastian Carr got to his feet. "Let me know if you have any other questions in future, Detective Greaves."

"I expect I'll see you in court, Mr. Carr."

The other man slapped his hat onto his head and stormed out.

Taylor, standing outside the office with two cups of coffee in his hands, deftly jumped out of Carr's way. "Want one, sir?" he asked, holding out one of the cups.

"No, thanks."

Taylor set one on Nick's desk anyway and glanced behind him at the station. "Guess Mr. Carr isn't so happy about his brother or his fiancée."

"I'm sure you can guess how much I care if the Carrs are happy," he said. "And make sure Tony Ingram's been released, will you, Taylor?"

His assistant grinned and ran off to take care of it.

• • •

"Everything is concluded, then," Celia said, standing at the window in her parlor, Nicholas at her side. "Another successful investigation."

"If the preventable death of a young woman can be called successful, Celia."

The fading daylight cast shadows on his face. All the meaningless deaths were wearing on him, creasing his skin. She wanted to erase the suffering he was carrying, but suffering was not as easy to remove as a smear of dirt upon one's cheek. Pain went far deeper than that.

She rested a hand on his sleeve. "We could not have prevented Emma's death, Nicholas."

"But if she'd told us—"

"What? That Preston Carr had gotten her pregnant?" she asked. "She could not foresee that her request to meet with him would lead to her death. As for the attempted poisoning, she may not have comprehended how her condition tied into that crime. She was likely unaware that Irene had come to believe Sebastian was the child's father, and if she'd witnessed Irene's unhappiness with him, why might Emma remark on that to you? Unhappy fiancées do not regularly poison their intendeds."

"You're right. Of course you are."

Being right did not restore Emma's life, though. No more than discovering the true identity of who'd paid to have Louise Ingram attacked would restore David Alonso's.

"Not even Miss Vanmeter, who knew that Preston had gotten Emma pregnant, could have anticipated that he might kill her. Especially after Emma was no longer with child," she said, lowering her hand. "So do not feel bad, Nicholas. There was nothing you could have done to change the outcome."

Her words had softened the creases, if only just a little, and they stood looking at each other for a few minutes. Lost in their individual thoughts until the gentle chime of the parlor mantel clock roused them from their woolgathering.

He retreated an inch; he was always retreating, unsettled by his feelings.

"My only wish is that I'd been more suspicious of Irene Bremerton and her lie about the fellow in the Turk costume. Dr. Schneider, as well," Celia said, returning to a discussion of the case in order to smooth over the awkwardness. "I am curious about one item, though. Since Irene did not murder Emma, where was she so early Sunday morning?"

"Out for a ride, like she'd told us. A ride that happened to go by the ferry ticketing station, according to the clerk there," he said. "She must've delayed her departure because she realized it would look too suspicious if she left town that same day."

"Ah." Her absence from the house had been suspicious enough, although not for the reason Celia had presumed. "I should inform you that Miss Ingram is doing well. The cut on her arm did not turn out to be serious, and Barbara did a wonderful job tending to it."

"Her brother's been released, by the way."

"Thank you, Nicholas. That is a relief."

She moved nearer to him because she did not want him to always retreat, to be unsettled. She felt the warmth of his body—was that even possible, with all the layers of clothes between them, or was she conjuring the sensation?—shimmer in the air between them.

He smiled and took her hand. "This has been an interesting way to have spent Valentine's Day, Celia," he said, lifting her fingers to brush a kiss across them.

"There is always next year to do something more romantic, Nicholas."

"You mean a murder investigation isn't romantic, Mrs. Davies?"

She laughed, and he quieted the sound with his lips.

• • •

He was still grinning like a fool when he strode through the front door at Mrs. Jewett's. He'd ask Celia to marry him soon. Really soon. The time was right. His landlady would be overjoyed when he did.

"Hello, Mrs. Jewett," he called out.

She was huddled on the staircase, hunched in a ball against the railing. Upstairs, Riley was barking, over and over again, stirred into a frenzy by Mrs. Jewett's sobs.

Nick rushed over to her. "What's wrong?" He started running his hands down her arms, searching her for any sign she was injured. "Are you hurt?"

"I'm not hurt, Mr. Greaves," she said, brushing him off. "That fellow was here again. The one who brings the letters. He came with a package this time. There it is, over there." She pointed toward the parlor where the parcel sat on the floor. "He's a beast."

"Did he hurt you? I'll kill him if he did. Did he?"

"No, no. He just . . . I don't like the way he looks. The way he talks." She peered at Nick, worry creasing every part of her face. "He means to cause you harm. I know he does."

Nick blew out a breath. He needed to stay calm. For Mrs. Jewett's sake if not his own.

"Here, let me help you stand. And come into the dining room where it's warm," he said, getting her to her feet. She was trembling so hard he swore he could hear her knees knocking. "Let me get you some tea or coffee."

He led her to a chair then went off to find some hot water. She'd been interrupted preparing tea, it looked like, and he brought the cup and the teapot out to her.

"Did he make threats? What exactly did he say?" Nick asked, setting them down on the table.

"Not much. Other than he wanted to make sure you got that package. That it was important and somebody would be contacting you soon to hear what you had to say about what's inside." She glared at the parcel. "You should destroy it, Mr. Greaves."

"That wouldn't do much good, I think, Mrs. Jewett."

Nick pulled out his knife and cut the twine holding the package closed. Inside, he found a stack of letters wrapped in ribbon, covered in Meg's distinctive handwriting. Her letters and a note that wasn't from her. His heart slamming in his chest, he lifted the message to the light coming from the dining room gasolier.

Time to learn the truth about Meg. About everything. Before it's too late

Author's Note

In 1865, a man calling himself Dr. Jordan opened the Pacific Museum of Anatomy and Science in San Francisco, just one of several such museums opened by supposed doctors named Jordan in various cities around the United States. Lured in by the medical oddities on display (the contents Owen describes come from the catalog of the actual museum), vulnerable men were duped into paying fees of several hundred dollars, and sometimes more, to treat the illnesses Jordan convinced them he could cure. The scheme was lucrative for several years, and the museum, in various guises, continued to exist until the mid 1910s. The original Dr. Jordan, however, appears to have skipped town long before then, his ultimate whereabouts uncertain.

A key setting for *No Justice for the Deceived* is the Carrs' masquerade ball. In Europe, the masquerade balls held during the pre-Lenten carnival season had been widely popular as far back as the seventeenth century. In San Francisco, the largest were those hosted by the German-American societies, who'd brought the tradition with them from their home countries. Costumers regularly advertised having ensembles on hand to rent for such occasions.

The origins of celebrating Valentine's Day in the United States are vague, although it's clear that by the 1850s in San Francisco, cards were bought and sent to loved ones. D. E. Appleton owned a book and stationery company in the city in the late 1860s, delivering gifts and cards via his Valentine Express and its ten-horse team. The service was a short-lived business, although Addie certainly enjoyed having Mr. Taylor treat her to the spectacle.

Two characters in the book—Kate Kennedy and Philip Alexander Bell—were actual citizens of San Francisco. An Irish immigrant, Kate Kennedy found work as a teacher when her family moved from New York City, becoming a highly regarded instructor and principal. Paid less than her male counterparts, she would fight all her life for equal pay for equal work, enjoying some success but an even greater amount of notoriety. As for Philip Alexander Bell, he was an abolitionist who began his journalism career with several newspapers back East before moving to San Francisco. In 1865, he founded the *Elevator*, a newspaper with the goal of promoting black suffrage and education opportunities. His interactions with Celia are, of course, the product of my imagination.

Lastly, a word to my readers—Celia and Nick and all the folks who inhabit these books would not exist without your support. Thank you.

About the Author

Nancy Herriman left an engineering career to take up the pen and has never looked back. She is the author of the Mysteries of Old San Francisco, the Bess Ellyott Mysteries, and several stand-alone novels. A winner of the Daphne du Maurier Award, when she's not writing, she enjoys singing, gabbing about writing, and eating dark chocolate. After two decades in Arizona, she now lives in her home state of Ohio with her family.

www.ingramcontent.com/pod-product-compliance
Lightning Source LLC
Chambersburg PA
CBHW051138190726
48290CB00006B/1894